ARIA HARDING

Also by Aria Harding

* * *

Stand-Alone Novels

Chasing Infinity

Everything In Between

Wonderstruck

The Cedar Ridge Series

Loathing Ryan

Liberating Bells

Just Josie

His Perfect Art Trilogy

His Perfect Canvas

His Perfect Muse

His Perfect Melody

Editing: Indie Proofreading

Cover Design by: Indie Sage

First Edition published 2024

ISBN (E-Book): 979-8-9883784-8-8

ISBN (Paperback): 979-8-9883784-9-5

Foreword

Below is a list of Content Warnings associated with this novel. Please read with your own discretion.
Some of these content warnings may contain plot spoilers.

- Themes revolving around infertility
- Child loss/infant loss
- Themes revolving around grief
- Family member dealing with substance abuse
- Loss of property to fire

Chapter 1

Josie

I drop my forearms against the cool wood counter of the bar, cringing when several pairs of eyes turn in my direction. "Give me two shots of the strongest liquor you have," I say firmly, holding up two fingers.

"You okay there, champ?" the bartender asks as he puts two shot glasses on top of the bar in front of me. He reaches for a bottle of tequila and then pours it into the glasses. Surprisingly, he doesn't spill any, and I find myself becoming enamored with how easy he makes this whole process look. "I thought your speech was excellent," he says, pulling me back to reality.

I take the first glass and throw it back, the liquid burning my throat as I swallow. Within seconds, my muscles unknot after the stress of having to put on that song and dance. "Whew, thanks. I just need this to take the edge off." Not that I mind too much. Ryan has quickly grown to be my closest friend, and I'd do anything for him. But it doesn't make the sheer number of eyes staring at me any easier.

He mindlessly cleans the already clean glasses stacked near

the bar, ready for more drinks. I read once bartenders keep their hands busy, cleaning glasses or wiping down the bar, to make their patrons more comfortable. No one likes someone glaring at them while they drink, and it's safe to say I appreciate that extra effort right now. "I can respect that. Public speaking isn't really my thing either. Nice get up, by the way." He tilts his head toward me, referring to the suit I'm wearing.

Looking down, I run my hands over the black slacks and tug on the fitted suit jacket, making sure they're still in good condition. I was excited when I came up with the idea to wear this outfit after Ryan asked me to stand next to him on his wedding day. I did my best to make sure the outfit was still flattering, but appropriate for a best man to wear. But under the scrutiny of this stranger, the black bowtie around my neck starts to feel a little too tight, and I swallow thickly before glancing back at him. He's watching me with a soft smile on his face, and I relax a bit, realizing he means what he says.

Standing a little taller, I give him a proud grin. "I'm the best man."

He nods twice, as if everything makes perfect sense, and is not weirded out by the fact the best *man* is, in fact, a woman. "Explains the speech."

I'll never forget the intense honor that overcame me when my best friend Ryan asked me to stand up next to him while he married the woman of his dreams. He could've asked any of his guy friends he's known since high school, or even his stepfather, but he asked me.

It's something that means more to me than I think he'll ever know. Ryan and Izabel have become such important people in my life. It was a great honor for me to be up there while they finally solidified their happy ending.

I never expected the anxiety that came with giving a best

man speech in front of a hundred plus people. Although, I'm not sure why I'm surprised by any of that since I've never been a fan of being the center of attention. With the reminder of my speech, I reach for the second shot, shoot it, and then drop it on the bar. My body is still vibrating with nerves, but the alcohol seems to soften it slightly. I slouch against the counter and look up at the bartender. "I hate talking in front of crowds. I didn't stutter, did I?"

He observes me with a coy smirk and then shakes his head. "No, really, you were perfect. I thought it was the best speech of the night."

"You have to say that, guy behind the bar. You're paid to make people feel better."

"It's Josh," he states, chuckling. "And no, I'm paid to pour drinks. The free therapy is an added bonus."

I let my eyes wander over Josh: the guy behind the bar. He really is quite handsome. He has light-colored shaggy brown hair barely draping over his eyebrows and warm chocolate eyes that remind me of a puppy dog. Josh is wearing the classic all-black attire the event staff is dressed in, but the way it hugs his narrow hips and broad shoulders makes him look more delectable than the others.

He holds up the bottle of tequila, and I shake my head. Two is more than enough for me. I normally don't drink at all, though tonight's festivities necessitated a bit of liquid courage.

"They're an adorable couple," he says as he pours me a glass of water instead. He motions his head over to where my friends, Ryan and Izabel, who just got hitched, are still doing their first dance. Izabel says something to her new husband that has him throwing his head back in laughter.

"They are," I respond, taking the glass of water and swallowing a big sip of it.

"That's the dream, you know?" he comments. "Finding someone who makes you smile like that."

I turn and look at Josh, narrowing my eyes. "What if it's not just *one* someone, though? What if I have many someones who could make me smile or laugh?"

He shrugs and leans on the bar. "Nothing wrong with that, I suppose, but don't you think that there's one person made for you out there? Who just sees you and understands everything you're made of?"

"No," I reply a bit too quickly. Then I backtrack when he recoils from me. I have to bite back the urge to roll my eyes at the reaction I always get. Why, as a woman, am I always expected to agree wholeheartedly with this? What if I'm perfectly happy spending my life alone? I take a moment to realize that this conversation about love and fate with a stranger might be a little too steep for his pay scale. "I mean, I don't know. I'm sorry, I think my head is still jumbled from the whole 'speech thing,' you know?" I say, trying to wave it off like I meant nothing by it.

Josh nods his head and watches me. "It's okay."

"Do you have to work the whole night? Or do you get to switch with someone?" I ask him. He's pretty cute. Maybe we could take this elsewhere and have a party of our own. And I can forget that I'm in a room surrounded by strangers who keep eyeing me weirdly.

He offers me a polite smile. "I don't mean to be rude, but I think I know where this is going, so I'll just call it here. I have a girlfriend."

I press my lips together and smile tightly, embarrassment exploding inside of me. Of *course* he's got a girlfriend. That would perfectly explain his enthusiasm for true love. "Of course you do. Why wouldn't you have a girlfriend? I'll just go light myself on fire now. Josh, it was great talking to you."

I grab my glass of water to walk away in shame as Josh protests, "Wait, I didn't mean—We can still talk if you want."

"No, I actually just remembered that I, too, have a date—with a bucket of gasoline and a match—so I'll have to take a rain check. Bye, Josh."

I saunter back toward the bridal table and collapse into my chair. My face burns with embarrassment, and I close my eyes, trying to center myself. Juliet, Izabel's maid of honor and oldest friend, is sitting two chairs down from me.

She looks at me with a perfectly manicured eyebrow raised. "You okay? I saw you chatting with that cute bartender. It looked like it was going well."

"Nope. Just ended up making a total ass of myself. He's got a girlfriend," I say, shaking my head and chuckling. "Can't say I'm surprised, though; he's charming."

"I'm surprised you didn't bring a date. Wasn't there anyone you asked?" Jules asks.

I sigh and look out at my best friend with his new bride, feeling a little sorry for myself, as I realize those days of just me and Ryan shooting the shit together might be few and far between now that he's officially tied the knot. Though my present relationship status is all of my own doing, seeing everyone else around me so hopelessly in love with their significant others always reminds me of the loneliness surrounding my life. "Nope. It was always just me."

"Where'd Liam go?" I ask Juliet to get the subject off me.

She looks at me and then motions over to the door. "He took Ashton to go to the bathroom. They'll probably be back soon, though I think we might bounce after they cut the cake."

"Life as parents, huh?"

Jules laughs. "No kidding. They're fun, but you can pretty much kiss any type of social life goodbye. Be thankful you still have your freedom while you can."

I feel the unintended deep stab of pain in my gut. I force a half-hearted laugh and look back out at the dance floor. I can't hold the comment against Jules; she doesn't know anything about my painful past. Not even Ryan and Izabel, the two people I'm closest to in this damn town, know the truth.

If my life hadn't turned upside down that night all those years ago, my baby girl would have been almost ten years old by now. I wonder if she'd be like Ryan's little sister, Thalia. Would she be rambunctious like me? Or would she have played more on the careful side, like her father?

The thought leaves a sour taste in my mouth, and I take a big gulp of my water to try to wash it away. No matter how many years go by, the wound still stings. I do my best to put up a good front, pretending that I'm invincible.

But frequently, I find myself thinking about the life I could've had. I usually try to nip the thoughts in the bud before they can grow into anything substantial. That life will not happen for me, so why go through the pain of entertaining it?

Thankfully, the man of the hour comes by after his dance with his mom. Ryan holds out a hand to me, asking me to dance with him. My feet are aching from the high heels I'm wearing, but I can't turn him down. I shoot him a sly smile and take his hand, letting him lead me out onto the dance floor. He pulls me around until we're facing each other. One of his hands rests on my lower back, and his other holds my right hand out to the side. I put my left hand on his shoulder, and we start dancing.

"So, how's it going? Was today everything you hoped and dreamed and more?"

Ryan looks off to the side as his lips pull up in a boyish grin. "More, it was definitely more. It all still feels like a dream." I let the hand on his shoulder fall down to his arm. Then I pinch the fleshy part of his bicep through his suit jacket. He startles and shoots me a glare. "Ow! What the hell was that for?"

"Just wanted to prove that this is definitely not a dream. Or I guess it's your dream come true, but it's reality. I'm so proud and happy for you, Ryan," I tell him.

Ryan's eyes trace my face, and he gives me a soft smile. "I know I've said it a few times already, but I hope you know how grateful I am that you're my friend. I don't think I could have pulled through like I did without you."

Last year, Ryan went through a multitude of ups and downs and hit some of the lowest points in his life. It was hard watching him go through it, but all I could do was try to be there to help him in any way I could. Ryan Miller is strong, but sometimes even the strongest people need someone they can rely on. I'm happy I was able to be that person for him.

I wave him off. "You would have. If I've learned anything, it's that you always get what you want because you work hard and you put in the time. Good things come to people who make an effort, Ryno. And I've never seen anyone fight for a person like you've fought for Izabel. You deserve this happy ending."

He beams at me. "Thank you."

"Thank *you*. I'm just glad I got to be a part of it. You two are living the dream now," I say, repeating what Josh noted earlier. I truly am happy for them. Even though my story is anything but a dream, I'm glad someone like Ryan got his. He deserves it. And seeing it unfold acts as a reminder that that sort of love is still out there for those who deserve it. But as more time passes, I can't help but wonder what I did in this life or a past life to not deserve these moments for myself.

Once the song is over, he pulls me into a crushing hug before heading off to Izabel once again while I take my seat.

The rest of the evening goes as any other wedding: cutting the cake, garter toss, and bouquet toss. Reluctantly, I join in the silly tradition with the other single women. I mostly stand to the side to avoid getting trampled by the overly eager women. I watch as Izabel readies in her stance and my stomach churns. What would happen if I caught it? Would there be some cosmic intervention that might lead to my own happiness? Surely not. Deciding that I have no business being a part of this, I take another side step, ensuring I won't be anywhere near the trajectory of the flowers. As the bouquet launches from Izabel's hands, a small form darts between everyone else and grabs it out of the air.

I look down and am pleasantly surprised to see the winner is Ryan's eleven-year-old sister, Thalia. She holds up the bouquet proudly and cheers. The women around me clap and praise in amusement, despite the stiffness in their shoulders giving away their annoyance. Izabel runs over and wraps her new sister-in-law in a big hug before allowing the photographers to take a few pictures of them.

I leave the group and wander over to the side where Ryan has his arms crossed, shaking his head. "She better not be thinking about getting married anytime soon. I'll kick his ass."

"You know, I've heard a lot about this Tyler fellow," I tease him. "Maybe they'll have a playground wedding!"

He groans and rubs his face with his hand. "Thanks, Jos. I really needed that visual."

"Always looking out." I laugh as I pat his shoulder. "I think it's your turn to toss her garter, though."

The evening winds down after that. There's still plenty of dancing and drinking going on until it's time for them both to leave. Before long, they're changed and disappearing into the limo. I watch as Ryan pulls Izabel into a scorching kiss, which results in loud cheers. And then they're driving off to their future together as husband and wife. I hang around for a while, even after the other guests begin to disperse, making sure nothing is left behind—staying committed to my bridal party duties until the very end. Then I give one last look at the event hall and head on my way, too.

After driving home, I pull my car into the driveway and grab my things. Clicking the doors shut behind me, I stroll up the few steps to the porch and unlock the front door. The neighborhood is quiet, just like it always is, and just the way I like it.

When I throw open the front door, exhaustion, both physical and emotional, threatens to take hold. I manage to slip off my heels once inside the comfort of my home, but that perception of comfort dies quickly, and I immediately know something's off. I'm not sure if it's a sixth sense or what, but I can feel in my bones that something is not right. I peer inside the dark house, straining my ears to hear if anyone's inside. I hang my purse up on the hanger and reach for the wooden baseball bat I keep next to the door.

Carefully, I walk into the house, trying not to make too much noise. I have the bat at the ready over my shoulder as I tiptoe down the front hallway. When I get to the living room, something crunches underneath my feet. I look down and see shards of glass littered all over my floor. My eyes dart to the front window, which has a giant hole in it. The sheer curtains that hang above it float in the wind.

I scan the room, gripping the bat tightly in my hands. I hear a groan across the room, and I stare at the source. A man is passed out on the couch. His face is turned to the side, mouth open and snoring like a chainsaw. A dribble of drool slips past his lips and falls to the ground. A bottle of Jack lays on its side, the contents spilled all over my white rug.

As I observe the man, I let the bat fall, immediately recognizing the figure as my poor excuse of a twin brother. As drunk as ever. I take a few steps closer and then extend the bat toward him. I nudge his shoulder with the end, but he doesn't budge. I nudge harder.

"Alex," I hiss at him, hoping he'll wake up. But again, no luck. Surprise, surprise.

Glaring at my waste-of-space brother, I pull out my phone and consider calling the police. He technically did break into my house. They'd be able to lock him up for tonight, but then he'd probably be at it again tomorrow.

Generally, in a situation like this, Ryan would be my go-to. But obviously—aside from him not even knowing I'm a twin— he's not an option tonight. He's probably busy ravishing his new bride, as he should be, and I don't want to interrupt that.

But Alex is too big for me to move around on my own. The utter weight of him would crush me. Even though he's supposed to be the male counterpart of myself, I am still much smaller than him. Alex isn't overweight by any means, but he's tall. He's like our dad, where I'm the carbon copy of our mom. I'm going to need someone big enough to manhandle him.

I sigh as I stare at my brother. There's only one logical person to call. But I really don't want to. He makes the most sense because he knows Alex so well, and he *knew* me so well.

I bite the inside of my cheek as I scroll through my phone, searching for his number. A chill runs up my spine when I find it.

I haven't talked to him in five years; what if this isn't even his number? What if it's some creepy pizza guy or an ax murderer or something? My thumb hovers over the call button as I weigh the pros and cons of calling him.

This is a really terrible idea. I know calling him will be like opening Pandora's box, but at the same time, I'm confident he's the best person to help me out of this situation.

Stop being a wimp and call him.

I tap on his name before I can talk myself out of it. I put the phone up to my ear and settle in an armchair where I can keep an eye on my brother. My heart is thundering in my chest as I wait for the familiar deep voice to pick up on the other end of the line—the phone rings and rings.

I'm about to hang up and call the cops when, finally, I hear the click, a pause, and then a low, incredulous voice that has my skin breaking out in goosebumps. "Hello?"

"Hey, Ace," I squeak. "Uh, it's me. I need a favor."

Chapter 2

Conner

I DON'T KNOW WHAT I WAS EXPECTING WHEN I WALKED through that door, but it certainly wasn't Josephine dressed up in a tuxedo holding a baseball bat.

Surprise filled me from head to toe when her name flashed across my phone screen this evening. And when I answered the phone and realized it was really her? I nearly fell over. Given that I hadn't heard from her in years, I was half expecting someone to be playing a cruel prank on me. But the sweet, melodic sound of her voice through the phone immediately sent my pulse racing into overdrive, and I almost choked on the whiskey sour I was drinking.

"Hey, Ace. Uh, it's me. I need a favor."

I jumped on that opportunity quicker than hell. Even though it's been years since I've heard from her, she's never not been on my mind. I'd probably do anything for her at this point just to even see her again. So, it had been easy for me to agree to go help her out.

When she asked that I come up to Cedar Ridge to help her with something, I took a deep breath and counted my lucky stars that I just so happened to be in Chattanooga for a conference. Chattanooga was only an hour or so drive from her house, whereas Atlanta, my permanent residence, is about four hours. And I just didn't have that time to waste. I needed to get to her.

I was in my car in record time, driving to the address she texted me. Though the drive was short, I was a mess of nervous energy, knowing that, with each minute that ticked by, I was closer and closer to seeing her. My fingers drummed on the steering wheel as my mind was a mess of memories of everything we had been through in our time together.

When I pulled into her driveway, the house was dark. I noticed the broken window right away and hurried up to the front door. I didn't even bother with the doorbell; I just pushed it open, letting myself in.

I find her in the living room, clutching a baseball bat to her shoulder and glaring across the room. It's a sight that catches me off guard, and I pause in my footsteps.

I stand there, wordlessly taking her in, for a few moments. Even though she hasn't turned toward me yet, she's still a vision. Dressed in a fitted black suit jacket, long slacks, and fuck-me black stiletto heels. She's every bit as beautiful as the last time I saw her all those years ago.

A sense of longing overcomes me, and I want to close the distance between us and take her in my arms—where she belongs. But I have the feeling that's the opposite of what she wants from me right now.

I know she knows I'm standing behind her. I wasn't quiet when I walked through the door, but she still doesn't turn around. Her muscles are bunched up tightly, her shoulders nearly to her ears, like she's gearing herself up to see me, too.

The silence becomes too much, and I finally announce myself, the curiosity of why she's dressed in slacks and a suit jacket too much for me to ignore.

"Why are you in a tux?" I ask. My deep voice cuts through the tension like a knife, and she spins around, pulled out of her frozen state.

Her hazel eyes find mine, and she sucks in a deep breath at the sight of me. Her jaw goes slack as she rakes her gaze over me. It sends tingles all over my body, having her attention on me after so long. When she makes it back up to my face, she rapidly snaps her eyes away from mine, looking down at her clothes.

"I, uh, was the best man at my friend's wedding tonight."

"Ah," I remark, sticking my hands in my pockets as if that's the most normal response in the world. I let my gaze roam over her again, taking her in, too. Even though I'm sure she's had a hell of a long day, she's still beautiful.

Her brown hair is piled on top of her head in an elaborate updo, though her face is framed on either side by loose curls that seem to have escaped from their spots. Those hazel eyes that still haunt my dreams glint in the darkness, but I sense a weariness as we take each other in.

She's so familiar, yet so distant. It's a hard reality to grasp that I hardly know this woman in front of me, when, at one point, I knew her better than the back of my own hand. This is not the way things were supposed to be between us.

"So, are you just going to stand there like a statue, or are you going to help me?" Josephine asks bluntly, as if the awkwardness of being in each other's presence again isn't affecting her as much as it is me.

But I know better. Josephine wears all her emotions on her sleeve, the expressions flitting across her delicate features as clear as day. I can see the way her eyes are shifting around, telling me that she's just as uncomfortable as I am.

"Well, you neglected to tell me what you actually need help with, Josephine," I say, flexing my fingers in my pockets where she can't see them. She didn't need to, honestly. All she had to say was that she needed me, and I'd be there. Which is exactly what happened.

All I want is to run over to her and take her in my arms—to feel whole for the first time in ages. But I can't. We don't know each other like that anymore. It's been way too long, and things have changed.

She scowls at me and stands up, still gripping the bat in her hands. I watch her coolly, knowing already she's not going to use that on me. "First of all, it's *Josie*. Second of all," she points the bat to the couch, "*that* is what I need help with."

My eyes travel across the room to the couch, where I see the passed-out form of her twin brother. A puddle of drool is collecting on the wooden floor underneath his mouth. An obnoxious snore tears out of his lips, echoing through the living room. He's out cold.

"Well, shit," I mutter.

"You're telling me," Josephine snarks. "I don't even know how he found out where I live. I purposefully didn't tell anyone."

Her mouth snaps closed, and she looks at me out of the corner of her eye. She didn't tell anyone, including me. She didn't tell *me* where she was living now. My heart constricts at the realization of how far we've actually fallen apart.

"Alex is nothing if not resourceful," I say as I rub the back of my neck absently. "So, what do you want me to do?"

"I don't care, Conner," Josephine says, crossing her arms over her chest. "Just get him out of here."

"Why'd you call me?" I ask her, knowing I probably won't like the answer. I've dreamt of the moment when we'd actually see each other again for years, but so far, this is not what I expected. A long time ago, I used to believe there would come a time where we would reconcile what happened. There would be hugging, meaningful kisses, words of encouragement—but that dream has long passed. I'm not naïve enough anymore to believe it will be that easy. "I didn't even realize you still had my phone number."

She sighs and then walks over to the armchair, where she curls her legs up underneath her again. "I don't know why. I guess because you were my only option."

Great. I think to myself. I used to be the number one person on her list. Now I've been demoted down to the last resort. Memories of the two of us storming the world together flash through my mind. All these years later, and it still stings to see the amount of distance that is between us now.

"That's great, Jo."

"Jo-*sie*," she snarls.

I chuckle darkly. "What, you think you can just give yourself a new nickname and pretend that the past never happened? Move away to a new city and live a new, perfect life?"

She stands up again, holding her body in a defensive position. "You don't know anything about me, Conner."

"That's not true, and we both know it," I shoot back at her, matching the heated tone that she's throwing at me.

"Whatever. Get out. I'll just call the cops and let them handle this."

"No, you called me here to help, so I'll help."

"I clearly see that that was a mistake. I should've known better, *my bad.*"

I cover my face with my hands and groan. What the fuck is wrong with me? I haven't seen Josephine in *years*, and this is how I react right out of the gates? There's nothing I've wanted more than to talk to her again, to hold her in my arms again. But I should've known this is how it would go. Anytime we're together, it's fireworks. Will we create a beautiful, colorful explosion or start a wildfire? Good or bad, but never in between.

Josephine had been my whole world at one point, and I haven't forgotten that. The utter devotion I have for her is still rooted in me. She turned to me for help tonight; at the very least, I can try to be nice to her without stirring up too many wounds from the past.

"Look, I'm sorry," I say, dropping my hands. "It's just, seeing you after so long is really throwing me. There's a lot of unresolved shit floating through my head right now."

Josephine's shoulders drop, and she exhales. "I know."

Her quiet admission means more to me than she could ever know.

"I'm glad you called me."

She stares up at me, her expression still hard. "I didn't really have any other option. Alex shouldn't be here. And I don't want him here. He's your best friend, so you can deal with him."

I frown. "He's not."

"Okay, well, he *was*. So you know how to handle him when he's like this." She waves her hand at her brother, who is still passed out.

"What am I supposed to do with him?" I ask her. Josephine shrugs and turns on her heel.

"Hell if I know, Ace. Just figure it out." She stalks down the hallway.

My feet are following her before I can comprehend what I'm doing. "Don't do that."

Josephine spins around and faces me again. "Don't do what?"

"Don't run away. I'm tired of watching you retreat from me like I'm the bad guy." There have been too many nights when all I could picture was her retreating form and feel that empty ache inside of me. It was like clockwork, no matter how good she looks walking away from me, it doesn't ease the ache that she leaves in her wake.

"I have nothing left to say to you, Conner. I called you for a favor. That's it. Just take care of Alex and be on your way."

Irritation builds up in my chest, and I clench my fists. "Well, I have lots to say to you, starting with I miss you."

"You don't even know me," she says, shaking her head. "You can't miss someone you don't know."

I could tell her that's not true. That I do know her. I remember everything, every little quirk and habit, every kiss and touch. She was my shooting star, a unique speck of beauty that streaked unwarranted into my life—my one chance for all my dreams to come true.

But I don't.

Instead, I squeeze my eyes shut, taking in a deep breath and counting to five before opening them. I take in all that is Josephine, standing in front of me in her tuxedo. Her bowtie is a little lopsided, makeup a little smudged, but she still looks beautiful. As beautiful as the last time I saw her, maybe even more so. She's grown into a beautiful woman; any man would be crazy to deny it. I can't leave her yet.

"I like your place," I state, changing the topic abruptly as I look around the house. And it's the truth. It's a small ranch-style house, but it's cozy—like a home.

"Thanks," she says hesitantly. "It was my aunt's."

I nod my head. The aunt that she ran to when things got tough. The aunt who shielded her from the rest of us when she decided that running was more manageable than facing problems head-on, not caring about who got hurt in her wake. "Where is good old Aunt Melinda?"

Josephine crosses her arms again, putting that defensive

front back up. "She passed away two years ago. Left the house to me."

"Oh, I'm sorry. I didn't know…"

"I know." I don't say anything else as she stares at me, unmoving. "How did you get here so fast, anyway? I thought you would've been on the road for longer."

"I was in Chattanooga for a conference," I explain. "Might have sped a little bit, too. I was anxious to get here. To see you."

"I see."

I take a step toward her, and to my utter surprise, she doesn't recoil from me. I test the waters again, moving even closer into her space. I can smell her perfume, the exact same scent she's worn for years. It smells familiar, as if it's awakening locked memories from years ago.

Carefully, I raise my hand up to her cheek. Josephine starts a little bit, but I hold her gaze, trying to convey that it's okay. She stares back at me and stills. My hand slides against her jaw, my fingertips rubbing along her silky hairline. My movements are methodical, careful. I don't want to spook her.

As soon as I touch her, the memories flood me. The hours I used to spend running my hands through her dark curls. Her head on my lap, her breath evening out as she'd fall asleep.

Her hazel eyes are still glued on mine, but I see her lean into my touch. She's hesitant, but she can't resist. The point of contact between our skin is charged with electricity, but it doesn't burn. My touch is familiar to her—I know it, she knows it. It's been so long, but even time can't erase the bond we had with each other. She can fight and deny all she wants, but I know she senses the same tug between us that I do. The same tug that has always drawn us together.

I take one step closer until I can feel her body heat seeping into mine. "I miss you, Jo."

"You can't."

"You stopped coming home for the holidays," I observe.

"There's nothing left for me there," she argues back.

"What about me?"

Josephine exhales in defeat and then lets her eyes fall shut. "Especially you. Can you please just get Alex and go? Please don't make me regret calling you more than I already do."

I let my hand drop away from her cheek. Immediately, my palm cools in the absence of her. I clench my fist, ignoring the ache in my chest, and then offer her a brisk nod, averting my gaze. "If that's what you want."

She nods her head and wraps her arms around her middle. "Just get him out of here. Don't worry about the mess. I can take care of it."

"You got it," I say as I turn around and head over to where Alex is still out of it. I shove his shoulder, trying to get him to wake up. I'd rather not have to carry him. That's nearly two hundred pounds of dead weight that I don't feel like hoisting tonight. I'm not sure I could manage the weight of his body on top of the agonizing weight of Josephine and myself still on the outs.

Alex doesn't budge. With a groan, I crouch, drape his arm over my shoulder, and use the strength of my legs to lift him into a semi-standing position—Alex grunts at the disruption and scrambles to his feet.

He looks around groggily, seeing me next to him. "Ace? What're you doing here?" he slurs. "Jo better not find out you're here. She'll throw a bitch fit."

I glance over at Josephine, who's still got her arms wrapped protectively around her middle. She's frowning at her brother, but she peeks at me when she senses my stare. She doesn't outwardly react to her brother's statement, though I'm sure she probably has some choice words that she's biting her tongue to keep from saying.

"Alright, come on, big guy. Let's get you out of here," I tell him, patting my hand against his chest. Alex's head slumps forward, and he lets me drag him toward the door.

I turn and look at Josephine one more time before opening the front door and manhandling Alex down the front stairs toward my 1970 Chevelle. I manage to open the passenger side door of my car and let Alex slump into the seat. He throws his head back against the headrest and then groans.

"Uh, Ace, I don't feel so good."

I sigh. "I bet you don't. Look, I'll be right back. You better not throw up in my car, you moron. Otherwise, your ass is walking back to Atlanta."

Alex's eyes are closed, but he sticks his lips out in a pout. "So mean."

I roll my eyes and then close the car door, making sure his fingers aren't at risk of getting smashed. Against my better judgment, I walk back inside Josephine's house. She's in the living room, on her hands and knees, attempting to wipe up the spilled liquor on the floor.

Josephine hears my footsteps and sighs before looking up to see me standing in front of her. "Conner, I told you to just leave me alone."

I take a few steps toward her. She stands up to face me, nearly falling over in those heels she's wearing. I reach an arm out to steady her, but she swipes her hand at me. "I will. I need to say something first."

Josephine huffs in annoyance but nods her head once. "Fine. Go ahead."

"I just want you to know that whenever you're done playing pretend here, that I'll be waiting. When you're ready to act like a grown-up and address the things that happened to you—to *us*," I correct myself. She wasn't the only one who was hurt that night. And I might be calling her out, but maybe that's exactly what she needs. "You have my number."

"Why do you think I'd need you for that?" she asks, narrowing her eyes at me. "We're not together anymore, Conner. What if I have a boyfriend who has already helped me move past everything?"

"You don't," I say assuredly. "I can see it in your eyes, Jo. And whenever you're ready, I'll be here. But don't try to act like you're fine, 'cause you're not. And I know, probably better than anyone, what that's like."

"It's Josie," she grits. "You don't know anything, and until you can start calling me by my name, I don't have anything else to say to you. Get out."

"What are you going to do about that window?" I ask her. Josephine's eyes go wide at the change of subject, and she looks at the shattered glass. She obviously hasn't thought that far ahead yet.

"I'll figure it out."

"I can—"

"No." She firmly cuts me off. "I don't need your help any further. I have everything under control. Now, please, just go."

"Okay," I say, raising my hands up in surrender. By now I know there's no point in fighting her when she's like this. "But just don't forget what I said. Whenever you're ready, Jo. I'm all in."

I turn to head out the front door again when I hear her throw the towel down on the floor. "That's not fair, Conner! You can't just storm back into my life and pretend that we mean anything to each other anymore. You and I are *done*. We've been done since—"

"Since when? Since you decided to take it upon yourself to make all the choices regarding our relationship? I wasn't done, Jo. I wasn't even close to being done. But you decided that I was. All by yourself," I shoot back, frustration growing that she would have the audacity to toss that in my face.

I haven't seen this woman in five years. But now, all it took was thirty minutes in her presence and everything is spewing out of me like a Mentos in Coke. I'm thrilled to see her. I'm dying to take her in my arms and to kiss her, but I need to get things off my chest first. Some things were never said between us that have been festering for years. I'm tired of it. So, if we need to throw it down here and now to resolve things, then so be it.

"Leave. Now. Before I call the cops on you for trespassing."

My shoulders sag in defeat. Looks like we're not resolving anything anytime soon. "Okay, have it your way. I'll see you around, Jo."

I turn and head toward her door again, and smile when I hear her growl at me, "It's *Josie!*"

Chapter 3

Josie

I GROAN INTO MY PILLOW AT THE ANNOYING *WHIRRING* sound of a drill. The noise travels straight to my bones as a screw is situated into place. After that, the repetition of a hammer hitting a nail has me gritting my teeth and cursing under my breath.

"What the actual F!" I shout as I throw back my comforter and storm out of my bedroom. My bare feet pad against the hardwood floors as I walk into the living room. I throw open the front door and stalk out onto the porch.

There, I see Conner-freaking-Reynolds, standing on a stool, hammering a board up over my broken window. Conner Reynolds, my high school sweetheart slash baby daddy. I put my hands on my hips and glare at him. "What the hell do you think you're doing?"

He looks down at me, a few nails stuck between his teeth. He removes them and then shoots me that boyish grin of his that sends my chest fluttering. "Morning, Josephine. Sleep well?"

"No," I state. "Because some psychopath decided it would

be a good idea to do construction on my house at six thirty in the morning."

Conner chuckles and picks up his drill and another screw. "You're welcome for helping you fix up your window. I got the measurements, and I put an order in at Home Depot to get you a new one. But this will have to do for now."

I cross my arms over my chest, feeling the cool October chill. I'm only wearing a tank top and sleep shorts. Definitely not enough to keep me warm in this fall weather. "I could've done that myself."

Actually, I probably couldn't have. I honestly hadn't been sure what I was going to do about the window. Conner asked me about it last night and I put on a brave face, as I usually do, and pretended like I had it covered. But again, in that situation, my go-to would probably be Ryan, who is not an option right now. Worst-case scenario, I'd probably call his friend Liam and see if he could help me or hire someone off the internet.

So, truthfully, Conner helping me out with this takes a huge load off my shoulders, but he doesn't need to know about that.

"I know," he says. "You've got everything under control. I just felt like lending a helping hand."

"Well, thanks, I guess."

"And I kind of felt bad about last night," Conner says. He looks at me with his golden-brown eyes.

My mind involuntarily jumps to Josh: the Guy Behind the Bar from the wedding. He had brown eyes, too, though his reminded me of a puppy. Conner's brown eyes have always reminded me of liquid amber. Ringed in rich dark brown but with a warm honey center.

"I shouldn't have ambushed you like that, given our history," Conner continues, pulling me out of my thoughts about the familiar color of his eyes. "Seeing you for the first time in so long really messed with my head. And I'm sorry."

I narrow my eyes at him. I can't deny that I had the same reaction. I was hesitant to call in the first place because I knew an encounter with him would work out exactly like it did. There's too much history between us. Frankly, I thought it would've been worse.

"It's okay," I say.

"It's not," Conner argues, and I clench my jaw. Always disagreeing with me. "But that's why I'm doing this. It's the least I can do."

"Okay," I respond. I stare at him for another moment before going back into the house, trying to wrap my head around the last twelve hours.

My house was broken into.

Not by a stranger, but by my alcoholic twin brother, who hardly anyone knows about. Leaving me with no choice but to reach out to the one person who knows Alex exists: Conner. Conner is now one of two people from my former life with my address, and he is still *here*.

Conner is *here*.

Fixing my window.

That my alcoholic brother broke.

Everything's fine.

I wander into my kitchen, hearing the sound of Conner's drill starting up again. I pull down my can of Folgers and put enough into the coffeemaker for two people. It's debatable if Conner will get that second serving, as my brain needs all the extra caffeine it can get this morning. The coffee pot bubbles when I turn it on and begins brewing the coffee.

I hurry back into my bedroom and find a pair of flannel pants and tug them on, as well as a sweater. I run my brush through my hair, yanking out the tangles and smoothing it all out. Then I run some warm water and splash it on my face, scrubbing the sleep away.

When I walk back out to the kitchen, the coffee is done, and I pour two mugs begrudgingly, carefully carrying them outside to the front porch. Conner looks down at me when I step outside.

"Here," I say, handing him the mug of coffee.

Conner's dark eyebrows raise in surprise, but he doesn't decline my peace offering. He takes it in his hand and takes a sip. His nose crinkles up and he glares down at the coffee. "You didn't have to do this, Jo."

"It's Josie," I correct him for the hundredth time, which is a lot, considering the very short amount of time he's been back in my life. "And you need coffee. It's the least I can do for you getting up early to fix my window." I pout, and then an idea pops into my head. "What if I take you to breakfast? I have no food in the house, but there's a nice diner down the road."

"You want to have breakfast with me?" he asks incredulously.

I shrug. "Not really, but you're doing me a favor. So, I can suffer through a meal with you."

Conner throws his head back and laughs. The deep sound of his voice tugs at something in my gut. "You really know how to make a guy feel special, Josephine DiMarco."

"Whatever. How much longer do you think you have?"

Conner looks back at the board he's setting up and rubs the back of his neck. "Maybe twenty minutes. I want to make sure it's on tight enough, so it won't come crashing down."

"Great, I'll get changed into some real clothes and then we can go." I step back into the house and let the front door close behind me. I go back into my room and find a pair of jeans and a simple long sleeve t-shirt before locking myself in the bathroom to make myself more presentable.

Thirty minutes later, I find Conner sitting on my couch flipping through TV channels. He looks up when I step into the room and shuts off the television.

"Ready?" I ask him, grabbing my keys.

"Yeah, I can drive. I know it's been a while, but I haven't forgotten that your driving is almost worse than your coffee," he teases me.

I roll my eyes, but follow him out to his car, anyway. Once I'm settled into the front seat, I sniff. "It smells really good in here."

Conner looks at me sheepishly. "Yeah, Alex threw up on the way to the hotel last night. So, before I came over to your place, I made sure to scrub that shit out. I think I used an entire bottle of upholstery soap and conditioner."

"Seriously? What time did you get up this morning? Did you even sleep last night?"

"Uh, no. I was too wound up from everything. I tried, but it just wasn't happening."

"So, you didn't sleep at all last night?" He shakes his head. "How do you even function? I need all the sleep I can get."

"I remember," he chuckles. "You sleep like the dead. I'm surprised I woke you up this morning."

I get an unsettled churning in my stomach. Conner and I are talking like two people who know each other intimately. This isn't what I want. I don't want to laugh and recall things about each other. I don't want to acknowledge that the one person who knows me best in the world is sitting right next to me. I don't have time for the issues that's going to dredge up, and I don't want to hurt him again by pushing him away.

I'm in a lose-lose situation right now.

Conner pulls into the parking lot of the diner, and we get out. We walk side by side, and the waitress sits us at a booth in the corner. Conner looks at his menu for a minute before peeking at me over the edge.

"You'll have to tell me what's good here."

"Pretty much anything. It's a mom-and-pop diner; you can't go wrong," I say.

"Then an omelet and chocolate chip pancakes it is," he says, shutting his menu and folding his hands on top of it. "What are you going to get?"

"I usually get an egg white omelet with ham and mixed veggies," I tell him. "And bacon on the side."

"Gotta have the bacon," Conner says, winking at me. I get that unsettled feeling again in my stomach, and I take a sip of water to calm it.

The waitress comes by and gets our orders. Then she pours each of us a cup of coffee. Conner takes a sip and then sighs happily. "That's better."

"Okay, Ace. I get it. I suck at coffee."

Conner messes with a packet of sweetener between his fingers and then looks up at me with a thoughtful expression. "You and Alex are the only ones who call me that anymore."

"Ace?" I clarify and he nods his head. I shrug my shoulders. "That's who you are."

"Not anymore. That ship has sailed."

"I guess your shoulder never fully healed from the injury?" I ask him.

"Nope. And no D1 college is going to take a volleyball player with a bum shoulder. Probably not even a community college team would let me play."

"I'm sorry, Conner," I say as I shake my head. I mean it, too. Volleyball was one of Conner's big-time dreams. He was so good; they were watching him for Olympic potential. I remember sitting on the bleachers cheering him on, game after game. They called him Ace for a reason—he was the team's secret weapon. But one distraction, a bad play, a torn rotator cuff, and two botched surgeries later, his volleyball career was done for.

Just another thing I have to feel responsible for.

"It's okay. Out of all the things I lost that year, that was the most inconsequential," he states. His eyes hold mine as he waits for his words to sink in.

But I don't let them. Our food arrives moments later, and I dig right in, not letting myself stew in the underlying meaning of his words. The buttery flavor of the egg white omelet explodes in my mouth when I take a bite, and I have to control myself from groaning. This diner is one of my favorite places to eat; they never disappoint.

By the time I'm halfway through my omelet, Conner's downed his two pancakes and is working on finishing off his omelet, too.

He's zeroed into polishing off his breakfast, and while he's distracted, I take the opportunity to really study this new version of him. Conner has always had an excellent physique, from all those days running drills in the gym and conditioning in the weight room. Though, now, the man sitting in front of me is a lot more filled out than the wiry volleyball player I used to date in high school.

His shoulders are much broader, his arms more bulky. His hair is longer than I remember, too, the dark chocolate strands falling slightly over his ears. He could really use a trim. I've always found Conner attractive, even as a boy. But now, he's all man, and it is doing unspeakable things to my insides.

The waitress comes by to collect our dishes when we're all finished, topping off our coffees and telling us to take our time.

Conner watches me with his warm eyes as he reaches for his coffee. "I'm going to ask you something, and I don't want you to get all defensive like you do, okay? It's just an honest question coming from someone who cares about you."

My muscles go on high alert, anyway, my shoulders stiffening in response, creeping closer to my ears by the second. "Do you have to?"

He leans forward and holds my gaze. "Yes, I think I do."

"Well, just get it over with, then."

"Have you talked to anyone about what happened? Have you gotten help?"

I stare him down for a moment, considering telling him to buzz off and that it's none of his business. But really, it kind of *is* his business as much as it is mine. Despite our history, I find myself lying to him through my teeth. "Of course. Have you?"

Conner narrows his eyes at me. "You've never been good at lying, Jo. You know I can see right through your bullshit. Tell me the truth."

Suddenly, my breakfast is not settling well in my stomach. My belly sours and threatens to protest the uncomfortable line of questioning. "I've got everything under control."

Conner sits back with a sigh and continues to stare me down. Not in a menacing way, but just enough to let me know that he sees me. "I guess that's how we're going to play this. If you don't want to talk about what happened, just say so. Don't lie and feed me a line about how everything's 'under control,'" he says, making air quotes with his fingers. "I know you're not fine because *I'm* not fine. And I can't even imagine that what I went through was even a fraction of what you did."

My breath catches in my lungs. He's not fine? What does that even mean? It's been almost ten years; how could he not be? But then again, I'm really not over it all, either, as much as I pretend that I am.

"The thing about loss," Conner continues softly, "is that

you have to face it head on to heal. You have to address it to properly move on."

I'm definitely going to throw up.

"Conner," I mutter as I squirm in my seat. "I'm really okay. I've done what I need to do to move on. I don't need you to shrink me in a diner, okay? Let's just finish our coffee and go our separate ways."

"I would accept that if I thought it were true, but I can tell it's not. You're still hurting, Jo. I can see it clear as day. And it's okay," he says gently. "Because I'm still hurting, too. I know you've convinced yourself that you had to go through it all alone, but you didn't, you don't. I'm here. We can work through it together."

The thing about burying emotions for so long is that the false pretense eventually becomes your reality. In my mind, I don't have unresolved feelings of grief or mourning. To me, everything really is fine. I have a good life, good friends, a good job. I'm happy where I am. So, when someone threatens that pretense, things often have the tendency to get heated, quickly.

"We can't because there's nothing to work through," I shoot back, my blood heating up and threatening to boil over. My internal defenses flare, and I glower at him. "I don't need you to *fix* me because I'm not broken. I've already done all the fixing I can do."

"Jo, that's not what I meant. I don't think you're brok—"

"For the last fucking time, it's *Josie*," I say through gritted teeth. I reach into my wallet and pull out two twenties, leaving them on the table. Without another word to him, I get up and storm out of the diner, not caring if I look like I've completely lost my mind.

"Josephine!" I hear Conner call after me as if I didn't *just* tell him what I wanted to be called. He mutters a quick "thank you" to the waitresses as he runs past and follows me out the door. "Would you wait up?"

"Go away," I mutter. My lower lip trembles, and my eyes start to sting. If he keeps pushing me, I'm going to cry right here in the middle of the street, and I really don't need that today.

"Hey, come here," he says, reaching out and wrapping his hand around my wrist, halting my movements. I spin around, and his face falls. "*Shit,*" he mutters before pulling me into him and encircling his arms around me. I bury my face against his chest, allowing a few traitorous tears to leak out, and let him hold me right there in the diner parking lot.

My body warms as he holds me. I close my eyes against his shirt and breathe him in. How is it that, ten years later, he still smells the exact same? It's not a cologne or body spray, it's just Conner.

The familiarity of being in his arms soothes me. Just as it did last night, my body has a primal reaction to his touch. All he did last night was touch my cheek, and yet, my stomach felt like molten chocolate.

Gradually, every nerve ending settles a fraction as he holds me. I don't want to react this way, but I can rationalize it. Conner meant so much to me for so long, it makes sense that I would still react to him the same way, even all these years later.

I haven't seen Conner in five years, but we've been split up for ten. After everything that happened with the accident and the baby, I ran for the hills and barely looked back. There was so much pain left over that I couldn't bear to face it, so I left. For the first five years following that, I would still return home for the holidays, Thanksgiving or Christmas, and Conner would be there every time, waiting for me, with that big goofy smile on his face that I loved so much.

But then I didn't go one year, and I haven't been back since. I didn't think anyone missed me. My parents, who had gotten a divorce shortly after the accident, never reached out to me. I'll occasionally get a birthday letter in the mail, but that's about it. Alex is too drunk most of the time to even care, and Conner... he eventually stopped trying, too.

The way I saw it, that chapter of my life was over. The Josephine everyone knew died that night in the accident. I didn't have any regrets. But now that Conner's back in my life, asking all these questions and holding me tightly in a parking lot and letting me cry all over him, I'm wondering if that's actually true, or if I've been living a lie for years.

Chapter 4

Conner

Josephine's sniffles against my shirt finally cease, and I'm confident enough to let her go. I push her back a little, keeping my hands on her shoulders so I can look at her. Her beautiful hazel eyes are red and blotchy, and I instantly feel like the biggest prick in the world.

I don't know why I jumped right into this sensitive topic again. Given her reaction last night, I should've known better. I can see her hurting right in front of my eyes, and I want to do something. Josephine has always been one of the most important people in my life, and I don't ever want to see her hurt or crying.

Like she is now.

I let out a shaky breath and run my fingers underneath her eyes, collecting the tears. "I'm sorry."

Josephine chuckles and then sniffles again. "You keep saying that."

"I know. I can't help it. I just keep fucking up."

She shakes her head and then looks away. "It's okay."

"It's not. I wish *you* would stop saying *that*," I tell her. "Do you think we could start over, for real this time? I promise not to bring up the bad stuff anymore."

Josephine exhales. "I don't know if that's possible with us. There's too much..." She trails off and then shrugs. "Maybe?"

"I can work with maybe," I say, giving her a small smile. "Let's get you home."

She follows me to my car, where we both get settled. I pull out of the parking lot and start heading toward her house. We're about halfway there when my vehicle jolts us forward. The engine stutters and makes a loud bang. As the car slows to a stop, smoke billows out from under the hood.

I swear out loud as I put my car into park. Josephine's leaning forward, looking out the windshield. "What happened?"

"I don't know, but it can't be good. Stay here," I instruct her. I hop out of my seat and walk around to the front of the car. I pop open the hood and cough as a plume of smoke comes out from the engine.

"Do you think you blew a gasket or something?" Josephine asks. I whip around to see her standing right next to me, because why *would* she listen to my request for her to stay?

"I better not have," I grumble. "I'll have to call a tow truck. Do you know of any good mechanics around here?"

"Yeah, there's one a few blocks down," Jo says. "But he's not open on Sundays."

I dial up the tow truck and explain what's going on and where I'm located. Josephine stands next to me, her arms crossed over her chest from the chill. Once I hang up the phone, I turn to her. "Do you want me to call you an Uber to take you home? I don't want you to have to wait."

She shakes her head. "No, it's okay. I'll stay with you."

I stare at her for a second before I decide not to question

her motives. I'll just take what I can get with her. "Let's wait in the car, then; you're freezing."

Josephine follows my lead as we get back into the Chevelle. I reach behind us into the back seat and grab a hoodie. "Here, you can put this on." I offer it to Josephine. She gives me a smile as she slips it on over her head.

"Thanks," she says simply, snuggling into the warmth of the sweatshirt.

I rub my hands together. It's not terribly cold outside, but chilly enough that I wish I could turn my car on to get the heat blowing, but given that I don't actually know what caused it to break down, I refrain. I don't want my car blowing up on the side of the road. "Well, this is an unfortunate turn of events," I muse. Jo chuckles next to me and agrees. "So, let's play a game."

She eyes me warily. "What kind of game?"

"How about twenty questions?" I ask and then continue speaking when I see her mouth open in protest. "I swear only safe questions, okay?"

Josephine stares at me a second before relenting. "Fine. But I get to go first. What do you do for work?"

"It's really boring. I work for my dad's company as a marketing data analyst," I explain. "I get to look at qualitative and quantitative trends to help other companies, our clients, determine the best strategies for their marketing processes."

Josephine crinkles up her nose. "That does sound boring. I thought you wanted to be a pilot."

I lean my head against my headrest. "Yeah, when I was sixteen. Then I wanted to be an Olympic volleyball player. But life has a way of surprising you."

"Ain't that the truth."

"After everything happened," I clear my throat, hoping Jo doesn't pick up on the emotion hiding behind my words, "my dad offered me a position at his company. Not really having any other prospects, I took it. Now, he's getting ready to retire, and he's training me to step up and take over once that happens."

"That sounds like a great opportunity for you."

"Yeah, I guess so. What about you? What do you do?"

Josephine looks down at her fingers and messes with the cuticle on her thumb. "I'm an architect."

I raise my eyebrows in surprise. "Wow, I wouldn't have guessed that. Didn't you hate geometry in high school?"

She shrugs and looks out the window. "Yeah. But for a while, it seemed like everything in life I touched I ruined. I wanted to go to college to learn how to build things. Architecture is what I landed on, and now I get to build things that last."

"What do you mean, you ruined everything you touched?" I ask her, not liking the tone her voice took on when she dropped that overarching statement.

Her hazel eyes find mine again, and she stares at me accusingly. "I thought you said no deep questions."

I hold up my hands. "You're right. You just brought it up. Sorry."

She sighs and then looks out the front windshield. "My brother is an alcoholic. I ruined our relationship. My parents got a divorce because of me. I lost our baby," Josephine adds softly as her voice breaks, confirming my suspicions that she definitely isn't as fine as she says she is. "I ruin things."

A thick silence blankets us. I don't know what to say to her. How could she possibly believe that's the truth?

She shakes her head. "*Anyway*, with this fresh start, I decided that I was going to *build* things instead."

"I like that," I say. I want to challenge her, force her to see that she's one of the most incredible people I know—but then I realize that I don't know her. At least I don't know this version of her, so I let it be.

"Yeah," Josephine agrees. "I work in a small firm with my best friend, whose wedding I was at yesterday. I do mostly commercial projects, but someday, I'd love to do residential."

"Like fixer-uppers? Think you'll have your own HGTV show?"

She chuckles and shakes her head. "Yes, on the fixer-uppers. Hard no on the TV show."

"Why don't you do that, then?" I ask her. "Start doing a few residential projects."

Josephine shrugs. "I don't really have time right now."

"Maybe you should make time," I suggest. "If it's something you feel passionate enough about."

She laughs. "You are really trying to turn my world upside down, aren't you, Ace? You come in with your guns blazing and try to stir shit up."

"Our relationship was short-lived, but I think that's what we did best. Don't you? We always pushed each other to be the best possible versions of ourselves."

"Do you ever wonder where we'd be now if that night never happened?" Jo asks hesitantly after a beat.

"All the time," I answer honestly. The memories of the fear and helplessness play on the edges of my mind, but I dampen them. "Do you?"

She looks out the window. "I try not to, but yes."

"Your turn to ask a question, Jo," I say. She doesn't want to talk about the deep stuff, so I won't push her.

"Is that the tow truck?" she asks, looking over her shoulder.

I turn to look as well, feeling my mood sink. That was quick. "Yup, looks like it."

I get out of the car and meet the driver, explaining to him a little bit about what happened and where I want the car taken. Josephine stands close to my side, seeking warmth from my body heat. The driver gets to setting the car up on the pulley system.

"You kids need a ride somewhere?" he asks. His voice is rough, but his eyes are kind.

"No, we're good. We'll call an Uber," I explain. He tips the brim of his hat toward us and goes back to work.

"I think we should get separate rides," I say to Josephine. "That way, you can go home, and I'll get a rental. Then I'll sort out the situation with your brother."

She nods her head and then pulls out her phone, opening up a rideshare app. "About five minutes for my car. Well, thanks for coming all the way up here and for fixing my window."

I stick my hands in my pockets and observe her. "You're welcome. I'm glad you called me. Maybe Home Depot will get your window in before I leave, and I can install it for you."

Josephine shrugs and offers me a smile that doesn't reach her eyes. "If you want. Otherwise, I can find someone else to do it."

"I can do it."

She eyes me a moment and then nods, giving me a soft, uncertain smile.

Her car comes a minute later, and she gives me a little wave before getting in.

I watch her disappear around the block, and then I pull out my own phone, typing in the address of the closest car rental place. As my driver takes me there, I think about the discussions I had with Jo this morning. I'm glad we left on a good note. She seemed almost reluctant to leave me alone on the side of the road, which I'll take as a good sign.

I'm not trying to fix her, but I can tell that she has put up some reinforced walls to protect herself. She's so different from the girl I used to love, but at the heart of it, she's still my Jo; she's just hurting and wounded. Despite how well she tries to hide it, I can see right through her façade.

I don't want to fool myself into thinking that I'm going to be the catalyst that helps her heal, but maybe I can at least put her on the right track. Our story might be over, but I still want her to live a happy life without the shadows of our past following her everywhere she goes.

Jo said she ruins everything she touches, and it breaks my heart that she would think that about herself. I don't hold her accountable for anything that happened, and I don't want her to blame herself. What happened wasn't her fault, but I don't know how to convince her of that. No one back home blames her for it. If anything, it's her idiot brother's fault, but even then... sometimes bad things just happen to good people.

After getting situated with a rental car, I drive back to the hotel and take the elevator up to my room. When I open the door, I run straight into Alex DiMarco, who's coming out of the bathroom, rubbing at his hair with a towel. He shoots me a scowl, then goes back toward the bedroom.

"What are you doing here, Ace?" he asks. He's not slurring his words today, so hopefully, he's sobered enough.

I drop my keys and phone on the table in the room and cross my arms. "I should be asking you the same thing. What are *you* doing here?"

Alex frowns and then rubs his shoulder. "Honestly, dude, I don't even know where *here* is."

I have to keep myself from rolling my eyes. Same old Alex, different town. He knew he was at Jo's house last night, which tells me he must've been past the point of no return by then. "You're in Cedar Ridge. You broke into Jo's house."

Alex has the decency to look surprised. "Oh, I bet she didn't like that."

"No, she didn't. What the hell are you doing with your life, man?" I ask him. "Also, how did you know where she lives?"

"I have friends in high places. Also, it's not hard to do a Google search. Don't be mad because I found her first," Alex snarks at me. Then he chuckles when he sees my expression. "Shit, that's it, isn't it? You're mad because I found her, and you couldn't."

"Don't be stupid. I didn't try to find her because I respected her privacy."

"Right. So, what, she calls and asks you to come to save her from me? Playing hero again, huh, Ace? I bet you really got your rocks off on that."

"What were you doing there in the first place?" I ask him, not taking his bait. Alex used to be my best friend until he got involved with the wrong people. Now, I barely even recognize him. And so is my trend with the DiMarco twins.

"I needed money," he says, as if that's the most normal reason in the world. "I know she's pretty well off, though you wouldn't guess that based on that dump she's living in."

"Why do you need money, Alex?" I prod, even though I already know I really don't want to know the answer.

He waves me off and scrubs at his dark hair again with the towel. "It's nothing. I got a little cocky and bet more than I had at poker last week."

I close my eyes and take a deep breath. Alex is just as bad at lying as his sister. Their matching hazel eyes get all shifty, and they can't look you straight in the eye. "How much?"

"A grand."

"Okay, I'll tell you what. I'll front you the money if you promise to stay far away from Josephine. Do you understand? I don't want to catch wind that you're anywhere near her."

Alex looks up and stares at me for a second, his expression suspicious. "You still have feelings for her, don't you? Even after everything that happened." He whistles lowly. "You poor bastard."

"You don't know what you're talking about. Do we have a deal or not?"

"I can see it written all over your face, Ace. You got that mopey puppy dog look that you always used to get whenever she'd come around." Alex chortles. "This is just too good. Does she know you still love her?"

I reach into my back wallet, pulling out a folded up blank check. I scribble the amount and then sign my name with the hotel pen before handing it over to Alex. "Just take the money and go. I don't want to see you around here again."

"Are you expecting me to pay this back?" he asks.

Now it's my turn to laugh. "If I thought you were good for it, maybe. But since I know you're not, no. As long as you stay far away from Cedar Ridge and your sister, you and I are square. Got it?"

Alex snatches the check out of my hands and stands up straight. "I get it. I'd say thank you, but I don't really feel like it." He sneers at me.

"Whatever, dude. Get out of here."

"Have fun with my sister. Don't knock her up again," he calls as he walks out of my hotel room.

When he's gone, I slump onto the edge of the bed and rub a hand over my face. Every interaction with Alex DiMarco is less than desirable. I just hope he listens for once in his life. The money I loaned him will hurt, given that I'll likely have car repairs that need to be paid for, but it's worth it to keep him out of Jo's way.

I pull out my phone and dial my dad's number. He answers on the second ring. "Conner?"

"Hey, Dad. Look, I'm not going to be in for work tomorrow," I tell him. I've been working under my father for the last few years, training and learning as much as I can before he retires and leaves it all to me. It's been the plan since I started there; my dad concocted it all on his own once we both realized I had no other professional prospects.

"Why?"

"Because I'm in Cedar Ridge and my car broke down, and I don't know when it will be ready to go."

"Where the hell is Cedar Ridge?" he asks. I can hear my mom on the other end of the phone, asking if he's talking to me and to tell me hello. "Your mother says hi."

"Hi, Mom," I say back. "It's in Tennessee."

"I thought you were in Chattanooga, at the conference."

"I was, but a friend called me and needed my help, so I drove up here," I explain. I can practically hear the gears clicking around in my dad's head, and I'm not surprised by his next follow-up question.

"Who's the friend?"

I close my eyes and sigh. "Josephine."

"Josephine DiMarco? Are you kidding me?" He laughs on the other end of the phone. "Well, good luck with that, son."

"Thanks. I might just take the rest of my vacation," I tell him. I haven't used any of it this year, so I have two weeks' worth sitting in the bank. It's October, and it doesn't roll over into the new year. Might as well just burn through it.

"Sure. Just put it in the portal if you get a chance," Dad says. "Thanks for calling, son. We'll talk soon."

I say goodbye and then hang up. I flop back onto the bed and groan. I might be overstaying my welcome here, but I don't care. This way, I can make sure that Josephine's window gets installed properly. Maybe I'll get the chance to spend some more time with her, too.

Alex's observation that I look like a mopey puppy might not

be that far off. He's right. I do always get like this whenever Jo's involved. I just can't help it.

I remember when I first met Alex and Josephine. They moved into the big empty house down the road from where I lived. It was the greatest thing ever to happen to me because there were no kids my age in the neighborhood, but then, the DiMarcos moved in, and I had *two* friends my age. We were thick as thieves from the start. The three of us were inseparable.

But quickly, I learned that one twin took priority in my heart over the other. Josephine was magnetic from the first moment I met her. She was a wild card. I never knew what to expect with her, and that's what made her so appealing to me.

Alex was my best friend throughout middle and high school, until he started getting mixed up with the wrong crowd. But Josephine was so much more.

We officially started dating when we were sixteen. I remember building up the nerve to finally ask her out officially. Up until that point, it was soft smiles, hidden moments. I'd hold her hand underneath the blankets during Friday night movies. Or I'd give her a quick kiss when no one was looking.

Once I finally did grow the balls to ask her out, our relationship took off like a rocket. My world revolved around her. I'll never forget the night after Junior Prom, when we finally made love. That night was all heated kisses and breathy sighs as I got to know Josephine on a much more intimate level. That part of our relationship had been building for a while until we finally made the leap together. It was just Jo and me, and nothing could get between us.

We found out she was pregnant right before our senior year started. While it opened up a new path for the two of us, I wasn't scared. I could easily see myself loving her for the rest of our life. And knowing that we had created a life together just made our love all that more real.

That's part of the reason why it hurt so badly when she cut everyone off. She was hurting, I understand that; what happened to her was unspeakable. But I never wanted her to feel like she was alone. We were a team. There was no better person for either of us than each other. Now I just have to remind her of that.

Chapter 5

Josie

"Good morning, Lori," I announce as I walk into the lobby of our office. The older woman looks up from her computer and grins at me.

"Good morning, Josie. How was your weekend?"

I pause. How was my weekend?

Lori was at Ryan and Izabel's wedding on Saturday, so I saw her then. But other than that? My weekend consisted of a blast from the past with my old high school sweetheart, including many uncomfortable conversations and a surprising amount of nostalgia hitting me straight in the heartstrings.

"It was fine," I tell her and leave it at that. "Are there any messages?"

"Just a voicemail from the Jackson Association about their designs for the hotel. They keep calling about that."

"And I keep telling them my deadline isn't until next week, so that's why I haven't finished them yet," I huff, frustrated with one of my bigger clients right now. I was excited to start working with them, knowing the project would be a huge win for our firm, but so far, they've been nothing but a pain in my ass. "It's like they expect me to be tied to my computer at all hours of the day or something."

Lori chuckles and shakes her head. "Have you heard from Ryan?" she asks.

"No, and I'm glad I haven't. They're probably all mushy gushy in love. He'll be back in town Friday, though, so I'm sure he'll be checking in at some point."

"You did such a nice job with your speech. I know you were worried about that."

I offer her a tight-lipped smile. "I'm just thankful I didn't pass out in front of all their guests. That would've been embarrassing."

Lori and I chat for a moment longer before I tell her I'll be in my office, and I disappear. I set my things down on my desk and swivel around in my chair to boot up my computer. As the machine whirrs to life, I reach into my bag and pull out the breakfast sandwich I got from McDonald's. I told Conner yesterday that I didn't have much food in the house, and I wasn't exaggerating.

Conner.

I take a bite of my sandwich and watch my computer screen display the boot-up logo. All day yesterday, I kept replaying our conversations over and over in my head. It didn't make sense that Conner could come back into my life for two seconds, and I was already spewing all my secrets.

I usually kept those secured behind a pretty tight lock. My past mistakes and regrets would keep me up at night if I let them, so I made an effort early on to bury them deep and not worry about them much. Aside from the occasional nostalgia or melancholy, I typically have everything under control.

Until Conner comes around and starts opening up old wounds.

I don't know what he was trying to accomplish. He kept telling me that he could see that I was still holding on to stuff. I'm not sure what that means. But I shouldn't really be surprised. Conner always saw me for *me*, more so than anyone else.

As much as I don't want to admit it, I enjoyed spending time with him yesterday. For a long time, Conner Reynolds was my best friend, my number one confidant. You don't just forget a relationship like that. Even romantically aside, I trusted Conner with everything in me. I'm sure a part of me still remembers that all these years later.

I lean back in my chair and munch on my breakfast sandwich. It had been nice seeing him. I couldn't deny that, while he was around, part of me felt lighter. I could put up all the walls I wanted to, but eventually those walls might start resembling more of a confinement rather than a stronghold.

Once the computer finishes booting up, I start my working music playlist. It's a collection of soft instrumentals that helps me focus a little better. I don't like sitting in a quiet room all day long. I get straight to work, pulling up my to-do list and starting on the first item. I like lists when I work. They keep me organized and focused. Since Ryan's out of the office, I have to do a little double-time to help him stay on track with his projects, as well as keeping up with my own. I have a few permits to order and a couple sketches to submit, and I'll finish the day with a couple of consult calls.

I run through my emails right off the bat and respond to those that need immediate attention. The phone rings a few times, a couple clients asking for updates or inspectors working on getting appointment times set up.

Once that's all taken care of, I start working on my big hotel project. I find myself getting lost in the work, excited to get this project rocking and rolling. This is going to be *huge* for Ryan and me, from a professional aspect. The Jackson Association is easily one of the biggest clients we've had, with cross country establishments that our firm will have contributed to. With the excitement and the big dollar signs in my eyes, comes a wave of trepidation—I can't mess this up.

Time flies, and before I realize it, the clock reads fifteen minutes to noon. Lori buzzes me on the intercom, and I pick it up. "Hello?"

"Josie, there's a very handsome man here who says he brought you lunch. Should I send him on back?" she asks.

My lips traitorously pull up into a grin. *Conner.* "Yes, send him back, please."

I hang up and then finish up what I was working on. There's a knock at my door, and I stand up and start to smile as the door opens. And then it quickly falls when I see who it is.

"Chris," I say, surprised, and I'm even more surprised when a feeling of disappointment settles in my stomach.

"Expecting someone else?" he asks with a coy grin. He holds up a white paper bag in offering. "I haven't heard from you in a while, so I wanted to stop by and bring you lunch."

"Oh, that's kind of you. I've just been swamped here at work. I'm sure you understand."

Chris Bruno—a one-night-stand gone wrong—nods his head and steps further into my office, seating himself in the chair in front of my desk. He plops the paper bag in front of him, and the smell of burnt cheese and onions wafts into my nose. I nearly gag.

"What is that?"

"Cheesesteaks!" he announces happily.

I try not to wrinkle my nose up. I'll definitely need to go get a salad or something next door after he leaves. "Thanks."

"Anything for my favorite architect," Chris says as he leans back in the chair. He notches his hands behind his head and looks at me cockily. "You know, Josie, I've been thinking..."

There's something new, I think to myself, but bite my tongue. I give him a small smile as he continues.

"I really love spending time with you. You're brilliant and gorgeous, and I think we should take this to the next level." He leans forward, so his elbows are leaning on his knees, and looks at me intently. "I'd like for you to go out with me. Let's see where this goes. I could be the greatest thing to ever happen to you."

"I have a boyfriend!" I blurt. This whole encounter is making me incredibly uncomfortable. The cheesesteaks are stinking up my office, and Chris's arrogant confidence makes me want to poke him in the eyeballs.

Chris raises his eyebrows and then laughs. "Right. That's funny."

I cross my arms and stare at him. "What does that mean?"

"You told me you didn't date."

I narrow my eyes at him. "So, then *why are you here*, propositioning me?"

"Because you're a catch, Josie. I'm trying to shoot my shot here. Maybe I can be the guy that rocks your world."

"Well, I'm serious, Chris. I have a boyfriend. We just got back together," I lie. I just want this guy out of my office. I've hooked up with Chris maybe two times, and he's here practically proposing marriage. I am barely holding the full body shudders at bay with that thought.

He looks at me with an amused stare. "Call him, then. Your boyfriend."

My stomach drops. "I don't have to prove anything to you."

"You're right. But I'm not going to give up unless you do. I feel very strongly about you, Josie. I'd love to have you by my side. We'd be unstoppable."

Good God, this guy is persistent. I glare at him as I pull out my phone and find Conner's contact information. He'll probably play along. I hit the dial button, and the phone starts ringing. I put it on speakerphone. I hold Chris's gaze the entire time, and he watches me with a smirk playing on his lips.

"Hey," Conner answers after a few rings.

"Hi, honey," I respond, trying to sound chipper. Conner goes eerily silent, and I can practically hear the gears clicking in his head. "I just wanted to call and see how your morning went."

"Uh, it went well. How about yours?"

"Oh, it's been good. One of my clients stopped by to bring me lunch, and he didn't believe me when I told him I had a boyfriend. But hopefully, he gets the message loud and clear now."

Conner chuckles, quickly catching onto my scheme. "I hope so, cause I'm not letting go of you anytime soon."

My lips turn up into a smile, and it takes me a moment to realize that I'm not pretending for Chris's sake. "Well, I think he's got the message. I'll see you at home this evening."

"Looking forward to it, baby." Conner's deep voice takes on a heated edge, and my stomach clenches involuntarily.

"Okay, talk to you soon," I whisper, and then hang up the phone.

I set the device on my desk and then look at Chris again. "Satisfied?"

"He's one lucky bastard," Chris says as he stands. "I can take a hint. Enjoy your lunch. I'll see you around."

I watch him walk out of my office, closing the door behind him. I fall back into my chair and let out a deep breath. From the first time I met with Chris for his office remodel project, I knew he would be a giant pain in my ass.

I hear him say a few words to Lori on his way out, and then

the office is silent. I wait for a few moments before picking up the bag and taking it out to the front lobby. I raise it up and ask Lori, "Want a cheesesteak?" She shakes her head with her lips pursed. "Me, neither," I say and then step outside and drop it in the trash can.

Chapter 6

Josie

Time ceases to exist as, once again, I get lost in my work. Lori took off around four, so I'm the last one. I take my time finishing up my projects for the day and then head home.

As I pull into my driveway, I smile when I see a broad-shouldered figure standing on my porch. He turns around and waves when he sees me, then goes back to working on the window. I grab my bags from the passenger seat and get out.

Conner looks up when I step onto the porch and winks at me. "Hey, babe."

I roll my eyes and set my stuff down. "Thanks for that. I was kind of in a pinch and panicked."

Conner shrugs. "Happy to be of service." He turns and looks at the window he's installing. "This got delivered today. Thought I'd get you all squared away."

I roll forward on the balls of my feet. Why do I feel so awkward all of a sudden? It's just Conner. "Thank you. How much do I owe you for that?"

He waves me off and bends down to one knee to inspect something on the window. "Don't worry about it."

"Conner, come on. You don't have to buy me a new window *and* replace it for me. I can pay you back."

"How about you pay me back by spending next weekend with me?" Conner asks, catching me off guard. His brown eyes are warm as they gauge my reaction. "I am your boyfriend, after all, right?"

I bite my lip. "Don't you have to get home?"

He shakes his head. "Turns out my transmission is shot, so I have to get that repaired. I decided I might as well blow my vacation days. Looks like you're stuck with me. I'll be here through next week."

My heart skips a beat for no apparent reason, and I nod my head, chalking it up to acid reflux from my lunch of fast food. "Okay."

Conner raises his eyebrows in surprise. "Okay? Just like that?"

I shrug, too worn out from the day to put up too much of a fight. "You're really helping me out, so yeah. Okay."

His lips pull back in a satisfied grin, and my pulse increases. Why is Conner so handsome? And why am I reacting to him like a love-struck schoolgirl?

"Um, do you want to stay for dinner? I could run out and grab a few things while you're finishing up?" I offer hesitantly.

Conner still holds my gaze, but then he nods. "Yeah, that would be great."

"Okay, is there anything you'd prefer?"

"Whatever you want to cook is fine with me."

"Great, then I'll just get out of your way." I take a step toward the door, but then pause before going inside. "Thank you again, Ace. It really means a lot to me."

He smiles at me. "You're welcome, Jo."

I chuckle as I open my door. "I really wish you'd start calling me Josie."

Conner shakes his head. "No can do."

I scowl at him, but go inside, anyway, to change out of my work clothes. After freshening up, I wander into the kitchen to see if I can scavenge something together because I really don't want to go to the grocery store tonight... or ever. I find some frozen ground beef in the freezer and set that out on the counter. Then, after rummaging through my pantry, I locate some spaghetti noodles and sauce.

This will work.

I toss the ground beef into a pan, let it start thawing, and then fill up a large pot to put the noodles in. Every so often, I hear Conner grunt as he works, and I smile to myself. A warm bubbly feeling settles in my stomach. It's nice not to be alone. Usually, it's just me after I get home from work, but the presence of another person in the house is a welcome change.

After a while, he comes wandering in from outside. He pulls off the work gloves he had on and sticks them in his back pocket. "You're all set. You now have a fully functional, un-smashed front window."

"Thank you again. You're the best," I tell him. My cheeks heat for no reason, and I turn away to drain the noodles.

"What are you making?" Conner asks, as he comes poking into the kitchen. He peers into the pot of sauce on the stove and sniffs. "Spaghetti?"

"Is that okay?" I ask, suddenly worried that maybe he's not a fan of tomatoes or something.

Conner gives me a wry grin and nods his head. "I love spaghetti."

I breathe out a sigh of relief. "Oh good, why don't you go wash your hands, handyman, and I'll get it all plated up."

He gives me a warm look before disappearing down the hallway. I hear the sink turn on as he washes his hands. I plop a healthy serving of noodles on a plate for him and douse it in the red meat sauce. Then I sprinkle a little bit of parmesan cheese on top.

Conner comes back into the kitchen, and I hand him his plate. He looks at it and then at the container of parmesan cheese in my hand. "I'm gonna need a little more of that."

I hand it to him and then laugh when he pours a mountain of it onto his food. "You crack me up, Ace."

He chuckles with me and then walks over to my little Ikea dining room table and takes a seat. His hands rest in his lap as he waits for me to dish my plate up. I also grab two wine glasses from the cupboard and pour both of us some wine. He takes his with a thank you and then watches as I sit across from him.

I hold my wine glass up and purse my lips. "I suppose I should give a toast or something over this heavenly dinner I've created for us."

Conner smiles. "I suppose you should."

"Well, um, here's to reconnecting with old friends who fix your broken windows and make you spaghetti."

"I'll drink to that," he says, lifting his glass to clink with mine before taking a sip. "You're pretty good at speeches."

I bark out a laugh as I dig my fork into my spaghetti. "Right. It's because I had to give a best man speech at the wedding this past weekend. I'm a professional now."

"You looked super cute in your tuxedo. I'm surprised the groom didn't decide to marry you right on the spot," he says, looking at me slyly over the rim of his glass. "I would've."

My mouth goes dry, and butterflies erupt in my stomach. I laugh lightly. "You don't know the groom. He's absolutely mad about his wife. Literally, nothing could have stopped him from marrying her right then and there. The world could've been hit by an asteroid, and they still would've said, 'I do'."

"Good for them, then. That's the goal, right? To find

someone who you want to spend forever with?" he asks, taking a massive bite of his dinner.

I blink. I'm pretty sure Josh: the Guy Behind the Bar said something like that at the wedding, too. What's with that? In my experience, men are typically the ones who aren't looking for something serious, and now, I've had two men say that to me, two days in a row. Am I the odd one out here?

Honestly, that type of life just hasn't been my priority. Maybe at one point in my life, it would be, but now? Not so much. I'm damaged goods. No one would want to spend forever with me when they could have someone less... flawed.

"So, where are you staying?" I ask him, changing the topic.

"At a hotel downtown. It's nothing fancy, but they have a good workout room and a pool."

"That's good. Oh, don't let me forget to give you back your sweatshirt from yesterday. I have it in my room."

Conner shakes his head and meets my gaze. "You can keep it. I remember how weird you are about sweatshirts."

The butterflies start doing flips. I definitely wasn't about to admit to him that I slept in his sweatshirt last night and hoped that he'd never ask for it back. But it belongs to him. The polite thing to do would be to return it.

"No, it's yours. I don't want you to—"

"Jo," he cuts me off, reaching across the little table and taking my hand. He holds my stare steadily. "I want you to have it. Just think of it as a souvenir from our little rendezvous."

My cheeks flame. "Why do you always insist on calling me Jo?"

"Cause that's your name."

"No, my name is Josie," I correct him. "Just Josie."

Conner chews a bite of his spaghetti and then stares at me. "Do you remember the first time I called you Jo?"

I frown. "No."

"I do," he says with a chuckle. "It was right before our first eighth-grade dance. You nearly took my head off with your shoe. You were so mad. Up until that point, no one called you anything other than Josephine."

"Well, I like Josie now."

"Jo isn't that far off from Josie," he says. "You'll get over it."

I sigh and then push my plate away. "You're annoying."

"And you're my Jo. You'll always be my Jo."

"Rude," I say.

He raises an eyebrow. "Adorable."

"Pompous."

"Beautiful."

With a groan, I reach over and grab his plate. "Are you finished?" His plate's empty, so I don't wait for him to respond before picking it up and taking it over to the sink.

Once I'm done washing up, I turn around and face him. He's standing at the edge of the kitchen, watching me. "Now what?"

Conner sticks his hands in his pockets and shrugs. "I don't know. I guess I should get going."

Pure alarm rips throughout my system. I'm not ready for him to leave. I'm not ready to be alone again. The realization takes me by surprise, but it's not entirely unwanted.

"You can stay," I offer hesitantly.

Conner stares at me, assessing the situation, before briskly nodding. "Okay. Want to watch a movie or something?"

"That sounds good," I agree. We head over to my small couch and settle in. I turn on the TV and scroll until I find a movie.

Conner laughs when he sees what it is. "*The Notebook?* Really? You're going to Notebook me? Maybe I should go."

I shrug and pull my feet up underneath me. "No one's keeping you here."

He exhales and looks at me with amusement. "Alright, hand me that blanket."

I do, and he covers the both of us up. I've seen this movie about a hundred times, and at least a third of those have probably been with Conner when we were younger.

The love story takes off. I polish off my glass of wine and then find my eyes growing heavier and heavier. Usually, after staring at a screen all day at work, I can barely keep my eyes open past eight o'clock, and then having a drink on top of that conks me right out. My head bobs forward as I doze off.

I startle when a big, warm hand lands on my shoulder. "Shh," Conner mutters softly as he pulls me toward him. "Come here."

Still half asleep, I let him pull me into his body. I settle my head against his chest and sigh happily when his arm wraps around me. This feels like home. I blink at the TV, trying to recognize what scene we're on. Conner's hand runs over my hair and then rests on my hip.

"I love this movie," I mutter unintelligently.

His chest rumbles with his gentle laughter, and he presses his lips against my hair. "I know."

I close my eyes again, breathing in the familiar scent of Conner. "You smell good."

He chuckles again. "Thanks. You do, too."

I can hear the movie playing in the background, but my eyes are too heavy to open and watch it. Conner's hand is rubbing slow circles on my back, and I melt even further into him, if that's even possible.

"I do," I mutter again. I don't know why I'm trying to talk to him in this state, but suddenly, it feels imperative that he knows something. It must be the few glasses of wine that are running through my system.

"Hmm?"

"I do miss you, probably a lot more than I should," I admit, definitely courtesy of the wine. "You're the Noah to my Allie."

He wraps his arm tighter around me. "I miss you, too."

"I'm just tired of being alone." I finally get my eyes to open and peek up at him. "Don't leave me alone."

Warm brown eyes meet mine and hold me steady in their gaze. His hand brushes against my cheek and leaves tingles in its wake. "Never."

Chapter 7

Conner

When the movie ends, I stay where I am. Josephine is sound asleep against my chest. My hand rubs small circles against her back, and she presses herself further into me. Soft noises escape her lips as she exhales in her sleep, and I smile down at her.

Her request for me not to leave her alone gutted me right to my core. Is that how she's been feeling all these years? Alone? That makes me sad, but also angry, because ultimately, she's the one who chose this path for herself. Hell, for the both of us. I would have never left her alone. But she's the one who cut ties, not me.

I sit there for a while, enjoying her resting against me, until I finally give her a slight nudge. It's getting late, and she should probably sleep in her bed tonight. "Josephine," I murmur softly. She moans against me and scrunches her nose up. "Jo, wake up."

Jo's eyes flutter open, and she squints at the TV, which is now showing some movie I've never seen before. She presses her face further into my chest and inhales. "I don't wanna."

I chuckle and brush a few strands of hair away from her face. "Do I need to carry you?"

"Yes," she says as she lazily nods.

I catch her legs and bring them around until she's sitting on top of me, straddling my hips. Those hazel eyes are wide as her arms automatically go around my neck, and she gasps at our new predicament. She has an imprint on her cheek from my t-shirt. In a swift move, I stand up, holding her in my arms.

When I have a secure hold on her, I walk us down the hall to where I think her bedroom is. The house is small, so there are really only so many options. I see one bathroom and an office before I find a bedroom at the end of the hallway. This must be it.

I push the door open the rest of the way and step into her bedroom. I glance around, taking it in. There's a queen bed in the middle of the room, with nightstands on either side. A dresser sits off to the left of the door frame.

"Conner," Jo breathes. Her face is close to mine, and I meet her eyes. My hands tighten on her rear, and I move her over to the bed.

I drop her onto the mattress, but she locks her ankles around my hips, bringing me down with her. If I thought our positioning was a predicament before, I didn't know what I was talking about.

Now, I'm lying on top of her, my body weight pressing hers into the bed. Our hips are aligned precariously, her warmth seeping into me. Her ankles are still wrapped around me, pulling me closer into her. I brace my elbows on either side of her head, pushing myself up so I can look at her.

Josephine holds my gaze for a moment, but then her eyes drop to my lips, and she exhales before meeting my eyes again. In a languid motion, Josephine arches up into me, capturing my mouth with hers.

I groan against her the moment we collide. Time seems to stop as I get my first taste of her in years. And even though it has been so long, it feels like no time has passed at all. For a moment, everything finally shifts into place, as if this is where I'm meant to be, as if I'm finally home.

I can still taste the bittersweetness of the wine on her lips, and all I can think is that I want more. More of her, more of this, more of us.

I break away, and her mouth reluctantly parts with mine. We're just barely touching now. My eyes flash up to hers for a moment, and then I'm kissing her again, unable to stay away. My fingers find their way into her hair, tangling through the silky strands.

Josephine arches her spine, pressing her breasts against my chest. Her hands claw at my back, pulling my shirt up and slipping under the hem to touch my skin. Throaty moans escape her as I move my mouth against her, and I'm addicted. I never want to stop kissing her.

Reluctantly, I do pull away, putting some distance between us. I press two more kisses against her lips and then give her a wild grin. Her hazel eyes are heated as she watches me, her cheeks flushed with pleasure.

"Your lips are so soft," I say, leaning forward and kissing her again. "I could kiss them all night."

Josephine arches again, making her intentions clear. "No one's stopping you."

I laugh softly as I lean down and rub my nose against hers. "You're right, but I think we should press pause."

She pouts, sticking out her lower lip. I want to suck it back into my mouth and kiss that frown off her face. "I don't like that idea." Shit, neither do I, but the sudden change from distant Jo to this Jo has me pausing.

"It's for the best, baby," I whisper. "Trust me, I don't want to, either, but you've had a few glasses of wine, and you're exhausted. When we take this further, I want you fully present. At that time, trust me, there is nothing in the world that could stop me from ravishing every inch of you."

Jo drops her head against her pillow. "Fine. I guess I can't argue with that."

I kiss her again, lingering against her lips, getting my last fill of her. "Okay, I should go now."

Josephine grabs my jaw, pulling me down again. I sigh against her, indulging myself one last time. Then I pull away, untangling my hips from her feet. Jo stretches out languidly on the bed, and I watch her, a gnawing ache forming in my stomach. There's nothing I want more than to crawl back onto that bed, rip both of our clothes off, and close the distance that's been between us for so long.

"Don't forget your sweatshirt," Jo whispers and then points at the dresser where it's folded up.

I step over, pick it up, then throw it to her on the bed. "Keep it. It's yours."

She catches it and smiles widely at me, her whole face lighting up. She holds it close to her and snuggles into the fabric. The sight makes my chest ache. "Goodnight, Conner."

"Goodnight, Jo," I say with a wink, chuckling when she scowls at me.

I give her one last appreciative glance before I walk out of her bedroom. I close the door behind me, and then make sure all her lights are off in the house before leaving. My drive back to the hotel is quick, but I can't get her out of my head. I'm sure I have a full on mopey puppy expression on my face the whole way, but I don't care. I'm all in.

* * *

The next morning, I wake up and work out in the hotel's fitness center. Then I shower before heading down to the dining room to grab breakfast. I have no idea what I'm going to do today.

My thoughts are still consumed by Josephine. I wonder if she slept well. Is she feeling okay? Does she regret the kisses last night?

I take a huge bite of my apple as I walk out of the hotel toward my little Malibu. The fleshy fruit crunches between my teeth, and I chew, contemplating what my next move is. I want to make sure she understands that this isn't just a one and done with me. There's a lot to unpack still between us, and now, I'm really getting a glimpse into this version of Josephine DiMarco. I can't lie and say it's not a little concerning that she's still so shut off. I could forgive her if she had worked through our history and still had no interest in me whatsoever—I would never fault her for that. But I can't help but notice how much she's still hurting, and that breaks my heart.

All I want to do is help her. I want her to live a fulfilled and happy life. And hey, in the process of that, if she decides she's open to something more, I'll jump headfirst back into a relationship with her.

These last few days have proven to me that nothing has changed between us. We're still Ace and Jo. All those emotions from before are still fully present, and I'm more than willing to explore what all that entails.

I drive through the city, looking around, getting a feel for Cedar Ridge. As I'm sitting at a stoplight, I glance over to my right and see an office front with the logo of a log cabin on the front window. Underneath the logo, in white lettering, is *Miller-DiMarco: Engineering and Architecture.*

Jo's office.

The light turns green, and I pull forward. As I drive, an idea forms in my head, and I find myself pulling into a florist parking lot. I run inside, picking out an arrangement, and then hop back into my car and drive over to her office again.

As I walk inside, an older woman looks up at me and smiles. Her eyes fall to the bouquet of red roses I'm carrying, and her grin gets wider. "Can I help you?"

"I'm here to see Josephine DiMarco."

The woman holds up one finger and then presses the intercom button on her phone set. She must put it on speakerphone because I hear the ringing out loud.

"Yes ma'am," I recognize Jo's voice as she answers.

"Josie, there's a handsome man out here with a bouquet of flowers for you," the woman explains, still smiling.

Jo swears and then grumbles. "You tell that douchebag that I told him I have a boyfriend and to stop harassing me. Oh, and that I don't even *like* cheesesteaks!"

The woman glances at me in alarm and then picks up the receiver of the phone. "It's not him." Pause. "No, I promise it's a different guy." Pause. She surreptitiously glances at me and then whispers, "Dark brown hair, brown eyes, big shoulders. Yes."

The secretary hangs up the phone and gives me a big, awkward smile. "She'll be right out."

I suppress a laugh and smile politely back. "Great."

Only a moment later, I hear an office door open, and Josephine appears from around the corner. She smooths out her black pencil skirt and looks at me, her eyes then falling to the bouquet of roses I'm holding. Something flashes in her hazel eyes, but she quickly smothers it.

"Conner, come on back." She motions for me to follow her and then waves at the woman at the front desk. "Thanks, Lori."

I follow Jo into her office, and she stands by her door, letting me walk in, before closing it behind me. She walks to her desk and then looks at me warily. "What's up?"

I hold out the flowers, raising an eyebrow. "I brought these for you."

Josephine hesitantly takes them and sets them on the desk, then she shoots me a tight smile. "Thank you, but I don't really like flowers."

Holy ice queen, I think to myself. What the hell happened in the twelve hours that we were apart?

"Okay..." I trail off, looking at her in confusion. "Everything okay, Jo?"

She glares at me. "Call me that one more time, see what happens."

I take a step back and hold my hands up. Someone's having a rough morning. "What the hell is going on here? I thought we were good... you know, after last night?"

Josephine sighs and then rubs her hand over her face, pinching the bridge of her nose. "We were. We are. I don't know. You being here is turning everything upside down, and I don't know what to do with it."

"Okay," I say again, still confused. "Do you want me to help clear anything up for you?"

"I just don't want you to get the wrong idea."

"And what idea would that be?"

"That we're together. Dating, or whatever."

Ignoring the sting and the massive weight crashing down onto any and all hope I might have, I raise an eyebrow at her and then smile hesitantly. "What if I *do* want that?"

"Trust me, you don't."

I take a step closer and hold her gaze. "That's not for you to decide."

Now she raises her eyebrows. "You want to date me? *Really*, Conner?"

I have to keep my brain from exploding. This whole encounter is not what I thought it would be. "Well, yeah. I thought I made that obvious last night when I said that I would ravish every inch of you."

Her cheeks flame, and she crosses her arms across her chest. I try to keep my eyes from darting down to her neckline, where her arms are pushing her breasts up into full display. "Why?" she asks.

"Because you're you, and I'm me," I offer as explanation enough. "And besides, I thought I was already your boyfriend, so why are we wasting time by having this conversation?"

"That was just for shits and giggles, and to get Chris off my back," she mutters.

"I see," I mutter. "Well, what do you say?"

"What do I say to what?"

I roll my eyes. "Go on a date with me this weekend. Nothing fancy, just the two of us again. Like it used to be."

"I'll have to think about it."

I chuckle and step forward until we're in each other's faces. "You're impossible," I whisper, my hand coming up to cup her jaw. Against her better judgment, her face leans into my palm, and the tightly wound muscles of her shoulders relax. "Just give me a chance, Jo. I promise you won't regret it."

"You can't know that," she whispers back. Her green-brown eyes fall to my lips. I can feel her soft breath against them.

"I guess you'll just have to trust me," I tell her, before closing the distance between us again. Her eyes fall shut as I move my mouth against hers.

Just like last night, everything slides into place as I kiss her. The world around us fades into nothing. Nothing matters except her.

When I pull away, she's breathless, but still hesitant. She eyes me suspiciously, as if she suspects I'm up to no good. "One date?"

"One date," I confirm. "For now."

Josephine sighs and steps away from me, going to sit behind her desk. "When?"

"I'll pick you up on Saturday. Can I text you the time?"

She nods her head, looks at her computer, and then back to me. Her hands fold in front of her and she wrings her fingers nervously. "Thank you for stopping by."

"You're welcome. I like your office."

"Thanks," Jo says, darting her eyes around her space. "I guess I'll see you around."

I wink at her as I take a step back. "Saturday."

She finally smiles at me, though it doesn't reach her eyes fully. I can tell she's still unsure. The wheels of her mind are rapidly spinning, trying to predict every possible outcome of her agreeing to hang out with me. "Saturday."

I give her a chin-up nod and head toward the door, pulling it open. Before I shut it behind me, I turn and glance back. Josephine has her eyes on the bouquet of flowers, a soft secret smile playing on her lips as she runs one finger over a red petal.

I grin to myself as I walk out of her office. I'll get through to her, one way or another. I know my shooting star is still in there somewhere. I just gotta remind her that she's still there, too.

Chapter 8

Josie

"Where's my other boot?" I shout out to no one in particular. I stalk out of my room and into the living room. As I peer underneath the sofas and the chairs, I mutter to myself, hating that I'm this way. How hard is it to keep a pair of shoes together? I could wear a different pair of shoes, but these are my favorite and they give me a surging sense of confidence.

And I need some confidence today.

Tonight's my date with Conner, and as much as I want to try to pretend to be grumbly about it, I'm actually excited—and incredibly nervous. I haven't been out on a *real* date with a guy since Ryan, and I gave it a shot and then quickly learned that we're better off as friends—we don't speak of those times much.

Or at all.

Besides that, I've had hookups or flirtatious encounters at a bar. But I haven't had the inclination to get to know anyone further than a one-night stand. I simply haven't needed or wanted to give them any more energy than the bare minimum. Getting close to someone means they usually expect you to offer snippets of yourself. The good, the bad, the ugly. It's typically expected. And I don't have any interest in that.

My secrets are closely guarded for a reason. They don't consume me the way they used to, but they're still there, lingering beneath the surface: the fewer people who know my past, the better. I don't like the apologetic or pitying looks. I just want to live my life and move on.

But with Conner... He already knows about all those demons because he has the same ones. I don't have to pretend to be anyone other than who I am with him. I never have. Even when we were kids, falling in love, I could always be me. Just Josie.

I still have some reservations, even with Conner. I don't want him getting too close because that will only end up with us both getting hurt, and Lord knows we've both had enough of that in our lives. Not to mention, he doesn't even live here. He's four hours away, where he has a life, a home, his family. And I have absolutely no intention of leaving Cedar Ridge.

So, I'll take advantage of the time I have with him now, but it won't go any further than that. It can't. I don't think either of us wants that or is prepared for what that might look like. And besides, he deserves better than what I can offer him.

"Gotcha!" I exclaim as I find my shoe stuck between the wall and the TV stand. I don't bother trying to contemplate how it would have ended up there.

I quickly pull on the boot, securing the zipper against the side of my calf. Then I dart back into my bedroom to observe my outfit in the full-length mirror on my closet door. I turn side to side and make sure I don't have any embarrassing stickers stuck to my new leggings or tags left over from the store. After I got home from work yesterday, I dug through my closets looking for something to wear today, but quickly realized that I've worn all these clothes out.

That didn't feel right to me, so I got up this morning and hit the strip malls, looking for a fresh new outfit for my date with Conner tonight. I settled on a new pair of dark brown faux-leather leggings and paired a cream-colored sweater tunic over them. It has a loose-fitting neckline that dips in a V-neck down my chest so I can wear a cute necklace. Around my waist, I cinched a brown leather belt that matches my boots perfectly.

I fluff up my hair in the mirror, watching it settle in the reflection. I did my usual soft curl with my hair but decided to go a little more glam on my makeup. I'm not sure what Conner's planning for today, but I'm looking forward to it. And worst-case scenario, at least I'm dressed to impress.

I make a few final adjustments to my getup before I hear the doorbell ring. Although the anticipation is revving me forward, I take slow, calculated steps toward the front door to not appear too desperate. When I open it, the wind gets knocked out of my chest.

Conner's standing there with one red rose in his hand. He's got that boyish grin on his face as his eyes roam over my body. He's wearing a dark wash pair of jeans and a dark gray sweater that seems to hug every swell and dip of his broad shoulders.

"Wow, Jo, you look beautiful," Conner says breathlessly as he holds out the single rose for me. "This is for you."

I take the stem delicately in my fingers, trying to avoid the thorns, and shoot him a smirk. "Is this to go with the others?"

He shrugs and sticks his hands in his pockets. "If you want. Or you can sleep with it next to you on your pillow."

"I threw away the other ones," I say, deadpan. That's a total lie. They're sitting on my dresser in my bedroom. Every morning, they're the first thing I see when I wake up, and it gives me some sort of calmness that I haven't felt in a *long* time.

"That's a shame," he says back, his tone telling me that he doesn't believe me even the slightest. "Ready to go?"

"Sure, let me just grab a few things," I tell him and step inside to set the flower on my kitchen counter. I grab my little crossbody bag and meet him on the porch. "Where are we going?"

"Do you like beer?"

"Not as much as I like whiskey." I shoot him a wink. "I'm a Tennessee girl now, you know."

Conner grins, and we get into his rental car. I guess he still hasn't gotten his Chevelle back from repairs. "There's a beer festival at a park close by that I thought we could check out, then we could grab dinner and watch a movie or something."

He starts the car up, and I look at him suspiciously. "Trying to get me all drunk so you can kiss me again?"

Conner turns his head and pulls his lips into a crooked smile. "Trust me, I don't need you drunk to get you to kiss me."

"Jerk," I say, laughing as I reach an arm out and slug his shoulder.

"Hey! Don't hit the driver! I don't want to crash and die," he exclaims. When he realizes what he said, he clears his throat uncomfortably and glances at me out of the corner of his eye. "I'm sorry. I wasn't thinking—"

I offer him a reassuring smile, though the darkness of the past lingers around us like a storm cloud. "It's okay. I'm not made of glass, Conner. You don't have to tiptoe around me."

I can tell he wants to argue with me on my statement, but he bites his tongue and refrains. We drive the rest of the way to the park, making small talk. He asks about my week at work, and I tell him. I haven't seen him since he stopped by my office on Monday, which kind of bummed me out, but it made me anticipate our date even more.

We park the car and walk a little way to get to where the booths are set up. As we're strolling on the sidewalk, Conner reaches down and takes my hand, lacing our fingers together. I look down at our hands and then up at him, and he beams at me.

The park is all done up with booths and displays from breweries across the area. There must be at least fifty vendors, a big turnout for a small town like Cedar Ridge. I look around excitedly at everything that's going on. People are bustling about, all cheery from the amount of beer they've sampled already.

"Where do we even start?" I ask Conner. He shrugs, still holding onto my hand, and tells me to lead the way.

I go to the first vendor I find that doesn't have a line. Risky, maybe, but I don't care. The woman running the stand greets us and tells us about the seasonal craft beers they're selling today. I order two and hand her a few dollars before taking my glass and handing one to Conner.

We do a little toast, tapping our cups together, before drinking. I keep my eyes locked on Conner as I take my first sip, savoring the cold flavors of the beer as they explode in my mouth. I run my tongue over my lips, picking up any lingering droplets. Conner pulls his cup away and makes a confused face.

"Does that taste like *chocolate?*" he asks.

I laugh and nod my head. "Yes, almost like slightly over-cooked, almost burnt, chocolate! And maybe some other weird spices in there, too."

He takes another sip and shakes his head. "That's bizarre. I don't think I'm a fan."

"Then why do you keep drinking it, you goon?" I ask him, still laughing as he downs the rest of the beer.

"Cause it's beer," he says as he sticks his tongue out at me. "Come on, let's find a better one."

We wander through the festival, stopping at a few intriguing booths and getting some cups of their brew. After we're each balancing a flight of three tasters, we waddle over to a section of the festival where there are wooden picnic tables set up in front of a stage. There's a folk-rock band up on the stage, playing guitars and singing their melodies into the microphones.

Conner and I settle in at a table and work through tasting the new beers we got. The first one that I try is particularly disgusting. I make a face, and Conner chuckles. "That bad, huh?" I hand it off to him, and he takes a sip, his face scrunching up to match mine. "Oh, God, that's awful."

He takes one for the team and dumps it out in the grass. Then he goes for one of the beers he collected. It's got a rich brown color to it and creamy foam on the top. He raises the cup to his lips and takes a deep swig. When he lowers the cup, he's got a foam mustache, and I burst out laughing.

"What's funny?" Conner asks, a smirk playing on his lips from my laughter.

"You have a mustache!" I finally get out, pointing at his upper lip. Conner sticks it out, rolling his eyes down to try to see it, making me laugh even harder. "Stop, you're going to make me pee my pants," I say in between belly laughs.

"Will you get it off for me?" he asks, leaning over the table toward me.

"What, no! You do it yourself!"

"Come on, Jo, meet me halfway here," he teases.

I stand up with an exaggerated sigh and meet him halfway across the table, noting how little of a fight I put up about this. I press my mouth to his and swipe his upper lip with my tongue, getting the foam off for him. We both sit back down, and Conner looks at me with a happy smile.

"Wipe that grin off your face, Ace. You're incorrigible."

"Yeah, but you love it." He winks.

I don't bother denying it, his confidence making a nervous

twinge go off in my belly. We finish off our beers and listen to the band play their songs. I sigh happily and rest my chin on the palm of my hand. After they finish a song, I dart my eyes to Conner, who has traded his seat across the table to one right next to me.

"What now?" I ask.

"Want to walk around?" he suggests. I agree, and we stand up, collecting our empty cups and tossing them in the trash before setting off. He takes my hand in his again as we walk. "How about a game?" he proposes after a while of walking and people watching.

"What game?"

"Have you ever played Kiss or Dare?"

"*Kiss* or Dare? Don't you mean truth?" I ask him.

"That's baby stuff," he explains with a scoff. "And besides, you're not ready to divulge all your deepest, darkest secrets to me yet, so we'll just swap out the truth for a kiss, or you can take the dare if you're not a chicken."

I don't miss how Conner uses the phrase *yet*. "Okay," I say. "You're on. You go first, kiss or dare?"

His lips pull away into a dangerous grin, and he stops walking. He steps around, so we're facing each other, and his hand comes up to cup my jaw. "Kiss," he murmurs before leaning down and pressing his lips to mine. I freeze, unable to wrap my head around what's happening.

Suddenly, I'm consumed by Conner. The light stubble on his face tickles my lips as he moves his mouth against mine. I smell his cologne, and I'm surprised and saddened to realize that it's the same one he used to wear back in high school—surprised, because it's so familiar, and saddened, because it's *so familiar*.

In the split second that he leans down to kiss me, my mind flies through replays of our time together, and all of those shared emotions flood me, threatening to take me over. Oh, how I loved him. It was a hard lesson to learn that when you love someone as much as I loved Conner, losing them was excruciating.

The pain and the hurt strikes me like a thousand tiny daggers, and I pull away, unable and unwilling to live through that again.

My eyes burn with unshed tears as I put distance between us. I shouldn't have agreed to play this game. Taking one for the team, I plaster on a smile and hope he can't see the despair lingering inside of me. "Doesn't this give you an unfair advantage?"

"Oh, it absolutely does," Conner agrees. "But I promise I won't always choose a kiss. Okay, Jo, your turn. Kiss or dare?"

"Okay," I say, my voice shaking. Zero chance I'm going to pick anything but dare. "Dare."

I ignore the way his face falls. He was hoping for another kiss, but I physically don't think I'm capable of that. He masks it quickly, though, replacing the crestfallen look with one of mischief. "I dare you to do a cartwheel."

"I can't do cartwheels," I mutter, embarrassment overtaking suddenly. "I look like a kicking donkey."

"You've been dared, Jo. Go for it." He nudges me with his elbow.

I'm steadier now that the intense wave of emotion has passed from Conner's kiss, and ignore the twist of self-consciousness that tells me I'm about to make a fool of myself. Giving a big dramatic sigh, I take a few steps forward, where there aren't many people that I could potentially kick. I lift my arms straight up in a salute, like the Olympic gymnasts do, then I attempt to maneuver my body into a flawless cartwheel.

Except it's anything but. I have no doubt—based on the way Conner's chuckling a few feet away from me—that I was spot on with the kicking donkey comparison. I manage to keep my hands on the ground, but I cannot get my legs straight up into the air, so my lower half is kind of bent at a lopsided 90-degree angle. My feet flail out behind me, and then I try to round off and stand up.

My face is no doubt red from being upside down, but I raise my arms again in a salute and give him a big grin. He claps his hands slowly, shaking his head in amazement as I walk toward him.

"That was marvelous," he says.

Despite myself, I toss my head back with a laugh and wrap my arms around his middle. Conner doesn't hesitate, wrapping an arm around my shoulder and pulling me into his chest.

"There's a reason I'm not a gymnast," I say once my laughter has eased. "Okay, your turn to pick now."

Our game goes on like that for another hour or so. Conner must have picked up on the overwhelming feelings I experienced after that first kiss. Thankfully, he followed my lead from that point on, only picking dares. One time, he dared me to go around asking people if they'd seen my phone, but I had to be holding my phone in my hand when I asked. I got many funny stares until one kind elderly man took me off to the side and gently showed me I was holding it.

I dared Conner to go try a new beer. The catch was that he had to finish it all while still standing at the booth, and then slam it down and start howling like a wolf. And bless his heart, the guy did it!

Our afternoon together goes quickly. I actually find myself having so much fun that I don't know what to do with myself. I don't think I've laughed this much in one day, in who knows how long. The festival starts thinning out as people head home.

Conner and I are still strolling along the pathway when my

stomach rumbles obnoxiously loudly. His eyes dart down to me, and he raises an eyebrow. "Hungry?"

I put a hand on my stomach and nod. "Ravenous."

He chuckles, and then we do a roundabout toward where his car is parked. He reaches over and takes my hand. I shoot him a quick glance but surprise myself when I don't pull away. Conner threads his fingers with mine and butterflies explode in my belly. I fight off a smile as we walk, feeling happier than I have in a long time. Once we're settled in the car, Conner starts the engine and asks what I want to eat.

We decide on Chinese food, and I direct Conner toward my favorite place. As we drive, he turns to me and takes my hand. "Did you have fun, Jo?"

I ponder his question and find myself answering truthfully. "More fun than you even know."

Chapter 9

Conner

Josephine and I order a shit ton of Chinese food.

When our hands are full of paper bags, we get back into the car and I turn to her. "Where do you want to take this? Your place?"

She looks back at me and shrugs. "Whatever. I'm fine with anywhere."

I wonder if she actually means that. I noticed right away the way she shut down after I kissed her in the park. Though she'd never admit it, she kissed me back initially, with just as much longing and yearning that I felt for her. But just as fast as that happened, she pulled away and shut down. The sight of fresh tears pooling in her eyes was enough for me not to push my luck and do it again. The last thing I want is to hurt her.

With that in mind, I'm hesitant when I suggest going to my place, but I'm not ready to take her home. "My hotel is right down the road. Want to just go there and we can hang out for a while? Then I can take you home, if you want."

Josephine offers me an encouraging smile. "Okay."

So, that's how we end up on my bed in my hotel room, with

cartons of Chinese food surrounding us. I, at least, had the good sense to lay down one of the bath towels on the bed in case we drop a noodle or a piece of chicken. She settles against the headboard, leaving plenty of space between us, and I pretend that I don't notice.

The spread is impressive. Chicken fried rice, crab rangoons, egg rolls, General Tso's chicken, beef and broccoli, lo mein. I'll be surprised if I can even walk after all of this.

Josephine is attacking the General Tso's chicken like no one's business. We're mindlessly watching home improvement shows while we stuff our faces with carbs and MSG.

"They should've knocked out that wall in the reno," Jo says, pointing to the TV with her chopsticks.

I glance at the TV, trying to see what she's referencing, though most of my attention has been on her all night. "Yeah, that might work."

She scoffs. "It *would* work, trust me."

I chuckle and shake my head. "You're pretty confident."

Jo shrugs and grins, stabbing a piece of chicken with her chopstick and raising it to her mouth. "Yeah, I guess I am."

I reach over to the side table and grab my bottle of soda we got from the vending machine. Neither of us got drunk, or really even buzzed, at the festival, but I am perfectly fine drinking soda or plain water tonight with our dinner.

After a while, we're both stuffed and we get rid of our empty boxes, then stuff the leftovers in the mini-fridge in my room. We both crawl up the bed and sit against the headboard while the rest of the show plays.

I keep glancing over at her out of the corner of my eye. Jo's paying attention to the TV, but I can hear her breathing is slightly labored. Her hands rest on her lap, but she's fidgeting, knotting her fingers together and then unknotting them. I slowly move my hand across the distance to grab hers and entwine our fingers together.

The action makes her breath hitch, and my heart rate increases. I'm not sure why; we've been holding hands all day. Maybe it's the fact that it's just her and me now, in a hotel room.

My body is hyper aware of hers next to me. There's enough space between us that we're not touching anywhere but our hands. I can sense her body thrumming, though, the energy and excitement radiating off her. She doesn't say anything, but I hear her swallow thickly. She's just as affected by our proximity as I am.

All the nerve-endings in my body are on high alert. All week, I've been imagining what might happen this weekend on this date. I want so badly to touch her, to close the distance between us and watch her come undone underneath me. But I don't want to push her. It would be a dream come true to reacquaint myself with her on that level, but the last thing I want is for her to feel like she's too vulnerable and to throw up those defensive walls again.

When the show goes to commercial break, I clear my throat, giving her hand a tight squeeze. "Kiss or dare, Jo?"

Josephine looks over at me, her pupils slightly dilated. I watch every possible thought flit across those hazel eyes. She hesitates, weighing her options before she breathes, "Kiss."

The air in the room grows thick. I breathe in; she breathes out.

Then she's on me.

She moves so swiftly my brain barely has time to catch up. One minute, she's sitting next to me holding my hand, the next, she's straddling my hips, rocking her pelvis over the seam of my jeans and claiming my mouth with hers. I groan into Jo's mouth as she traces her tongue around the seam of my lips, and I give in, opening and letting her take what she wants. Lord knows that I would give her anything she wants, anyway.

I let my hands travel up her back until I get to the nape of her neck. My hand grips the muscles of her neck, and I use that as a leverage point to adjust our position. I maneuver from being underneath her to hovering above her. I press my weight against her, pushing her into the mattress.

I break our kiss and move my lips from her mouth to her jaw, down to her neck. My tongue laves against her clavicle, coaxing out mewls and sighs from the woman underneath me. The neckline of her sweater goes low, but I still don't have the access I'm looking for. I want to kiss her *everywhere*. Re-learn what it's like to truly love Josephine DiMarco.

But I don't.

Before we get too carried away, I pull back, putting the same distance she initiated earlier between us.

Josephine looks betrayed as she quickly scrambles up and wraps her arms around herself. Her voice is small as she asks, "Why'd you stop?"

I run my hands over my face, wishing that things were different between us and I could kiss her the way I want to. "Because I saw the way you reacted earlier, Jo. Even though you tried to hide it, I saw how much that kiss hurt you."

"I'm sorry."

I drop my hands and give her a sad smile. "Don't be. There's a lot of unsaid shit between us. It's stupid of me to come here and pretend like the past didn't happen, so *I'm* sorry." She runs her tongue over her teeth but doesn't say anything. "I guess I should take you home."

Her eyes widen. "I don't really want to go home yet."

Blinking, I register her words. She doesn't want to leave me yet. I let that realization ease some of the heartache I feel for her.

"Okay," I say. "Want to watch a little more TV? Then I'll take you home?"

She nods, and I try to calm my racing heart. This is progress. It might be slow going, but it's progress, nonetheless. Both of us settle back against the headboard and turn our attention back to the screen.

My focus stays on the television, though I'm hyper aware of her still sitting stiffly next to me. Slowly, over the next half-hour, she starts to relax. Eventually, she tosses back the blankets of the hotel bed, curling up underneath and bunching a pillow up under her head. I don't protest, watching her get comfortable.

The next time I glance over at her, her eyes are closed, lashes fluttering against her cheeks as she dreams. Fighting off a smile, I contemplate my options. For the first time all day, she finally looks at ease. I decide to just let her sleep. I can take her home in the morning.

Staying on top of the comforter, letting it act as a sort of barrier between us, I settle back against the pillows and fold my hands on top of my chest. I close my eyes and let the very presence of her next to me ease some of my apprehension. Sleep overtakes me soon, and all I dream about is playing Kiss or Dare with Josie, where every time, each of us picks *Kiss*.

Chapter 10

Josie

Conner's jaw slackens and his breath evens out in light snores. His hands are folded against his chest, and one arm twitches—one of his tells that he's asleep. I let my eyes trace across the features of his face. Those delicious full lips that were kissing me senseless only a little while ago. His angular jaw is strong and firm, and I want to run my fingers over the hard edge.

This whole day has my head spinning. I had so much fun with Conner at the festival that I don't even know what to make of it. I'd honestly forgotten what it was like to be with someone who compliments you so perfectly, who knows when to push and when to concede. This evening in his hotel room only further drove that home.

My chest aches as I watch Conner sleep. I want so badly to have the confidence to jump headfirst like him, but I'm worried if I do, I won't be able to swim. Being with Conner these last few days has been confusing. There are so many years that have passed between us, but yet, at the same time, it's like no time has passed at all. When I look at him, I'm reminded of the teenagers who fell hopelessly in love without realizing what all that entailed.

For me, back then, the sun rose and set with Conner. I knew I didn't stand a chance against him because he made it so easy. Just as he's making it easy now. I could see myself falling for Conner Reynolds again in this lifetime, and honestly, that terrifies me. Everything that I felt for Conner when we were younger is still there, bubbling right below the surface. Being around him is natural, seamless—like muscle memory. Today proved that. It was as if we just slipped right back into who we used to be.

I'm concerned because we are *not* the same teenagers that fell in love all those years ago. We're grown now, and there are too many skeletons in the closet for us to go back to who we used to be.

I let myself put those concerns aside and imagine for a moment what that could be like if I let myself fall for him the way I had before. Ryan mentioned to me that I could have everything he and Izabel have if I wanted. Every day could be like this. Fun dates where we goof off the whole time. Nights spent getting lost in each other. Having someone day in and out who appreciates me for exactly who I am. It could be perfect.

But it could also be catastrophic. Loving someone that intensely puts a person in a constant state of vulnerability. It requires trust and faith that your person will hold you up rather than tear you down piece by piece. And after I've spent all these years building my walls back up and learning to stand on my own, I'm not sure if I can risk breaking again.

I run my fingers against Conner's cheek, appreciating the contrast of his rough stubble beneath my sensitive skin. This man once held my whole world in his hand. I'm just not sure if I want him to have that much power over me again. Not that he would ever abuse that, but just knowing that every aspect of your life now revolves around another person is... daunting.

For the longest time, it's just been me. I've lived my life to the fullest all by myself. I have a great job and great friends, and that's all I've needed. I've worked so hard to make sure that I'm not vulnerable. I find comfort in knowing that I'm in control. That's how I'm able to stay strong.

Conner could ruin that, single-handedly. He knows me better than anyone. If anyone could have the power to rip me to shreds, it would be him. While, at the same time, giving me the support and love I need to flourish.

Falling in love sometimes feels like evaluating a risk-benefit analysis. There are risks to putting your heart on the line. But at the same time, there are overwhelming benefits of giving up yourself for another person, which I am acutely aware of. And then with that data in mind, trying to determine which path to take, that leaves you with the greatest benefit potential, with the least amount of risks.

It's impossible.

I snuggle into the pillows again, trying to let sleep find me once again. I must succeed because I'm startled awake a while later when Conner rolls onto his side with a sleepy sigh and drapes his arm over my hips. Unconsciously, his arm tightens around me, as if he's going to pull me closer. Heart racing, I peek over at the alarm clock on the table, and it reads four o'clock.

I wiggle out from under his arm, push aside the covers, and use the flashlight on my phone to maneuver through the hotel room to the bathroom. The urge to get out of here is over-whelming suddenly. I don't want to wake up again in the morning and face the awkwardness of lingering where I'm not wanted. Or, on the flip side, be ambushed by Conner asking too many probing questions again.

I need time to think, to assess. And I won't be able to keep a clear head with Conner right in front of me.

After using the bathroom, I step toward the hotel room door. Before walking out, I chance a glance back at him again. Through the shadows, I see the comforter has fallen down his body, displaying his broad chest to me. My heart wants so badly to curl up against him again, but my brain tells me to get out of Dodge. Sticking around will only lead to uncomfortable conversations in the morning. And we need to talk. I know that, but I need to have the advantage here. Otherwise, Conner will totally disarm me with those warm brown eyes, and I'll be putty in his hands.

I quietly sneak out of the hotel room and run down to the lobby, pulling up the rideshare app on my phone. The driver is only a few minutes away, and soon, the hotel is disappearing behind me as I drive away.

I'm so conflicted. Conner's only been in my life again for a *week*, and here I am, making a risk-benefit ratio of building a life with him again. How outrageous is that? We barely know each other. And true, I had a lot of fun with him yesterday, but a relationship is more than that, and I don't know if I'm willing to put it all out for him.

Not to mention his life is back in Atlanta, where mine is here. I have finally laid down roots and created my own little family here in Cedar Ridge, and I have no intention of leaving. Would Conner have any desire to leave a bustling city like Atlanta and come to the small-town life? What would I do if he didn't? Would I even *want* to pursue a long-term, long-distance relationship?

These thoughts plague my mind, and when morning comes, I'm still wide awake, worrying over all of them. Feeling unmoored, I decide I need an objective party to talk this through. Maybe that will help me get some better insight or a different perspective. I've isolated myself from all my friends growing up who knew Conner. And my brother, Alex, is right out.

Wrapping myself up in the blanket on my couch, I pull out my cell phone and send a quick text to Ryan. He's my best friend. And knowing his rocky history with Izabel, hopefully he will have some idea of what I can do. Or what I shouldn't do.

Chapter 11

Josie

RYAN DOESN'T BOTHER KNOCKING WHEN HE ARRIVES, BUT just strolls in like he owns the place, holding a mug of coffee in his hands. I put my phone down and acknowledge him.

"I'm surprised you're up this early on a Sunday," I observe.

He chuckles as he walks around and sits beside me on the couch. "You and me both. But it's nice for once not to be the person needing support through their life problems. What's going on with you?"

"It's a long story."

"I got time," he says, shooting me a small smile and stretching his arm out along the back of the couch.

I take a deep breath and look at the guy who has claimed the role of my best friend. Ryan watches me with his kind eyes. I see no judgment, no predetermined opinions—just my friend, wanting to help in any way that he can.

The part of me that has put up those walls for so long screams at me that I shouldn't trouble him with this. He's finally gotten his life back on track. The last thing he needs is to take on the weight of all of my problems.

But the part of me that sees his happiness, and wants it for myself, tells me that it's time to be brave. That it's time to trust that the people who care for me want me to allow them to help.

I tell him.

"Well, it started when my brother broke into my house the night of your wedding. He was passed out drunk on my couch, and I didn't know what to do. So, I called my ex-boyfriend over to come get him."

Ryan frowns, not liking the sound of me believing I had no other options. "Why didn't you call me?"

"Are you serious? It was your wedding night. I wasn't about to do that to you, and I sure as hell wasn't about to do that to Izabel."

He nods. "Fair enough. Go on."

"So, Conner comes over, and it turns into a whole big thing because he thinks I'm burying all the bad stuff and not coming to terms with it."

Ryan holds up a hand. "Who's Conner again?"

I bite my lip. "My ex-boyfriend."

"And? I can see there's more you're not telling me."

"And my baby's father," I add in, quietly.

Ryan's face goes stock still as he processes my admission. He blinks a few times and then his green eyes scour my face, looking for something. Gently, he reaches over and takes my hand. "Okay. Look, Jos, I want to help you, but I need you to talk to me. I can't help if I don't know the whole story."

I take my hand back and pick at a hangnail absentmindedly. I know he's right, but it's hard opening up about something I've spent years burying. It's all right there on the tip of my tongue. All I have to do is tell him. Just bite the bullet and trust someone else to share this burden with me. "You're right."

"I promise you're safe with me," Ryan adds. "Nothing that

you say is going to make me think anything less than you. You're still my best friend and my partner. But I think you need to take a load off. Let me help you."

Ryan's words hit me right in the center, and the assurance of the safe place he allows for me is all it takes for the truth to come tumbling out of me. I fold my hands in my lap, take a shaky breath, and start talking.

"I grew up with Conner. My family moved into the same neighborhood that he lived in when I was eight. We hit it off with him right away."

"You and your brother," Ryan supplements.

"Yes, my twin," I say, watching Ryan's reaction. I never told him I was a twin. His face remains neutral, waiting for me to continue. "Conner and I always had a stronger connection than him and Alex, right from the get-go. There were a lot of hidden touches and lingering glances in those early teenage years. When we finally were old enough, we started dating. And then one thing led to the other, and I got pregnant when I was seventeen."

"And was Conner okay with that?"

I smile, thinking back to the day that I told Conner I was pregnant. It was right before our senior year. I was so nervous, but finally broke the news to him. He froze for only a second as he processed before a blinding smile took over his face. He rushed toward me, picking me up and spinning me around. "Yes, he was very okay with it. We were going to be a family. I'm sure we would've eventually gotten married, and I just—I wanted it so much."

"So, then, what happened?"

"It was February. I was six months pregnant. Conner was out of town for a volleyball tournament. It was the weekend of the winter formal at my school. I went with Alex because

Conner was gone, and I didn't want to miss out. After the dance, we decided to go to an after-party. And Alex got wasted."

"This is the brother who," Ryan pauses and hesitates, "has *issues* with alcohol?"

I nod my head and bite my lip. My pulse is steadily increasing, memories of that night flooding in now that the floodgates are open. I remember having so much fun at that party. The most popular girl in our grade was hosting it at her huge mansion of a house. I had been ecstatic to have even been invited. It wasn't all that it was cracked up to be, and now, in hindsight, I wish I never would have gone.

"Alex drank way too much, but I didn't realize it because he was good at hiding it. His words slurred, but his actions weren't jerky or out of control, so I thought he was fine. I told him I wanted to leave and that I was going to call my mom to come pick me up so he could stay. But then he got really mad because he didn't want our parents to know that there was alcohol at the party.

"As if they didn't already know," I scoff, shaking my head. Parents know everything. "But he insisted on driving me home, saying that he had only had, like, one drink and acting all offended that I didn't trust him. And I was so concerned with getting home that I didn't care.

"So, I gave up and got in the car with Alex, and everything seemed okay. He was singing along to the music and making funny faces at me, just like always. But then he hit a patch of black ice, and his motor skills were so impaired that he wasn't able to control the car once it started sliding out of control."

I glance at Ryan, whose eyebrows are pulled together. He's frowning at my story but waits for me to continue without interruption. He reaches over and retakes my hand, giving it a squeeze, letting me know it's alright to continue.

"It's kind of fuzzy after that. I just remember the car spinning, and I felt like my stomach was in my throat. My hands were clenched around my belly, trying to stay grounded. The cops told me later that the car slid right into the oncoming traffic of an intersection, and since it was snowy, the other cars couldn't stop in time.

"The doctors said that both Alex and I were lucky we made it out of there alive. We were both unconscious when we were rushed to the hospital. When I woke up, I was told that I had suffered a severe placental abruption, and they weren't able to save my baby.

"It was a girl," I say, the admission washing over me like I've been doused in cold water. "Conner and I had wanted to be surprised, so we didn't find out the gender. I found out when they brought her to me afterward. Conner doesn't even know that I got to meet her. I never told him."

"Didn't he come see you in the hospital?" Ryan asks, confused.

I shake my head and wipe away a few shameful tears. "Conner's tournament was in Wisconsin. That weekend, a huge snowstorm was blowing in, so the airplanes couldn't fly out, and his parents refused to let him drive in the snow to get to me. That was the same tournament where he blew out his shoulder. Because he was so distracted by me, he wasn't paying attention. He made a bad play and tore his rotator cuff, ending his volleyball career."

"God, Josie," Ryan breathes, his hand still gripping onto mine tightly. "I'm so sorry."

I sniffle. "It was just a perfect shit show of a weekend, honestly. I got to hold her for a few minutes before I told the nurses to take her away. The pain was too much. I couldn't— My parents handled all the logistics for me because I couldn't. I know where she's buried, but I haven't gone to visit her."

"Even after all these years?" he asks. I nod, feeling embarrassed, ashamed, and deeply gutted, reliving the loss all over again as I recount it to my friend.

"I came to Tennessee almost right after that. As soon as I was released from the hospital, I packed up my bags and ran as fast as possible. I couldn't be there anymore. I couldn't even look at Alex, who never apologized or took responsibility. I couldn't talk to Conner because I thought he was upset with me. I was so irresponsible with our baby, I was sure he would hold it against me forever.

"I came to live with my aunt here in Cedar Ridge, and that was that. I finished courses for high school online and forced myself to go home for the holidays for a few years in a row. Conner would be there, waiting for me. He would hug me and give me a kiss, and we just pretended like it never happened. Like we were just old friends. But then, when I was in college, I stopped going home. And he never came looking for me."

"But he's here now," Ryan fills in. I nod again.

"He's here now, and I don't know what to do. It's all just too much, too fast. I'm not prepared to deal with everything that comes along with Conner."

Ryan moves forward and pulls me into a hug. I rest against him, wrapping my arms around his middle and accepting the comfort. "Josie, I wish there was something I could do to turn back time for you."

"Yeah, me too."

He pulls away and looks me dead in the eye. "You are so strong. I don't think I could have gone through that and come out better for it like you have."

I shake my head and wipe away more tears. "I'm not strong. I buried one of the worst things a person could go through so far down so fast, trying to burn it from my memory. I pushed the most important person in my life away when I needed him most. I'm so messed up, I don't know what to do with myself most of the time."

"I think you need to talk to him," Ryan says gently. "You two have a lot of unresolved history floating between you, and I'm not sure if you can move on with that lingering."

I let out a laugh and sniffle. "You sound like Conner."

"Well, that only tells me that he does want to move forward with you. If he wants to address all the demons, then that means he wants to find a life with you without them."

"Maybe. But he keeps calling me Josephine."

Ryan raises an eyebrow, and his lips pull off to the side in a smirk. "Isn't that your name?"

"No. I mean, yes, it is, but no. My name is Josie. Josephine is what everyone used to call me growing up. I didn't have a nickname or anything. Conner called me Jo, but besides that, to everyone, I was Josephine." I pause and take a shaky breath. "But Josephine died that day her baby did. And he doesn't realize that. So now it's Josie, just Josie."

"Maybe you should explain that to him," Ryan suggests.

"But I'm scared to," I admit. "I don't think I can give him what he wants. He deserves a family, and someone who can give him that, but that's not me."

"You don't know that. You might be exactly what Conner wants. You won't know until you talk to him, though."

I bite the inside of my cheek, knowing that there's more to the story that Ryan doesn't know and that he won't ever know. I've already shared plenty, but I can't get myself to tell him the rest. It's too embarrassing, too personal. My shortcomings as a woman don't necessarily concern him. But overall, he might be right. Conner might be the guy for me. I just don't know if I'm the girl for him.

"Do you think that he could forgive me for what I did?" I

ask him, knotting my fingers together. "Even though I hurt him by turning my back on him?"

"I think he probably has forgiven you already," Ryan says.

"You'd forgive Izabel for something like that?"

Ryan's eyes go soft, and he nods his head. "There really isn't anything that I wouldn't forgive Bells for, and trust me, we've had our share of ups and downs. We've hurt each other, but we've gotten past it, together."

I wipe my face again and sigh. "Well, I didn't mean to get all teary on you."

He chuckles and nudges my shoulder. "I'd be more concerned if you hadn't. You've been through a lot, Josie. Give yourself a break."

"I guess I should call Conner and talk to him. Do you think we could play a game first? I need to de-stress a little bit before I go see him. I should have a clear head. And nothing clears my head like *Call of Duty*."

Ryan chuckles but reaches forward to grab one of the controllers. I turn the TV and my gaming system on with the remote and grab the other controller. I pull up the game, and soon we're shooting at all the bad guys and trying to win. It's therapeutic. I find relief, getting lost in the game. And before I know it, I'm smiling and laughing at my best friend's usual side comments and jokes.

After we finish a round, I turn to him and grin. "Thanks, Ryan. I appreciate you coming over and listening."

Ryan rests his arm on the back of my couch and offers me a reassuring smile back. "Anytime. You've helped me through my darkest days, so I figure it's about time I return the favor."

I move forward and wrap my arms around him in a hug.

I hear my front door fly open and footsteps pounding through the hallway from behind where we're sitting. "Josephine!" Conner's deep voice calls through the house. "We really need to talk. And don't try to run away this time, please. We need to figure this out."

I pull away from Ryan just as Conner rounds into the living room. He stops short, his chocolate brown eyes zeroing in on Ryan and me on the couch. He sticks his hands in his pockets and narrows his eyes at me.

"Sorry, am I interrupting something?"

Chapter 12

Conner

JOSEPHINE MOVES SWIFTLY AWAY FROM THE GUY SHE'S draped all over. Her beautiful hazel eyes go as wide as saucers when she sees me standing there. I keep my face cool as I stare at them. The guy is looking at me in surprise, sizing me up. I glare back at him.

"Conner," she breathes. "I was going to call you."

"Right," I say. "I'm sure."

The guy pats Josephine's leg and then stands up. "I'll give you two some space."

I frown even harder as he walks around the couch. He extends a hand toward me, but I take a step back. "Don't."

"Easy there. This is nothing like you think it is," the guy says to me.

"You have no idea what I'm thinking," I deadpan.

"He's married, Conner," Josephine interjects, as if that means anything. "I was the best man for his wedding. Remember the *tux?*"

The guy holds his left hand up for me to see the wedding

band. "Is that supposed to make me feel better?" My tone is likely sharper than it should be.

"*Okay,*" the married guy mutters. "That's my cue to leave. I'll talk to you later, Jos."

She waves at him, and he walks out of the house. I glare at Josephine from across the room, and she scowls right back. My blood is boiling, and I take a deep breath, so I don't yell at her.

"So, he can call you Jo, but I can't? I'm the one who gave you that nickname in the first place."

Josephine's eyes dart to the ground. "He calls me *Jos*, with an *s*. Short for Josie."

I stare at her for a second, trying to discern if she's serious, and then shake my head in disbelief. "You're actually crazy, you know that, right?"

Her shoulders drop in defeat, and she looks up at me with troubled eyes. "You're probably right. I'm sorry, Conner."

Her admission takes me off guard, and I falter. I move closer to her but still leave distance between us. "Why did you leave? I would have driven you home if you wanted me to. Did I do something to offend you?"

Jo shakes her head. "No, of course not. I just—I had to leave."

I let out a humorless laugh and finally close the space between us. I walk around the couch and take her in my arms, encompassing her in a hug. She responds by standing up on her tiptoes and pressing her cheek into my neck. I hear her take in a deep breath and then melt into my arms.

"I need you to stop running away from me." I let go of her and brush my fingers over her cheek. "Just trust me that I'm not going to hurt you."

"Sorry," she whispers. "A lot is going on in my head. That's why Ryan was over. I felt like I needed to talk things through with someone. Figure out what this is that I'm experiencing inside."

I drop my hand, feeling helpless suddenly. "Someone other than me."

She shakes her head again and grabs onto my hand. "No, that's not it. I don't want to push you away anymore, Conner. I think you're right. I do still have a ton of shit I need to work through, but I don't want to do it alone. You being back has just —it's just made me realize that I... I need to start taking some accountability." She huffs the last part out, like she is finally accepting defeat. Except that's what she doesn't realize. She took some hits, yes, but she is so strong.

My eyes trace over her face as I look for any hesitation. "Do you mean that?"

"I think so," Josephine admits, glancing down.

"Okay, I need you to trust me for a moment. Obviously, something's weighing on your mind, and I need to know it before we can ever move forward. Let's play a new game called 'One Truth.' You tell me one truth, then I tell you one truth."

Josephine shakes her head. "That's not a real game."

"Indulge me."

She sighs and then squeezes her eyes shut. Her words are hurried as she says, "I'm scared that you blame me for our baby dying."

My heart shatters in my chest, and it takes me a moment to pull myself together after that nuclear bomb. Slowly, I place a finger under her chin, lifting her gaze up to me. She opens her eyes and looks at me dismally.

"Losing our baby was not your fault. It wasn't even Alex's fault," I say. "Though, I would have appreciated a little more responsibility on his part. But what happened, happened. It was an accident."

"But me running away wasn't an accident."

"No," I say, hesitantly. "But I understand that's what you needed to do then. I've never hated you for that. I've just missed you."

Her eyes go soft as she gazes at me. "I've missed you, too." Her voice breaks, and I feel my resolve go with it. My lips pull into a smile.

"Okay, now I'll tell you my truth. I worry you resent me for not being there with you when you lost the baby."

"Conner," she whispers, surprise lacing her tone.

"I should've been there. You needed me more than ever, and I was too busy playing a dumb volleyball game."

"A game you loved. I've never resented you for that. I know that, if you were able, you would've been by my side the whole time."

"Would it have changed anything?" I ask her the question that's been weighing on my mind all these years. If I had been there with her, helped her through everything, would we still be together?

Her hazel eyes go wide as she considers my question. Finally, she exhales and shakes her head. "No, I don't think so."

"I guess that's just the part that confuses me so much," I admit. "Why did you run? We were great together, Jo. We barely fought, though we drove each other crazy ninety-nine percent of the time. It was just you and me against everything until it wasn't."

I can't ignore the pang of hurt that catapults through my chest. Clearly, I'm still not over the way she up and abandoned me—abandoned *us*. If she would've just given me the chance, I wouldn't have hesitated standing by her side as we weathered the storm together, but she took that away from me. At the end of the day, I don't doubt she would've left, anyway, to figure out life on her own at some point, and I wouldn't have stopped her. It just would've been nice to have been considered.

"I don't have any excuses for how I reacted right after that. The pain was—" she pauses, trying to calm her increasing breaths, proving how difficult reliving these memories are for her, "stifling."

"Baby, look at me." Her hazel eyes meet mine, and I let out a breath. "I wish I could take away that pain for you. I would move mountains for you if I could. I don't care if it takes days or weeks or years; I want to help you. And I'll do whatever it takes to show you that I mean that."

"I'm not good at this," Josephine says. "Relationships."

I offer her a small smile. "That's okay. We'll figure it out together."

"I'm worried that I'm not what you want. How do I know that you won't find someone better? Who can give you every-thing that you want?"

"Jo, *you're* what I want. I've wanted you for as long as I can remember. Since we were kids playing kickball on the street. With your pigtails flying all over the place. Trust me, if I have you, I don't need anyone else."

Josephine stares at me with glossy eyes. "I just—"

"Come here," I interrupt her, putting my hand on the back of her neck and pulling her into me. Our lips touch, my tongue swipes across her bottom lip, begging her to open for me. When she does, I devour her, trying to convey just how much she means to me in one little kiss.

Josephine's hands tangle in my hair, and she grips me to her. The tears now streaming down her face wet my lips as I kiss her, but I don't mind. When I finally pull away, her cheeks are flushed, her eyes red from crying.

"I think we're done with the truth-telling. Let's just take this one day at a time, okay?" I ask her. "We don't need to jump into anything, but I don't want you to push me away anymore. Can you do that?"

Josephine nods her head. "I think so."

"Good," I say, pecking her lips again. "And for the love of God, Jo, stop running away. I'm faster than you, so I'll catch you. Every time."

She laughs through the tears still leaking out of her eyes. "How do you know you're faster than me?"

I grin. "I just do."

Jo snorts and wipes at her nose. "Arrogant."

"Stunning," I respond, remembering this game from a few days prior.

"Delusional."

"Exquisite," I press another kiss to her lips, and she loses all resolve beneath me. We fall together on the couch, and I wrap her up in my arms.

We stay there for a while, soaking in the comfort of each other, letting the small touches and whispered words heal some of the hurt we've both felt for the last few years. We both have a long way to go, but I have no doubt that we'll be able to finally heal if we do it together.

Chapter 13

Josie

THE MINUTES OF THE DAY SEEM TO BE TICKING BY AT A snail's pace. Mondays are always some of the hardest days of the week coming off the weekend, but today seems especially brutal.

Thankfully, there's only an hour or so left in the workday, which is good because my eyes feel like they're going to burn out of my eye-sockets with the intensity with which I'm staring at this project.

A text message comes through my phone, and I glance away from the computer to read it.

Conner: I'm bringing you dinner tonight. What do you want?

I bite my lower lip, trying to decide if I want to see him tonight or if I want my space. This weekend was a lot, but I do think we left things in decent standings. I know there's a lot more ground I have to cover with Conner, so I suppose there's no better time than the present. I reach for my phone and type out a response.

> Josie: Taco Bell. Same order.

I smile to myself as I send it, and I wonder if he remembers. Conner and I were frequent fliers at Taco Bell when we were dating as teenagers. I would always get the same thing—a bean burrito (with no onions), a soft taco, and a side of chips and nacho cheese. It's nothing extravagant, but it's comfort food at its finest.

> Conner: You got it. Be there around 6.

> Josie: That sounds perfect.

> Conner: You sound perfect.

I laugh under my breath and roll my eyes. He's such a damn flirt. I don't know what to do with him most of the time.

Rolling my lips together, I glance at the clock on my desk. A little over an hour. Ryan's already bounced for the afternoon to go meet some contractors on site, so I'm here by myself. I've got a crazy deadline, but my burning eyes convince me that it's time to call it a day.

After shutting everything down, I head home, hop in the

shower, and pull on a pair of my favorite lounge pants. Curling into my favorite spot on my couch, I wait for Conner to arrive.

It's only a few minutes past six when he knocks on my door before opening it and coming into the living room, holding a heaping bag of Taco Bell up like a trophy.

Laughing, I motion to the small table in front of my couch, and he sets it down, taking a seat next to me and looking me over.

I squirm under his gaze and wonder to myself if I should've put a little makeup on after my shower. I'm sure he's noticing the massive pimple on my chin. Then I realize how ridiculous of a notion that is—this is *Conner*. He's seen me at my best, my worst, and everything in between.

"Why are you looking at me like that?" I ask him, my voice soft.

He continues to trail his gaze over my features and his lips curve up in the corners. "Just memorizing you."

My heart skips a beat, and I avert my eyes.

Conner turns away and reaches into the bag, pulling out the items he ordered for us. He sets three things down in front of me and I can't fight the grin off my face—a bean burrito, a soft taco, and chips and cheese.

"I can't believe you remembered after all these years," I mutter, reaching for the chips and grabbing one to dip in the gooey cheese.

"You're hard to forget," he says. "And your order isn't that complicated."

"Did you remember to get no onions on the burrito?" I ask, putting him to the test.

"It's the very first thing I ordered," he nods solemnly, assuring me that he knows the importance of the customization.

Though his words send my pulse skyrocketing, I can't fight the sudden apprehension that surrounds me.

"What are we doing, Conner?" I ask, souring the mood in zero-point-two seconds flat.

He looks at me with narrowed eyes. "Eating? That's what we do best."

"No, I mean… what's the goal here?"

Conner leans back against the couch. "I thought we agreed yesterday that we would figure it out. Is that not what we're doing now?"

I shake my head and wrap my arms around my middle. I don't know where this anxiety came from, but it's causing my chest to tighten in ways I don't like. "There's just so much we have to talk about still."

He nods. "Then let's do it. Where's your head at, Jo?"

I look at the bag of Taco Bell sitting on the table, remembering how we used to enjoy this very meal as teenagers. "We were so young. How did we ever think that we could have done it?"

"We had each other. And that was enough then," Conner says, his voice sure.

I raise an eyebrow. "Is it enough now, though?"

"It is for me." He nods. "But is it for you?"

I shrug. "I don't know. There's so much more to a relationship than what we used to think. A lot more that we have to consider."

"There is," he agrees. "But ultimately, it comes down to whether or not you can picture spending the rest of your life with that person. Everything else falls into place after that."

I shake my head. "Sometimes it doesn't. You have to be willing to compromise, and concede, and make sacrifices that you may not really want to make."

Conner studies me for a moment, silently. Then he says,

"All of those things I'm ready and willing to do for you, Jo. What's holding you back?"

What *is* holding me back?

"I don't know," I say again, honestly.

He heaves a big sigh. "Well, I'll be here when you figure it out. I told you I wasn't going anywhere, and I meant it. I'm in this for the long haul."

"Okay," I whisper.

Conner nods again briskly, and then reaches for his food before digging in, conversation officially shelved for now.

The rest of the evening passes uneventfully. I snuggle into Conner's side as we watch mindless TV until it's late.

When Conner gets up from the couch, he stretches his arms over his head. His t-shirt rides up just a bit at his waist, teasing a hint of muscled skin underneath. He turns to me and gives me a sideways grin. "I guess I should get going; leave you to your beauty sleep."

He leans down and presses a kiss to my cheek. It's confusing to me for a moment, the feeling of panic that I have at the idea of him leaving. With a rash decision, I blurt, "You can stay. Spend the night." He blinks and I panic even further. "If you want."

His dark eyes light up. "Yeah, I'd like that."

Together, we walk back to my bedroom. I pull out a spare toothbrush for him, and we stand together at the sink in my bathroom, brushing our teeth. It's something so mundane, so natural, that it sends my head spinning.

Even as we crawl into bed and Conner curls his large body around mine, my head swirls with thoughts and worries and dreams.

This could be every day.

But do I want it to be every day?

In the dark of the bedroom, I close my eyes and let myself

imagine just for a moment what that might look like. I can't seem to settle on one version, and my head ends up hurting the more I try to think about it.

Conner's already fallen fast asleep, his gentle breathing whispering against the skin of my shoulder. I take a deep breath, trying to ease some of the nervous thoughts racketing through my brain.

Finally, after an eternity, I manage to sleep.

In the morning, when I wake up, Conner's already awake, soft brown eyes tracing every inch of my face and fingers stroking through my hair. My heart flutters, and I snuggle into him more, feeling cherished and loved. Without a doubt, I already know that today is going to be a good day.

Chapter 14

Josie

The rest of the week flies by. Conner takes up all of my free time and keeps me entertained with his jokes and games. We spend every evening together, having dinner, watching a movie or a show, and then falling asleep holding each other.

Before I know it, it's Friday, and I'm sitting at my desk about to tear my hair out. The Jackson Association representative that I've been working with has decided that everything we've done up to this point is precisely *not* how she wants it, so now it's back to the drawing board to start from scratch. I hit *delete* on the file on my computer and bury my head in my hands.

Anxiety claws at the back of my mind. I can't mess this project up. They've already paid a hefty advance that Ryan and I have allocated to different facets of the firm. It would be bad news bears if they decided to pull out last-minute, and we had to refund them for the rest of the project.

I can imagine how that conversation with Ryan would go.

Me: Hey, Ryan, sooo about that major project that you're counting on me to deliver...
Ryan: Yeah?
Me: Well, they've decided to go a different direction.
Ryan: You're fired.

Of course, I know Ryan wouldn't fire me. At least I hope he wouldn't. We've been through a lot together. Still, I can't help but be worried that, if this project goes sideways, it will be my ass on the chopping block.

I can't wait for this day to be over so I can go home and let myself be utterly distracted by Conner for the rest of the weekend. So far, everything between us has been perfect. Each day, we've gotten to know each other a little more, and slowly, the demons are stepping into the light, only to disappear completely. All my free thoughts are beginning to be consumed by Conner, and I find myself counting down the minutes until I can be with him again.

I let the work suck me in until I'm interrupted by a message from Lori up front, letting me know someone's here to see me. I grin ear to ear, already knowing that it's Conner. I save my work and then grab my bag, wandering up to the front desk.

Conner's standing there talking to Lori. He looks up when he sees me enter and gives me a wide smile. "Hey, baby. You look as beautiful as I left you this morning."

I feel my cheeks heat, and I smile back. I can't find it in me to complain when Conner calls me baby. It makes those traitorous butterflies act up again and causes my heart rate to spike —and honestly? I like it. "Thank you."

"Lori, would you mind—" Ryan strolls out of his office, but then pauses when he sees the crowd by his secretary's desk. He pushes up his glasses and looks around. "Oh, hey."

Conner glances at me, then moves forward, extending a

hand. "Hey, man, sorry about last weekend. I'm Conner Reynolds."

Ryan chuckles but takes Conner's peace offering, giving his hand a firm shake. "Ryan Miller, nice to meet you. And don't worry about it."

"I didn't mean to jump to conclusions," Conner sheepishly adds.

Ryan waves him off. "I know walking in on something like that can get your head spinning, regardless of how innocent it was. *Trust me.* Been there, done that."

"I'm just dropping by to pick up Jo here for lunch."

"Good. She's been over there swearing like a sailor all morning," Ryan says. I open my mouth to protest, but he shoots me a smirk. "I can hear everything in your office. We share a wall. Just keep that in mind."

My cheeks flare even more, picking up on his implication. Little does he know that we're nowhere near that point. "*Okayyy*, we'll be going now."

I grab Conner's hand and drag him outside, to the front of the office, where his Chevelle is sitting. He's still snickering as he gets behind the wheel and pulls away from the office. "When do you have to be back?"

I glance over at Conner. He's driving with one hand on the wheel, the other on the center console. He looks back at me, the sunlight playing off his chocolate eyes, giving them a warm glow. I offer a shrug of my shoulder and smile. "Whenever. An hour or so, maybe?"

"Perfect."

We drive for a few minutes until he pulls into the parking lot of Lancer Park, a Cedar Ridge favorite hangout spot. He reaches to the back seat and pulls out a lunch box. Together, we walk over to a wooden picnic bench by the lake. It's unseasonably warm today, so we'd be crazy not to take advantage of the weather.

"This place is nice," Conner observes, squinting his eyes against the sun as he looks out at the lake. Unzipping the lunch box, he pulls out two homemade sandwiches and a bag of chips to share.

We dig into our lunches and remain quiet for a bit until Conner breaks the silence by clearing his throat. "So, I have to be back at work on Monday."

I wipe a dollop of mustard off my bottom lip and look down at the table. I knew this was coming sooner or later. The inevitable, 'it was fun, but...' that always seems to come. "So, you leave on Sunday?"

"Yeah, probably early Sunday afternoon. That way, I can have the evening to get settled for the week."

I nod and glance up, smiling awkwardly. "Well, I guess it had to come to an end sometime."

He frowns and gives me a baffled look. "Jo, I don't want this to end."

"You don't?"

"No, of course not," Conner says, reaching across the table and taking my hand. "We've had the best time this week, and I don't think I'd be able to survive knowing that we didn't take the leap when we could have."

Butterflies take flight in my stomach. "I thought we weren't leaping yet."

"Is that what you want?" he asks me before taking a bite of his sandwich. His eyes are thoughtful as he watches me.

I toss his question around in my head. What *do* I want? Sunday, I told him I wasn't good at relationships, and Monday I had no answer for the same question, but it seems that Conner and I have been living in a version of a relationship ever since then. I look forward to texting him throughout the day and wait excitedly for his replies. We may be in the early stages, but this still feels like the beginnings of a relationship to me.

It's only been a week. I don't know how this will play out long term. Conner lives in Atlanta. His life is there; his job, his family. And I have no intention of leaving, so I don't know where that leaves us. Do we agree to long-distance before we really even know what we're agreeing to?

I realize he's waiting for my response, so I shrug, giving him the exact same non-committal answer. "I don't know."

He offers me a knowing smile. "You do, but it's okay. How's your sandwich?"

I look down at the remaining half of my lunch. "It's good."

We make small talk for a while, but his question is still playing in my mind. *What do I want?*

Finally, it comes to me, clear as day.

I want quiet nights on the couch, Conner rubbing my feet as we talk about our days and drink a glass of wine. I want holidays, and birthdays, and anniversaries, and every day in between. I want someone to look at me how Ryan looks at Izabel, and know that it's me who spins their world around.

As much as I've run from it in the past, I can see the door wide open in front of me. This could be my second chance at having that kind of love. But falling in love is a risk, and I'm not sure if I'm strong enough to risk everything that I've built if I don't know for certain that it will last.

After we finish eating, we toss our trash into a trash can and take a quick stroll around the lake. Conner's holding my hand, his thumb tenderly rubbing against my skin.

"I want to know if you mean it," I say suddenly. "You talk about not wanting whatever's happening to end, but I need to know if you really mean that."

"Of course I do, Jo."

"Even when I get crazy or bad things happen?" I ask

him. "I need to know that you'll be there to catch me or hold me steady through whatever happens. Because if I let myself fall for you again, Conner, I want it to be the last time," I say quickly, breathlessly, knowing that if I let myself fall for him again and it didn't work for some reason or another, I would not recover quickly. Maybe not ever.

His eyes trace my face, his lips set into an earnest line. "Josephine, I *promise* you that if you agree to give this a go, I won't let you down. As long as you're in, I'm in."

Well, how is a girl supposed to refuse that?

"What does that mean, though? You live in Atlanta. I'm here," I counter back.

"It's not that far. We'll go back and forth. I'll come up here on weekends, or vice versa."

"How about just holidays?" I offer, grimacing. "I'm not ready to be around my family that much yet."

Conner squeezes my hand and chuckles. "That sounds like a decent compromise. I don't mind coming up here on weekends, then we can spend Thanksgiving and Christmas down there."

I stop walking and turn to him. He follows my action and does the same. "Are we really going to do this?"

"Is this really what you want? Do you want to be with me?" he asks. I nod slightly, and his face breaks out in a grin. "Then I suppose we are, girlfriend."

Girlfriend.

"Is this too soon? It's probably too soon."

His hand comes up to cup my jaw, and he holds my gaze steady. "There are no rules for us. It's not like this is a new relationship. We're just coming back from a long intermission, is all."

"A ten-year intermission."

"If, by the time all is said and done, I have you on my arm, I would wait a hundred years. Ten is nothing."

I sigh and roll my eyes. "Conner Reynolds, how am I supposed to keep a clear head when you say things like that to me?"

He laughs and closes the distance, pressing our lips together. I hold him to me, loving the way his arms wrap around me in response.

Time seems to slow, and I let myself become consumed with Conner. When I'm breathless, he parts away.

His warm breath fans over my lips. "That's the point. If I have you swooning, you can't be mad at me." I reach a hand out and sock him in the gut. He pulls back from me with a groan. "Ow. Why'd you do that, woman?"

"I tripped," I say with a tip of my shoulder and walk back toward the car, a smirk playing on my face. I hear Conner's feet behind me, then his arms are wrapped around my waist, lifting me in the air and spinning me around. "Put me down, you brute!"

"Apologize!"

I throw my head back and laugh as he spins me around and around. "Never! Seriously, though, put me down, or I'm going to throw up all over you."

Conner relents and sets me down, his hands gripping my hips and holding me steady. He kisses me again. "Now that I've kissed you again, I don't think I'll ever be able to stop," he mutters, rubbing the pad of his thumb over my bottom lip. "I don't know how I'm going to survive once I'm back in Atlanta."

"I do," I say slyly.

"And how's that?"

I stand up on my tiptoes so that my lips are next to his ear. Even before I say what's on my mind, my cheeks flush bright red with the insinuation. "*Phone sex.*"

He groans lowly as his strong fingers dig into my hip bones. "You're killing me, Jo."

"I never said I was going to make this easy," I say as I take a nibble of his ear. "In fact, I think I might take extra steps to make sure it's very, very *hard*."

Conner swears and then pushes me away, his hands on my hips, moving to turn me toward the car. "Okay, you evil little vixen, let's get your hot ass back to work before you make me self-combust over here."

He starts pushing me toward where his Chevelle is parked and then swats me on the ass before stepping over to his door. I snicker as I buckle myself in.

"This is going to be fun," I remark.

He groans and runs a hand through his hair, but then shoots me a wink. "I don't know what I just signed up for."

Chapter 15

Conner

SUNDAY COMES FAR TOO QUICKLY.

Josephine and I lay in bed early this morning, watching the sunrise through the blinds in her bedroom. She's got her head laying on my shoulder, her fingers running through the coarse hair that covers my chest. I've got my arm wrapped snugly around her waist, idly tracing patterns onto her shoulder through her t-shirt.

There's really no other feeling like waking up next to her in the morning. Even with us not having sex, the intimacy from holding her close all night fills me with a deeper satisfaction that I never knew I needed. If she were the first thing I saw every morning, I'd be the happiest man on the planet.

"I don't want you to go," Josephine says softly, so softly that I almost don't hear her.

I take a deep breath and shift us slightly so that I can look down at her. Those hazel eyes stare up at me, twinkling in the soft light of dawn. "I don't want to go, either."

"Good," she says, snuggling into me more. "Then just call your boss and let him know you won't be back."

A low laugh rumbles out of my chest. "I don't think he'd be too happy about that."

"Can you work remotely?"

I look down at her again. "I can, but I really need to go back into the office, Jo. As much as it physically pains me to do so."

Josephine sighs and adjusts her head a bit on the pillow. I run my fingers through the silky strands of her hair. "It's been nice having you around, just like old times."

"Just like old times," I agree. "But I want new times, too, you know. I can't wait to see where this all takes us."

I feel her smile against my chest, and she falls silent again. I bend my neck and press a kiss into her hair, smelling the sweet scent of her perfume. We stay like that for a long time, watching the sun stream in through the blinds.

If I fall for you, Conner, I want it to be the last time.

Those words have been on repeat in my head since she said them this weekend. She wants everything I want; she's not ready to admit that I'm what she wants, though. That's okay. I'll wait for however long she needs me to wait.

I grip her waist and pull her against me, her body flush against mine until she's practically on top of me. Our lips join in a heated kiss, and I pry her mouth open. She gives in, letting me devour her.

My hands trace the curves of her body, down her torso, to her hips. Then they dip underneath the hem of the oversize shirt she's wearing. I meet her eyes for a second, and she nods, giving me approval. I push the material back up her body. Jo lifts slightly, raising her arms so I can pull it off of her.

Then I get to work on her underwear, pulling them down her glorious legs until she's lying on the bed, absolutely bare. A strangled moan comes out of my mouth when I gaze at her. Her arms are over her head, her back slightly arched up, and her luxurious brown hair is splayed across the white duvet, creating a dark contrast.

"*Fuck* me," I utter as I look at her. "You're beautiful."

She grins. "You are slightly overdressed, Ace."

I smirk at her and stand up, pulling my t-shirt up over my head until my chest is bare. She sucks in a deep breath as her eyes trail across my chest and abdomen. A trail of fire licks my chest, following in the wake of her attention.

Josephine sits up, her hands coming to my hips and finding the band of my athletic shorts. Jo presses a kiss against my stomach, making my abdominal muscles flex against her lips. I let my head drop back and sigh. Josephine keeps her lips against my stomach as she rids me of my shorts, along with my briefs, until I'm just as bare as she is.

I suck in a deep breath and push her back down on the bed, my mouth encasing one breast. Her quick reaction of a gasp, followed by a seductive moan, has me grinning, and I flick out the tip of my tongue, rewarding her for her responsiveness. Unable to bear being apart from her much longer, I break our connection and crawl over her until we're pressed against each other. The feel of her skin on mine has my body practically exploding.

My hand snakes around to her back, and I push between her shoulder blades, trying to bring her impossibly closer. I'm finally finding that missing puzzle piece. Jo's hands are trailing over my back, running over the ridges of my muscles and then kneading my rear end.

I move down her body, leaving open-mouthed kisses all over her. I spend some more time on her breasts, rolling my tongue over her nipples until she's writhing on the bed. Then I kiss down her sternum to her belly button. As I'm exploring her skin, my eyes dart down to her hipbone, and everything comes to a crashing halt. There, right next to the bone, is a dark-lined tattoo. My heart stammers into my throat as I trace the outline with my thumb.

"Conner," she pleads brokenly. But I can't ignore it. "Please."

I want to cry as I observe it. My jaw tightens as I try to fight off the overwhelming emotion of the sight right before me. The tattoo is small, so small that I didn't see it until I removed her underwear. It's beautiful, though. Two angel wings, etched into her skin, with a halo hovering right above them. To anyone else, it might just look like a beautiful angelic tattoo.

But I know better. I know what this ink means to her.

I lean down and press my lips to the tattoo, closing my eyes and breathing her in. Jo shivers underneath my lips as our alternate reality flashes before my eyes—a life we could've had together, a family. But sadly, that was over before it even began. I make the quick decision not to linger. I don't want Josephine to lock up, like I know she will if I pay too much attention. We can talk about it later. And we *will*. But now, I need her more than I need the air I'm breathing.

I keep moving lower in my exploration of her, coming to rest between her thighs. I don't hold back. I show her everything I want to say, but can't, as my tongue moves expertly against her. Her fingers grip into my hair, her knees bending and pressing against my head, almost crushing me.

"Conner," Jo breathes.

I look up at her from my position between her legs, and I get her message. She's ready. I move back up her body, positioning myself where I can finally take her. Her heat surrounds me, sending my thoughts into a tailspin. Before I enter her, I pause and look around.

"Condom," I mutter. Shit, did I even bring any with me? I'm sure there's some here somewhere. In my suitcase, maybe?

Jo's hands clasp on my cheeks, and she pulls me back down to look at her. "It's okay, I'm good."

"You're on the pill?"

She shakes her head but says, "Something like that. Trust me."

I do. I trust her implicitly. After the pain she went through with her first pregnancy, I know she wouldn't be reckless. Even with me. Especially with me.

Our gazes lock, her hazel eyes burning into mine as I push into her. Her warmth envelops me for the first time in years and reminds me exactly how we are meant to be together. For the first time since our last time, all those years ago, I finally feel like I'm right where I was always meant to be—with her. It's as though she was made for me—her body, her heart, her mind. If I could bottle up this moment right here, I would in a heartbeat. Every inch of her surrounds and consumes me from head to toe. Breaking our gaze, I finally bottom out inside of her, and I have to close my eyes, exhaling sharply to get control of myself. She feels too good. Too right.

Jo pulls me down into her and kisses me, arching her back to press into me further, encouraging me to start moving. I groan as I roll my hips against her, pulling out and then pressing deep into her again.

Josephine throws her head back and moans when I thrust into her. I press my lips against her neck, doing it again, getting the same reaction. "You like that, baby?"

"God, yes!" she cries. Her hands claw at my back and hold me tightly to her. I continue to move against her, already losing myself in everything that is Josephine. I do it over and over again, until she's shivering beneath me. "I'm close. Don't stop!"

I pause, grabbing each of her hands and pinning them above her head, holding her wrists down against the bed as I pound into her. "That's it, Jo. Come for me."

Jo screams, arching her back against me. I keep thrusting into her through her climax, appreciating the way her walls constrict around me. Josephine goes rigid as the waves of her orgasm roll over her. I slow down, keeping my eyes on her the whole time, never wanting to miss a moment of her. I don't stop moving in her, but let her catch her breath.

I capture her lips in mine, and she kisses me back with fervor, her hands snaking into my hair and gripping against my scalp. I'm moving against her now with more passion rather than frenzy. I get closer to the edge with every movement I make, but I try to keep control of myself. I never want this to end.

Josephine wraps her legs around me, digging her heels into my lower back and driving me forward. "Conner," she whispers against my neck. "You feel so good."

I moan against her, my body swelling with need for her. Josephine keeps whispering dirty words in my ear, each driving me closer and closer to the edge. I catch myself losing control and my thrusts get more erratic. I never want this to end, but I know I'm close.

Jo's teeth nibble on my ear, and she gives the lobe a light tug. "Come for *me* now, Conner."

Her words toss me over the edge. I throw my head back with a loud groan and bury myself deep into her, finally finding my release. My arms give out and I collapse on top of her, my cheek pressed against her chest. I can hear her heartbeat hammering in my ear. Her pulse is just as wild as mine is.

Her fingers comb through my hair as my body calms down. I take deep breaths in and out, not quite ready to move from my position. I hold her tightly to me, thinking about how I never, *ever* want to let her go again.

Josephine and I are fireworks, and this is just an example of just how good it can be with someone. With her.

Over the years, I've been with my share of women, each of them beautiful and special in their own way. But none have ever, nor ever will, compare to what I've experienced here with Jo. She's wrecked me.

I finally muster up the strength to push off of her. Her greenish-brown eyes find mine and they sparkle. I lean forward and kiss her again, my body humming with the lingering effects of our lovemaking. I pull away from her lips and then roll onto my side, allowing her to wiggle away.

Jo runs into the bathroom to clean up, and I pull back the covers on the mattress. When the bathroom door opens, she bolts back over to the bed. I hold up the comforter and she slides in next to me, laying on her side facing me.

I smooth a hand over her hair, pushing it from her glistening forehead, then trail down to her waist where I pull her naked body flush against mine. Her smooth legs tangle with mine and she wraps her arm around me, trying to get impossibly closer.

"That was—" I start to say, but then trail off, unsure of how to finish my sentence.

"Perfection," she whispers back, her eyes holding mine.

"Perfection," I agree. I inhale happily and look at Jo through half-closed lids. "Where have you been all my life?"

She preens and presses against me, nuzzling into my chest. "Nowhere. Everywhere."

I fall silent for a moment, my fingers idly tracing patterns over her bare back. "When did you get the tattoo?"

Josephine's spine stiffens slightly, but then relaxes slowly, like she had to coach herself down. "I got it about a year after."

I shift a little bit, my shoulder starting to ache from how I'm laying on it. All these years later, and it's not fully healed. The scars run deep. I'm sure Josephine can relate.

"I really like it," I tell her.

"Thanks, I do, too."

"Do you have to explain it a lot?" I ask. She understands my question. Does she have to explain it when she's intimate with others? I fight off the scowl, thinking of her being intimate with any other man than me. I'm not naïve enough to think she hasn't, as much as I dislike the idea.

"No. Most guys I'm with don't even notice it. Too caught up in the moment, and if they linger, I'm quick to distract them," Jo explains, not beating around the bush.

My hand flexes against her back, and I look down at her. "But you let me linger."

"You're..." she hesitates, trying to think of the right way to say it, "different." I laugh lowly, and she smiles. "I don't have to explain myself because you already know," she adds.

"I do."

"I like that. It feels nice."

I close my eyes and hold her close, never wanting to let go. If I were to die right now, I'd be a happy man. There's no other place that I'd rather be than buried deep inside her, watching her come undone beneath me.

Josephine lets out a long breath. "Her name was Madelyn."

I freeze as her words wash over me. "Madelyn?"

She nods her head against me, then pushes up onto her elbows so she can look at me. "Madelyn Hope. A girl."

My heart is beating so hard it's almost painful. I'm worried it might beat right out of my rib cage. My fingers swipe a section of hair off Jo's face as I search her features. "Madelyn Hope DiMarco."

She offers me a small smile and then shakes her head *no*. "Reynolds."

I inhale a shaky breath and then close my eyes. "You never told me."

"I know."

A girl. I could've had a daughter. A little girl that looked just like her mother. The pain shatters through me as I kiss Jo, and I let it. I let myself imagine what that could've been like, even though it hurts so badly. I'll relish in it now and let it pass. Josephine and I can get through this eventually, together.

For the first time since I found out that Josephine was in the hospital, I feel my eyes burn with unshed tears. I pull away from her lips and then lean my forehead against hers. "Thank you. For telling me."

Her eyes hold mine, and I can see moisture brimming at the lids of her own eyes. "You're welcome. I got to hold her for a little bit after everything. But then, I couldn't. My parents handled all the logistics from there, but I made sure that they knew her name."

"It's beautiful," I tell her. And I mean it.

"She's buried in Atlanta," she says, looking down. "I've never been, but I've been thinking that maybe we should go. Together."

My hand cups her cheek, and I hold her eyes steady. "I would *love* that, Jo."

"Maybe at Thanksgiving. Since I said I'd be there for the holidays."

"We can definitely make that happen," I assure her.

"I'm trying," Josephine hesitates. "I want to be better. I don't want to let this consume me anymore."

I watch her for a second before I grip her waist and spin us around until I'm hovering above her. Her legs automatically wrap around my hips until we're pressed together in the most intimate way. I hold her gaze and offer her a compassionate smile.

"I don't know if the pain will ever go away. But maybe together we can make it not hurt so much. There's so much life for us to live. I think it's important that we work through everything together."

"I agree." She bobs her head.

"And maybe at some point, we'll get to a place where we can try again," I say hopefully, looking down at her. Her eyes go wide with panic, and I quickly backtrack. "At some point, maybe. But not anytime soon. Right now, all I want is to spend my last few hours committing you to memory."

And I do exactly that.

For the next hour or so, I roam over every inch of her, learning what parts of her body make her squirm, and what areas cause goosebumps to rise on her skin whenever I linger too long.

I want to become a master of all things Josephine. She already commands my heart and my soul. I want to be able to repay her and show her just how much she means to me.

Eventually, against my wishes, we get out of bed. We make it all the way to the shower before my hands are on her again, soaping her up and teasing her, eliciting sexy little gasps from her lips. I take her in the shower and then wrap her up in a towel, holding her to my chest.

She sighs as my arms hold her tightly. "I'm going to miss you."

My lips find her hair. "Me too. It won't be for long, though. I'll come stay the weekend in two weeks, and then, before you know it, it will be Thanksgiving. Do you think Ryan will let you take that whole week off?"

"Probably. I kind of make my own schedule."

"Then that's perfect," I say, kissing her hair again.

Josephine shivers, and then her hand is on my jaw, guiding my mouth to hers again. It's like we're newlyweds. We just can't seem to get enough of each other. I scoop her up, still wrapped in her towel, and take her back into her bedroom, laying her on the bed.

I brace my arms on the mattress, looking down at her. She's splayed out underneath me, still in her towel. My eyes trace over every inch of her. This version of Jo will be burned into my brain forever, and I wouldn't have it any other way.

"I really need to start moving," I say softly. "There's nothing I'd love more than to sex you up all day, but the real world awaits."

Josephine drops her head back with a groan and covers her face. "Don't remind me."

I chuckle as I locate my jeans and briefs on her bedroom floor and pull them on. She's lying on the bed still, propped up on her side. Her hazel eyes watch my every move, tracing over every dip and curve of my body. I smirk and strike a pose.

"See something you like?"

Jo winks at me. "You don't even know."

Oh, but I think I do.

Two weeks. That's all it took for us to find happiness in each other again. Even after I thought it would never happen, here we are. Two weeks.

Imagine what we could do with a lifetime.

As the morning passes and she cooks breakfast before I have to leave, I can't help but be overrun with my feelings for her.

I love her.

Call me crazy, but I don't know if I ever *stopped* loving her.

I'm not about to let that loose and scare her off because I know for a fact she's not there yet. But the fact remains true. Josephine DiMarco is the only woman for me. She has been since the first moment I saw her.

Eventually, the time comes that I have to head back to Atlanta, and despite the brave faces we're putting on for each other, it hurts. I see the displeasure etched all across her face. I would give anything just to kiss it off, sweep her off her feet and carry her off to bed, where I'd give her a much more pleasurable expression to wear on that pretty face.

"Okay," I say finally. We're standing by her front door. My bags are already in the Chevelle, ready to go.

Jo has her arms crossed over her chest. "Okay."

I reach up and cup her cheek. She leans into my palm, slightly turning her head to press a kiss against my skin. Then she turns her eyes up to me, the green-brown hue glossy. It's goodbye, but just for now.

Leaning down, I capture her lips one more time. Jo responds by standing on her tiptoes and wrapping her arms around me. When I finally pull away, her cheeks are flushed, and a single tear streaks down the side. I wipe it away with my thumb.

"It's only a few weeks. I'll call you every night if you want."

"What if I don't want to talk to you?" she asks me, a teasing glint sparking.

"Then I'll leave you voicemails," I respond with a wink. "Okay, goodbye, Jo."

Josephine closes her eyes and exhales, squeezing my hand in hers. Then she opens them with a grin. "Goodbye, Ace."

I take one last look at her and then turn around to head out the door. I'm down the steps and on the sidewalk when she steps out onto the porch behind me.

"Oh, and by the way..." she says. I turn around to face her. "My name is fucking *Josie*."

A grin splits across my face, and I laugh. Jo joins in with me. And I'm laughing all the way back to Atlanta.

Chapter 16

Josie

IN THE DAYS FOLLOWING CONNER'S DEPARTURE, I DO MY best to get through the workdays without thinking about the empty house I have to go home to at the end of the day. It took me by surprise how much I miss having Conner around. I knew I would, but now that it's just me again, it's really becoming apparent that I despise being alone.

I'm ready to put this part of my life behind me. I think I'm ready to say goodbye to solitude and embrace sharing a life with another person. Not that I'm planning on moving in with him anytime soon, but knowing that he's there helps quiet some of the lingering anxieties.

As if on cue, my phone starts ringing the minute I put my car into park in my driveway. Conner's name flashes across the screen, along with a goofy picture that we took together while he was here. He's been true to his word and has stayed in touch plenty throughout the week. Which helped ease the loneliness.

"What do you want?" I tease him, answering the phone.

"Uh, yes, I'd like to place an order for one sexy architect

with a side of attitude." His deep voice echoes through the receiver, making goosebumps break out across my arms.

"Sir, I don't think that's in your budget."

Conner sighs dramatically. "Damn, you're right. Guess I'll just have to take you as a consolation."

Now I laugh. "Jerk."

He joins in with me. "I miss you."

"I miss you too, Ace," I reply. "How was your day?"

"Ohhh, it was a long day. Bunch of garbage meetings and end-of-year projects getting assigned. Somehow, I always seem to draw the short stick on these types of things. My dad considers it good training for taking over the company someday."

I laugh as Conner launches into a big, dramatic tale about how his coworkers are all after him. I listen and chime in where I need to as I wander off to my bedroom to get out of my work clothes. I put the phone on speaker and let his voice echo throughout my room, making it seem like he's actually here with me.

Once I'm in my comfy clothes, I head out to the living room and crash on my couch. I pull up the pizza app and start ordering while Conner's still regaling me with his office drama.

"And so, I told her, like, hey, I'm doing my best to make the transition of leadership as smooth as I can, but I can't do that with you purposely sabotaging me every chance you get." He goes on and on. I listen with an amused smile on my face; fired-up Conner seems sexy. I only wish I was there to fully appreciate this version of him.

"Well, enough about me. How was your day?" Conner finally asks after a particularly heated rant. "Were you able to get everything settled with that client of yours?"

I groan and then flop on the couch. "No, she's still being super indecisive. Ryan thinks I should just suggest that she go find another firm, but I don't know. It's a huge account, and they've already paid us an advance. I don't want to risk the firm losing money on them, simply because she can't make up her mind and I'm getting tired of being strung along."

"If she's driving you that crazy, maybe you should. It's not like you won't be able to find another high-end client. You're good at what you do, Jo."

"Thanks. It's just frustrating."

"I think I know what could make it better," I can hear the mischief lacing his voice, and I smirk into the receiver, waiting for him to continue. "What are you wearing right now?"

I laugh and look down at my getup. "A ratty t-shirt, old sweats, and granny panties."

"Mmm, the good old period panties, huh?" Conner teases me. "My favorite."

"I'm sure," I snicker. I don't bother correcting him that they're *not* period panties. That's not exactly something I have to worry about most months. But that's a dreaded conversation for another time.

"Seriously, though, I was promised phone sex. It's been almost five days," Conner whines.

"Poor baby." The doorbell rings, and I look over toward the general area. "We'll have to take a raincheck. I think my pizza's here."

Conner groans. "Fine, but I better get some sexy pictures of you eating the pizza, at least."

"I'll see what I can do. Goodnight, Conner."

"Night, baby."

I hang up the phone and walk over to the front door, reaching for my cash as I swing it open. "Hey—" I start to say, but quickly cut my sentence short when I realize who's standing on my porch.

It's definitely *not* the pizza guy.

"Alex, what are you doing here?" I ask, crossing my arms over my chest.

My brother looks me up and down. He's got his hands in his pockets, and he's bouncing on his toes. He's only dressed in a pair of ratty jeans and a t-shirt. He must be freezing.

"Hey, sis, can I come in?"

In a split second, I weigh my options. The reasonable, rational part of me knows that dealing with Alex in any capacity can only lead to bad, but the tenderness of my heart makes it so difficult to turn him away.

"Why?" I deadpan, keeping my face level.

Alex laughs and then shakes his head. "Because it's fucking freezing out here. Come on, Jo."

"Fine. But you're not staying." I give in to the good side of me, unwilling to let him freeze to death outside. Although, the thought is tempting. Tossing open the door, I turn on my heel and head back into the living room.

Alex follows me. I hear him shut the front door behind him, and then he saunters after me into the living room. I lean against the back of the couch, resting my hips on the edge. "What do you want, Alex?"

"First of all, good to see you, too. Second of all, I wanted to apologize," he says. "For your window. I was kind of out of it, and I wasn't thinking clearly."

"No shock there," I snark at him. "I'd accept your apology if I was surprised, but I'm not. That's your MO, Alex."

"I'm trying to be better," my brother argues back.

I tilt my head back and bark out a humorless laugh. "Right, and I'm trying to become an astronaut."

Alex stays silent, but he looks around. He's still moving, bouncing and jerking his head back and forth. "Nice place you got. Good old Auntie did well."

I narrow my eyes. "Are you on drugs?"

His head snaps back to me, and he frowns. "What, no! Why would you ask that?"

"Because you're jerking around like a crazy person. You can't stay still. Come here," I move into his personal space before he can protest and grab his chin, pulling his face down toward me. Alex is a few inches taller than me, so I have to reach up.

I stare into the hazel eyes that are the mirror image of my own. Depending on the light, they flash from brown to green to any mixture in between. I frown as I observe his dilated pupils and the way his eyes are shaking, even though he's staying still. Burst blood vessels surround the whites of his eyes. I feel white-hot rage, mixed with disappointment, settle in my belly.

"What are you on?" I ask as I release him a little too forcefully.

"It's nothing, Jo. I was just playing a little poker with the guys, and they had some. We all did a line. It's fine."

I cross my arms again and scowl at him. "It's not fine. You need help."

"Don't pretend to care, baby sister. I know I fell off your radar years ago. I'm only here because you're my last option," he sneers. I don't bother correcting him that he's only *two* minutes older than me. That doesn't equate to me being his *baby* sister in my head. But I'm not on crack, so there's that.

"Your last option for what?"

"I need some money," he explains. I'm already shaking my head before he can finish, but he persists. He steps closer and takes my hands. "Please, Jo, just listen to me. Conner gave me enough, but I made a bad choice, and I bet too much on a shitty hand in poker, and now it's gone."

I blink. *Conner* gave him money? Steeling my resolve, I cross my arms over my chest, deciding to talk to him about that later. "How is this my problem?"

"Seriously. The people I bet against are *bad* news. If I don't get them that money, they'll find a way to take it."

"Again, I ask how this is my problem?"

"Because you're my only option. And it's not like you don't have money. I know you have a nice little office downtown, and you own the house 'cause Auntie paid it off. I'm sure she left you something when she died, too." He squeezes my hands. "Please, Jo, I'm desperate here."

"I can't help you," I grit out, pulling my hands away. "Go to a bank or something."

"You're not listening. These are bad people, Josephine," Alex sneers. His eyes are hard, but his hands are still shaking from his high, so I can't really take him seriously.

"You need to leave."

"They'll kill me," he says. I shrug a shoulder, and then he changes tactics. "I'll send them after you. After Conner. They'll get their money one way or the other. Even if they kill me, they'll still expect the debt to be paid. I'll just casually drop that your boyfriend's living large in the big city, and they'll go after him."

My pulse pounds as I consider his words. What kind of people did Alex get involved with? The freaking mafia? Good Lord. Rationale tells me that he's probably bluffing. But the way he's begging me makes me take a pause.

What if he's not bluffing? What if he really could send them after Conner or me? I watch Alex closely as I consider his words. He knows he hit a tender spot because he continues taunting me.

"These guys won't hold back, I promise you that. Their money's all they care about. If I don't get it to them by tonight at midnight, you can consider yourselves on a hit list."

I close my eyes and curse myself for what I'm about to do. "How much?"

"Ten grand."

My stomach drops, and my eyes shoot open. "*Ten grand?* Alex, I don't have that much! What the fuck were you doing betting that kind of money?"

He holds his hands up. "It was a shitty situation, I'll be the first to admit. I made a bad play."

I cover my eyes with my hand and try to control my breathing. "Okay. Shit."

"Look, if you don't have the full amount, you can just give me whatever you do have, and I can try to hit up a few of my buddies to spot the rest."

"Do you even fucking hear yourself, Alex?" I yell. "What happened to you?"

Alex holds his hands up in surrender; they shake as he holds them in the air, like he can't control them. "Okay, okay. Calm down. I know this is a lot to hit you with, but I wouldn't be here if this wasn't serious."

"I don't have that much money, Alex," I tell him again weakly.

"I'll just take whatever you do have. That will be plenty. I'll figure it out from there," he pleads. "Come on, Jo. I came here because I knew you'd be the only one to understand."

I know I shouldn't do this. I shouldn't give him the money. I don't know if it's the fact that he's my twin brother, therefore a part of who I am on a deep level, or because I'm hoping this will save him, but my resolve cracks, and I hate myself for it.

"Fine. Wait here," I tell him before stalking down the hall into my bedroom. I close my door to make sure he's not watching and then head toward my closet.

My aunt might have been a little paranoid about some things. She always told me that you should have an extra cash reserve, just in case. When I moved in after she died, I discovered her little stash, tucked behind a panel in the master bedroom closet. I move my purses aside on the top shelf and reach for the shoebox.

As I pull it down, I lift the lid and see the stacks of twenties and tens that she often squirreled away. I can't say I blame her. My aunt was estranged from her family. She was all she had in the world, so she had to be prepared.

I haven't had to touch it, but this might prove to be the perfect time. Last I counted, there was about $2500 in here—nothing close to the dollar amount Alex needs, but maybe it will get him by until he finds the rest.

I carry the box out to Alex, who's still twitching around in the living room. As I walk toward him, a smile plays on his lips. "You're the best sister ever, Josephine. Really, I knew I could count on you."

"Alex, listen to me," I say sternly, still holding tightly to the shoebox. "If I give this to you, you have to *promise* that this will be the end. You need help. You can't keep living like this."

"Sure, I promise. Now can I have it?"

I stare at him for a moment, knowing that he's just feeding me a line. He's practically holding out his hands, saying, *'gimme, gimme.'* But I hand the box over to him, anyway. "There's about twenty-five in there."

His eyebrows raise hopefully. "Thousand? Twenty-five thousand?"

"No, you dipshit, twenty-five hundred. I know it's not much, but maybe it's better than nothing. It's all I have."

Alex moves toward me and then envelops me in a hug. I rest my head against his shoulder and close my eyes. For a moment, I can pretend that everything between us is okay, even though it hasn't been for so long. Growing up, Alex was my best friend, my confidant. Aside from Conner, he was the most important guy in my life.

As we grew older, and he started mixing with the wrong

crowd, things between us started getting a little stressed. And then the accident was the final straw. After that, our relationship was never the same. Truth be told, I miss my brother. I miss the connection we used to have when we were little, and I miss knowing that my counterpart always has my back. Maybe that's why I inevitably cave and give him the money that I know I shouldn't.

"Okay, I should go. Thanks again for this, Josephine. I really appreciate it." Alex gives me one last squeeze and then lets me go.

I cross my arms over my chest and stare him down. "Remember what I said. You have to get help, Alex."

"I know. I will."

I don't believe him. Not for one second. But I try to convince myself that I do. He'll take the money and then figure something else out to pay off his debt, and then maybe he'll try to figure himself out. I would love to have him back, but I don't think that's ever going to happen.

I watch Alex saunter out of the living room and to the back door. He turns back with that wild grin that he's always had. It makes my chest hurt. "I'll see you at Thanksgiving, sis."

I press my lips together and nod my head. And then he's gone. I fall back into my couch and pull my knees up to my chest, resting my forehead against them. Taking a few deep breaths, I try to tell myself that I did the right thing in giving him that money. Maybe this was the catalyst that he needed to realize what a shit show he's gotten himself into.

I try to steer my thinking in that direction, but the rational part of my brain knows that he will never change. This was just a stop so he could get himself out of trouble. This cycle that he's gotten himself into will likely never end. And now I'm just an enabler.

My pizza delivery arrives a few minutes later. I thank the

worker and give him his tip. I open the pizza box and see the gooey-pepperoni goodness, the smell of melted cheese and pizza sauce wafting up into my nostrils.

Usually, this would have my stomach growling in anticipation, but instead, I just feel nauseous thinking about Alex. I've always thought that I ruin everything I touch. I hope this curse doesn't seep over into Alex's wayward life. I want him to get help; I want him to be better. I stare at the pizza for a minute or two before I close the box and stuff it in the fridge. There's no way I'm going to be able to get myself to eat that tonight.

Instead, I strip off my clothes and step into the shower, letting the water wash away the painful thoughts of my prodigal twin.

Chapter 17

Conner

Now Entering Cedar Ridge: Population 35,637

I grin to myself as I see the big green sign on the highway. It's been two weeks since I've seen Josephine, and I am ready to wrap her in my arms and never let her go. I know I sound seriously whipped, but I don't care. Not in the slightest.

I was supposed to come in tomorrow, Saturday, but I decided to surprise her early. I took off work a few hours early today and hit the road to get to Cedar Ridge by the time she finished work. I'm like a little kid on Christmas Eve.

It's dark already by the time I pull up in front of her house. I leave my car on the street so she can park in her driveway when she gets home and then walk up to her porch. Jo told me she keeps a spare key hidden underneath the cap of a post on the porch, so I sleuth around until I find it, then let myself in. Her house is quiet, telling me that she hasn't arrived yet.

I make myself comfortable, dropping off my weekend things in her bedroom. Then I head back out to her living room and kick off my shoes, settling onto the couch and scrolling through my emails to make sure I didn't miss anything by leaving work early. Not long after I settle in, I hear her key in the front door. I pop off the couch and walk around, a big grin on my face.

Josephine opens up the door and smiles back at me, though it doesn't reach her eyes. "Hey, Ace."

"Hey, what's going on?" I ask her, immediately knowing something is not quite right.

She raises an eyebrow at me as she sets her bag down by the door. "Why do you think something's going on?"

"I just know. Everything okay?"

Jo steps toward me and wraps her arms around my middle, pressing her head against my chest. "I've just had a really long day. All I want is a glass of wine and someone to cuddle with."

I rub my hand up and down her back, chuckling slightly. "Well, lucky for you, I know just the guy for the job. Are you hungry?" Jo shakes her head against me. "Well, then why don't you go run a bath, and I'll grab the booze."

Josephine holds me for just a moment longer before letting me go and walking toward her bathroom. I hear the door shut, and then the sound of the tub filling up. I go to the kitchen and grab a bottle of red wine and two glasses. I also search her kitchen cabinets until I find a few candles and a lighter.

I follow her toward her bathroom and knock on the door. When I open it, Jo's already sunk deep into the tub that's filled with shiny bubbles. Her work clothes lay discarded in a pile by the door. She's submerged up to her collarbones, and she looks at me with a smile. Her curly brown hair is wrapped up in a knot on top of her head, the steam already causing some frizzy pieces to fall out.

I've never seen her more beautiful than right now.

I open the bottle of wine and pour us each a glass, handing one to her right away. Then I place the candles around the bathroom strategically and light them.

"Are you going to come in?" Josephine asks me.

I shoot her a wry grin and get to work on my belt buckle. "You think I'm going to let you be all naked in there without me? Hell yes, I'm coming in."

Jo's hazel eyes watch my every move as I strip for her. Her gaze traces over the hard planes of my body and the length of my legs. She doesn't hold back in showing me how much she appreciates my body. When I'm not wearing a stitch of clothing, she scoots forward in the tub, making room for me.

I try my best to crawl in behind her, making the water slosh over the edge with my large frame. I sink into the bubbles, and she leans back. I shift a little, trying to get comfortable, but this standard tub is not big enough for both of us. My knees stick out of the water, my torso feels all crunched, and I am horribly uncomfortable.

"So, Ms. Architect," I murmur into her ear once she's resting against my chest. "Tell me what your perfect house would look like. If you could build it from scratch, tell me everything you'd want to put into it."

Her fingers frolic in the water. "Why are you asking?"

"I just want to know what's going on in that brilliant mind of yours. Would you fix up this house? Or find a new one?"

Jo laughs. "No, definitely not this house. This house has been here since the dawn ages. It would have to be totally gutted, and then I'm sure we'd come across some outrageous issues hidden underneath."

"You don't like this house?"

She shakes her head. "I love this house, but financially and logistically, it just wouldn't be a good idea as a fixer-upper. It's fine the way it is."

"So, then, tell me what your perfect house would be like."

She thinks about it for a moment. "I'd love something a little bigger, more open. This place just feels so closed off. I'd knock down that wall." She uses her hands to illustrate what she sees in her mind, waving them around in the air. I try to picture what she's picturing. "And I'd have a big open kitchen with a window above the sink."

"Do you like something more modern or rustic?"

"Maybe a little bit of both? I don't know. I'm more into the architecture of a space rather than the interior design."

I chuckle. "Makes sense."

"And it would need more rooms. My perfect house would probably have maybe three or four bedrooms and two or three bathrooms. That way, I can have the master bedroom, an office, and a guest room."

Or a baby room, I think, but I bite my tongue.

"You should draw it up," I suggest, my arms tightening around her.

"Why would I do that?"

I shrug. "I just want to see what you can come up with. That way, if I'm strolling around and I find the perfect house, I can jump on it for you."

"You're not buying a house, Conner," Jo says, her tone telling me she thinks that's the most outrageous idea ever.

"You never know. If I find your perfect house, then you bet I'm buying it for you." Her silence is deafening, and I laugh under my breath. "Too soon?" I ask.

Josephine gives me a little nod and then looks sheepishly over her shoulder at me. "I'm sorry. I can't get as excited about this as you are."

"Don't apologize," I say, rubbing my thumb over the smooth skin of her belly.

"You just seem so sure—"

"I am," I cut her off. "I am sure. And you'll get there. I won't give you a choice. Once you figure out that I'm in this for the long haul, you'll get excited, too."

"It's nothing against you," Jo adds quickly. "I trust you, Conner. I'm just hesitant. I don't want to get too comfortable and then have you decide that I'm not what you want."

"That won't happen," I assure her, leaning forward to press a kiss to Jo's cheek. She sticks her bottom lip out in a pout. We sit together in the tub for a while longer until I can't take it anymore. The muscles in my legs have cramped up, and I have to call it quits.

"I don't think this is working." I slide out from behind her and grab a towel, wrapping it around my waist. Then I sit down on the floor next to the tub. I cross my arms on the ledge and rest my chin on top. "I have a request for the perfect house."

Jo raises a perfectly shaped eyebrow at me. "What's that?"

"A big jacuzzi tub that can fit the both of us," I tell her with a grin.

She smirks back. "I think we can make that happen."

"You better," I tease. "Now, tell me about your day."

Josephine sighs and sinks even further into the water. "It was stupid. I got into a big fight with Ryan about a project we're both working on. He pulled rank, and it just pissed me off because I felt like I was right."

"What exactly does Ryan do? Is he an architect, too?"

Jo shakes her head and reaches for her glass of wine. "No, he's an engineer. So, when we're working on a project together, he's usually working on the structural aspect of it, making sure the building is stable and won't crumble to the ground. I draw up the initial building plans based on what the client wants, and then he makes sure that it's possible to build it."

"So, what was the fight about?"

"He didn't particularly like one part of my drawings because he said it wouldn't be structurally sound or feasible. But I ran them through our program before I even turned it in, and it should've been fine. But he can be bullheaded sometimes when he thinks he's right. The issue is that, by doing what he needs to do, it's going to change the entire design of the building."

"Will the client still be satisfied with the outcome?" I ask her.

She sighs. "Yes, Ryan wouldn't compromise the client's satisfaction for anything. So, with this one, I just let him have it. It's annoying, though. Both Ryan and I have specific training. I'm more design-focused, and he's more technically focused. Which usually works out, but sometimes ends with us at each other's throats."

"I'm sorry, baby," I say, reaching across the ledge of the tub to take her hand. I entwine our fingers together. "When we build our perfect house, you can have all the control. You can design it however you want from top to bottom."

She chuckles. "I'd probably still let Ryan look at it. I don't want our house to fall in on itself."

"I'm sure he didn't mean to hurt your feelings. Want me to beat him up, anyway?"

A grin splits her face, and she shakes her head. "He didn't hurt my feelings. I'm just annoyed because he's probably right. Architects sometimes get lost in the design. We have all the fancy dreams that we want to see built to all their glory. The engineers then get to come in and tear it all apart because we aren't realistic."

"Was today any different? Why did it bother you so much?"

Jo grabs a handful of bubbles and then blows them away, the suds flying across the length of the tub. "I don't know. I've been off all week. I think I'm still reeling from Alex dropping by last weekend."

I frown at her. "What are you talking about?"

"Didn't I tell you?" she asks, and I shake my head. She most certainly *did not* tell me. "Alex came by last Friday and was asking me for money."

"That slimy little bastard," I mutter. "I told him to stay away from you."

"Was that when you gave him money, too?"

I freeze for a moment, but then opt for the truth. "Yeah, I considered it a business transaction. I gave him some money to keep him out of trouble, and he said he'd stay out of your way."

Josephine narrows her eyes a little. Behind those hazel eyes, I can see the displeasure that I'd do any type of business with her brother, but she tucks away her thoughts for later. "Well, he didn't listen. Shocker."

"How much was he asking for?"

"Ten thousand dollars." I open my mouth to remark, but she continues. "Obviously, I couldn't give him that. I don't have that much money. But I did give him twenty-five hundred out of my aunt's old emergency fund."

"Jo, you shouldn't have given him anything. It's just going to lead to him harassing you more."

"I know, but he said he was in big trouble. I guess he played a bad game of poker and bet across some dangerous people."

"That's on him. It's not our problem that he's a moron."

"He's my brother, Conner," she says. "I had to give him something."

I have a sick feeling in my gut that there's more to this story, but I nod my head at her. I don't like that Alex came to her asking for money, especially after I already gave him some. That only tells me that Alex is on a quick spiral to rock bottom. And he could take Jo down with him.

Before these last few weeks with Josephine, I hadn't heard from Alex in months. He would occasionally reach out to chat or grab a drink, but he'd been radio silent. Until that night he broke into Jo's house and she called me out of desperation.

Now that Alex knows Josephine might be willing to lend him money, there's no telling how far he'll take it. Alex used to be my best friend, but I don't trust the guy. Not even for a second. And that has nothing to do with his poor judgment when it came to his sister and his unborn niece. He's a sketchy dude, plain and simple. He only ever thinks of himself and how everyone else can aid him.

"If he comes around again, I want you to call me," I tell her. "I don't trust him, Jo."

"I will. I think he was on drugs, too. He was acting all weird and jittery."

The knot in my stomach tightens. Drugs amplify everything. The thought of him coming here and threatening his sister makes me want to throw up, then beat him into a pulp. "All the more reason to stay the hell away from him. If he comes by again, call the cops first, and then call me."

"He said he'll see me at Thanksgiving. Do you think he'll be there?" she asks me with wide eyes.

I sigh. "Probably, he usually is. But I'll make sure that he doesn't bother you." Thanksgiving with Alex typically ends up with him passed out drunk in his parents' living room. I would imagine this year will be no different.

"Thanks, Conner, for everything." She pauses and then looks around. "I think I'm ready to get out."

"Do you need help rinsing off?" I ask her, my lips pulling up into a smirk.

"Are you offering?" Jo asks. When I nod my head vigorously, she giggles. "Then, yes, I suppose I do need some assistance."

I reach for her wine glass and put it next to mine on the sink. Then I help her stand up in the tub, holding onto her hand, so she doesn't slip and crack her head open. The bubbles from the bath are sluicing gloriously down her skin, and my mouth waters.

Josephine pulls on the stop to let the water drain from the tub, and then she turns on the showerhead, squealing when the cold water hits her. I laugh as I drop the towel around my waist and step in behind her, closing the curtain behind me, so the water doesn't go everywhere.

When we're both underneath the water, Jo turns toward me and stands up on her tiptoes, wrapping her arms around my neck so she can press against me. My hands trail over her bare back, coming to rest on her hips where I pull her into me. I claim her mouth with mine and kiss her thoroughly for the first time all night.

God, I've missed her. It's crazy how someone can be totally out of your life one moment and then utterly consume your life the next. Three weeks ago, Josephine DiMarco was just a memory. But now, she's all I think about. I don't want to go another day without her in my life. Now that I know what life with her can be like, there's no way I'm going to give that up.

I pull away and cup my hand around her jaw, tilting her face up to mine. My gaze traces her face, landing on her eyes, which are a swirling mix of greens and browns. Starlight dances across her bright eyes as she watches me back with a smile on her lips.

"There you are," I whisper.

She raises an eyebrow. "Hm?"

"My shooting star. You're back."

Jo looks a little confused, but she also doesn't look concerned by my admission. She leans her head up again to kiss me, and I kiss her with just as much enthusiasm. My hand reaches behind her until I find the bottle of shampoo sitting in the caddy.

When we part again, I squirt a quarter-size amount into my hand and then grin wickedly at her. "Turn around."

"Conner, what are you doing?"

"Nothing, just helping you rinse off," I say, feigning innocence. My intentions are the exact opposite of innocent. I rub my hands together, creating a froth of shampoo, then stick my fingers into her hair, working the soap through her strands and massaging her scalp.

Jo leans her head back slightly, giving me better access. She moans out loud, and my body tightens and heats in response. The water streams down her front, and I watch the water droplets trace over every curve of her skin, feeling jealous. When I'm satisfied that her hair is thoroughly shampooed, I spin her around, so she's facing me, and her head is under the water.

The suds get rinsed out of her hair while I keep her lips occupied. Then we do the same routine with her conditioner. When I'm satisfied her hair is clean, I soap up her loofah and trail it all over her body. Josephine preens underneath my careful attention to her most sensitive spots. By the time we finish showering, she's breathless and flushed.

"Conner," she breathes once we step out of the tub, and I wrap her up in a towel. Desire shines in her eyes as she looks up at me.

"Yeah, baby?" I prod. Jo steps closer to me and presses her torso against mine. "What do you want?"

I watch her every move, and my blood starts to boil when she bites onto her lower lip. "You."

I don't give her a chance to process anything else as I scoop her up into my arms and drag her out into her bedroom. I deposit her on her bed before ridding us of both of the fluffy towel barriers. Neither of us wastes any time losing ourselves in each other.

After we're both sated, we lay together underneath her covers, our arms wrapped around each other.

"I missed you," Jo says, tracing patterns on my chest.

Tightening my hold on her, I press my lips to her forehead. "Same here."

Thoughts consume me, and I mull over how badly I want this to be my life. Full time.

I might be moving fast—too fast for her, that is for certain—but I'm ready. Before we broke up, I was prepared to commit everything to her. I would've given her the ring, the wedding, the house—the whole enchilada. There has only ever been her. And now that I'm back here, all those feelings are returning full force.

I wonder what it would take for me to get a transfer here. I could work remotely full time and then just travel whenever I'd need to. I could easily run the business from anywhere, with everything being mostly online these days. It would all depend on whether Jo would be into that. She said she missed me, but I don't know if she's to that point yet, and I don't want to push her.

We've been making solid ground, working through some of the skeletons lingering in the closets, but I know she still has a ways to go. It's so appealing, though, imagining what life could be like just the two of us. Coming home from work each day and knowing that the other is there to take care of you. Having someone to listen to the griping and complaining about coworkers.

Josephine looks up at me with an adorable smile. I bend down and kiss the tip of her nose. She rolls her eyes but smiles at me. Yes. I'll start looking into what it would take to transfer. Now that I have her back, there's no way I'm letting her go.

Chapter 18

Josie

"ARE YOU READY?" CONNER ASKS, STEPPING BEHIND ME IN the mirror.

I finish adjusting my earring and then meet his eyes in the mirror. "As ready as I'll ever be."

Conner places his hands on my shoulders and gives me a comforting squeeze before wrapping one arm across my chest and pulling my back into his front. He leans down and presses a kiss to my cheek. "You look lovely, Jo."

I close my eyes, relishing in the sensation of his lips lingering against my skin. I don't respond but offer him a smile in the reflection of the mirror. My heart has been racing a mile a minute ever since we woke up this morning. We're getting ready to go to my mom's house for Thanksgiving dinner. Though my parents got a divorce shortly after the accident, they'll both be in attendance. It will be the first time I've seen them in years, and I'm not sure how everything will play out.

I'm glad Conner will be there with me. His parents will both be there as well. And Alex said he would make an appearance, but who knows if he'll actually follow through. Hopefully, today goes smoothly.

"Should we go?" I ask Conner softly.

"I don't know. I think I might just want to stay here. I can have you for Thanksgiving dinner," he hums against my neck.

I wiggle out of his grasp and step back into his bedroom. "We should go."

"You got it, boss."

I roll my eyes and then find my purse amongst the mess of my things. I've been in Atlanta since the beginning of the week, but Conner and I haven't done much else except bask in each other. I didn't want to go out and risk running into my family or their friends. I figured I could wait until Thanksgiving Day to put myself through their scrutiny.

And besides, I've missed Conner like crazy. There is nowhere I'd rather be than with him. We've done a lot of ordering in and vegging out with Netflix-binge sessions. And honestly, it's been the best week of my life.

Conner and I get into his car, and he revs the engine, tearing out of his parking lot and speeding toward the small cul-de-sac where we grew up. I stay quiet most of the drive and keep my eyes trained out the window, watching the familiar neighborhoods and shopping centers pass by. I knot my fingers together in my lap until Conner notices and takes one of my hands in his.

He catches my eye and grips my hand. "It will be okay, Jo. Just breathe. I'll be with you the whole time."

I nod my head, but my adrenaline is still spiked. Maybe I could jump out of his car and run. I probably wouldn't get too banged up in the process. A little gravel never hurt anyone too bad, right? It might be better for me than living through an awkward encounter with my family.

I manage to make it through the whole drive without

attempting an escape. But my stomach churns and I worry I might throw up. My mom got to keep the house after the divorce, and Conner's family still lives in his childhood home, so it's really like stepping into the past. The treehouse that we played in is still standing proudly in my backyard. And the stones we printed our handprints on are displayed around Conner's family's mailbox for everyone to see. Three sets of handprints: red for Alex, blue for Conner, green for me. The colors are faded, but they still hold the memories.

It feels like another lifetime.

Conner parks his Chevelle in front of my parents' house and turns to me, offering me a supportive smile. "Okay, do we need to do a pep talk? Need a shot of whiskey or anything before we face the parents?"

My heart flutters, but not because of nerves this time. I stare at Conner for a second and wonder how I got so lucky to find him again. It's not every day that you come across someone who understands you so completely and accepts you without question. It's like, somehow, he's found the perfect glue to piece me all together again. I just hope I don't ruin whatever we have together, too.

I shake my head but squeeze his hand. "No, let's just do this."

He leans forward and presses a chaste kiss to my lips. "You'll be fine. And if we need to leave, you just say the word, and we're gone, okay?"

I love you. The thought startles uninvited across my brain, and my stomach lurches. I quickly swallow it down, unable to process that on top of everything else stacking up today. We can address that later.

"Okay, let's go."

Conner and I walk, hand in hand, up to my mom's front door. In my other hand, I grip onto the neck of the bottle of wine I brought as a peace offering. Conner rings the doorbell and then reaches for the handle, letting himself in. I follow his lead and step into my childhood home.

I'm immediately hit with the homey smell of Thanksgiving —a mixture of rosemary, melted butter, and fresh bread. The dining room table is set up elegantly. There are candlesticks lit in the middle, giving off a warm glow. Loud chatter and the sound of pots clanging together rings out from the direction of the kitchen, where I'm sure my mom and her friends are busy fixing dinner. In the living room, I hear a bout of deep laughter. Likely, the men all crowded around the TV, watching the football game.

"I'm going to go say 'hi' to my dad," Conner tells me. "Are you okay by yourself for a second, or do you want me to stay with you?"

Those three words trickle across my mind again, but I dampen them. No time today. "I'll be okay, Ace. Thanks, though."

He nods his head and kisses my cheek before letting go of my hand. He disappears off to the family room, and I'm alone. I take a deep breath and steel myself as I head toward the kitchen. I can hear my mother's voice, as well as Conner's mom, and a few others that I can't place.

The moment I step across the threshold into the kitchen, the room goes silent. I grip the wine tighter and bite the inside of my cheek as I look around, catching my mother's eye. "Hi, Mama," I whisper.

My mother stares at me as if she's seen a ghost. Her bright eyes that match mine are wide. "Josephine."

I nod my head and then step farther into the kitchen, right as my mother lunges for me. She wraps me up in a big hug, and I hug her back. I haven't seen my mother in years, but her hug is the same. Her hold is comforting, warm. I rest my head against her shoulder and breathe her in. She smells like home.

Mama steps away and holds her hands on my arms, looking me up and down. Her eyes are teary, and a smile glitters across her face. "You look beautiful, Josephine. It's so good to have you home."

"It's good to see you. I brought wine," I say, holding the bottle of wine up to show her.

My mom offers me a polite smile and takes the bottle. "Well, that's lovely. Thank you, Josephine."

"If it's not too much to ask," I start hesitantly, holding her gaze, "I prefer to go by Josie now."

My mother stares at me, and then another big smile parts her lips. "Josie. It suits you. Come in, come in."

I look around the kitchen, my eyes landing on Conner's mom, Sylvia. She offers me a wink and a smile, and I nod back to her. My mom leads me over to the counter, where she hands me a big bowl and a whisk.

"You remember how to make the mashed potatoes, right, Josie?" Mama asks. I acknowledge her and then set to work.

"Conner told us you two were seeing each other again," Sylvia announces. "We couldn't be happier."

My mother looks up, surprised. "What? You two are together again?" She shoots Sylvia an accusatory stare. "Why didn't you tell me?"

Sylvia shrugs and smiles as she takes a sip of her wine. "I figured I'd let your beautiful daughter be the one to tell you."

Mama turns to me with raised eyebrows. "Well?"

I swallow thickly. "Yes, Conner and I are seeing each other again."

My mother claps her hands. "Well, that's just marvelous! You two made such the perfect pair. I was heartbroken when you broke it off. I know Conner was a wreck afterward."

I smile tightly, and Sylvia offers me a sympathetic look, but nothing more is said on that topic, thank God. I know they're trying to be nice, but jumping right into the subtle guilt trip has left me feeling nothing but uncomfortable and awkward. Mama goes back to hustling around the kitchen, checking on dishes in the oven, and peeking into the turkey roaster to check on her bird.

After whisking the potatoes, I help myself to the wine I brought and pour myself a hefty glass. So far, this hasn't been as bad as I imagined it would be, but I am still wildly uncomfortable, minus the previous conversation. Any second, I'm worried the ball will drop, and the shots will start firing. I can't let myself lower my armor, just in case. I take a deep gulp of the wine, appreciating how it settles in my stomach with a warm, tingling sensation.

A while later, Conner comes strutting into the kitchen. I breathe a sigh of relief as soon as my eyes set on him. He's looking sharp in his dark jeans and a black button-down shirt. Conner leans over to press a kiss to his mom's cheek and then comes and stands next to me, his hand snaking around my hips.

"Everything going okay, baby?" he mutters under his breath, so only I can hear him.

"Surprisingly, yes," I whisper back.

He leans forward and presses his lips to my temple. "Good. Just giving you a heads up, Alex just got here."

My eyes flash to his, and I raise my eyebrows. I notice my mother's gaze on us, and I peek over at her. She has a knowing grin plastered on her lips, and she looks at Conner and me approvingly.

Only a moment later, my brother saunters into the kitchen. He walks straight to our mom and gives her a hug. "Hi, Ma."

My mother hugs Alex and then pulls away and ruffles up

his hair. Then she looks over to me with a smile. "How long has it been since I've had both my babies home?"

Alex, only just realizing I am standing there, turns to stare at me. His eyes trace my face, and then he dips his chin slightly at me. I return his gesture but remain impassive. He looks sober enough, but I don't trust him for a minute.

"Ah, the DiMarco twins," one of the other ladies in the kitchen states. "Such a beautiful duo. I remember when they were little rugrats, always running around, getting into trouble."

The ladies all laugh in accord, and I grit my teeth. I'm just a few years shy of thirty, but somehow, as I stand in this kitchen, I feel like I'm eight years old. Not to mention that Alex and I haven't been on the same page in over a decade. Not sure I would call that a 'beautiful duo.' My brother still holds my gaze and then jerks his head off to the side, insinuating that he'd like to speak with me.

I glance up at Conner, and he meets my eyes, body tense. His gaze searches my face as if waiting for me to give him a hint of what I'm thinking. When he finds what he's looking for, he gives me a slight dip of his chin, and I take a breath. Reluctantly, I step out of his grasp and follow my brother out of the kitchen and into the dining room. I hear Conner's footsteps shuffling behind me. I'm grateful that he isn't letting me do this alone. Alex waits for us with his arms crossed.

"I just wanted to say thanks for spotting me that money," Alex says, watching me carefully, his eyes darting over to Conner, too.

"Were you able to pay off your debt?" I ask him.

"No, but it helped."

"I thought I told you to stay away from her," Conner chimes in, his voice deep. There's a menacing tone that I haven't heard from him before. Alex turns his full attention to

Conner. Conner has his arms crossed over his chest as he watches me and my brother, his face unreadable but firm, as if he's silently warning Alex not to test him.

"Well, I was out of options, Ace. And besides, you don't get to boss me around when it comes to *my* sister."

"The hell I don't!" Conner fires back. His shoulders are stiff, and his chest puffs out in defense as he drops his arms to his side, hands curling into tight fists. I'm worried we're two seconds away from a full-on brawl between the two men. I don't think Alex would stand a chance against Conner, but that's not a theory I'd like to test.

"Guys," I plead, holding my hands up between them. "Let's just drop it. Alex, I'm glad I could help you this time, but I can't be your cash cow every time you make a bad decision. Do you understand?"

My brother presses his lips together but nods his head briskly. "Good," I say. "And Conner, I appreciate your concern, but Alex isn't going to hurt me. This was a onetime thing. It's over. Let's just move on now."

Conner's shoulders drop, and he sighs. "Fine. But I don't like it."

I rest my hand on my boyfriend's arm. "Thank you."

"Well, isn't this just adorable?" Alex sneers at the two of us. "Glad to see you two have made up. Really gets me in the jellies."

With a dramatic roll of my eyes, I say, "No one asked you. Come on, Conner."

Conner rests his hand on the small of my back, and we walk back into the kitchen. My mom eventually announces that everyone can find a seat at the table, so we all pile into the dining room and claim our seats. My mom and Sylvia each hustle around, bringing dishes out to the table and setting them around.

Conner and I settle next to each other on one side of the table. Alex sits across from us. He takes a sip of his water and gives me an unsettling smirk over the rim of his glass. The confrontation with him earlier wasn't the worst thing to happen, but my brother is notorious for making things into a bigger deal than they need to be. Especially when he feels threatened.

When all the food is laid out, my mom takes her seat opposite my dad at the head of the table. She clasps her hands in front of her and then motions to my father. He clears his throat and bows his head. Following his lead, I close my eyes as my father says grace, and then the feasting begins.

My father carves up the turkey, and the dishes are passed around the table. Everyone takes spoonfuls of their favorites, then moves on to the next, until our plates are heaping with various flavors. Cheerful conversation floats around the room as we all enjoy our dinners.

"So, Josie," Sylvia begins, "how's life going for you in Tennessee? We haven't seen you in years. What are you up to these days?"

I pat the corner of my mouth with the napkin and smile at her. "It's good. I love Tennessee. I'm actually a partner at a small structural design firm. My best friend is an engineer, and he hired me for architectural work."

"That sounds lovely, dear."

"How wonderful that you get to design buildings and then actually see them come to life," Conner's dad muses. "That must be very fulfilling."

"It is," I tell him with a grin. "I love my work."

"And we're so glad that you and Conner were able to make it this year. It's such a joy seeing you two together again," Sylvia looks at her husband as she says this, and he nods along.

"Indeed it is," Alex chimes in. He snickers as he stabs a bite of turkey again. "The power couple, back at it again."

I frown as I look at Alex. My mom glares at him as well. "What is that supposed to mean?" I ask.

Alex shakes his head. "Oh, nothing. Just that the golden couple is back, which means that everything gets to be about you two again. I'll skip the formalities and ask what everyone else is thinking. I have nothing left to lose. When's the wedding?"

"Alex—" I try to interrupt, but he's on a roll now. I brace myself for the impending disaster that is my brother out of control. There's only been a few times I've seen him amp himself up like this, but in all of those cases, it has left everyone in his vicinity reeling and hurt.

"Probably soon, right? I can't imagine good old Ace here has been able to keep his paws off you. Probably want to get married before you start showing this time, huh? Don't want to look like a planet on your wedding day."

"Alex!" my mother admonishes.

My cheeks heat, and my eyes burn. I know I'm not expected to, but I feel like I need to defend myself. Conner is stiff in his seat next to me. When I glance over at him, his eyes are ablaze with fury. "I'm not pregnant."

"Yet," Alex sneers. "We all remember how fertile you two are together. I mean, holy shit, there will probably be an army of babies before we know it. Maybe this time will have a better turnout than the last, eh?"

"Enough!" Conner explodes and the China on the table rattles. My brother cowers from his deep baritone voice.

"Alex, you're excused," my father says firmly. His expression is hard as he stares at my brother. Even though we're both adults, the authority of our father rings true and Alex's eyes go wide.

Alex makes a big show of standing up and tossing his napkin on his plate. "Fine. I got better places to be, anyway."

"Alex," I say, trying to stand up after him. Conner grabs my hand and pulls me down. When I look over at him, he briskly shakes his head, telling me *no*. He releases me when I sit down again.

"Hope you all have a Happy Thanksgiving. Sorry for being such a colossal disappointment all the fucking time," Alex spits before he storms out of the dining room. "Enjoy your perfect dinner with your perfect daughter!"

The front door slams behind him, and I flinch in my seat. Everyone's eyes are still on me, but I keep my attention trained on my lap, where I'm knotting my fingers together in embarrassment. Conner's glaring after Alex and then he's pushing his chair back and striding out of the dining room, too.

My eyes dart between the other people sitting around the table, who are all staring in the direction Conner stormed off in. I give them a tight smile and hold up one finger. "I'll be just a minute."

I excuse myself from the dining room and hurry into the living room, just in time to witness Conner grabbing Alex by the shirt collar through the front window, his expression pure fury. Alex snarls at him, his mouth moving with words I'm sure are intended to maim. Conner freezes for a moment and then his arm is swinging back and flying forward, catching Alex in the jaw. The force from the punch forces Alex to the ground in a heap.

I can't help the gasp that escapes me, and I cover my mouth with both hands. But I can't look away. Conner doesn't throw another punch. He just stands over my brother, fists balled at his sides and posture rigid. He says something else that I can't make out, and then he's stalking back into the house.

He hesitates when he sees me standing there, but then he

lets out a long breath and wraps his arm around my shoulders, drawing me into him. "I'm so sorry. I'm so sorry," he mutters over and over into my hair as he holds me.

My fingers grip the fabric of his shirt, but I can't say anything back. I'm numb to everything happening around me.

Eventually, he leads me back into the dining room. Our parents and their guests all offer us tight smiles, but nothing else is said on the matter.

I remain quiet throughout the rest of the dinner. My parents make small talk with their guests, but politely don't address me any more than they have to, and I don't offer much input. Conner keeps shooting me worried looks, but I try my best to ignore him, too. I've never felt more awkward in my life. They're not saying anything, but I can feel their pitiful glances spear me like little knives, and I can practically hear the thoughts running through their heads.

Is Josie going to have more babies? The poor thing. I wonder if she would put herself through that again? I'm so glad I never had to go through that. Bless her heart. Maybe having children just isn't for everyone.

We finish dinner, and my mom serves slices of pie and whipped cream. I take a small piece but can't get myself to stomach it. I'm not sure why I'm so troubled by all of this. It's nothing I haven't told myself before, but Alex's outburst left me with a sourness churning in my gut.

Once I can't take it anymore, I push my chair back and stand up. "Excuse me," I mumble before bolting out of the dining room and toward the guest bathroom down the hallway.

I hear Conner mutter something to the table before his footsteps follow me. I slide into the bathroom and close the door, locking it behind me. Conner comes and stands outside, tapping his knuckles gently against the wooden door.

"Are you okay, Jo?"

I turn on the water in the sink and wet my hands. I bring them up to my neck and let the cold water calm me. "I'm fine. I just need a minute."

"Baby—"

"I said I need a minute, Ace. Please."

Conner lets out a sigh from the other side of the door, but he walks away. I know what he's thinking. There goes Josephine, running away again. But I'm not running. I just need to catch my breath. I need to take a moment and recenter myself after my twin brother verbally attacked me.

I brace my hands on the sides of the sink and stare at my reflection again. I try not to let myself feel like a failure. *Maybe this time will have a better turnout.* It wouldn't. It never would. And now, I get to live with that truth forever. I know I should talk to Conner about this, but I clam up every time I think about it.

Alex might think that he's the colossal disappointment, but really it's the both of us. Alex, with his vices, and me with my insane ability to destroy everything I touch. Our poor parents really hit the lottery with us. The DiMarco Twins. Double the trouble, double the disappointment.

I take a few deep breaths and then unlock the bathroom door. Conner is waiting for me at the end of the hall. He's leaning against the wall with his head tilted back, eyes closed. He perks up when he hears me coming closer, and he steps toward me, arms open. I let him wrap me in a hug, and I press my face against his chest, breathing him in.

"You have nothing to be sorry about, Jo," he whispers, before pressing a kiss into my hair. "You're a beautiful and brilliant woman. Nothing that you could ever do would change my opinion of you."

Again, those three words dart across my mind. I only tighten my hold on him, thankful that he's here to ground me. I don't acknowledge his endearing words, but I let them warm me from the inside out.

"Can we go?" I ask him.

Conner tightens his hold and then pulls away. "Of course. Do you want to tell them, or should I?"

I shake my head and wrap my arms around my middle, worried that if someone's not holding me, I'll break into a million pieces. Conner tilts his chin forward, then disappears to let our families know we're leaving. I take the quiet moment to look around the living room, the house I grew up in. All the happy memories I have are now tarnished by the realization that my family is broken. My parents, though friendly with each other, don't love the way they used to. The strain from the accident was too much for them to bear. My brother only comes to me when he needs something. And I'll always be the black sheep, the one who ultimately tore this family apart.

I need to get out of here. I'm ready to start new, start fresh. When Conner rounds the corner, he offers me a grin. My heart stutters, and I settle a bit at the sight of him. My world finally feels like it's back on its axis now that he's in my life again. I don't know why I ever ran away from him to begin with. I should have been running toward him.

I'm ready for a new start, but I want this man by my side the whole way. We are better when we have each other, and I'll never let myself forget it.

Chapter 19

Conner

THE INCESSANT BEEPING OF MY ALARM CLOCK WAKES ME up. I groan and roll over, smacking the thing to turn it off. I haven't been able to get on board with the clock app on my cell phone like most normal people. I'm too worried that I'll sleep right through it. So, I keep to the classic alarm system that catapults me into consciousness.

I sigh and roll over onto my back, rubbing the sleep from my face. When I turn to look at the spot next to me, I'm surprised to find it empty. I brace myself up on my elbows, peering around the room to see if she's still in here.

"Jo?" I ask out loud, but I don't get an answer.

Jesus Christ, I think to myself. She better not have run away again. Yesterday turned into a disaster with her brother's attacks. I spent all evening trying to console her and help her ease her worries and fears, to no avail. Josephine has been knocked down one too many times in her life, and while I know she's getting better, we still have a long way to go. But I don't care what it takes; I'll help her get there.

I throw back the covers and step out of bed, padding over to my bedroom door and wandering out into the main living space. I find Jo sitting out on the small walkout porch from my living room. She's wearing a sweater that's one size too big for her and has a mug of coffee in her hands. Her knees are pulled up tight against her chest, so she looks small.

I pull open the sliding door and lean against the frame. "Morning, beautiful."

Jo turns around and offers me a smile. Her eyes still look tired, and I can see a hint of her hurt leftover from the night before. The wounds are still fresh and healing. "Good morning. There's coffee in the pot if you want some."

"Thanks, I'll get some in a minute. You doing okay?" I move out onto the porch and pull out the chair next to her.

"Yeah, I guess. I'm still thinking about everything that happened yesterday."

I reach across the table and hold out my hand. Jo places her hand on top of mine and intertwines our fingers. The action acts as a reminder of the punch I threw at her brother yesterday. My knuckles, though not bruised, are a little sore today. "Just let it go. Alex doesn't deserve any more of your thoughts."

"It's not just Alex," Jo explains. "I've been reflecting on everything."

I chuckle under my breath and then stand up. "I think I'm going to need coffee for this conversation. Hold that thought."

When I'm settled back on the porch with my own steaming mug of coffee and Jo's topped off, I motion for her to begin.

"I'm tired of being this version of myself," she says honestly. "I'm ready to just be me. Josie. I thought that by running away and moving to a different state, I might escape that image. I might be able to make a new version of myself, and become successful in my career. But yesterday made it very clear that that wasn't the case."

I frown. "How so?"

"After Alex's outburst, everyone just kept looking at me, their eyes filled with pity, like they didn't know how to talk to me after that. I'll never just be Josie. I'll always be that DiMarco twin who got in the car accident and lost her baby."

I narrow my eyes, watching her. She's still curled up on her chair, like she's trying to hold herself together. It breaks my heart. "What do you want to do?"

"I'm ready to move on. I want to put that part of my life behind me. There's too much at stake if I don't. I can't risk losing you or all that we've gotten through already."

My chest tightens as I take in the implications of her words. She's ready for a new life with me. Finally.

I scoot my chair closer to her and hold her gaze. "Tell me what you need me to do, Jo, and I'll do it. If you want to say goodbye to Atlanta for good, then that's what we'll do. I'll start packing right now."

"That's the thing, though. After seeing my mom yesterday, I realized that I want her to still be in my life. Same with my dad. They were nothing but welcoming to me. And it felt good to be home with them. But how do I do that without having to relive that horrible night over and over again?"

I sit back and think about it. "Maybe you should talk to them. Just you and your parents. Lay it all out and clear the air."

"You're probably right," Jo admits with a sigh. "But honestly, I'd rather get my nails ripped off."

I laugh lightly, though it's not funny at all. "I know things between you all have been stressed, but they love you, Jo. They don't hold anything against you because none of it was your fault. They will be happy to do whatever it takes to be in your life. Just like me."

Josephine smiles and shakes her head. "I don't know how you turned into such an amazing man, Conner Reynolds. You used to be this punk ass jock, and now, here you are, sitting in front of me, acting like a dream come true."

"What can I say? The ladies love me."

She laughs. "But seriously. You're the kind of guy love stories are written about. What are you doing with a girl like me?"

I frown and give her a firm look. "First of all, I need you to start seeing yourself the way I do—beautiful, smart, caring, funny. I know you want to put the past behind you, but that includes valuing yourself. Second of all, why couldn't my love story be with you?"

Josephine sighs and sips at her coffee. "I can't answer that. It would break your first rule."

"I'm glad you're starting to see it my way," I tease her. We fall into a comfortable silence for a while, listening to the sounds of Atlanta waking up for the Black Friday madness. "So, what's on the agenda for today?"

Jo cuts her eyes back to me, and she looks nervous. "I thought we were going to the cemetery. Are you not wanting to do that anymore?"

My lungs constrict, but I force it away and look at her warmly. "Of course, I still want to. As long as you're comfortable with it."

Josephine's eyes dart down at the mug she's gripping in her hands. Not meeting my gaze, she nods her head. "I think we need to. It's time to properly say goodbye."

And so, that's how we find ourselves in the Chevelle an hour or two later. We both take the time to ease into our mornings, finishing up coffee, and then taking a shower together—because *hello*, conserving water. Josephine doesn't bother trying to primp or put makeup on. She throws on a pair of jeans and a shirt, and then we're off.

We drive in silence. I ask Jo if she needs any food, but she just presses her lips together and stays quiet. I drive through McDonald's and get myself a large coffee, since Jo's disaster of a pot didn't cut it. Once we're on the road again, she doesn't say much, until she needs to give me directions. I've never been to the cemetery we pull up to, but it's gorgeous.

We're a little ways out of the city, so the road is quiet. The gates to the cemetery have the name of some saint that I'm not familiar with. I know Josephine's family are devout Catholic, though Jo isn't these days. I didn't grow up going to church, but I wouldn't be opposed to it if she wanted to go back. Maybe it would help her. Once we're parked, we both get out of the car. I immediately take her hand, and she looks at me with appreciation.

Josephine walks through a few different rows until she comes up to a plot. There are a few larger stones, but the one she stops in front of is flat, level with the ground that it's pressed into. She lets go of my hands and sinks into the grass in front of the flat stone. I follow her lead and settle in next to her, crossing my legs underneath me.

Josephine runs her hand over the granite stone marking. The words etched into the stone break my heart.

Madelyn Hope Reynolds
February 25, 2014

Josephine takes in a shaky breath as she traces her finger over Madelyn's name. "Sometimes, I imagine what she would look like." Her voice sounds wistful, and I tilt my head and watch her but remain quiet. "She would be tall like you. She'd be right around fifth or sixth grade now, so she'd probably start playing volleyball, like her daddy."

I'm filled with sorrow as I imagine it. Going to pick out Madelyn's first knee pads, teaching her how to bump a volleyball—passing with intention versus flailing your limbs everywhere. I wonder if she'd be a hitter like I was. Or maybe a setter, or defense. Whatever position she chose, she would've excelled. It would've been amazing. I would have *loved* playing my game with my daughter.

"I bet she would've been breaking hearts already," Josephine laughs, her voice heavy with emotion.

"Just like her mama," I tell her. I fell in love with Josephine the first time I saw her, when we were only ten years old. I know that Madelyn would've been exactly like her, and it kills me that we never got to see it out.

Jo reaches up and swipes a tear from her face. "Do you believe in heaven?"

"I think so," I reply, thinking back to my musings about church earlier. "Do you?"

She nods her head. "But I'm not sure what it's like. When I die, I know she'll be there waiting for me. But will I recognize her? Is she going to be a baby still, or grown? I don't know."

"You'll recognize her," I assure Josephine. I place my hand on her upper back and rub soothing circles. "You're her mother. I know that without a doubt."

"I think Madelyn would be happy to know that we're together again," Jo says. "Maybe she's been the one pulling the strings all along. She probably put a good word in with the Big Guy Upstairs."

I laugh and grip Jo's shoulder. "That sounds like something you would do. Like mother, like daughter."

"It's weird to think about. That if I hadn't gotten in that car with Alex, we'd be parents right now. I'd have a daughter."

I press my lips together. "It is weird."

"We'd probably be married and have a house, a dog—"

"Oh, we'd definitely be married," I cut her off and shoot her a cocky grin. "You're a fox. No way I wouldn't have put a ring on that as soon as possible."

Finally, I get a chuckle out of her, but she mellows quickly. "I wonder if I'd be an architect still."

"You always wanted to be a teacher."

"Ryan's wife is a teacher. She loves it, but I don't think that's for me. I wouldn't be able to put up with that many kids in one room."

"Me, either. I don't even know how some of these parents do it, with their families of three or four," I say.

"I would've been happy with just one," Jo whispers, and my heart cracks again, straight down the middle.

My hand rubs up and down her back. "If I could, I would kiss away all your scars. I wish I could make this better for you."

She shakes her head. "You can't. But thank you. I'm glad you came with me today." Her eyes meet mine again, and she offers me a weak smile.

"I'm glad you asked me to come with you. I think we both need this."

Josephine stays quiet for a while. I can tell something's weighing on her mind, but I don't want to push her in fear that she'll shut down right in front of my eyes.

"Do you want to have children? Again, I mean. At some point?" she finally asks hesitantly.

I smile and nod my head, taking her question as the go-ahead to conversation again. "With you? Yeah. I'd have all the babies with you, Josephine DiMarco. I can just imagine what they'd look like. I hope they have your beautiful hazel eyes that are an endless blend of color and mischief."

She falls quiet again. Her fingers still methodically trace over the engraving on the stone. The wind blows gently through her hair, rustling it against her back and wafting the smell of her shampoo toward me.

"Conner," she says weakly, then turns her gaze to mine. I see her eyes glisten with her unshed emotion and my stomach sinks.

I sit up straighter and scoot next to her, wrapping my arm around her waist. "Hey, what's wrong?"

"I need to tell you something."

Chapter 20

Josie

"WHAT IS IT? YOU'RE SCARING ME, JO," CONNER SAYS, HIS voice hesitant. He's sitting close to me on the grass. His hand moves methodically over my back in an attempt at comfort. I can smell his cologne through the wind, and I try to memorize the scent, knowing full well that what I have to tell him might push him away for good.

How the hell do I even start?

Just rip the Band-Aid off, get it over with. "I can't have children," I say, trying to keep my voice level. My eyes remain trained on Madelyn's gravestone. I can't get myself to look at Conner. I know the disappointment that I'll see written all over his face, and I just don't know if I can bear it.

He stills next to me. I can hear his breathing, so I know he didn't die of shock. I don't say anything more for a moment, letting the implications of my words sink into him.

Finally, his hand drops from my back, and then he folds his hands together in his lap, looking over at me. "How?"

I sigh. Might as well tell the whole story. "In my first year of college, I was seeing this guy in one of my design classes casually. We'd hook up here and there, nothing serious. But finally, one day, I realized that I hadn't had my period in two months, so I thought I was pregnant again.

"I went to the doctor, and they did their pregnancy test and an exam, and they told me I wasn't, thank goodness. I was a wreck during that time, and I knew a baby would complicate things. But they informed me that I wasn't pregnant, but also that I likely wouldn't ever be."

"But why?" Conner asks. I finally look at him, and he's frowning, his dark eyebrows pulled together in confusion. "We had no issues getting pregnant before."

"That was before I was in a serious car accident and had a traumatic miscarriage," I say, a little harsher than I mean to. "That car accident ruined *everything*, Conner."

"Okay," he whispers, retaking my hand. "I'm just trying to understand."

I pinch the bridge of my nose and try to focus on my breathing. I'm more vulnerable than I ever have been in my entire life. I'm laying everything bare—no more secrets, no more quiet suffering. I just have to get it all out, and then he can decide if he wants to move forward with someone who can't give him the life he deserves.

"They call it Asherman's syndrome," I explain. "It's when scar tissue develops in the uterus after trauma. It usually happens after surgeries."

"Did you have to have surgery after the accident?" he asks.

Biting my lip, I shake my head. "No, they gave me medicine to induce labor with her, so I delivered her. But they said there was something unusual with how my placenta grew. They made it sound like it was growing into the walls of my inner muscles, and so, when they removed it, my body's response to the trauma was to develop scar tissue. That condition is incredibly rare."

"Well, maybe they're wrong," Conner says. "Doctors are wrong all the time. Have you gotten a second opinion? We can go see a specialist."

I shake my head again. "Listen to me. I don't think I'm going to be one of those miracle cases, Ace. I've seen the specialists and the doctors. I've had the diagnostic tests. And they all tell me the same thing. Another pregnancy likely isn't in my future. It's just not going to happen for me."

Conner stares at me, his shoulders slumped in defeat. "Oh."

My eyes start to burn, and the panic sets in. I stand and wrap my arms around myself. "I know this isn't what you wanted to hear, but I understand if you want to end things. You deserve someone who can give you babies, a family."

Conner flashes his eyes up to mine in alarm. "What are you—"

"I'm sorry," I choke out, the tears finally falling down my cheeks. I turn away from him and start to walk in the opposite direction of the car.

I hear Conner swear, and then his footsteps are trailing after me. He grabs my arm and pulls me around to face him. "Josephine, stop. Stop running."

The tears are coming full force now, and I can't even see him. My vision is so blurry. "I'm sorry. I'm so sorry."

"Shh," he soothes, gathering me up in his arms. "It's okay, baby. I'm here."

"I just want to be normal. I want to give you the normal house and the normal family," I sob. "But everything I touch, I ruin, even my own damn uterus."

"Josephine," he coos. "It's okay."

"It's not. It's not okay!" I cry. I'm on the verge of becoming hysterical, but I can't stop myself. "It's too much. I have too much baggage. You deserve someone who's easy, who you can have everything with."

"That's for me to decide. And luckily for you, most of our baggage matches. So, just let me help you carry it."

"You can't; it's too much!"

"Baby, for you, nothing is too much," Conner tries to assure me. "I would carry the world on my shoulders for you if I had to."

I break down into more tears. I'm sure we look like a spectacle. Or maybe not. I suppose, if I was going to have a complete and utter mental breakdown, a cemetery is an excellent place to do it. No one is a stranger to grief here.

Conner holds me until I calm down. I'm still sniffling and snotting everywhere, but I can finally get myself to speak again. I pull away slightly and wipe at my eyes, trying to laugh it off. When I look up at Conner, he's watching me with sympathy. I sigh.

"I wish you would stop looking at me like that."

"Like what?" he asks, confused.

"Like you pity me. That's all anyone ever does when they find out."

Conner brushes some hair away from my face that is stuck to my cheek by the salty tears. "I don't *pity* you, but I am empathetic. I wish I could help you. But I don't know how."

"Nothing will help; I'm a lost cause," I say.

Conner tilts my chin up with one finger until I'm looking deep into his warm chocolate eyes. How easy would it be to get lost in those eyes if I'm not careful? "You are *not* a lost cause. And you do *not* ruin everything you touch."

Opening my mouth to protest, Conner swiftly slides his finger over my lips, shushing me as he continues. "I know you saw all the doctors, but we'll see better ones. And if that doesn't work, then we can adopt. Josie, *I love you.* I want to be with you and make a life with you just because you're *you.*"

Suddenly I'm crying again. Conner wraps his arms around me tightly again. "It's okay, you're okay," His deep voice rumbles against my cheek as I cry into his t-shirt.

"You called me Josie," I sniffle.

Conner pulls away slightly and cups his hands around my face. He offers me a wry grin. "Well, that's your name, isn't it? Just Josie?"

The sound of my preferred name coming through in his deep voice is doing things to my stomach. The tears keep falling, but despite myself, I smile through the despair. I tilt my chin up slightly, conveying to him what I want without using words.

Conner picks up on my action and leans down, pressing his lips to mine. He kisses me like he loves me, and I have never felt happier. When we part, I look into his gentle eyes and smile.

"I love you, too, Conner Reynolds."

Maybe we're crazy. Crazy in love, perhaps. When it comes to Conner, though, I want it all. He's talked about it before—the house, the dog, the ring. And the more time that I spend with him, the easier it gets to see myself living that life right along with him.

Especially now that he knows my truth, a weight is lifted off my shoulders. He doesn't want me solely so I can give him babies. He wants me because I'm me. I've never felt more relieved in my life.

"You're not mad at me?" I ask him quietly.

He searches my face with tender eyes and then shakes his head. "Of course, I'm not mad at you. Why would I be?"

"Because you want a family," I respond, my lower lip quivering. "And I won't be able to give that to you."

Conner's lips turn up at the corners, and then I'm

enveloped in another hug. "If we want to have a family some-day, we will. There are different options. But if you don't want to have children at all, then we won't. We don't have to live our lives in a certain way. We can make it up as we go, Jo."

"I guess you're right."

"I am," he says confidently, squeezing his arms around me tighter. "So, now that we got this out in the air, are you feeling better?"

I nod my head and bite my lip. "I've been carrying it around by myself for so long."

Conner brushes his fingers over my cheek. "We're in this together now. Whatever you're dealing with, I deal with, too, okay?" I bob my head again, telling him I understand. "Good. Now, do you want to spend more time with our girl, or are you ready to go?"

I direct my eyes toward where her headstone is. We head back over together, hand in hand. I crouch down in front of the stone and place my hand on it. I don't say anything out loud, but I think of my goodbye in my head.

Wait for me, Madelyn. I'll see you again one day. Goodbye, sweet girl.

Conner stands a step behind me, his hands folded in front of him, watching. When I'm done, I turn toward him, the pressure on my chest lighter, allowing me to finally breathe again. I smile, and he grins back.

"Ready?"

"Ready," I reply.

He steps toward our daughter's headstone, closes his eyes, and breathes deeply as if he's fighting back his own emotions while tempering the flood of mine. His hand lifts to his lips, where he presses a delicate kiss, before placing it onto the top of the stone. By the time he turns around to face me, his eyes sparkle with tears that he blinks away quickly and replaces with his lopsided grin.

We get back in the Chevelle, and he revs it up before looking at me. "Where to? Home?"

I fiddle with my fingers in my lap and then peek over at him. "Actually, do you think you could take me to my mom's house? I need to talk to her."

Conner smiles at me tenderly and pulls away from the cemetery. I keep my eyes trained out the window, watching the gravestones pass. We drive back to our families' neighborhood, and Conner pulls into my mom's driveway, putting the car into park.

"Do you want me to come in?" he asks quietly.

I shake my head. "No, I think I need to do this by myself. Can I just call you when I'm ready to go?"

Conner leans over the console and cups my cheek with one hand, pressing his lips to mine. "Of course. Just let me know."

I kiss him back once more before getting out of the car and walking up to my mom's front door. I wrap my arms around my middle after I ring the doorbell, as I wait for her to answer. Finally, after a few moments, my mom's face comes into view behind the door.

Her eyes brighten, and she smiles widely. "Josie, come in, come in."

"Hi, Mama," I say gently. "I don't mean to barge in on you."

Mom waves me off and walks into the living room. I follow her. "You're not. I'm always happy to see you. I'm just setting up the Christmas tree today. Do you want to help?"

I look around the living room at all the boxes she has laid out full of Christmas decorations. They're all neatly labeled with what room they go in or what the contents of the box include. My mom's big artificial Christmas tree stands proudly in the front window, the white lights already strung around it.

"Sure," I say, the corners of my lips turning up in a smile.

We set to work. My mom hands me a box to rifle through, full of ornaments that she has collected over the years. Many have sentimental value to her, while some are traditional ornaments.

"I can't even remember the last time you kids helped me decorate this tree," Mom muses. She doesn't sound upset, but rather, wistful.

"It was probably before we were in high school. After that, we were always too busy with our friends."

"Or boyfriends," Mom adds in with a wink, and I blush. "It was so nice seeing you and Conner together yesterday. That man loves you, Josie. He always has."

"I know," I say, my throat thick with emotion. "I love him, too."

"That makes me so happy to hear. That's all we've ever wanted for you, to find someone who you can love and who loves you right back."

I smile to myself but remember my purpose for coming here today. "I'm sorry about running out on dinner yesterday," I tell her.

My mom meets my eyes, then sets down the ornaments she's holding. She walks across the room and wraps her arms around me. "It's okay, darling. I know your brother made you feel unwelcome, but trust me. There was nothing that could have made that day better for me than having you here. Even if it was just for a few hours."

I hug her back and sigh. "I don't understand Alex. I tried to help him, and he turned around and practically stabbed me in the back."

My mom pulls away and sets her hands on my shoulders. I can see her thinking through her words carefully. "Your brother is... lost. I know you want to help him, but Alex needs to help himself first before he will ever be open to others' help. Your father and I are worried about him, and we're doing all we can to bring him back."

"Like tossing him out of Thanksgiving?" I ask her before I can stop myself.

She chuckles. "Well, that was probably necessary. Alex can be extremely toxic when he wants to be. And with having you back for the first time in years, I think your father made the right decision."

I think back to what my brother said yesterday. He kept jabbing at me, calling Conner and me the *golden couple.* "Maybe that's the problem," I say. "Do you think he's jealous of me?"

"Alex has always been jealous of you, sweetheart. That's nothing new. While you kids were growing up, your dad and I always tried to make sure we gave both of you equal attention. We love you both the same. And you three kids were insepa-rable for many, many years. But I think when you and Conner announced you were pregnant, the dynamic changed just slightly, and Alex felt it. All of a sudden, it wasn't the three of you anymore, it was you and Conner, and then Alex, on the sidelines."

"He needs help," I muse. I consider what I'm about to tell her and wonder if it's a good idea. "He came to my house a few weeks ago and asked me for a lot of money. He was acting weird."

My mom frowns. "Weird how?"

"Like he was on drugs, weird."

Mom narrows her eyes and turns to the tree, placing an ornament on a branch. "I'll have to let your father know. We'll take care of it."

While a part of me is reassured by her taking this on for me, the other half is full of doubt that she'll be able to do anything for him. Like she said, my brother is lost, with little hope of being found unless he decides he wants to be.

"Will you tell him I stopped by?" I ask her, following suit and putting an ornament on the tree. "I should apologize to him, too."

My mom looks over at me and smiles. "Of course, sweetheart. He doesn't hold anything against you, either. We understand."

"Even all those years that I never called or spoke to you, or when you and Dad got a divorce..."

"Shh," Mom shushes me. "My dear, you went through something that no woman should have to go through ever, especially at your age. You will always be welcome here, Josie. Even if you don't want to be around, we will never turn our backs on you. And what happened between your father and me is absolutely not your fault. Stop apologizing."

I stare at her for a moment, frozen, before I get back into action. I let her words wash over me, and I make an effort to take them to heart. "Thank you."

My mother's love wraps around my shoulders like a warm blanket. We continue to decorate the tree, and I continue to count my blessings. I might not be entirely healed, but today has been therapeutic for me. I was finally able to say goodbye properly to my daughter. My mom welcomed me into her home and assured me that I'm still loved and welcomed, despite my bad behavior. I have an amazing man waiting for me at home who would move mountains for me if I asked.

My life is good. It might have taken a minute for me to realize it, but now that I have, I don't think I'll be taking it for granted again.

Chapter 21

Conner

I watch Josephine walk into her mother's house, closing the door behind her. I rub my thumb over my bottom lip, thinking about everything she's divulged already today. My poor girl will be exhausted by the time all is said and done; there are way too many emotions flying around. Maybe I should take her to a nice dinner or do something else for her.

Everything she told me today at the cemetery is still sitting like a rock in my gut. Nothing she said changed how I feel about her, but it's definitely put a damper on some of my plans. I can't believe she's been carrying this around by herself for so long. No wonder she reacted so badly yesterday when her brother was running his mouth.

Thinking about Alex verbally attacking her gets my blood boiling again. I suddenly know what I'm going to do to kill time while Jo's with her mom. I put the car into reverse and back out of the driveway.

When I pull up to the run-down apartment complex, I inhale deeply, knowing that this probably is a bad idea, but not caring. I walk to the second building and go down the stairs to the lower units. The building smells like mildew and smoke. There's dirt bunched up against the hallways' kickboards, and the carpets are torn up at the edges.

My fist pounds against the door, and I hear a scuffling inside. "It's open!" the occupant yells.

I step inside and am immediately hit with a cloud of smoke that smells suspiciously like weed, though it's masked with the unmistakable odor of tobacco. Alex is lurking around, pulling the cushions off his couch and tossing them behind him. One hits a side table with a lamp, and it goes crashing to the floor.

"You tell Jordy that I'm working on getting his money!" he cries, not bothering to see who his visitor is. "I know I got something I can pawn around here somewhere."

"Who's Jordy?" I ask, sticking my hands in my pockets.

Alex whips around and glares at me. He's only wearing a pair of low-slung jeans and has a cigarette sticking out the side of his mouth. His dark hair is a rat's nest on top of his head. His clothes hang off his unhealthily skinny shoulders.

"What the fuck are you doing here, Ace?" he sneers at me, pulling out his cigarette and tapping the butt, allowing ash to fall wherever.

"I'm here to talk about yesterday." Alex rolls his eyes and goes back to tearing his apartment up. I glance around at all the beer cans and pizza boxes littering the space. "Jesus, Alex, when's the last time you cleaned up in here?"

"No one asked you. Now get out."

"I thought we could talk. I'm not here to attack you," I try to tell him.

"Well, I'm busy."

"Who's Jordy? You owe him money?" I ask. I don't care if I have to pry the answers out of him. I will.

Alex runs his hand through his hair and sighs. "Jordy's

someone you don't want to know. Consider yourself lucky. But yeah, I owe him money. A lot of money."

"What about the money Jo gave you?" I prod.

He falls silent before saying, "I don't need your fucking lecture, Ace. I'm a screw-up, I get it."

I frown at the man who used to be my best friend, his deflection telling me all I need to know. "You need help, bro. Look, the only reason I'm here is to let you know that you really upset your sister yesterday. I was hoping you'd maybe take that to heart and think about talking to her yourself."

"You think I don't know that?" Alex sneers as he spins around toward me. "You think I didn't see the way her face fell and the pure disdain that she had toward me?"

"Honestly, Alex, I'm not sure what you know these days. You're pretty inconsiderate when it comes to her."

Alex laughs humorlessly. "Oh, I see. You're back in her life now, so you get to act all high and mighty again, is that it?" I go to clap back, but now Alex is on a roll. "All I did was tell the truth. It's not my fault she's so sensitive these days."

"You don't know the first thing about what's going on with her," I snap. I've always been protective over Josephine, even more so after what she told me this morning.

Alex stares at me for a second, tonguing the cigarette hanging out of his mouth. Then he lets out a shaky sigh and presses the heels of his hands against his eyes. "Yeah, I fucking know that. You think I *like* the fact that my sister can't even stand to be around me?"

My shoulders drop as I watch him. He looks like he's about a second away from a complete breakdown. "What do you mean?"

"I get to live with the guilt of what I did to her *every day*, Ace. And part of that penance is not having her in my life. So, *no*, I don't know about what's going on with her because she doesn't want me to know."

"You need to talk to her," I tell him, crossing my arms over my chest.

"What's the point? I don't deserve any more breaks. I've done enough," he mutters, dropping to his knees and peering underneath the couch.

"Josie is the only one who gets to decide that. And you know how she is. She'll forgive you if you ask her to."

"She won't," he says, his voice echoing from beneath the furniture. "And frankly, I don't want her to. I'm a ticking time bomb. I don't want to get all cozy with her again and then just fuck it up even worse than I already have."

"Talk to her, Alex. That's all I came here to tell you. If you want to be a part of our lives moving forward, you have to talk to her and work things out."

Alex slaps the floor with his palm. "And yeah, see, that's just it! You said *our* lives, as in you and Josephine. Where do I fit in on that, huh?" He turns his eyes toward me, and I can see the hurt there. "I'm just the fuck up drunk brother who ruined her life."

"You don't have to be. There's time for you to turn everything around, you know."

He chuckles darkly and looks down. "I don't even know where I'd start."

I take a step forward, my arms still crossed over my middle. "You start by getting sober. Then you talk to your sister, and you let her forgive you, and you move on."

"Easier said than done, Ace," he grumbles. "Now, if you don't mind, I have a lot of money that I have to pull out of my ass, and I don't have time for your self-help shit."

I throw my hands up in the air. "Whatever, man, just think about it. Ball's in your court now."

I turn on my heel and start to walk out when I hear him mutter, "The ball has *never* been in my court."

I pause, but walk out of his apartment, closing the door behind me. I can't help him. He has to be the one to make that decision. I'm not going to waste any more energy trying to get him on the straight and narrow. All I can do is tell him that, when he's ready, he might not be turned away like he thinks he will be.

I get back in my car and drive around the city until Josephine calls me and lets me know she's ready to be picked up. I go back to our neighborhood and find her waiting for me at the end of her mom's driveway. She hops in the passenger seat when I pull around and leans across the console to kiss my cheek.

"How'd it go?" I ask her, my eyes roaming over her face. She doesn't have a hint of makeup on, and her eyes are still glossy from the crying she did at the cemetery. Her cheeks are flushed, but the corners of her lips are curved up. She's freaking gorgeous.

"It was good. I'm glad I decided to go talk to her today," Jo says, as she settles into her seat. "What did you do?"

I grip onto the steering wheel so tightly my hands hurt. "Nothing much; just drove around." I exhale and then decide to go with the truth instead. "Actually, I went to talk to Alex."

"Oh?" she asks, raising an eyebrow.

I nod briskly. I briefly regale the conversation I had with her brother and then look over at her sheepishly. "Are you mad at me?"

Jo looks at me with wide eyes. "Why would I be mad at you?"

"I'm butting into your DiMarco twin business. You used to hate it when I did that."

She laughs under her breath. "Well, there really isn't much

business between my brother and me these days, so I have nothing to be mad about. If Alex wants to figure things out, then I'd be open to that, but until then, I'm not holding my breath."

I reach across the car and grab her hand, bringing it up to my lips to press a kiss on the back. "I love you, Jo."

She looks at me, her eyes sparkling with the most intimate expression we've shared with each other. "I love you, too, Conner. Now can we go back home? I'm hungry and tired. It's been a long day."

"It has," I agree, squeezing her hand. "But I think I know how to make it better."

Josephine peers at me from the corners of her eyes, and I smirk, driving away from her mom's house. I keep a hold of her hand the entire way home until I have to let it go to get out of the car. But then I jog around to her side, scooping her up into my arms when she steps out onto the pavement.

Jo squeals as she wraps her arms around my neck. "What are you doing?"

I press a kiss to her cheek and grin. "I'm taking you upstairs to bed. Because you're very *tired*, remember?"

She laughs, but doesn't protest, as I carry her into the building. Jo presses the button for the elevator, and we get in. She stays in my arms the whole way, helping direct me through obstacles, such as the front door of my apartment. I do as I say and carry her all the way back to bed.

Jo bounces slightly on the mattress when I drop her on it, but then she settles back, stretching her arms above her head and arching her back. My blood starts to simmer as I watch her little display. She watches me with smoldering eyes, conveying everything she needs to without words.

"Look at you," I mutter to her. "You're the most gorgeous thing I've ever seen."

Josephine smiles and wiggles her hips on the bed. I reach behind my shoulder, gripping onto my shirt and pulling it over my head in one smooth motion. I hear Jo's breath hitch when it's off, and she's watching me like a hawk. I hold her eyes as I set to work on my belt, unhitching the buckle and pulling it out of the loops.

Jo sits up then and hooks her fingers in the loops of my jeans, pulling her toward me. My stomach muscles flex when she presses her lips against my skin, right next to my belly button. I thread my fingers through her hair and tilt her face up to look at me.

"You're wearing too many clothes," I whisper, leaning down and capturing her lips. My fingers reach down to the hem of her shirt, and I pull it over her head. Then, reaching to her shoulder blades, I unclip her bra and pull that off as well.

When she's bare on top, I hook my arms around her, lifting her up and depositing her back into the middle of the bed, where I crawl on top of her. My lips find her skin and leave open-mouthed kisses all the way down. Across her collarbone, down her sternum. I spend a few extra minutes on her beautiful breasts, ensuring each gets the attention it needs before moving on.

I kiss down to her belly button and then work my fingers nimbly on the button of her jeans, yanking them down her hips once they're loose. My eyes spot the tattoo on her hipbone, and I press my lips against it. I close my eyes and inhale against her skin.

"Conner, I need you," Jo whimpers. I know what she means. It's been an emotional few days, and she wants me to make it better, ease the strain. I ache to be inside of her, to be one with her and help put her back together.

I move back up to her face and kiss her thoroughly, parting her lips and tangling my tongue against hers, as I work to rid us of the rest of our clothes. When we're both naked, I pull away, spreading her knees and settling against her center. In a gentle thrust forward, I slide home, and we both groan in relief.

I swear softly as I start to move inside of her. Josephine's hands are everywhere—on my shoulders, my back, and then on my hips, pulling me impossibly deeper into her. She throws her head back when I snap my hips forward, pressing as hard against her as I can.

"*Yes*," she hisses. "So good. Conner, please."

My lips latch onto her breast again, flicking over the tip of her nipple, causing her to writhe against me on the bed. Her orgasm hits her fast, and soon, she's clenching around me as she cries out. I keep moving in her, coaxing it on.

"So beautiful," I murmur, taking her lips against mine again. She scrapes her fingers through my scalp and kisses me back. "I love you, Josephine."

Jo whimpers against me. We keep at it until we're both spent and exhausted. I collapse against her chest; perspiration from my forehead beads and slips down my skin. I'm still buried deep inside of her, not ready to break our connection. My nose nuzzles the swell of her breast, and I exhale, perfectly content.

I could spend all day here. There's nowhere I'd rather be than with Josephine like this. Vulnerable, intimate. Today felt like someone took a wrecking ball and smashed it through every hope and expectation. But that's okay. Being with her here and now, I start to build new dreams. We can still have our happily ever after, though it might not be how we both initially imagined it. As long as Josie's in my life, I'll be a happy man. She's all I need.

Chapter 22

Conner

"OHHH, CONNER, IT'S GOING TO HAPPEN AGAIN."

"I know, baby, just relax."

"No, no, no," Josephine groans as she leans over the toilet and dry heaves. I wince as I hold back her hair and try to rub soothing circles on her back. We've been here for hours now. She's thrown up a few times and is still suffering through the motions as her body tries to rid itself of the bad stuff.

Not quite my idea of ringing in the new year, but I suppose that's how it goes. Last night, we met with Ryan and Izabel at a bar that was hosting a New Year's Eve Party. We had purchased the all-inclusive tickets, which included an open bar and all-night buffet. Which, in theory, sounded like a great idea, but it turned into an outright disaster.

I don't think I'll ever be able to forget the sudden flip of the switch from Josephine riding on top of me, enjoying the pleasure of our bodies together, to suddenly jumping off and running into the bathroom to spew her guts up. Once I regained my bearings, I followed her into the bathroom, and we've been here ever since.

"I'm so sorry," Jo cries once she's done. She braces her elbows on the edge of the toilet and buries her face in her hands. "I shouldn't have eaten those lobster puffs. They were sitting out all night."

I chuckle softly and brush some hair away from her sweaty forehead. "Well, you live and you learn, but now you know why I steer clear."

She groans but lets me pull her back to rest against my chest. Her cheek presses against my shoulder, and she takes in some deep breaths. Every few seconds, her body shivers from the exertion of throwing up.

The sun is just now starting to shine through the window in her bathroom, bringing us into the light of day. I lean against the wall, offering my body for Jo to rest on until she has to throw up again. I'd rather act as a pillow for her than have her curl up on the cold tile. It's not like she's contagious. Even if she were, I wouldn't mind. She needs me right here, right now, so this is where I'll stay.

Through sickness and in health.

The thought rings through my brain, but I dampen it. I remember the ghostly expression Jo's face took on when I handed her the jewelry box on Christmas. She's not ready for that conversation yet, and so I'll wait. I'll wait a thousand years if I have to. My commitment to her isn't in question. I don't care if I have to sit on the floor listening to her throw up for the next three days. My feelings won't change.

Josephine groans against my chest, and I wrap my arms tightly around her. "Can I get you anything?" She shakes her head against me as she presses her hand against her stomach.

"The thought of eating or drinking anything makes me want to puke."

"Do you think you're going to throw up again?"

She shrugs her shoulders. "I don't know. I don't think there's anything left in me to throw up."

"Let's get you to bed then, and I'll find a trash can to keep by you, just in case."

Jo groans as I carefully pick her up in my arms. "I'm so sorry, Conner."

"Would you stop with that? You're sick. There's nothing you can do about it." I carry Jo back into her bedroom and lay her on the bed, pulling the covers up to her shoulders and sitting next to her on the edge. She shivers again, and I put my hand on her forehead to gauge her temperature. I don't think she has a fever.

Josephine closes her eyes and snuggles into her pillow, taking deep breaths through her nose. I get up and grab the trash can from her bathroom, and set it by her on the night-stand. Thankfully, the trash bag is empty, so if she has to throw up again, she won't get a face full of used tissues.

I go to the other side of her bed and lie down on top of the comforter, resting my hand over her hip. "Try to get some sleep."

Josephine moans in response, shifts slightly under the covers, but then settles down into sleep. I lie there with her, listening to her breath even out, until I know she's asleep. I doze with her for a few hours until I'm awakened by the sound of the doorbell ringing.

I sit up gently, making sure I don't jostle my patient. Jo still remains dead asleep. I quietly pad out of her bedroom and toward the front door. When I pull it open, I almost shut it again on the visitor.

"Wait, wait," Alex says, reaching out to stop me before I close the door in his face. "I'm here to talk to Jo."

I squeeze my eyes shut and give a groan of frustration. "Why?"

"Because you gave me hope that I might be able to have a relationship with her again."

I glare at Alex DiMarco. "Am I supposed to believe that?"

"Uh... yeah?" he asks, like it's a question.

I run my hand over my face and sigh. "Look, this isn't really a great time. Josie's sick and we were up all night—"

"She's sick? Is she okay?"

"She'll be fine. She just ate something bad and was barfing it up all night. She's finally sleeping right now."

"Here, hang on. I got something that might help." I watch in confusion as Alex bolts back to his car and rummages around on the inside. When he comes back up to the front door, he's holding a small bag of peppermint candies—the kind you get at restaurants or doctors' offices.

"What are those for?"

"It might help with nausea," he explains. "We always used to eat them when we were sick as kids."

"I see. What are you doing here again?"

"Really, Ace? I told you I just want to talk to her."

"Did you figure your shit out with that guy?" I ask Alex abruptly, changing topics.

He won't meet my gaze but shrugs his shoulders. "Yeah, as well as I could have."

"Alex—"

"Chill out, Ace," he retorts, now turning to glare at me. "I don't need you on my case all the time, okay? I handled it, and now I'm here to make up with Jo, like you suggested. You should be bouncing off the walls instead of up my ass."

I glare right back at my old friend. He might be right, but I can't risk him hurting Josie with his utter lack of anything other than himself. That's not a risk I'm willing to take.

"Alex?" Josephine's weak voice echoes from down the hallway. I turn and look at her. She's wearing a pair of lounge pants and her blue fluffy robe. Her face is still ghostly white, but her eyes hold confusion as she stares at her brother. "What are you doing here?"

Alex sticks his hands in his pockets and watches her. "Just thought I'd come and chat for a moment, but I hear you're not feeling well."

Jo manages a weak laugh. "I might have gone a little crazy on the lobster puffs last night at the buffet."

"Lobster puffs? Okay, well, I'm not sorry for you anymore. You should stay away from seafood at a buffet. Everyone knows that."

I laugh, and Josie glares at me as she responds to her brother. "Yeah, well, now I know."

"Here, I grabbed these out of my car," Alex states, handing over the candies he retrieved. "Remember when mom used to give them to us when we were sick?"

Josephine takes the red and white striped candies and twists them around in her fingers. "She always said the peppermint was good for our stomachs."

"Right, well, I always keep a bag on hand now..." He trails off but lets the implication linger in the air. He always has peppermints on hand for when he's coming off a hangover to fight off the nausea. "But I think you could use them more than me right now."

"Thanks," Jo mutters, watching her brother with a confused expression. I stand against the wall, watching the whole interaction silently. My arms are crossed over my chest, but I don't say anything. I'll leave the DiMarco twins to figure this out themselves.

"I guess I'll get going, then. I hope you feel better, Jo," Alex says, bouncing on his toes. He turns to head back toward the door.

"Wait."

Alex freezes and then turns back toward his sister. Josephine is still twisting the peppermint candy in her fingers, but she looks at Alex sheepishly. "You don't have to go... if you don't want to. I'm not really up to much today, but you could still hang out."

"Are you sure? I don't want to impose or anything—"

Jo waves him off. "It's fine. We can watch a movie or something."

"That sounds great," Alex says, with a small smile on his face. He steps farther into the house and then follows Josephine over to the couch, where he sits next to her. Jo grabs a blanket and tosses it over her feet and onto Alex's lap.

The twins discuss what movie to watch, then Josie turns it on. I watch the pair of them with a mixture of amusement and awe. Even though Jo's probably still feeling like garbage, she's making an effort for her brother to bring him back in. I admire her for that.

I step around the couch and settle into the armchair so I can watch the movie with them. Alex hands Josephine a few more peppermint candies, but doesn't say much else. The three of us watch the movie, and I can't help but succumb to a tiny hint of nostalgia. This is how it used to be all the time between us. This is how it *could* be all the time with us.

A flicker of hope burns in my stomach when I catch Josephine watching her brother out of the corner of her eye instead of the screen. She studies him closely, almost as if she's searching for a catch. But she doesn't find one. When her eyes go back to the TV, I can see a sense of satisfaction playing on her lips.

They might have a long way to go, but I suspect we're entering into a phase of healing for these wild DiMarco twins. I just hope no one gets hurt in the process.

Chapter 23

Josie

My eyes flutter open at the sound of rain hitting against my bedroom window. We've had unseasonably warm weather this winter, and instead of snow, all we've gotten is rain. I blink, looking around. The curtains are still drawn, but there is a faint sliver of light peeking through. I stretch out my muscles, noticing that the bed is empty beside me; Conner must have already gotten up for the day.

I can hear rustling in the kitchen down the hall, and I smile, hoping that he's making breakfast for me. My stomach rumbles in response to the thought of pancakes and coffee, and I breathe a sigh of relief. Hopefully, the food poisoning has worked its way through my system, and I can start eating regularly again.

I think after that bout of sickness, I'll be adopting Conner's philosophy of avoiding buffet seafood at all costs.

Yesterday is somewhat of a blur in my mind. I remember being sick all night and then spending the rest of the day on the couch watching movies with my brother and boyfriend. I was too ill to really let the shock of him arriving at my doorstep hit me, but now that I'm better, it seems surreal. Alex and I haven't exactly had the best history, and I know his friendship with Conner is still strained, too. I'm hoping now that the white flag has been drawn that that might be able to change.

I toss back my comforter and find my new favorite pair of comfy pants. They were a Christmas gift from my mom and have wiener dogs patterned around the pink fabric. They're a little big around my waist, but I pull them on anyway and pad out of the bedroom to the kitchen. Instead of finding my boyfriend behind the counter, I come face to face with Alex. I stop short, and he pauses what he's doing, looking at me with wide eyes, as if he's been caught red-handed.

"Uh, morning," he mutters sheepishly. I stay silent, just staring at him as he measures out coffee grounds. "I hope it's okay that I crashed here last night. I don't really have money for a hotel, and I didn't want to drive all the way back home."

Finally, I convince my brain to get myself moving again, and I wave him off, walking over to the breakfast bar and pulling out a stool. "It's fine."

"Are you feeling better?"

"I think so." My stomach growls again. "I'm a little hungry, so that's probably a good sign, right?"

Alex looks around and rolls his lips between his teeth. "Do you want me to cook you breakfast or something?"

I smirk at my brother. "No, thanks. I'd rather not have my house burned down."

"Ha ha. But seriously, I could make you toast or oatmeal or something else that's bland and disgusting."

I peek around the kitchen, then glance back at him. "Maybe. Where's Ace?"

"He said he had to take his car for an oil change or something," Alex says with a shrug. "You were still passed out, so he just told me to tell you to call him if you need him."

I nod my head in acknowledgment, glancing over at the

clock on the stove and see that it's ten o'clock. I really must have been sleeping like the dead. I slide off the barstool and head over to the refrigerator to pull out the carton of eggs. Alex returns to brewing his coffee, and I set to making myself a light breakfast of scrambled eggs and toast. Not entirely keeping with the I-just-puked-all-my-guts-up diet, but I need some protein. I make enough for Alex to have some, too, and toss a few bacon pieces on for him.

We move about my kitchen in silence. When breakfast is ready, we sit down at my dining room table. I glance at my brother between bites, trying to catch his gaze, but his attention is focused on his plate in front of him.

Finally, I clear my throat, and his eyes snap to me. "So, I know we didn't get much time to talk yesterday. How are things going for you?"

He finishes chewing his bite of eggs and then looks at me sheepishly. "Fine, I guess. I don't know. I'm just trying to take it one day at a time right now."

"Are you sober?"

No point in pussyfooting around the giant elephant in the room. My brother has his share of demons that he has to work through, just like Conner and I do. Though Alex's solution to his issues tends to be found at the bottom of a bottle of Jack versus trying to confront our hurtful past.

"I'm trying to be," he mutters. "I haven't drunk since Christmas, and even then, it was only a glass or two."

"And the drugs?" I prod him.

Alex's eyes flash to me, and I'm hit with how clear they look. I don't think I've seen him this lucid in ages. "I haven't used them in a while. I don't even remember the last time I was high."

"Good," I say briskly, taking a bite out of my toast. "And the money?"

At that question, my brother shifts in his chair, clearly uncomfortable with this line of interrogation. "Uh. It's sorted out."

I narrow my eyes at him. "Really?"

He lifts a shoulder in a shrug. "Mostly. I've paid them back all I can, and now I'm picking up odd jobs, trying to get the rest back."

"What kind of odd jobs?"

"Jesus, Jo. What's with the third degree?" he mutters, but then sighs. "Anything. I've been doing some UberEats deliveries when I can or helping some of my neighbors with construction projects. Oh, and last week, I was a nude model for the community college art class."

I snort, spraying my drink of water everywhere. Alex watches me with a twinkle in his eye, clearly amused at the display. "You were a *nude model?*"

"Yeah, I might be scrawny, but I still got the goods."

"Gross," I say, wrinkling up my nose and making Alex chuckle.

"It pays pretty well, surprisingly. A quick way to make a few hundred bucks. All I have to do is get naked and sit there for a few hours. You should try it sometime."

"I think Conner would have a coronary if I told him I was going to go sit butt-ass naked in front of twenty people," I say, laughter lacing my tone. I hear the front door open and close, then footsteps echo through the entryway.

"You never know, good old Ace might be into sharing these days."

"Into sharing what?" Conner asks, his brown eyes narrowed suspiciously as he steps into our conversation. He's got his jacket draped over his forearm and a plastic bag from the drugstore down the road in his hand.

I rest my chin against the heel of my hand and look at my

boyfriend appreciatively. He's wearing his worn-out jeans and a plain gray t-shirt that's almost too small for him. The sleeves bulge around his biceps, and I have the desire to reach out and squeeze the muscle. "Alex was just telling me about how he's a nude model."

"You're a *what?*" Conner's eyes dart to Alex.

My brother stretches his arms up and behind his head, reclining into the back of the chair. "Yep, a nude model, for artists."

"And then he was telling me that I should look into doing that, too. Easy way to make some quick cash," I fill Conner in on the rest as I rub my fingers together in the universal sign for money.

Conner narrows his eyes at my brother and then frowns. "Absolutely not. If you want someone to draw you naked, I'll do it. Just give me a piece of paper and a pencil."

I see the mischief flit across my brother's face, and before I can stop him, he's hopping up from the table and bolting down the hallway to my office. When he comes back, he has one of my notebooks in his hand and a few pencils. He drops them on the table and motions to Conner.

"Knock yourself out, Ace."

I crack up at the expression that crosses Conner's face. He's looking between Alex and me helplessly, as if he can't tell if this is a joke or not. "I'm gonna have to pass on that one, but thanks. But it's somewhat disturbing that you'd be interested in watching me draw your *sister* naked." He walks over to me as Alex cracks up and bends to press a kiss to my head. "How are you feeling, Jo?"

"A ton better. I had some eggs and toast, and it seems to be settling okay. I'm not as worried that I'm going to spew it back up anytime soon."

"That's great, babe," he says, his eyes tender as they trace over my face. "Hey, I got a message from work this morning. I'll probably have to head back down to Atlanta for a bit. They're doing their beginning-of-year projection meetings."

I force a smile through a pit of sadness that flares in my gut. "Okay, when do you have to go?"

Conner grimaces. "Probably tonight. It would be great if I could be there tomorrow."

My energy levels plummet at the thought of Conner leaving. I've gotten so accustomed to having him around, I'm not sure what I'll do with myself when he's gone. The house is deafeningly quiet, and my life is just a little less bright and exciting. But thankfully, I have a few new projects lined up for the next week or so. That will give me something to work on while Conner's back in Atlanta.

Conner pulls out a chair next to me and drapes his arm over the back of mine. He holds my gaze, concern etched in his chocolate brown eyes. "Are you going to be okay by yourself?"

I nod my head sullenly. "I'll be fine. I'm always—"

"Fine," Conner finishes for me, a smirk on his lips. "I know."

"You two are weird," Alex mumbles from across the table.

"Thanks," I tell him, smiling back.

My brother rolls his eyes and then crosses his arm. "I could always hang around, too, if you want. I have nowhere to be."

"What, no art classes you have to pose naked for?"

"I think I can make room in my schedule for you if you need me to," Alex replies nonchalantly, but I can hear the lace of hope in his voice. He doesn't want to leave. He tries not to meet my eyes, but I know my brother well, despite being estranged for years.

"Yeah, that would be cool," I concede. Relief etches across his face, and I have to force my lips into a flat line to keep from smiling.

"Good, well, I'm glad that's decided," Conner says, and he sounds pleased. "I'm going to go shower, and then I'll start packing."

He scoots the chair back and then gets up from the table. I watch him saunter down the hallway, fully appreciating the view of my boyfriend's backside. I know I must be feeling better because my physical appreciation for my man is back in full swing.

Alex clears his throat, snapping me out of my thoughts. I turn back to him to see him smirking at me. "I would appreciate it if you didn't eye-fuck your boyfriend right in front of me."

I roll my eyes and then get up from the table, grabbing our dishes as I go. "Whatever, Alex. It's not like it's anything new."

He follows me into the kitchen and watches as I drop the dishes into the sink and turn on the water, scrubbing away at the leftover food on the plates.

"Oh, I know. You two were always like that once you hit puberty," Alex teases me.

I wrinkle up my nose at him, but turn back to my task. "Well, *I'd* appreciate it if you didn't say the word *puberty* in front of me."

He chuckles but remains silent. I finish up with the dishes and quickly dry them. I reach my arm up and pull open their cabinet. While I'm there, I decide to put a few other dishes away that are sitting in the dish rack. The wine glasses that Conner and I had out from a few nights ago are a little higher than I can reach usually, and I stand up on my tiptoes and stretch to put them away.

My too-big pajama pants slip slightly below my hips, and I hear Alex suck in a tight breath. I drop back down to my flat feet and then hike them up, knowing full well what caused that reaction from him. My eyes slip to his, and I observe him leaning forward on the breakfast bar counter, his attention trained on my hip but his face passive.

"I didn't know you got a tattoo."

I chew on the inside of my lip as I watch him. "There's a lot you don't know about me."

"What is it of?"

A shiver runs down my spine from the awkwardness of this topic. It shouldn't be awkward. This is my twin brother. The person I shared space with in the womb. Before everything went down between us, he and I were tighter than peanut butter and jelly.

But that's the past. This is now.

I close my eyes and exhale, debating if I want to show him. I finally throw caution to the wind and reach for the hem of my wiener-dog pants, rolling them down so he can see. I don't pull them too far, as it's a sensitive area, but just enough so he can tell what the ink resembles. I observe his face as he registers the meaning of my tattoo.

His eyes flit to mine for a brief moment and then dart away. I can see the despair and shame in his expression. We've never addressed this before, and I see it eating him up from the inside out. Sadness and anger flare in my belly as I remain silent, trying to dampen it. Alex stares out the window for a moment, collecting his thoughts, before he finally turns back to me.

"Jo, I—"

"Don't," I cut him off abruptly. I don't want to do this with him, even though I know we have to.

His eyes harden, and for the first time all day, he holds my gaze steadily. "No, I have to say this. I'm *so sorry*. I don't think I've ever actually said that to you, but I should have."

"Alex..." I trail off, my heart hammering in my chest.

"Look, I know that I'm a fuckup. I ruin everything I touch, everything I love, including you and Ace. So I'll understand if you don't want to see me again after today, but I need to get this off my chest.

"Conner told me that I had to talk to you, that I should try to put this all to rest so that we can both move forward. I didn't believe him then, but I decided that it was worth a shot. I'm so sorry, Josephine. I'm sorry that I was selfish, and I'm sorry that I put you in danger," he pauses and takes a deep breath, squeezing his eyes shut as if in physical pain, "and I'm sorry that I'm the reason your baby died."

A white-hot rod of pain pierces my heart, and I grip the counter, so I don't collapse. Ten years' worth of pain and anger swirls around me, making my head spin. I want to lash out, yell at him, and ask him how he could be so careless. But I know deep down that's not going to help me feel better. What happened, happened, and there's no use living in the past.

I think back to what my mother told me when I saw her last in Atlanta. She told me my brother was lost. Now, I can't help but think that maybe this is him finally wanting to be found. Mom told me Alex had to help himself first, and well... maybe he has.

I force myself to open my eyes and look at my brother. He's watching me as if he's worried I'm going to explode on him, attack him and scream at him. I let out the breath I've been holding and my shoulders drop.

"It's not your fault," I whisper. They're the same words that Conner has said to me over and over. Liberating words that finally gave me a chance to have my life back. Hopefully, they can do the same for Alex and maybe allow me to fully move on.

His face falls, and he looks down at the counter. His fingers scratch at something. "I know you're just saying that, and it's okay. I know you won't be able to forgive me, and that's—"

"I do, Alex," I breathe out. He meets my eyes again, his

wide with uncertainty. "I do forgive you. I don't blame you for what happened."

"How can you?"

I shake my head. "I don't know. But I can, and I do. I'm ready to put everything behind me. Conner and I have talked about this a lot, and we've decided that there's no point in dwelling in pain. It only ends up hurting ourselves and the people we love more."

Alex stares at me but doesn't say anything. I can tell he's not convinced. I walk around the edge of the breakfast bar until I'm standing in front of him. I carefully place a hand on his shoulder, and he turns around to face me. "Do you know what her middle name was?" I ask him. He shakes his head. "Hope. Madelyn Hope. I don't know why I chose that. I was a wreck when I named her. But maybe a part of me, deep down, knew that I would pull strength from her middle name at some point. Maybe I knew that naming her Hope would, in turn, give me hope. To know that pain gets better. It will never get easier; I miss her every day. But there is always hope that we can heal."

My brother lets out a shaky breath and wraps his arms around me in a hug. I hug him back, squeezing him tightly to me. "I forgive you, Alex. Now you need to forgive yourself."

With my arms wrapped around my brother, I notice the tension easing out of his shoulders as he holds me back. We stay that way for a while. Movement down the hall catches my eye, and I see Conner leaning against the wall, his arms crossed over his chest. His hair is still damp from his shower, a few strands hanging over his forehead. His warm brown eyes watch me with approval, and he dips his chin toward me.

I nod back at him. Everything will be okay. The door to healing has been broken wide open. And now, with both Alex and Conner beside me, I think I'm ready to walk through. I'm prepared to put the hurt and the pain behind us for good.

Chapter 24

Conner

THE SOUND OF A CAR HORN AND TIRES SCREECHING HAS my heart rate increasing. I watch as two cars in front of me on the road collectively roll down their windows and stick their middle fingers out at each other. I frown and narrow my eyes; I definitely do not miss living in the city.

I've been back in Atlanta for a total of two days, and I'm already over it.

I miss my quiet life back in Cedar Ridge, and if anything, this trip back to Atlanta has only made my mind up more. It's time for me to make a change.

I contemplate how that would look on the rest of my drive to the office. As I pull into the parking lot, I glance up at the building and a sense of dread falls over me. Today's going to be busy—full of meetings and progress reports. The whole week has been like that. But hopefully, by the end of the week, I'll have the approval to go remote and I won't be needed in the office anymore.

The first thing I did Monday morning was put in the request for transfer. I haven't heard anything yet, but it's only

Wednesday, and I'm not sure how long these requests typically take.

As I head up to my office, I nod and say good morning to the people I pass. A few of my buddies from marketing sidle up to me and clap me on the shoulder. At least someone's glad I'm back in Atlanta. I humor their ribbing for a few minutes before I excuse myself and hop into the elevator to get to my office.

The day passes slowly. I settle in and get to work. I catch myself losing focus a few times, my mind traveling back to Cedar Ridge and the love of my life. I wonder what Josie's doing at work today. She'll probably be grabbing lunch with Ryan at their favorite cafe down the road from her office. Or maybe Alex is still in town and she'll be having lunch with him.

My eyebrows furrow as I think about her brother. Things were okay between the two of them when I left Sunday evening. Alex said he'd hang around for a while. I want to trust him—I do—he was my best friend for so long. But our history aside, I have to put Josie first, and if he so much as says another mean word to her, I'll kick him to the curb. She's been through too much for her brother to disappoint her again.

A few hours later, a knock at my door has me looking up from the spreadsheets I'm going over once more. To my utter surprise, my dad stands in the doorway, his arms crossed over his chest as he stares at me. I push my chair back and stand up when I see him.

"Dad," I say in greeting.

"Hello, son. Thought I'd check in with you to see if you're going to that department meeting this afternoon."

I bob my head. "I am. I was just looking over some of the final spreadsheets beforehand."

"Good, good. I appreciate that you're always so prepared.

Are you still planning on coming by tonight to have dinner with your mother and myself?"

"Yes, I was planning on it, if that's still okay."

"That's fine. She's looking forward to it."

"Good," I say awkwardly. He still stands in the doorway with his arms over his chest. I frown and then rub my neck. "Is that all? You just wanted to check in, or is there something else?"

My dad steps further into my office and then closes the door behind him. My pulse rate picks up slightly. That's never a good sign. "Well yes, actually, Conner, there was something I wanted to talk to you about, but I didn't think it was an appropriate conversation for this evening, seeing as it's work related."

"Okay," I trail off, having a suspicion of where this is headed.

"A little birdie told me that you were inquiring about transferring. Want to tell me what that's all about?"

I relax a bit. I was worried he was going to grill me on some questionable reports I sent up the line last week. I had sent ample explanation for my stats, but I was still expecting to hear from someone higher-up about it.

"Things between Josie and I are getting more serious," I tell him. "The obvious next step for me is to move up there to be with her full time."

"I see," my father says simply, coming to sit down in the chair in front of my desk. He crosses one ankle over his knee and folds his hand in his lap as he studies me. I consider how I want to present my case to him as I study him right back. If I were to ever be curious about what I would look like in my late fifties, all I'd have to do is take a look at my dad. He and I have always been mirror images of each other, though now his dark brown hair is starting to gray around his scalp.

"I thought that I could work remotely from Cedar Ridge

because I'm very rarely needed in person here, anyway," I explain. "Even when you step down, I can run it remotely."

"Except for when meetings such as the one this afternoon come up," he fills in for me. "If you take this transfer to remote work, would you be traveling in for these department meetings?"

"There are different options that I may still attend. I could always video chat in, or even do it over the phone."

My father watches me carefully, and he scratches at his jawline. "I think you really need to take a step back and think about the logistics of what you're proposing."

I frown. "I have. Josephine's and my relationship is more important—"

My father holds up his hand, cutting me off. "I'm going to stop you right there, Conner. You know I love Josephine. She's a sweet girl, but I'm not sure I can condone you uprooting your career simply for her. We've been planning this transition for years. I'm not sure I can get behind you tossing that away. Given the circumstances."

"What circumstances?" I ask him, my body going rigid. When he doesn't answer right away, I narrow my eyes and can barely keep from growling, "Why don't you just come out and say it, Dad? I can tell there's something you're holding back."

He sighs and looks at me apologetically. "Your mother was over with Josephine's mother. You know they're good friends. And her mother let slip that Alex told her Josephine can't have any more children."

The features of my face turn down even more, if that's possible. Josie must have finally divulged the fact to Alex, who told their mom. A deep, ugly anger starts to turn in my gut. "And?"

"And son, well, that really upset your mother. She cried for hours after she got home. She's been anxiously looking forward to when you have children. She wants grandchildren."

I laugh under my breath and shake my head, unable to really believe I'm sitting here talking to my father about this. "I thought you said this was work related."

"It is. You're considering leaving your job for a woman who can't give you a future. We have a *family* business, Conner. You have a duty to the company. What's going to happen when you're ready to retire? Are you going to sell out? You won't have anyone to pass it down to. I'm your boss, but I'm also your father. I want the best for you in all aspects of your life, career and otherwise."

"I can't believe we're actually having this conversation right now," I grumble, running a hand over my face. "This is none of your business. This is between me and Josie."

My father nods his head. "It is, it is. I just want you to really think about what you're doing before you commit to something that might affect you long term."

"There are other ways that Josie and I could have children, Dad," I argue. "We could foster or adopt. Or we could get a surrogate."

"It's just not the same, Conner. You know that."

I've had about enough of this conversation. My anger and irritation bubbles over. "No, I don't know that. Cause no matter how Jo and I come to have our children, I won't love them any less than if she birthed them herself. And neither should you. If you want grandchildren that badly, I would hope that you would be understanding."

"Conner, please don't misunderstand where I'm coming from."

"No, you've made your position very clear. Now, you can see yourself out. I have stuff to finish before the meeting."

"Son—"

"Goodbye, Dad."

My father sighs, but gets out of his chair and heads toward the door. "I'll talk to HR about getting that transfer for you. I guess I'll see you later this evening. "

I squeeze my eyes shut. "Actually, you know, I think I just had something come up. Tell Mom I'm sorry for being such a massive disappointment. Close the door on your way out."

I glare down at my spreadsheets until I hear the door click behind him, and then I let out a loud sigh and bury my face in my hands. My body is fuming with anger and disappointment. Not so much at anyone in particular, but rather the whole situation.

I don't blame Josephine for anything. None of this is her fault, and I know that if she could change it, she would. I have no qualms about looking into other family options. I meant what I said to my dad—no matter how Josie and I come to have children, I will love them as if they are my own flesh and blood.

I don't know how my father can stand here in front of me and tell me that the woman I love isn't good enough because she can't have children. My stomach twists at the thought. I love Josie because she's Josie. Not because she was born with the right parts to bear children, but because of her fire, her spirit. Her overall Josie-ness.

Gritting my teeth, I shove down all the negative thoughts that are brewing in my head. I only have a few more hours of work and then I'll get out of here.

The meeting goes by smoothly. I ignore my father at the other end of the table as I give my presentation and reports, only answering him when he asks me a direct question. I keep the whole interaction very professional.

As soon as that clock hits five, I'm grabbing my work bag and bolting out the door to my car. I don't head home, though. I stop at the only place that I know where I can let my anger out in a healthy way.

I check in at the front desk and then find my locker in the locker room. As soon as I've changed out of my work clothes, I hit the gym floor, my tennis shoes squeaking against the shiny wood of the court. After a decent warm up, my shoulder feeling limber enough to run some drills.

I twirl the blue and yellow volleyball between my fingers, studying the net that's set up in the middle of the court. I kick the serving line a little with my toe, scuffing my shoe, before taking a few wide strides back. Breathing deeply, I launch into my serving approach.

My arm retracts behind my head before springing forward. My hand comes into contact with the ball with a solid sounding hit. The volleyball sails across my side of the court and over the net before landing in the far right corner of the opposite side.

My shoulders rise and fall as I breathe. I roll my shoulder back and forth, noticing the familiar twinge of my old injury. I'll never be as good as I was, but at least I can still play some.

Volleyball has always been an outlet for me, for as long as I can remember. There's nothing quite like landing a solid ace against the opposing team, or hitting a ball with such force that it blasts right through the other team's attempted block. There were days that I lived and breathed for this sport. It consumed almost every aspect of my life.

Except for Josephine.

She was the other constant. If it wasn't volleyball, it was her. And now, as our relationship grows, I'm learning that nothing has changed. Which I am more than okay with.

I run through a few more drills and motions before my shoulder is screaming at me that it's had enough. I put up my ball and then jog into the locker room to clean up. I dig through my bag, looking for my shower stuff, right as my phone starts to ring. Josie's name flashes across the screen and a doofy smile flits across my lips before I can stop it.

"Hey, beautiful," I answer, lifting my shoulder up to hold the phone to my ear, freeing up my hands. "How're you?"

"Hey, Ace. Fine, how are you?"

"Tired," I breathe. "I just finished tossing a volleyball around."

"That sounds fun," she says, though I know she's lying. If there's anything Josie's bad at, it's volleyball. "I just wanted to call and say that I miss you. It's weird not having you here."

I close my eyes and exhale. "I know what you mean. I'm doing what I can to get that transfer going. I talked to my dad about it today."

"Oh yeah? What did he think about it?"

I hesitate before answering. "He was on board. Told me he'd talk to HR about it."

"Well, hopefully that's a good sign!" Jo says cheerfully. "We're heading in the right direction."

My mind flits back to my conversation with my father. Though I fully am on the same page as Josie, my dad made it clear that he was not. A question burns on the tip of my tongue and I brace myself as I ask, "Jo, did you tell Alex about the baby thing?"

She hesitates on the other end of the phone. "What baby thing?"

"About us not being able to have another baby," I say carefully.

"Oh, well, yeah, it just came up the other day when we were talking. He asked about it, and I didn't want to lie. I'm done lying."

Despite everything, my chest swells with pride. I love this woman so much. "I love that you felt comfortable sharing that."

"Why do you ask?" she asks hurriedly, knowing there's something more.

I exhale. "He told your mom. And then your mom told my mom."

"Oh," Josie breathes. "So everyone knows now."

"Everyone knows," I confirm.

Josephine stays quiet on the other line for a moment and then sighs out loud. "Whatever. It's not like I can help it. This doesn't change anything, does it?"

My lips turn down at the uncertainty laced through her voice. "Of course not."

"Good. Well, now that that's settled, Alex just got home with takeout, and his face has an appointment with my fist for spilling my secrets two seconds after I told him. Do you have plans tonight?"

I smile at my feisty girl. "Nothing, just missing you."

"I miss you, too, Ace. Come home soon," she says. I can picture the expression on her face, her lids slightly lowered, big lips pouty. There's nowhere I want to be more than with her.

"I love you, Jo."

I can hear her smiling when she says it back. I close my eyes, lingering on the call until she hangs up first. I slide the phone into my gym bag and then hit the showers. When I'm done, I head out to the car, replaying pieces of our conversation over in my mind. Josephine handled the news of everyone knowing about her fertility much more gracefully than I could have imagined.

As much as that makes me proud, it also pisses me off. She shouldn't have to deal with everyone knowing because it's no one else's business but hers. And mine now. As I drive home, I think about how this will likely linger over our heads for a long time, just like I saw with my dad today. It will be a hurdle that we'll have to jump over repeatedly, and I hate that she'll have to subject herself to that when there's nothing she can do.

My resolve only solidifies as I mull this over. Like I told Josie earlier, this doesn't change anything. I still love her, and I still want to spend my life with her, children or not, and no one gets an opinion on that. Not Alex, not Mom, and certainly not my dad.

The only person who matters to me now is Josie. Now and forever. I make up my mind that, once that transfer goes through, I'll never leave her side. I won't let anything or anyone come between us, not even the family business.

Chapter 25

Conner

"Hey there, darlin'. What can I get you to drink?" the waitress asks me as I settle into the uncomfortable metal chair on the patio.

I look up at her and grin. "I'll take a Blue Moon, if you got it on tap."

"Sure thing," she says and writes it down on her notepad. "Is it just you today?"

I sigh and shake my head back. "No, I'm meeting someone here. If you could just get him a water to start, that should be fine. Thank you."

The waitress sashays off, giving me a wink as she goes. I chuckle softly to myself and lean back in the chair. She returns only a moment later with my beer and a water for Alex.

I had been having a perfect day up until the point Alex requested I meet him here at this pub because we 'had to talk'. To the best of my abilities, I've tried not to overthink whatever this meeting is going to entail and focus rather on my goals for the day, which I successfully completed.

I take a big gulp of my beer. I had two goals for the day:

first, talk to Josie's dad and ask him for his permission to marry her. An age-old tradition, I know. But I've known the man since I was a kid. Not to mention I've already knocked his daughter up once without his permission. I figured it wouldn't hurt to dot some I's and cross some T's for good measure this time around.

Mr. DiMarco had a good laugh and told me, "It's about damn time, kid."

I shook his hand, told him how much I respect him and his daughter, and then shortly thereafter, I headed to the jewelry store and picked up the engagement ring that I had specially designed for Josie.

It's something that I had always intended to give her. I had to dig through some of my old school notebooks to find the sketch that we had drawn together when we were teenagers. We had just been fooling around that spring day, playing tic-tac-toe in my algebra notebook, before we started sketching random things and her 'perfect ring' was drawn into existence. I'm sure it was meant to be brushed off or forgotten, but I made sure to keep it all these years, knowing that ring would sit on her finger one day.

I brought the sketch to the jeweler in town about a month back, and it was finally ready to be picked up today. I have no plan whatsoever on how or when I'm going to ask her, but having the ring sitting in my pocket is reassuring. It will happen someday. Soon.

I take another sip of my beer and look down at my watch. *Where the hell is Alex?*

He comes tearing into the parking lot a few minutes later in his beat-up car. He slams the door behind him once he's parked and hurries over to where I'm sitting, tossing nervous glances over his shoulder the entire way.

Alex pulls his chair out and falls into it, giving me a chin-up nod. "What's up, man?"

I narrow my eyes at him. "You called me here, you tell me."

Alex looks over his shoulder again and fidgets with his fingers. I'm hit with the most uncomfortable sense of déjà vu as I watch him break down into nervous neurotic habits. "Alex," I mutter. "What the hell is going on here?"

He reaches across the table and grabs the water cup that the waitress brought, downing it in a few big gulps. He drops the empty cup back on the table and then puts his head in his hands and groans. My stomach is bunching up into uncomfortable knots, and I know I'm not going to like what I'm about to hear out of this guy.

Finally, Alex pulls his shit together enough to talk. He looks up at me and his hazel eyes are rimmed with panic. "Okay. So, don't flip out on me, I just want to preface that I'm trying my best to handle everything. Don't go all Captain America on me or anything. I'm just telling you for the sake of being transparent."

What the fuck.

"Are you using again?" I ask him, not wasting time.

His eyebrows raise, and he shakes his head. "No. But it's related to that. Kind of."

I run my hand over my eyes and groan. "For the love of all that is *holy,* Alex."

Why can't I ever catch a break with this guy?

"I know, I know. Just hear me out," he says hurriedly, raising his hands up in the air as if in surrender.

"Fine, just get it over with."

"So, you remember around Thanksgiving, I think? When you barged into my apartment like a lunatic and I thought you were someone that," he clears his throat and looks around before leaning in closer and whispering, "Jordy sent after me?"

I frown at him. "Vaguely. Jordy's the tool you owed money, right?"

"*Shhhh,* don't fucking say his name that loud." Alex waves his hand at me before continuing. "But yeah. Kinda. But, *anyway,* I told you that I had all that shit handled, right?"

I frown even more. "Yeah…" I reply, trailing off, playing dumb, but already knowing that I'm sitting on the brink of a complete and utter cluster fuck.

Alex reaches across the table for my Blue Moon and polishes the rest of it off before finally looking me square in the eye. "Well, it's not handled anymore."

I stay quiet for a minute, listening to the rush of my blood in my ears. I try to keep my head on straight, but now the anger and panic are making their way through my system, and I really want to reach across this table and wrap my hands around Alex's scrawny neck.

"What do you mean, it's not handled anymore?" I grit out between my teeth. I'm clenching my jaw so tightly I wonder if I'll ever be able to open it again. "You better fucking explain yourself, DiMarco. You told me everything was fine. Are you in danger? Is Josie in danger?"

Alex looks like I just sucker-punched him in the gut. I wish I had. "I don't know, okay? That's why I wanted to meet you here instead of back at the house. You don't know what he's capable of."

"Who is this guy? Is he like the mafia or something?"

A bleak chuckle escapes my ex-best friend. "No, not mafia, but probably something close to that. He's like the dealer to my dealer's dealer."

My stomach starts hurting even more. "So, a drug lord. Is this *Breaking Bad* or what?"

"Shit, it might as well be," he mutters, his tone unhinged as he runs his hand over the back of his neck.

"What happened?" I deadpan. I'm instantly regretting letting Alex back into Josie's life. I should have slammed that door in his face the moment I saw him standing on our porch. I knew better, but I still let him in. Nothing is worth risking Josie's safety over, even if it is her idiot twin brother.

"I don't want to get into the nitty-gritty. The less you know, the better, honestly. Let's just leave it at the fact that I owe Jordy a shit ton of money, and now he's trying to collect. I thought I had paid it all back, but then he just informed me that I owe 'interest' that is just as much, if not more than, the original balance."

"Why do you owe interest to him?"

"I don't fucking know. Because he's a greedy bastard who likes to screw people over!" Alex exclaims. He gets a few dirty looks from the older couples sitting around us, and he waves sheepishly at them and then lowers his voice again.

"Did you steal from him?" I prod, still trying to get the full story out of him.

"No, not really," he sighs and then gives in. "It was a poker game. I played in a game and bet way more money than I had."

"And that's when you came and asked Josie for her help."

He nods his head. "Yeah, but then, like the fuckup I am, I blew all that money before I was able to give it to him."

"Jo said it was ten thousand dollars you were after," I say, surprised at myself that I can remember that fact, but the number popped right into my head. Alex presses his lips together and I know I'm not going to like what comes out next. "How much more?"

"Forty. Fifty in total."

My jaw drops open. Oh good, so it's not going to be stuck forever. "*Fifty thousand dollars, Alex? That's five times what you originally owed him.*"

"Thanks, Ace, I can do the math! I know, I know. It's bad."

"It's worse than bad, Alex. How are you going to pay that

back? I don't have that kind of money to just loan you. Neither does Josie. "

"I know," he says again, resigned. "I'm not asking you to do that."

"So, what are you going to do?"

"I'm going to leave and probably never come back. Look man, I know I've screwed up majorly here, and I don't want anything bad to happen to you or Josie. So I'm going to take myself out of the equation."

I stare at him for a moment, letting his words sink in. "Okay."

He exhales a sharp breath. "I just felt like it was time to fill you in on this because I got a message from Jordy this morning. He's onto me, so it's time for me to book it."

"What does that mean?"

"It means that he knows I'm here. And that I've been here." He dips his chin in acknowledgment when it all clicks together in my mind. "I don't know how long he's been scoping me out, so I wanted to make sure you knew. If you or Josie sense anything is off, or that something doesn't feel right, it probably isn't."

"Are they going to come after us?"

"Hopefully, they'll just follow me and leave well enough alone here."

I lean back in my chair and glare at him. "Hopefully?"

"Yeah. Hopefully."

I close my eyes and breathe through my nose. "Fuck you, Alex. Seriously."

"Yeah," he says again. I can hear the defeat lacing his tone. "I know. I want to be good, I swear. Life's just not letting me."

I don't have anything to say back to that, so I don't. We sit in silence for a few minutes, the weight of Alex's revelation hanging heavily over our table. Finally, I muster up the energy to tell him the news of my supposedly good day. I don't know why I bring it up. I guess I think it's something he should know, as her brother. "I asked your dad if I could marry Josie today."

Alex's eyes meet mine, and I see the surprise there before it's covered up with angst again. "That's great, man. I'm assuming he said 'yes'?"

I nod my head and reach into my pocket to pull out the ring box, dropping it on the table in front of my future brother-in-law. Alex stares at the box before picking it up and exposing the diamond ring inside. He whistles low as he tilts it in the sunlight.

"Damn, dude, this is flawless. She'll love it."

I manage a smile and hold my hand out, feeling significantly more comfortable once the very expensive ring is back in my possession. Though I know he wouldn't dare, part of me was wary that Alex would take the ring and run. Maybe pawn it for some of that money that's on his head.

"Have you told Josie any of this?" I ask him.

Alex shakes his head. "No, and I don't want her to know."

"So, you want me to lie to her," I throw out, irritated. "Great way to start off a future marriage, huh?"

"I'll come up with the lie. You just have to... play along."

"Whatever. So, what is this brilliant lie that I am supposed to tell her?"

He pauses and thinks for a moment before settling on a story. "Maybe just tell her I've checked into a long-term rehab facility in Arizona or something. I don't know."

"Fine. Anything else?"

"And that I'm sorry, truly," he says softly, his eyes meeting mine. "Really, Ace. I'm sorry."

"Okay," I say again. Unsure what else to tell him.

Our waitress swings by, and I get the bill from her before paying for it. Alex stays quiet the rest of our time together, which is good. I'm not sure how much more bad news I could take from him.

We walk out to the parking lot side by side. When we get to our cars, I stop and turn to him. He awkwardly extends a hand, but I just stare at it before looking off to the side.

"Well, goodbye, I guess," I mutter. "Good luck."

"Thanks, Ace. I'll see ya around."

I look at him again and shake my head one more time, making sure that he's aware of my disappointment, before getting into my Chevelle and firing her up. I drive home in silence—the sound of my thoughts loud enough. Today was supposed to be a great day. I was getting all my ducks in a row to marry the woman I loved so we could finally, *finally* get the happily ever after we deserve.

Alex told me before that he was a ticking time bomb. Well, it turns out that he was right. He was a time bomb that completely detonated today, taking down everything and everyone in his path. I will do anything in my power to make sure that everything turns out okay for Josie and me, despite the fallout we are now facing. A fallout that neither of us deserves to have any part in.

I try to think positively on my way home. *Everything will be fine, everything will be fine.* But regardless of my weak attempt at a pep talk, I have a horrible sense of foreboding that everything that I've worked so hard to pull together is about to completely unravel.

Chapter 26

Josie

"Wʜᴀᴛ ᴅᴏ ʏᴏᴜ *ᴍᴇᴀɴ*, ᴛʜᴇ ᴘᴇʀᴍɪᴛs ɢᴏᴛ ʟᴏsᴛ?" I sᴘɪᴛ into the phone receiver. This is not how I expected my morning to start.

The contractor on the other end of the phone sputters and lays out excuses that they're not actually *lost* per se, but more... misplaced.

"How can they be misplaced? They're supposed to be on file at the county's office," I say, trying my damnedest to keep my cool and failing miserably.

"I don't know, Josie. I'm trying to figure it out. I just wanted to tell you so that you know what's going on. Don't shoot the messenger, okay?"

I cover my eyes with my free hand and take a few deep, calming breaths. It's only eight-thirty. I can't be losing my shit this early in the morning on a Monday.

"Okay, okay. Here's what you're going to do. Keep with the project deadlines as best as you can, Clint, and find those fucking permits. We don't have time for this."

My contractor mumbles a few words of apology, and then

we hang up. I drop my head into my hands and groan, thankful no one is at the office yet. Ryan texted me this morning, letting me know he wouldn't be in until lunch, and Lori, our secretary, is out on spring break with her grandkids.

I grumble to myself and kick off my high heels underneath my desk. I don't have time for Clint's carelessness, and I definitely don't have time for shoes. I put this horrible wrench in my plan aside and try to focus on my other projects.

Springtime has always seemed to be the busiest time for me, even when I was working at different firms. Now that the weather is warming up, projects are starting to get underway, which means that anything that could go wrong, does.

The only good thing about putting out fires all day long is that it makes the time pass quickly. I get off another particularly bad call that leaves a foul taste in my mouth and bury my face in my hands, letting out a loud groan. I am grateful once again that I'm the only one in the office today, so I'm free to express my annoyance as loudly as I want. After a moment, I lift my head and glance at the clock on my computer to see that it's nearly lunchtime. I finish typing up my notes from the call and power down my computer. I walk down to the cafe next door and order a light lunch, knowing my stomach can't handle anything too heavy. My whole body is knotted in tension after all the brutal bad news I had today.

The day is surprisingly warm for late March. The sun is shining, and the promise of spring is in the breeze. There's still a slight chill to the wind, but it's a comfortable temperature where I can walk down the block in only my long sleeve sweater I'm wearing.

I get my food and thank the girl at the checkout before heading back toward the office. As I get closer, I notice Ryan's car parked in his spot and I grin, happy to not be alone for the rest of the day, though making a mental note that I need to keep my grumbling to a minimum now.

"Hey, Ryno," I call as I enter the front door. I can hear him shuffling around in his office. He calls back a hello to me as I stroll up to his doorway. Ryan's standing at the edge of his desk, flipping through a pile of papers. He turns around when he hears me settle against his doorframe.

"Hey, Josie, how was your morning?"

I shrug a shoulder and grin at him. "Oh, the usual. I'm probably an honorary firefighter by now, after all the fires I had to put out this morning." Ryan laughs lightly, but I can tell his mind is elsewhere. "Everything okay at home? You usually don't take late starts."

"What? Oh yeah, everything's great," he says, grinning at me, his whole face lighting up.

I narrow my eyes at him. "What, did you win the lottery or something?"

He laughs again and shakes his head before his eyes meet mine; they're glittering with happiness. "Bells is pregnant," he announces, and my stomach flips. "We had a doctor's appointment this morning to confirm it."

"Ryan, that's great! Congratulations!" I plaster on a wide smile as I step forward and give him a hug, even though I feel like throwing up.

His big arms wrap around me, and he hugs me back. "We've been trying ever since the wedding, but it doesn't seem real now that it's actually happened."

"I bet," I say against him as I try to ignore the deep pang of jealousy that sinks into my stomach and sours like rotten milk. I'm happy for him, I am. Ryan is my best friend, and I wish him nothing but happiness. He deserves to have things go right for him.

It still just stings, knowing that I'll never get the opportunity to share that kind of news with him. Ryan loosens the hug and places his hands on my shoulders, his green eyes scouring my face. I know what he's thinking, so I beat him to the punch.

"Don't, Ryan. I'm fine. You're allowed to share good news with me without worrying that I'm going to have a mental breakdown in front of you," I tell him, hoping he can't hear the shakiness of my voice. I mean what I say, I do want him to be able to tell me things without worrying about my history. It's not his fault I've had a shitty day today and am on edge. I can deal with my emotions myself, and honestly, knowing he's treading carefully almost makes the whole situation worse.

"Okay, I just don't want to make you feel bad," Ryan says gently.

"You didn't. I'm happy for you both, really," I tell him with a grin. "This is great news."

"Yeah, it is," he agrees, finally dropping his hands from my shoulders. One hand reaches up to rub at the back of his neck. "Bells and I were thinking of having a little barbecue out at the cabin to celebrate this weekend. Would you and Conner want to come out?"

"I'll have to ask him, but I would imagine he'd say 'yes'," I tell him.

"Cool, well, yeah, just let me know. I think it would be fun," Ryan says, shifting awkwardly on his feet. I know this is my fault—that Ryan feels like he can't be excited in front of me.

I sigh and tilt my chin toward my office. "I better get back to putting out those fires. They seem to be never-ending today."

"Oh yeah, of course!" he says, motioning toward his door. "Don't let me keep you."

I nod at him and offer a smile. "Seriously, though. Congratulations, I'm really happy for you both."

Finally, I get another real smile out of him and the pressure on my chest eases slightly. "Thanks, Josie. It means a lot."

I bob my head and then head back to my own office, my fingers gripping tightly into the takeout bag that my forgotten lunch is still sitting in. I don't waste time and just toss it into the trash can by my desk. There's no way I'm going to be able to stomach food right now.

My phone buzzes right as I settle down in front of my computer, and I glance down, seeing I've received a text from my brother. Sniffling back my tears, I pick up my phone and swipe it open. Alex has sent me a selfie of him giving a thumbs up. He's standing in front of a gas pump in an unknown location. I smile despite my bad mood and send him a supportive text back, encouraging him.

I can't believe what I'm about to admit, but I miss having Alex around. I came home from work last week to all of his stuff packed up and gone. When Conner came home that evening, he informed me that Alex was planning on checking into a rehab facility across the country and wasn't sure when he would be back.

While I am happy that my brother is doing all that he needs to do to get back on track, I miss seeing him every morning and sharing coffee. I went years without having him around, but now that I got him back for a time, I don't want to go back to how it was before.

Somehow, over the past two years, I've built myself a new family. I have Ryan and Izabel, and their friends. And then Conner bulldozed himself into my life again, followed shortly behind by my idiot twin brother. I don't know if I remember how to be alone anymore.

Though, as I'm sitting here staring at my blank computer screen, I'm wondering if being alone had its advantages. For so long, I was on my own. It was me, myself, and I, looking out for each other. There was less stress, less heartache, fewer worries. But also less joy, less love, less happiness.

I take a deep breath and decide that my life is definitely better now than it was before. Even though the past still hurts me, it's in the past. I steel myself and force the negative thoughts down and get back to work. I just have to get through today.

But the thoughts and sadness linger. I force myself to take the calls, deal with the situations that come up throughout the day, but I'm watching the clock tick down until I can go home and wallow. Ryan stays in his own office for most of the day, probably instinctively knowing that I need space, and I'm grateful. Finally, hours later, I say goodbye and head home.

I wander into the house and kick off my shoes, spying the back sliding door open just slightly. I know Conner's out there, probably having a beer and enjoying the night.

"Hey, Ace," I say quietly as I step out onto the back patio. His brown eyes find me, and he gives me a warm smile.

"Hey there, gorgeous." He brings his beer bottle up to his lips and takes a swig. "How was your day?"

I settle into the chair next to him and lean my head on his shoulder. "It was a Monday. Yours?"

Conner chuckles. "Same."

"Is your office still grumbling about you being here?"

"They are. It appears they are really struggling with the concept of having to email me versus just waltzing into my office whenever they want. I'm not complaining, though," he says, leaning down and pressing a kiss into my hair. "I'll take their moaning and groaning as long as I get to be with you every day."

I chuckle lightly and give his shoulder a shove. "You big sap."

"You love it."

I roll my eyes and then look out at the backyard. My heart is still heavy from Ryan's news this afternoon, even though I'm more than excited for him and Izabel. It's a weird place to be—when you want to be happy for someone but can't. The guilt eats at me, and I hate that I can't push my feelings aside and be happy for my friend, but that's how it is.

I'm quiet for a moment as I try to let Conner's closeness ebb the hurt away, but I know it's no use. "It's a nice night."

Conner exhales contentedly and looks up at the sky. "It sure is. I'm glad spring's right around the corner. I've had about enough of this winter."

"You and me both," I say, sighing along with him. My shoulders ache, and I'm seconds away from crumbling under the weight of the day. I swallow thickly, trying to push my emotions back down.

Conner startles next to me and then points up at the sky. "Look, a shooting star!" He turns his eyes down to meet mine and gives me a blinding smile, still fully unaware of the war raging inside of me. "Make a wish, Jo."

My fragile heart shatters in my chest, and I suddenly can't hold back the tears anymore. And I don't want to. I know that I'll feel better once it's off my shoulders. I let out a sob and then cover my face with my hands.

I hear Conner scooting around in his chair so he can face me. His hands wrap around my wrists so he can see my face. "Hey, baby, what's wrong?"

It takes me a moment before I'm able to answer him. I try to take calming breaths to level out the sobs, but I can't. It's uncontrollable now. I shake my head and mutter, "It's so stupid. I hate that I'm doing this right now."

Conner's hands move up to my shoulders, and his fingers

massage my muscles in comfort. "It's not stupid if it has you all torn up like this. Tell me what's wrong."

"Everything's falling apart," I whisper brokenly, and I look up to my man with tear-filled eyes. "My big project at work is turning into a train wreck. I miss Alex; I don't know why he couldn't have said goodbye. And Ryan's having a baby." I immediately see the compassion take over Conner's face as understanding sinks in. He moves forward, pulling me into his chest, and wraps his arms around me tightly. "I want to be happy for him. I *am* happy for him. For them. But I just—" My voice breaks as tears stream down my face.

I am overwhelmed with guilt and hurt, and longing, and excitement that my friends are growing their family and happiness that my brother is taking care of himself, but also selfishness because I miss him. I don't know how I can be experiencing all these emotions at once, and I'm overloaded.

"Shh, it's okay," Conner coos at me, running his large hand over my hair. He doesn't ask where this is all coming from or question me in any way. He just offers me comfort in the best way he can.

I shake my head against his chest. "It's not okay. I should be happy for him, but I'm not. I'm jealous and angry and... it's just so unfair. Why do I have to be like this? I just want to be normal."

"It's okay, Jo. I know it hurts. Just breathe."

"I want it so bad," I say finally, giving into the tears once more. "I want to be the one who waltzes into the office with great news like that. I want to give you a baby, but I can't."

"We'll get our chance, sweetheart. It will all work out some- how," Conner soothes me, his fingers threading through my hair and rubbing against my scalp. "I know it will."

"You can't know that. There's no manual on how our life is going to play out. Maybe your parents were right and you should find someone else to be with who can give you a future," I mutter as two big fat tears roll down my cheeks.

I remember when Conner came back to Cedar Ridge after being in Atlanta for a week or so. He seemed put off about something, and I finally was able to pry it out of him. I knew that my brother had blabbed about the baby situation to my mom, but Conner had conveniently left out the part about his dad confronting him about it.

I can't say I blame him. There's a part of me that wishes that Conner would take his dad's advice and go find someone who can give him what he wants, because I want him to have everything. But the other part of me, the one that's sobbing into this man's shirt right now, can't imagine life without him and is willing to hold on to him no matter how selfish it makes me.

I wipe at my cheeks and struggle to breathe through my clogged up nose. "I hate that this keeps coming up, but there's no way for me to turn it off. I'm stuck in this loop, and there's no way out. I'm sorry. I'm so sorry."

Conner's chest deflates with a big sigh and his arms wrap around me tighter. "Don't apologize, Jo. You have nothing to apologize for."

"I know," I whimper. "But I still feel like I have to. I'm supposed to be able to do this, to give you a family and I *can't*. It's devastating knowing that I'm the one at fault."

He's quiet for a minute or two as I try to regain control of myself. His fingers thread through my hair, running over the strands soothingly. "Jo, I would never *blame* you for something you have no control over. *You* are my family. I'm committed to you, regardless of anything else."

Another sob wracks my body, and I can't fight off the shame and despair from consuming me. "I just want to be able to give you a baby. I want to be a mom."

Conner holds me, letting me sit in my feelings and work

through them. Eventually, his shoulders tighten as he braces himself for what he's about to say. "Maybe we can look into other options."

I look up at him with watery eyes and sniffle. "Like what?"

Conner looks at me warily, as if he's trying to decide if he wants to commit to this conversation. "I think it would be best if we get an appointment with a doctor first to discuss things, and then we can go from there. I know we've talked about this before, but I'd like to get another opinion, and if that's a dead end, we can look into something else."

I really don't want to see another doctor. I've played that scene out before, the paper gown, the tests, the prodding, the hope. And every time, it was squashed. Now even going to my gynecologist for a yearly exam nearly puts me into a panic attack.

But I also know why Conner wants me to do this. As real as the diagnosis is for me, it's not, necessarily, for him. He hasn't gone through those moments where the doctor walks in, a grim expression on her face, only to deliver the truth. So, I can do it for him. One more time for him.

"Okay," I whisper. His arms tighten around me. "And when she says exactly what I've been telling you, then what?"

Conner signs, the corners of his lips dropping into a frown. I know he doesn't like my pessimism. "Then we can see about reaching out to an adoption agency or registering to be foster parents. There are so many kids already out there who would be lucky to have you as a mom. We'll find them."

I know Conner means well, but his words are not doing enough for me in the way of comfort. I just don't have the energy to put up much else this evening. I stare into his eyes quietly for a moment before nodding my head and resting against his shoulder. We stay that way in silence until I must doze off, and Conner carries me into the house and to our bed.

He presses his lips against my forehead gently and whispers that he loves me. But still, even half-asleep, my heart is heavy.

Chapter 27

Conner

"Hey, Conner!" Izabel chirps at me from behind the counter, where she's preparing a bowl of salad. She drops a few cherry tomatoes into the bowl and then brushes her hands off. "Anything I can get you?"

I grin at her as I slide onto the barstool at the counter and rest my arms on the granite. "I wouldn't object to a beer if you've got one of those in the fridge."

Izabel bobs her head and turns, grabbing a bottle of Blue Moon for me and popping off the top. "Needed a break from the Dynamic Duo?" she asks me with a sly smirk.

I laugh under my breath as I take a swig of my beer. "Yeah, it was getting just a little bit too competitive for me. I don't think I was destined to be Cornhole Champion."

Izabel rolls her eyes. "Me, either. Not the sport for me." She grabs a bag of croutons and sprinkles a few of them on top of the lettuce and tomatoes.

"This place is great, by the way. Thanks for inviting us out this weekend," I tell her.

Izabel's face splits into a grin as she continues to bustle

around the kitchen. "Thank you. Ryan really outdid himself on this whole project. It's my favorite place in the world."

"Better than what used to be here, huh?" I ask teasingly. Josie had filled me in on their epic beginning a while back.

Izabel laughs out loud. "Oh, definitely. The original cabin—if you could even call it that, it was more like a shack—was practically falling apart when we stumbled across it the first time. It definitely needed a makeover."

"I love that you will get to raise your kids where it all started for you," I say, looking around at the beautiful home. "It will make for a lot of great memories for them."

"I hope so," Izabel agrees wistfully. "And of course, your kids can come up here anytime, as well, whenever that happens for you two."

I take another pull of my beer and frown. "Hopefully, we get that chance. We have an appointment with a fertility specialist this week."

Izabel raises her eyebrows at that news. "That's amazing. Maybe a baby will be in the cards for her after all."

I hear Josie laughing at something Ryan has said, and I look out the window at her. Her face is lit up with amusement, and she shoves his shoulder before his deep laugh rings out as well. My stomach clenches. "I hope it is. She deserves to have everything she wants."

Izabel looks down at the counter and then brushes away some crumbs, clearly thinking over what she wants to say. Carefully she says, "Ryan was really worried about her after he told her about the baby. I know that was hard for her to hear."

"Yeah, she's so happy for the both of you, but I know it hurts her a little bit at the same time," I respond.

"You're good for her, Conner. I love seeing her so happy, and I know Ryan does, too. She's important to him."

I'm grateful that we have friends in the Millers. I know

Josie's friendship with Ryan played a big part in their relationship. Forever friends like that don't come around so often. "Thank you. I just hope I can live up to the example your husband sets."

Izabel laughs again. "Oh please, Ryan isn't perfect, but as far as I'm concerned, you're doing a great job. Don't sell yourself short."

"I appreciate it," I reply.

"Well, I think I'm all set in here. Do you think you have it in you to go tell Ryan that he needs to pause his game to start up the grill?"

"Hm, I dunno. I'd better let you do it. That man is hardcore when it comes to cornhole. He can't wallop you for interrupting."

"Wuss," she teases me, but heads outside to interrupt the Dynamic Duo's game. Ryan wraps his arms around her when she approaches and gives her a big kiss.

"Hey there, beautiful," he says, a grin forming on his face.

His wife pats him on the chest. "Time to start grilling, buddy. You and Josie will have to finish your tournament later."

Ryan pouts a little bit, but listens to his wife's instructions and hurries into the house to grab the hamburgers. Izabel follows after him, leaving Josie and me out on the lawn.

"I'm probably not as good as your bestie, but want to have a go?" I ask her, picking up a red beanbag and giving it a toss toward the other board. It misses completely, flying off to the side, not even close to hitting the target.

Josie gives me a look and shakes her head. "No, I'll save you the embarrassment."

"Thanks, babe, means a lot," I tell her with a wink.

Josie reaches her hand out to me, and I take it, following her lead onto the porch, where there's a swing. I sit down next to her and rest my arm against the back, allowing her to lean into my chest as we rock back and forth.

It turned out to be the perfect weekend for a mountain getaway. It's warm enough that we can sit comfortably outside when the sun is up, though I'm sure it will get a bit cooler once the sun sets. This is my first time out to this cabin, but so far, I'm not left wondering why Ryan and Izabel are so attached to it.

Josie and I sit until Izabel calls us in to eat. We settle around the table and dig in. We talk about Josie and Ryan's cornhole game for a moment, and I smirk as the two friends rib each other back and forth. The table falls into a beat of silence, and Izabel changes the subject.

"Conner told us about your appointment this week, Josie," she says. I take a bite of my burger and look at Josie. She's sitting there frozen, fork halfway to her mouth and her eyes wide.

She's quiet as her brain catches up, but then she jumps back in. "Oh, yes, that appointment, later this week."

"I just wanted to let you know that we're both behind you guys one-hundred percent. If you need anything or whatever, just let us know, and we're here for you," Izabel tells both of us, her blue eyes sincere as she locks gazes, first with Josie, and then me. I smile, but Josie is still taken off guard.

Ryan places his hand palm up on the table, and Izabel laces her fingers through his. He offers his wife a smile, happiness lighting up his eyes for a second before turning to us. "Absolutely. Josie, you helped me through some of the darkest times in my life. Whatever you need, we'll be here."

Josephine's cheeks flush a deep rose color, and she looks down at her salad again, moving a tomato around the bowl. "Thank you both. That really means a lot."

I grin and extend my arm across the back of Josie's chair,

resting my hand on her shoulder. As soon as I touch her, Josie's back straightens, and she pulls away from me, leaning forward in the chair, so my arm is hanging off into nothingness. I watch her out of the corner of my eye, but she doesn't look over. She reaches for her wine glass and takes a sip, listening to whatever Ryan's saying now and not giving me any type of acknowledgment.

Her silent treatment continues throughout dinner and into the evening activities. Ryan makes up a bonfire right outside the cabin, and we all huddle around it. Izabel leans against her husband, his arm around her waist and hand placed on her belly. There's nothing to note yet there, but soon, their family of two will turn into a family of three.

Josie is sitting in her own chair a few feet away from me, a blanket wrapped around her shoulders and her gaze staring straight into the flames. Ryan tries to engage her a few times. Still, her responses are clipped, so he eventually leaves her alone, picking up a conversation with me about sports.

After the fire has reduced to nothing but embers, Josie stands and stretches. "I think I'll probably head to bed. Do you guys need me to do anything beforehand?"

Ryan and Izabel share a look with each other, and I see my friend's arm tighten around his wife possessively. "I think we'll probably stay out here for a while longer. You two go on inside, though."

"Don't worry about cleaning anything up," Izabel adds. "I'll take care of it in the morning."

After we say goodnight to Ryan and Izabel, I follow Josie into our assigned guest room. She's still giving me the cold shoulder, and it's like I'm walking on eggshells. I clearly did something to upset her, but I don't want to push her into talking if she's not ready.

We get ready for bed in silence, pulling on our pajamas and

crawling underneath the covers. I settle in on my back, curling one arm up and underneath my head. Josie has her back to me, but I can hear her stuttered breathing. After a moment of contemplation, I throw caution to the wind and move onto my side, my chest pressing against her back. I wrap an arm around her hips and pull her further back into me.

"Hey," I murmur into her hair, nuzzling my nose against her ear. "Want to tell me what's wrong?"

She sniffs and shakes her head. I exhale in disappointment but still hold her close. If she's not ready, then she's not ready. I'm positive I'll be hearing about whatever I did whenever she's ready to talk.

We lay in silence for a while; the only noise is Josie's occasional sniffles. As soon as I start to doze off, giving up hope for a conversation, Josie turns around in my arms and comes face-to-face with me. I lazily open my eyes and meet hers.

"Hi," I say. She frowns at me, and I know I'm not out of the mud yet. "Are you ready to talk about it?"

She's quiet for another half a second before she lays into me. "I can't believe you told Izabel all of that, Conner. You really hurt me tonight."

"All of what?"

"That we were talking about going to see a specialist."

"But we are, Jo. I didn't realize that it was a secret."

Josie scoffs and reaches a hand up to swipe at her cheek. "I haven't even told Ryan any of that. They know about," she pauses, "*before*. But we've left it at that. I don't want to tell people before we know what's going to happen."

"They're our friends, and they love you. I thought it would be good to have friends supporting us through this."

"It wasn't your decision. I don't want anyone to know unless we have good news, okay? You broke my trust tonight, Conner. I'm really disappointed and hurt. I've *told* you exactly what is going to happen at this appointment, but I've agreed to go, for your sake. Do you know how terrible it's going to be for me now to not only crush *your* hopes, but to also disappoint our friends?"

A deep unsettling chill courses through my chest and down to my fingers and toes. I stare at Josie in the dark, trying to think of how I can make this better—but I don't think I can. "I'm sorry," I say, settling on my course of action. "I would never intentionally hurt you like that."

Josie sighs and closes her eyes. "I know. I just wish you would've talked to me before airing all our secrets out to them. Even if they don't mean to, once they find out there's no hope, they're going to look at me with pity—like I'm something that's broken."

My heart breaks into a thousand pieces, and the self-loathing sets in stronger than ever before. "I'm sorry. I'll never do it again. It's you and me in this, and if you don't want me to say anything to anyone, I won't. I swear."

"Thank you," she says weakly. Her head tucks underneath my chin to rest on my chest. I bury my nose in her hair and inhale, smelling the familiar sweet scent of her shampoo.

"And listen to me... You are not *broken*. You're perfect exactly how you are, no matter what happens."

Josie sniffles, and it guts me. I hold her tightly against me, wishing that neither of us had to be in this challenging situation. I wish Josie would never have known this kind of pain, but I can't change the past. I can only help her through to the future.

"I love you, Jo," I tell her. "No matter what happens at this appointment next week, that won't change. It will always be us."

"Thanks," she says again, rubbing her cheek on my shirt. I press a kiss into her hair and squeeze my arms tighter.

I've never seen my girl this distraught over anything. Before, she would always run and hide whenever the going got tough. Now, I know she's doing her best to face it head-on, even though it's hard. And I'm not ignorant enough not to recognize that she's only doing it for me. If anything, it makes me love her even more, knowing she's sacrificing so much—putting all that she is on the line.

The last thing I would ever want to do is betray her. I think about how Ryan and Izabel made it through so many obstacles to get where they are now, and I hope that can happen for Josie and me.

I want to be everything she needs so badly, but I know I can't fix this for her. As I hold her in the darkness, I close my eyes tightly and pray to whatever God is up there that we can get through this, that everything will go well this week. I don't want to see her hurting when there's nothing I can do about it.

I'm not asking for a miracle, but just hope.

Chapter 28

Josie

The room smells like antiseptic. The table is cold underneath me, a stark contrast to the clamminess of my skin. I already know that I'm not going to be able to get off of this thing because the bare skin of my thighs is going to be forever stuck to the vinyl exam table. Either that or the paper cover they have laying down will eternally be attached to my legs because of how much I'm sweating.

Conner is sitting across from me in a regular chair, flipping through his phone, unbothered by everything that is about to happen today. But I can't seem to get my heart rate to calm down. When we first arrived, the nurse who performed my blood pressure looked at me with a sympathetic expression and chalked the high reading up to "Nerves, totally normal."

Sure. As if I could *ever* be normal when it comes to this.

I finally gave in when Conner insisted that we meet with a new doctor. He made us an appointment at the best fertility specialist in town. The last week has been filled with tests and blood draws and conversations, and now, today, we're finally getting the news.

The nurse brought us into this exam room and gave me this atrocious paper gown, instructing me to change and that the doctor would be right in. Today, I'm being subjected to a transvaginal ultrasound to really see what's going on with the scar tissue situation. My doctor didn't seem too upbeat after seeing the images from the first ultrasound earlier in the week, so we're going in for a second look. *Lucky me.*

"Hey," Conner says, grabbing my attention away from picking at my cuticles. It seems he's finally noticed my anxiety levels. "Everything will be okay, no matter what happens today. I promise."

I press my lips together and nod my head, not trusting my voice right now. I turn my attention to my fingers and start picking at a hangnail that I almost have loose. Of course, Conner would say that everything will be fine; he's not the one who has to live with the fact that he's damaged. I appreciate that he's trying to be helpful, but I can't help but think that it's a waste of time and energy.

I'm trying not to be pessimistic. I really am. But the thoughts pop into my head every so often that he would probably be better off without me. A guy like Conner deserves to have a chance with a family. A real family, that's his. And despite his reassurance that he'll be happy no matter the outcome, I can't help but worry that he'll resent me down the road if we don't get the answers we want today.

I know it's not my fault. But at the same time, I realize that *I am the problem here.* Conner's sperm levels were tested earlier this week, and his results came back perfectly normal, perhaps even better. And yet, here we are, because Josie can't seem to figure out how to get pregnant.

A soft knock on the door has me sitting up, clenching my hands tightly together. "Come in," I mutter loud enough that whoever's on the other side can hear.

The door is pushed open, and a tech wheels the ultrasound machine into the room, my doctor following closely behind with a smile on her face. "Good morning, Josie, Conner." Conner stands up to shake her hand, then sits right back down, a hopeful expression on his face. "I'm just going to have Lacey here perform the ultrasound, and then I'll reevaluate the images, and we can see what's going on. This shouldn't take too long. Do you have any questions?"

I bite the inside of my cheek and shake my head. Conner asks her a few questions about the process and whether or not it will hurt me, and the doctor responds to him. Meanwhile, the tech instructs me to lie back on the exam table, situating me how she needs me and adjusting the god-awful gown around my hips. Once the doctor steps out, I'm instructed to bend my knees and spread my legs as the tech begins the test. I squeeze my eyes shut, willing everything to be over soon.

I wince at the intrusion of the ultrasound wand and try to focus on my breathing as she moves it around inside of me to get the images that she wants. I hear the shuffling of footsteps, and then I can sense Conner's presence at the table beside me. He takes my hand, lacing our fingers together and not commenting on the disgusting sweat that's lingering on my palms.

Lacey, the tech, finishes up her imaging and removes the ultrasound wand from me. She gives me a reassuring smile and wheels the machine out of the room, telling us that the doctor will be back in shortly.

Once she's gone, Conner leans down and kisses my forehead, and despite everything, a tear drips out of the corner of my eye. I grip his hand tightly in mine, praying with everything in me that the doctor will come back with good news.

The room is eerily silent. Conner helps me sit up and watches me tenderly as I throw away the paper gown and pull my underwear and jeans back on, but doesn't say anything. I don't think either of us really knows what to say or do not want to jinx anything.

I'd rather it be quiet. I don't think I could handle Conner being overly optimistic out loud, even though I know that's what's running through his head. He's a hopeful person by nature, and I'm... not. Not when it comes to this.

It takes a while, but finally, the knock on the door comes, and my doctor walks back in. I know immediately by the grave expression on her face that she doesn't come bearing good news. Conner, however, still looks at her hopefully as she sits on the stool in the room and pulls up the ultrasound images on the computer.

Taking a deep breath, the doctor meets my eyes. "I'm so sorry, Josie, but unfortunately, your ultrasound came back confirming what your previous provider told you." She points to a few spots on the black-and-white image. I don't know what I'm looking at, but she explains, "These spots here indicate a significant buildup of scar tissue, likely from your previous trauma."

I nod my head, understanding the implications, but Conner's not quite following, so he asks, "What does the scar tissue mean?"

"Unfortunately, this amount of scar tissue buildup means that it is unlikely that Josie would be able to become pregnant by natural means," the doctor explains.

"And what about other means?" Conner asks, frowning.

"I've seen some cases with this particular diagnosis where we were able to go in and surgically remove some of the scar tissue. That procedure helps implantation of an embryo," she says but then looks back to the screen. "However, there was significantly less scar tissue in those cases, so I'm not confident that it would be a successful procedure here. But if that's the route you wanted to go, we could certainly try it."

Conner looks at me with hopeful eyes, and my heart crashes and breaks into a million pieces. "What are the chances that my body could sustain a full-term pregnancy?" I ask her, knowing the answer already.

The doctor presses her lips together as she turns her gaze back to me. "We would consider you a high-risk pregnancy, meaning that your chances of miscarrying would be higher than normal."

I close my eyes and shake my head before turning to Conner. "I can't do it again."

Though I may be able to get pregnant, after all, the thought of losing another baby absolutely terrifies me. That's simply not something I'm willing to go through. His eyes trace the features of my face, and he nods slightly. It kills me to know that I'm taking this opportunity from him, but I simply can't go through that again.

"I'll have the nurses put together a few things for you, and we'll have that at the counter when you check out." She stands and closes down my chart on the computer. "I'll let you two have the room. If you decide on anything different, please don't hesitate to reach out."

Once the doctor leaves the room, the tears finally fall. Conner comes over to me and wraps his arms around my shoulders, pulling me into his chest. I bury my nose in his shirt, sniffling in his familiar scent. "I'm so sorry, Conner."

His hand smooths down my hair. "Shh, it's alright. Everything's going to be okay, Josie."

I let him hold me for a few moments while my tears subside, and then I'm ready to go. We grab our things and head up to the front counter to check out. Conner pays the copay, and then we leave, walking hand-in-hand.

For almost the whole ride home, I'm quiet, staring out the window, trying not to cry again. At one point, when we're stopped at a red light, Conner glances over at me and lets out a big sigh.

"You know, she said it wouldn't be impossible," he says carefully. "Just that it might be riskier."

I snap my attention to him and give him a glare, irritated and annoyed that he'd even suggest that. "Which is enough to deter me from ever trying it."

"I'm just saying that—"

"No, Conner," I tell him forcefully. "I agreed to go to the doctor for you, and she gave me the same diagnosis and expected outcome as the other doctor. I'm not putting myself through that again."

"I understand that, but—"

"No, I don't think you do," I cut him off again, my annoyance flaring. "You weren't *there*, Conner! You weren't there when they told me that our baby died, that we would never get to see her, never get to meet her. You weren't there. You have no idea what that was like."

I turn away from him again and swipe angrily at a tear that treks down my face.

"That's not fair, Jo," he mutters softly, pressing on the gas as the light turns green.

"I don't care. My answer is no. We'll look into other options like you said."

"Just think about it, okay? The doctor didn't take the possibility completely off the table. Don't close that door just yet."

"There is nothing to think about!" I raise my voice again, my throat thick with emotion. "I *told you* that I could never give this to you. If it's that important to you, go find another woman to have your baby, 'cause it will never be me. Do you hear me, Conner? I won't put myself through that again."

"Okay, I hear you."

"Thank you," I say softly, defeated. Conner's hands are gripping the wheel of the Chevelle so tightly that his knuckles are white. I look at his face, and I can see the tears threatening the edges of his eyelids. The sight makes my stomach twist, but I can't find it in myself to say anything else on the matter. We've been at each other's throats all week, each of us walking around on edge, waiting for today.

When he finally pulls into our driveway, he puts the car in park and turns to me, swallowing thickly. His eyes are red, as if the pressure from the built-up tears is making them bloodshot. "This doesn't change anything, Josie."

"How can you be sure? Also, why does it feel like it does?" I ask him in a whisper.

"Because when I close my eyes and imagine my perfect outcome, you're the only one I see that really matters," Conner tells me. "You're the one who is constant, every time. Every outcome of my future has you in it." He reaches across the center console, offering his hand to me. I tentatively slide my hand into his, breathing a sigh of relief when he wraps his fingers around mine and gives me a squeeze.

"I'd like to look into adopting," I admit softly after a few minutes of silence. "But will that be enough for you?"

"Of course it would be, sweetheart. I've already told you I'm fine with whatever path you choose." He shifts in his seat to face me fully, reaching for my other hand. When I give it to him, he brings both of my hands up to his mouth and presses a kiss on them. His brown eyes are sincere as they hold mine. "If this is what you want, we'll do it. We'll call the agency today if you want."

"What about earlier, when you wanted me to 'think about it'?" I ask him, the emotions from just a few minutes ago quietly threatening to come back.

"I only wanted you to think about it because I thought that's what you wanted, but if you don't want to do that, then we won't." He presses another kiss to my hands. "The last thing I want to do is cause you pain, Josie. You've had enough of that in your life. We both have. So, if you put your foot down on the matter, then that's it. No more."

I close my eyes and lean my forehead against his. "I don't deserve you."

He laughs under his breath. "I think it's the other way around, actually." Conner falls quiet for another moment, allowing us to bask in each other's presence. "Should we go inside, or do you want to sit out here in this hot car for a while longer?"

I laugh now and pull away. "Okay, let's go inside."

We both exit the car and walk up to the house. "I think we probably need some emotional support food tonight, huh?" he teases me as he puts the key into the front door, unlocking it. "What do you think?"

"Only if it's pizza with all the toppings and you're buying."

Conner throws his head back with a laugh, and it makes my heart soar. Finally, for the first time today, my spirits seem to lift. He always seems to have that ability. "That sounds like a deal."

I put my hand on his chest once we step into the house. He looks down at me with an eyebrow raised. I lift onto my tiptoes and press my lips to his. When I pull away, he smiles softly at me, reaching up with a hand to tuck a strand of hair behind my ear. I can still see the hesitance in his eyes from the stress of the week, but behind that is the familiar warmth that he saves just for me.

"What was that for?" he asks.

"Nothing, I just love you."

Chapter 29

Conner

"Jo, I'm home!" I call out as I step into the house. I had to take a trip to Atlanta for the week to work out some issues with a project. It was just easier for me to be down there in person than trying to work out conflicts via email or video calls.

I meander down the hallway, tossing my duffle bag into the bedroom to worry about later. I hear a rustling down the hall, and then Josie calls back to me to let me know she's in her office. Now, with my hands free, I step into her office space and walk up behind her. My hands find her shoulders and knead at her tight muscles.

"What are you working on?" I ask her. She's hunched over her laptop, but quickly closes it as soon as I ask.

"Oh, just this and that. We can talk about it later," Josie says as she turns around to face me and stands, wrapping me in a hug.

I frown but hug her back. It's been a few weeks since our appointment with the fertility doctor. In the week or so immediately following that, I found Josie often staring off into space, or I'd catch her crying to herself in the shower. Every time I'd ask her about it, though, she'd quickly brush me off and tell me she was okay. I was hoping that my being away for a week would give her the chance to work through some of these feelings independently, but I'm not sure if it worked out that way. She's still being shady.

"I thought we could go out to dinner tonight," I tell her.

She pulls away and grins at me. "That sounds great! Let me just change real quick, and then we can go."

As Josie's changing her clothes, I set about unpacking my duffel from my trip. My phone buzzes as soon as I unzip my bag, and I look down to see a message from Alex. I frown and pick up my phone, opening it up and reading what he sent: **Call me ASAP.**

I roll my eyes, deciding to worry about Alex later, toss the phone back on the bed, and get back to work unpacking my things. Just about everything goes into the laundry basket for later. I'm glad to be home; going back to Atlanta just reminds me of all the years Josie and I spent apart, which makes me all the happier that we've found each other again.

I glance toward the bathroom, ensuring that Josie is still in there before opening up my underwear drawer. I dig around for only a moment before my fingers brush against the black velvet box that has been hiding there since I got it. I quickly stuff the box into my pocket as Josie steps out of the bathroom, running a brush through her hair. She grins at me, unaware.

"Where do you want to go tonight?" she asks.

I stuff my hands in my jean pockets, my left hand grasping the box tightly. Tonight feels like the night. "Wherever you want, I'm fine with anything."

"Want to go to Rizzo's? I could go for a piece of lasagna right now. Oh, and their *breadsticks.*"

"Yeah, that sounds great," I say. Rizzo's is quickly becoming a staple in our household, not that I have any complaints about it. Their breadsticks *are* to die for. "Are you about ready?"

Josie looks at me with an eyebrow raised. "Sure, are you okay? You seem off."

I want to tell her that *she's* the one who's seemed off the last few weeks, but I refrain. I'm sure I'm acting jittery, thinking about the box sitting in my pocket or how she'll respond when I finally get down on one knee.

"I'm fine, just hungry," I tell her. She nods as if that makes perfect sense and then bounds out of our bedroom to the car. I follow behind her, shaking my head at her energy. She definitely seems to be in better spirits today, given the events of the last few weeks.

As I was coming home from Atlanta, I started working on a big proposal speech. I would tell her how I wanted to spend the rest of my life with her and how she was the one I wanted next to me when all of our dreams come true. I'd do anything to reassure her that we are meant to be with each other, that we're better together.

We drive over to Rizzo's and are seated relatively quickly. A waitress comes by and takes our orders, dropping off a basket of breadsticks that we can snack on in the meantime. When the food arrives, Josie's eyes light up, and she digs into her baked lasagna. A string of gooey cheese hangs off the fork as she takes her first bite, eyes closing in bliss.

"Is it good?" I ask with a chuckle as I take a bite of my spaghetti.

"Better than good," Jo replies, opening her eyes and meeting mine. "This is the best lasagna I've ever had."

We finish our meal, sharing a bit of conversation in between bites. Jo asks about my trip, and I fill her in on all the details. She tells me that things have been quiet at home since I've been gone.

The waitress comes by to take our plates and asks if we want any dessert. Josie jumps to answer. "Could we get a piece of your Black Tie Cheesecake to go, please?"

I grin and lean my cheek on my hand. I know that's her favorite. "In a hurry?"

Josie looks at me and shrugs a shoulder. "I'm just ready to head home."

"That sounds perfect to me," I respond. The box in my pocket is like a lead weight, but I decide to wait until we're home. I'll get down on one knee after we finish our dessert and ask her the big question. Josie will say yes and then throw herself at me. Asking her in private makes the whole thing more intimate. I'll wrap her up in my arms and take her back to our bedroom, where we'll spend the rest of the night.

Yeah, that sounds perfect.

I pay the tab, and Josie grabs our cheesecake to go, and we head home. Josie hums along to the music on the radio in the car, and I smile quietly to myself. Tonight has gone exactly as I hoped it would so far. I finally feel like I have my Josie back, and I'm never letting her go again.

I watch her, appreciating everything about her, as we eat our cheesecake. Josie meets my eye when we finish, and she blushes, looking down at her hands folded on the table. My own hand reaches into my pocket as I ready myself for the big moment. This is it.

"So, I was looking at adoption agencies today," Josie says, swiping a few crumbs of cheesecake off of the table.

I release the box back into my pocket. This is not it.

"Really?" I ask her, surprised. Though we've agreed that this is the path we want to take, she hasn't seemed gung ho about moving in that direction. I wasn't expecting anything to happen in that regard so quickly. I figured we had time.

"Yeah, I found a few promising ones, but uh, there's something I wanted to talk to you about."

I frown at her, unsure where she's going with this. "Okay?"

"Well, from what I've researched, we would make the perfect adoptive parent candidates, since we both are employed and we make a decent living. I think we could put in an application any time and be considered."

"That's great, Josie."

She fingers the tablecloth on the table and then looks at me warily. "Yes, and I've already filled out most of the application, but I thought that if you weren't busy tomorrow, we could go down to the courthouse and get married. I was reading that being a married couple might make an adoptive mother more receptive to applicants. That might mean we would have a better chance of getting chosen."

My blood runs cold as I stare at her. Oh, how the tables have turned. Her eyes dart from me to the table, then back to me and away again. "You want to get married tomorrow," I say, and she nods vigorously. "So that we'll be better applicants for adoption?"

"Yes, then when I turn in our application, I can say that we're married. I was reading a forum, and I saw a few couples on there commenting about how much easier things would have been if they had gotten married."

"And you want to do this tomorrow," I say again, unsure I heard her right. "Because..."

"Well, I want to get the application in as soon as possible."

I run my hand over my mouth to cover the frown on my face. "I see."

Josie rolls her eyes. "What does that mean? It's not as if we weren't ever going to get married. You're acting like this isn't what you want."

I scoff and sit up straight. "It's not. At least not like this."

She frowns at me. "What does that mean?" I clear my throat and grab our plates, walking into the kitchen and putting them in the sink. I hear her following after me. "Conner, answer me. I don't see the problem here."

"You're really making this sound like a business arrangement, Josephine," I tell her, trying to keep my voice level. The black box in my pocket burns like it's on fire. This isn't at all how I saw this night going. Specifically, this conversation.

"Well, historically, that's what marriage is!"

I spin around and glare at her. "Not for *us*, it isn't. I don't want that, Jo. I want the big ceremony and the reception. I want to watch you walk down the aisle toward me, making me cry like a baby in front of all our friends and family. I don't want to marry you in a courthouse because it's just business."

Josie crosses her arms over her chest and stares at me. "I think you're overreacting. I'm just trying to make sure that we get chosen as adoptive parents. So that you can finally get what you want."

I shake my head. "No, don't put this on me. I've told you time and time again that *you're* all I want. You're all the family I need."

"So, you don't want to get married? That's fine, if that's what you want. Just tell me."

"Did I say that? You're being irrational, Jo."

"Well, it sure sounds that way. I ask you to marry me tomorrow, and all of a sudden, you have a problem with it. I thought we were on the same page."

"Jesus Christ," I mutter as I run my hand over my face. "I want to marry you because we love each other, Josephine. Not because it's expected or to make us look good on an application. I want to marry you because I love you."

"Well, I love you, too, so I don't see the problem with just going tomorrow and getting it over with."

I close my eyes in frustration, trying not to let the 'getting it over with' comment affect me too much. I say as calmly as I possibly can, "You're not listening to me."

"And you're not listening to me!" she shouts back. "This will help us, Conner. As soon as the application is in, we will have a better chance of getting selected."

I reach into my pocket and pull out the black box, slamming it on the counter, finally losing my composure and unwilling to continue with this conversation. Josie's hazel eyes go wide as soon as they lock on the ring box. "This is *not* an arrangement for me. It never has been, and it never will be. So, no, I won't be marrying you tomorrow at the courthouse," I tell her. I can see the gears churning in her mind, and I see her planning to backtrack, but it's too late. I'm done for tonight.

"Conner, I—"

I hold up my hand, "No. I'm sorry, Jo, but I can't do this. I need to get out of here for a while." I brush past her out of the kitchen and to the living room. She trails after me, calling my name. "We can talk tomorrow."

"Wait, I didn't mean to—"

I turn on her. "No, I think you did, but what? You weren't expecting me to have gotten a ring already?" Her eyes are still wide as she's staring at me, tears welling up in the corners. "I've had it for months, Josie. Since the day Alex left. I've just been waiting for the right time, but congratulations, I guess you beat me to it."

"Can we at least talk about this?"

I let out a big sigh. "Oh, we'll absolutely be talking about this. But I can't right now, You've really hurt me tonight, Josie, and I just need to clear my head, okay?"

"Conner..."

I reach for my keys and open the door. "We can discuss the terms for your *arrangement* tomorrow."

I hear her protesting behind me as I open the door and step outside. As soon as the door is closed behind me, I take a deep breath of the night air into my lungs, trying to calm my shaking hands. Without another look back, I get in my car. I pull out my cell phone, powering it down before I drive away. I just need some time to think.

This is not at all how I intended this night to end, not that I should be surprised. When it comes to the woman I love, I should always expect the unexpected. That's just Josie, and honestly, I wouldn't want it any other way when it comes down to it. But for now, I need some time to myself.

I close my eyes and breathe for a second before opening them again, pulling out of the driveway, and driving off into the night.

Chapter 30

Josie

I STARE AT THE FRONT DOOR FOR A FEW MINUTES AFTER Conner walks out. My eyes burn from tears that pool along the edge of my lower lids. I can't believe he just *left*. I'm sick at the thought of running him out of his own house. Despite my position on the matter during our argument, I see where Conner's hurt and frustration are coming from. I certainly was insensitive to how he was feeling, and I hate myself for it.

I swipe at the moisture on my cheeks and turn away from the door, heading into the kitchen where the black velvet box is sitting right where he tossed it. I have to admit, I didn't see that coming, which makes me feel even worse.

Was he planning on asking me tonight and I totally blew it?

I pick up the box in my hands and turn it around, my fingers running over the soft black velvet. The temptation to open it is overwhelming, but I can't bring myself to actually do it. The romantic side of me wants to wait until Conner's in front of me on one knee to actually see the ring he picked out just for me. Peeking at it now would just add insult to injury.

I hold the box tightly to my chest and wander back to the

bedroom, not bothering to stop my tears now. I curl up on my bed, clutching the ring box close to me still, and pull up a blanket over my shoulders.

As I lay in my bedroom all alone, Conner's side of the bed empty and cold, the tears finally spill over the edges of my eyelids. I let myself cry, imagining all the ways I'll apologize to Conner when he comes back. Hurting him was never my intent, and I hate how insensitive I was to bring up the concept of marriage like that. I should have been more aware of how he might receive it. The tears fall until my eyes ache like they've been rubbed with sandpaper, and my lids grow heavy. Sleep blurs the edges of my vision, and when my eyes close, memories of Conner's brown eyes, shadowed with hurt as I deliver the verbal injury, fill my mind.

I'm startled awake when I hear two men arguing outside of my house. The house shakes as the front door is thrown open, and something crashes to the ground. I sit up in bed, gripping the blanket tightly in my hands, my eyes darting around my bedroom, trying to reorient myself.

What was that?

I hear the door open and slam shut again and then more yelling. I wrack my brain to try to remember if I had locked the door once Conner left, and to my horror, I don't think I did. The yelling gets louder and louder. Neither of the two voices belongs to Conner.

Carefully, I step out of bed and walk to the closed bedroom door, pressing my ear to it to try to hear what the intruders are yelling about. I can't fully make it out, but they're definitely fighting. I press my back to the door and pull my phone out of the back pocket of my jeans. It's late, I notice —nearly midnight —not a few minutes later, as I initially thought. Inhaling shakily, I dial Conner's number, and bring the phone up to my ear. The call goes straight to voicemail, and I swear under my breath. I repeat the actions one more time, to no avail. Voice-mail again.

The shouting gets louder, and then I hear a loud crash before the front door slams again. My body stills as I strain my ears to hear anything else. When I decide the house is empty, I take a few deep breaths to try to convince myself that I'm brave enough to venture out. I open my door as quietly as I can and tiptoe down the hallway.

As soon as I get to the living room, my nose is immediately assaulted by the smell of gasoline. My eyes are drawn to the image of my drapes caught on fire. "Oh my God!" I shout as I stumble back against the wall in shock. I'm about to make a bolt for the front door when I notice a pair of boots peeking around the corner of my couch. I hurry over and gasp when I identify one of the intruders.

He's lying splayed out on the ground. His shirt is disheveled and his hair rumpled, but it is unmistakably Alex. I'd know this crazy fool anywhere.

I crouch down next to my brother, who's out cold, and shake his shoulder. "Alex!" I hiss. "Alex, wake up."

But he doesn't budge. *Jesus, where did he come from?* I notice a reddish-purple bruise starting to form on his cheekbone. His lower lip is split, a trickle of blood falling down his chin and onto my living room carpet.

I hear the cracking of wood as the fire engulfs one of my end tables on the other end of the room. I glance over and my pulse picks up speed. Pulling out my phone, I dial Conner's phone number once more, praying he'll pick up. When I'm sent to voicemail this time, I leave a message.

"Conner, it's me. Something's happened. Alex is here, and he won't wake up, and there was another man who beat him up, and now the house is burning, and—"

I break off with a scream at the sound of my curtain rods

breaking in half and crashing to the ground. I drop my phone and turn around. The flames are still licking up and across the wall. I look around quickly and see that my entire living room and the kitchen are glistening in clear liquid. They've covered the place in gasoline and lit it up.

"Alex!" I yell as I shake my brother harder. I can't leave him here, but we need to get out soon. "Alex, you have to wake up!" When he still doesn't move, I swear loudly and get up, running to the bathroom to get something cold and wet. My kitchen is almost entirely engulfed in flames now, the smoke from the living room and the kitchen making it dark and hazy. I have to hurry.

I get two wet washcloths from the drawer, wet them, and run back to my brother's side, wringing the water out over his head. Alex sputters and then sits straight up, looking around. His eyes go wide at the sight of my house on fire, the flames reflecting back in his hazel eyes. He turns to me with horror etched on his face.

"What happened?" His eyes are frazzled.

I give an exasperated sigh. "I don't know, you tell me. All I know is my idiot brother broke into my house—*again*—got knocked out, and now my house is on fire."

"Jo, we have to get out of here."

I can't help it; I roll my eyes. "No shit. Come on." I stand up, covering my face with the second washcloth, and turn to make a run for the front door, but I stop dead in my tracks.

The front hallway is blocked by flames, and whoever was in here moved one of my couches to block the back door. That couch is now a burning, charred disaster, so there's no way we'll be able to move it. My heart breaks a little bit; that couch had been a great find, and now it's destroyed.

"How do we get out?" Alex asks behind me. His voice is muffled from the washcloth that he has covering his mouth. I look around. The entire living space is covered in flames and smoke. It's almost too dark from the black fumes to really see where we are.

I cough and point at the front window. "There!"

Alex steps up and tries to pry the window open with one hand, but it won't budge. "Come on, Alex, you've broken that window before; I'm sure you can figure it out."

My brother turns back to me and glowers. "Now is not the time to be funny, Josie. Get me something to break it with." His voice is muffled from the cloth, but I can hear the fear in his tone.

I manage to find a chair that hasn't burned yet, and I drag it over to my brother, who's crouched down on the floor to get away from the rising smoke. His eyes are bloodshot as they meet mine. I'm starting to feel a little light-headed, but I pull it the rest of the way to him. Alex drops the washcloth covering his face and picks up the chair, smacking it against the window.

Nothing happens.

"Fuck!" I yell. "Why'd he have to get such a good window!"

"Do you have a mallet?"

I glare at my brother. "Do I look like a person who would just have a *mallet* lying around?"

"A hammer, then? Or something?" he pleads with me.

"Yeah, Conner has a bunch of tools in the shed in the back-yard!" I yell at him while pointing toward the sliding door with the flaming couch sitting in front of it.

My brother groans and runs his hands through his hair. "Fuck!"

I huff in frustration, my eyes darting around my living room, trying to find anything that we could use to break this window apart. My eyes fall on a white-painted ceramic flower I bought at a craft fair a few years ago. I hurry over and pick it up, measuring the weight of it in my hands. *This might work.*

"Here, try this!" I instruct Alex and hand the flower over to him.

He looks at it hopefully before lobbing the thing at the window. It bounces off and clatters to the floor. We both look at it dumbly. "I remember hearing something on the news about how you're supposed to aim for the corners," I suggest, leaving out the fact that it was about breaking a windshield on a car. I figure glass is glass, right? "Something about surface tension being less there and easier to break."

Alex shrugs and picks up the decorative piece again, and aims closer to the corner of the window. I wince as he swings his arm back and crashes it against the window. A small ceramic petal breaks off and falls to the floor, and he looks back at me warily, but I'm still looking at the window.

There's a small crack in the glass where he struck it. "Do it again!"

Alex does what I ask, and he hits the window two more times, the crack in the window growing wider with each strike. The heat of the flames surrounds us, getting closer and closer. The washcloth covering my mouth is drying out and not doing as much to filter out the smoke from my lungs. Alex sways on his feet as he gets ready to strike the window again. He gives a grunt as he hits it with all the strength he has in him.

The glass shatters.

My stomach flips with relief, and I take a few steps toward the now broken window. The glass on the floor cuts into the bottoms of my feet, but my adrenaline is pumping so hard at this point that I can barely feel it. Alex is using the ceramic flower to try to knock the remaining glass off of the window frame so we can get out without slicing ourselves too severely.

Through the window, fresh air flows in, kissing my skin. It

dissipates the dark smoke around us only a little, but enough to allow me to breathe easier. I drop the washcloth from my mouth and take big greedy gulps before covering my face again. I meet Alex's eyes, and he motions for me to go through, but I shake my head.

"You go first. You're the one who was passed out only a moment ago; you shouldn't be in here. What if you got hit in the head?"

He glares at me. "I'm the fucking reason your house is on fire, Josie, so please, I couldn't live with myself if anything else happened to you. Get out of here."

I don't fight with him anymore and make my way toward our exit. I can hear fire truck sirens echoing through the crackle and roar of the flames, and I hope with everything in me that they're coming here.

Carefully, I grip the edges of the window. A few pieces of glass jab into the palms of my hands, but I don't have time to worry about it right now. I straddle the lower sill and push myself through, landing unceremoniously on my front porch with a *thump*. I sit there for a moment, trying to catch my breath and fully wrap my head around this reality. The sound of Alex grunting his way through the window shakes me back to the present, and I scramble out of the way so he can get out of the house.

When we're both standing safely on the porch, I whirl on my brother and give him a good shove with both hands. He looks at me and holds up his hands in surrender. "You idiot! What the hell happened?" I scream at him. "Explain yourself!"

Alex looks from me to the house and then back at me again. "Let's get further away, and I will. Or I'll try to. Come on." His arm wraps around my upper back as he leads me down the porch steps, toward the grass.

My whole body is trembling, and I can't stop it. My head is

foggy, as if this is a dream. The finer details of the last thirty or so minutes are hazy. This doesn't feel real. It can't be real. Any moment, I'm going to wake up in my bed, holding onto the beautiful ring that Conner bought me. He'll be sitting right next to me, and I'll tell him I'm sorry, and we'll kiss and make up.

I blink as Alex's arms tighten around me, and a part of my brain is capable of recognizing that this actually might be happening. My trembling intensifies.

The sound of sirens is getting closer now. I turn toward my house and look at it forlornly. Flames are now licking out of the window that we opened and crawling up the siding. At the sight of the burning house, my head spins and my stomach twists. I stumble a few paces back as it hits me.

My house is on fire.

My whole life is burning, and there's nothing I can do about it.

This is *not* a dream.

I hear Alex call my name, but everything around me is spinning too fast for me to answer. This is too much. My brain is about to tap out. My legs give out beneath me, and a pair of strong arms wrap around me, softening my blow to the ground. More shouting and deep voices are surrounding me, but I can't fully understand what they're saying. I'm skirting on the edge of consciousness, not willing to black out completely, but nearly there.

At some point, I manage to open my eyes. I'm met with the flashing red and yellow lights of a fire truck off to one side and a pair of profoundly concerned chocolate brown eyes off to the other.

"Conner?" I mutter. His hand smooths my hair away from my face, and he says something back to me, but I can't understand it. The smoke I inhaled must be affecting my brain in some way.

My body is lifted off the grass, and I'm placed on something soft, and then I'm moving again—rolling, actually. I hear people shouting all around me as an oxygen mask is placed over my mouth and nose. I inhale deeply, allowing the cold oxygen to fill my lungs.

A few minutes of receiving fresh air has me slightly more alert. I can open my eyes and glance around, even though I know that the insignificant action will wear me out. Paramedics are hooking me up to IVs and situating me on the gurney in the ambulance so we can leave.

My eyes dart around rapidly, looking for a familiar face, and suddenly, he's there.

"Shh, it's okay, Josie," Conner says, his hands coming to frame my cheeks and holding my eyes with his. "I'm here; you're safe. Everything's going to be okay."

"My house," I squeak weakly against the oxygen pushing itself into my respiratory system.

Conner shakes his head and leans forward to kiss my forehead. "Everything's going to be okay. Just rest now."

I listen to his instructions and fall back against the gurney, my eyes heavy from all the smoke, and my brain is foggy still. I take deep breaths and try to relax as he said. I tilt my head toward him and capture his gaze again.

"I'm sorry," I whisper.

He gives me a sympathetic smile. "I'm sorry, too."

"Are we okay?"

Conner's hand finds mine, and he tangles our fingers together. I try to smile back at him, but it might be more of a grimace. "We're better than okay, Josie. We're going to be fine."

"Good," I sigh, turning my head back on the pillow and closing my eyes. "I can't lose you again."

"Me, neither, sweetheart," he whispers, squeezing my hand. "Me, neither. Try to rest. We're going to be okay."

I finally let the black edges completely encase my brain, letting my consciousness slip, knowing that Conner's there. The weight of his hand in mine is comforting, grounding. No matter what happens next, we'll face it together. That I know to be true.

Chapter 31

Conner

"CONNER, IT'S ME. SOMETHING'S HAPPENED. ALEX IS HERE, *and he won't wake up, and there was another man who beat him up, and now the house is burning, and—"*

I sigh as I lock my phone. I don't know why I keep listening to that message. It does nothing besides amp up my anxiety and piss me off. The first time I heard it last night nearly had my heart jumping out of my chest.

I had only been down the road, sitting at a park, contemplating a few things—namely, how I wanted to address Josie's wayward proposal. Not even a mile away. But I had thought it would be a good idea to turn off my phone to give myself the room to think, and it nearly cost Josephine her life.

I'm not sure how I'll ever forgive myself for that.

It really is a blessing that I decided to turn my phone back on when I did. I was about to head home when I powered on my phone and saw missed call after missed call. I had just missed Josie's voicemail by a few minutes, and based on the fear in her voice and her scream as she cut off the message, I was able to call 911 right away and get them over to the house.

272

I pulled up right before them, my heart stopping as I saw the red-orange flames taking over our home. Alex was hunched on the grass, knees bent and his face buried in his palms, shoulders rising and falling as he sucked in deep breaths. Josie stood on the grass gazing up at her house burning, and then she started to sway. She began to fall right as I jumped out of the car and ran for her.

The rest of the evening played out in a blur. Josie was in and out of conscious thought. Though her hazel eyes were wide open, she wasn't looking at anything. Just blankness. The paramedics said that Josie inhaled a lot of smoke as she was trying to escape, so her brain would be a little foggy for a while. As soon as the paramedics had Josie and Alex loaded up, we drove off and didn't look back.

Now, I'm sitting at the hospital, just waiting for clearance from her doctors to go see her. We've been here for a few hours, and my butt hurts from sitting in this hard chair for so long, but I can't get myself to move. I don't know where we'll go. I don't know what state the house is in; if it's even still standing. The firefighters were just starting to put out the fire when we left, but I have no doubt that the damage had already been done.

Part of me is curious, but the other part wants to put it off for as long as possible. The thought of seeing our house in ruined ashes makes my stomach churn. And to think that just last night Josie and I were huddled around our table eating cheesecake, and now... I don't even know what I'm going to say to Josie. She loved that old house. It was her refuge when she didn't have any other place to go.

Now it's gone.

We'll be starting from scratch, and I don't know what that's going to look like. It's kind of terrifying. I run my hand over my face as my head spins. I glance up at the clock hanging against the wall: two-thirty. It's been a while since I've heard any sort of update, and I'm getting antsy.

"Conner!" I look up at the sound of a deep voice calling my name urgently. My eyes lock on Ryan and Izabel Miller hurrying down the hallway toward where I'm sitting. Both of them are sporting concerned expressions. I stand up as they get closer and run my sweaty palms down the front of my jeans.

As soon as the ambulance got to the hospital, I sent Ryan a text to let him know what was happening and that Josie wouldn't be at work tomorrow. I'm not surprised that he showed up. That's just the kind of friend he is.

"What happened?" Ryan asks as he offers his hand out to shake mine.

I grip his hand tightly, taking the strength that I know he's silently offering. "There was a fire at the house. I'm not sure how it started or what happened yet. Josie was pretty out of it the last time I saw her, and I haven't had a chance to see her since." I fill him in on the basics because, honestly, that's all I know.

"Oh, Conner, we're so sorry," Izabel says gently as she steps forward to give me a hug. I wrap my arms around her shoulders and hug her back, grateful for the comfort of friends. "Is there anything you need us to do?"

I step away from Izabel and shake my head. "I'm not sure. Everything is so up in the air right now. I don't know how long they're gonna want to keep Jo," I explain and then take a deep breath. "And I have no idea where we're even gonna go after that."

Ryan shares a look with his wife and then tilts his chin down in a nod. "I'll call my mom; they have a guest room that I'm sure they'd be willing to let you stay in."

"Do you want me to go by the house and see how things

are?" Izabel asks me hesitantly. "See if I can get any more information?"

My stomach twists at the thought of our house burned to nothing but ashes. "That might be helpful, as long as you're okay with that." I motion my head toward her barely there belly.

Izabel smiles and pats a hand over her stomach. "I'll make sure to keep a little distance. Hopefully, the first responders will still be there, and I can ask them a few questions."

"Thank you," I breathe, letting some of the weight lift off of my shoulders, then something else occurs to me. I fall back into it heavily and lean my head against the wall. Ryan talks to Izabel for a moment, and then she leaves, going to check on the house. I hear Ryan sit two chairs down from me, giving me enough space but still offering a presence.

"I think it was her stupid brother," I say after a few minutes of contemplation. Ryan mutters something under his breath, and I continue, "I had gotten a text from him earlier tonight that said 'Call me ASAP'. And I just figured it was him being him. So, I let it go."

I open my eyes and turn my head toward the man sitting next to me. This is Josie's best friend, but as I've gotten to know Ryan Miller better, he's turning into my friend just as much as hers. "What if I'm the reason this happened? Maybe if I would've just called him back, none of this would have happened."

Ryan shifts in his chair and turns toward me, his face grave. "This isn't your fault."

"I just—" My voice breaks off, and I inhale, trying to get my composure back. "Jo could've been killed."

"I know," Ryan says quietly, then louder. "But she wasn't. She's safe."

"When I see that little punk, I'm going to bash his face in."

"Oh, her brother is here, too?" Ryan asks, surprised.

"Yeah, he was there with her during the fire," I explain. "I don't know to what capacity, but I know he's involved in this. And he and I are gonna have words."

"Count me in on that," Ryan says, a devilish smirk growing on his face.

I start to ask him if he owns a shovel to bury Alex with, but a nurse steps toward us, holding a tablet in her hands. "Are you here for Josephine DiMarco?"

"I am." I stand up right away, wringing my hands in front of my stomach. Ryan follows my lead, getting to his feet after me.

"The doctors have looked her over, and everything checks out, but we're going to hold her for observation. She's awake now, if you'd like to come back and see her," the nurse tells us.

I can't seem to form any words, but I nod my head. She offers me a kind smile and instructs me to follow her. I turn back to Ryan, but he waves me off. "Go ahead. I'll wait here."

"Thanks, Ryan," I say sincerely before turning and following the nurse back to where Josie's being kept. Neither of us says anything as we walk. The only noise is the hospital phone ringing in the distance and the sound of our shoes hitting the tile floor. My pulse is whooshing in my ears, and I try to keep it cool.

We come to a closed wooden door, and the nurse smiles gently at me. "I'll just give you two a few minutes," she says and leaves me to face the closed door all on my own.

I take a deep breath and turn the handle, stepping into the room. It's dark, the only light coming from the lamp by the hospital bed. Josie's facing away from me, curled up on her side. I can see her shoulders rising and falling as she stares out the window.

When she hears me step in, she turns her head to see who it

is. Recognition crosses her face, and I see her shoulders slump, the tension releasing from her body.

"Hey, Ace," she whispers, and my heart splinters. I stagger into the room and around the edge of her bed until we're face-to-face. My eyes locate a rolling chair, and I move it over to sit by her. Josie offers me her hand, and I take it, gripping her fingers tightly in mine, bringing our fingers up to press my lips to the back of her hand. "You're here."

"Of course, I'm here," I breathe. I bend forward and rest my forehead against hers, relishing in her presence. "I told you I'd never leave you."

She hums in response and closes her eyes. We stay that way for a few minutes, until finally, I pull away and run my hand down her cheek.

"How are you feeling?"

Josie shrugs one of her shoulders. "My throat is scratchy. They say it's because of all the smoke I inhaled. But they checked my airways and told me everything looks okay."

I run my finger over the oxygen line that leads to her nose. Her eyes are a little bloodshot, and her voice sounds hoarse when she speaks, proof that her throat is as scratchy as she said.

"Do you remember what happened?" I ask her hesitantly. "If you feel up to talking about it."

Josie rolls from her side onto her back and grabs the control for the bed. She presses a button that tilts the bed up to an angle, so she's sitting up more. "I don't know how it happened. I was pretty... upset after you left. I fell asleep in our room, holding onto the ring box," she explains, and then her eyes shoot wide open with realization, and she looks at me frantically. "The ring! Conner, your ring was in the house!"

Her pulse monitor starts beeping faster, and she tries to sit up further. I put my hand on her shoulder and carefully press her back down.

"Shhh," I soothe. "It doesn't matter."

"It does matter! You spent all that money on a ring for me, and now it's gone!" Her pulse is still too high for my liking.

I take her hand and press another kiss to the back of it, holding her gaze with mine and hoping she'll calm down. "It's okay. All that matters is that you're safe, you're alive. I can get another ring."

Her pulse drops slightly, though it's still elevated. Her beautiful face pulls into a frown, and she looks off to the side. "You don't have to if you don't want to," she mutters.

"Why wouldn't I want to?"

Josie's hazel eyes flit back and forth, from my eyes to the window, and her frown pulls into something like a sheepish grimace. "Well, I was kind of a jerk last night."

I place my pointer finger underneath her chin and bring her gaze back to mine. When her attention is entirely on me, I smile softly. "Josephine DiMarco, I have wanted to marry you since I first saw you. If you think a little skirmish like that is going to scare me off, you're in for a surprise."

Josie stares into my eyes for a moment before she leans forward and presses her lips to mine. I kiss her back soundly, my hand cupping her cheek. When we're both out of breath, I pull away and tuck a few strands of hair behind her ear.

"Now, tell me the rest of what happened."

Letting out a long exhale, Josie continues on with her account of last night. "I was sleeping, and I heard a loud crash and arguing. I hid out in our room until it quieted down. When I went out into the living room, the place was already in flames, and Alex was knocked out." She raises her eyebrows and then looks at me in alarm. "Where's Alex now?"

I shake my head. "I don't know. There was another ambulance that took him. He's gotta be here somewhere, but I haven't heard."

"I'm gonna kill him," Josie mutters under her breath.

I let out a laugh, and she turns to me with an eyebrow raised. "Get in line, sweetheart. I think Ryan and I are gonna have a go at him first."

"Ryan's here?"

I nod my head. "Of course, he is. He's out in the hallway. Izabel was here earlier, but she went to see if she could find out anything about the house."

"It's so late, though. She should just go home. I don't want anything to happen to her or the baby," Josie pouts, looking out the window again, her lips twisting into a scowl.

"So, you saw Alex passed out in your living room?" I ask her, trying to get her back on track.

She explains to me the rest of what happened. I laugh when she tells me about the broken window that I already replaced once for her, but then we both fall into a melancholy quiet as we realize that our home is probably nothing but ashes at this point.

"What are we going to do?" Josie whispers.

"Well, first things first, you need to get some rest," I say, reaching for the remote to her bed and leaning her down. Josie yawns, driving my point home. "We'll worry about the rest later."

I stay on the edge of her bed and watch as she snuggles underneath the covers. "Don't leave, okay?"

I give her a soft smile and reach for her hand again, entwining our fingers. "Never."

Chapter 32

Josie

"Good morning, Josie," a gentle female voice rouses me from my sleep. I groan and crack open one eye to see who's disturbing me. A short, curly-haired nurse is standing beside my bed, typing on the computer. "I'm just here to check in on how you're feeling."

I groan again and try to sit up, rubbing my eyes. I glance around the room quickly until I find Conner slumped over in the recliner chair in the room. His elbow is propped up on the arm, and his cheek is smushed against his fist. His jaw is slack as he snores—completely undisturbed.

I answer all the nurse's questions, happy to find that my throat isn't as scratchy and my voice stronger than last night. She offers me a menu for breakfast, and I take it gratefully, my stomach rumbling. The nurse exits the room and closes the door just a little too loudly. Conner jolts awake with a snort and looks around frantically, checking for danger.

"Easy there, tiger," I tease.

Conner's brown eyes find mine, and I can see the relief fall across his features. He stands up and stretches his arms above his head, causing the t-shirt he's wearing to ride up across his belly. I watch the movement appreciatively. You won't see me complaining about Conner putting on a show.

"What are you looking at?" he questions, catching me red-handed.

My cheeks flush, and I look away. "Nothing."

Conner barks out a laugh and saunters over to me. "Well, that was rude. It's okay if you want to ogle me. I won't be offended." I roll my eyes at him. "How are you feeling this morning, sweetheart?"

"Kind of like I got stepped on by a hippopotamus," I reply. "Though my throat feels better."

"Can I get you anything?"

I hold up the menu that the nurse gave me. "I could go for some breakfast."

"You could always go for breakfast."

"Well, you're one to talk, Mister I'll-take-a-side-of-pancakes-with-my-pancakes," I tease.

Conner gives me a grin that splits across his whole face. "You are feeling better."

"Yeah, I guess I am," I say with a shrug. "Here, look at this menu and decide what you want."

Conner settles on—*shocker*—pancakes, and I decide to go with an egg white omelet with ham. Our food arrives not too long after we order it, and we eat in silence, watching the TV across from my bed. We've decided to forgo the news channels, knowing that my story might show up. I'm not ready to hear or see anything about my house yet.

The thought of it is harrowing. I know that there won't be much for me to return to once I get discharged from this hospital. My brain is already making checklists of everything we'll need to do: stop by the house, salvage anything we can, call the insurance company, call my parents... the list goes on.

And then the matter of where we're going to live is a whole other topic that is too daunting to dive too deep into.

Both of us look up at a knock on my door an hour or so after we eat breakfast. Conner glances at me, and I nod my head once as he yells for them to come in. The door clicks open and a pair of uniformed police officers step in.

I wring my hands together on my lap as they introduce themselves and ask us a few questions. I do my best to answer them, but when it comes down to it, I know my house was on fire, but I don't know *how* or *why*.

"We'll be going over to talk to your brother after we leave here," one officer tells me, and I nod my head. "Do you have any suspicions that he's behind it?"

Conner grimaces next to me and I purse my lips. "He's definitely involved somehow, but no. I don't think he lit the first match. But if you could rattle him up when you go over there, you won't hear any complaints from me."

The officers share a chuckle and thank us for our time before leaving to go talk to my idiot brother.

"So, who do you think did it?" Conner asks me.

I shrug as I lean back on the bed. "I don't know. That's not really Alex's MO, though. Sure, he's into destroying property— my window, for example, twice now. But it was probably someone who he pissed off and wanted to get back at him, more likely. So, he's definitely behind it, though he might not have been the one to start the fire. What is it?"

Conner's face has pulled into the most severe frown I think I've ever seen on him. "Someone he pissed off? I might know—"

Another knock at my door cuts off what he was about to say, and I turn to him and mouth '*later*' before hollering, "Come in!" The door cracks open to reveal the sheepish face of my best friend. Ryan pokes his head in and grins, looking between the two of us.

"Sorry, I didn't mean to interrupt. I can come back later," he says and starts closing the door again.

"No!" I stop him. "It's fine. You can come in."

Ryan steps into the room and sticks his hands into his jeans pockets. His hair is all messed up, and he has dark circles underneath his eyes. I remember Conner mentioning that Ryan was here early this morning, and I wonder if he got to sleep at all last night.

Conner stands up and leans over to press a kiss on my forehead. "I'll give you two some space. I'm going to go find some coffee."

I look at him gratefully. "Thanks, Ace. I'll take a coffee, too, if you find some!"

Conner winks at me and walks past Ryan, patting his shoulder on the way out. They mutter something to each other, quiet enough that I can't hear. Conner presses his lips together grimly and nods his head before stepping into the hallway.

When he's gone, I shoot my best friend a look. "What was that about?" Ryan walks over and sits in the chair that was just previously occupied by my significant other. He's got a frown on his face, and I can see he's hesitating to tell me. "Oh, come on, just spit it out. I can take it."

Ryan rubs the back of his neck—his tell for when he's nervous. "Izabel just texted me about your house. She stopped by there last night."

My stomach clenches in anticipation. "And?"

"And... it's not good, Josie."

I exhale loudly and fall back against my pillows. "Well, I'm not surprised. The whole place was in flames the last time I saw it."

"I'm sorry," Ryan says, and he means it, I can tell.

My throat thickens with emotion, but I tell myself that I'm not going to cry, so I throw up my best defensive mechanism.

"Well, I guess that's what I get for playing with matches as a little kid."

Ryan stares at me blankly and then says, "Could you not be morbid for like five seconds?"

"Sorry, I just don't know what I'm supposed to say. What do you do when your house, and everything in it, is literally burnt to the ground?" I shake my head, and my eyes start to prick. I'm *not* going to cry in front of Ryan. "All I can do is try to laugh about it."

"Except it's not funny."

"No, it's not funny at all." One little traitorous tear slips out of the corner of my eye, which I know he can see. I ignore it, though, and hope that he does the same.

Ryan's quiet for a moment, and I appreciate the silence. I pick at my fingernails, trying to come up with something to say, but he eventually beats me to it. "I spoke with my mom this morning. She and Derek said they would be happy to let you stay at their house until you and Conner figure out what's next."

"Thank you," I whisper, my chin beginning to tremble. "I mean it, thank you, Ryan. You didn't have to do that."

He offers me a smile and extends his palm toward me. He gives my hand a squeeze when I place it in his. "It's the least I could do. I only wish I could do more."

"I don't know what else there is *to* do," I say with a shrug. "I mean, there's a lot to do, but I don't really even know where to start."

"Maybe start by getting out of here," he teases, and I laugh.

"Yeah, that sounds like a good first step. But after, I'll have to call the insurance, right?"

"Probably. I'm sure there will be an investigation, too. You think it was arson?"

I nod my head. "Oh, definitely. There was gasoline all over

my living room and kitchen. Somebody lit it up on purpose. The cops know, too. There were two officers here just before you came in."

"Yeah, I saw them walking down the hall. Conner said your brother was involved somehow, too. Have you talked to him?"

I frown. "No. That slimy little toad is here somewhere, hopefully being interrogated right now, but I haven't heard from him. If he's smart, he'll jump ship and never come near me again."

Ryan raises his eyebrows at my tone, but I don't care. I can't help but be angry with my brother. Sure, in the thick of it, he helped me get out. I'm not sure if I would've been strong enough to break through that window without him.

But also, let's be honest. If it wasn't for Alex, I'd probably still have a house right now. And I wouldn't be racking up medical bills by the minute.

"Ugh, I don't have time for this," I groan after a beat, covering my face with my hands.

"Everything will work out, one way or another," Ryan says carefully.

"You sound like Conner." I shoot him a look. "I know everything will work out, but I just need to be crabby about it for a while, okay? Conner's just way too optimistic all the time."

"I think you need that balance," he retorts with a laugh. "Just relax and tackle one obstacle at a time. I know you like to be superwoman, but that's not going to work this time around."

I know Ryan's right on point. Conner's optimism *is* the perfect balance for me. I'm nice in my own way, but I can be snarky and sarcastic sometimes. I have a habit of building walls made of steel and hiding behind them when I get scared.

Conner breaks down my walls effortlessly, and he constantly helps me realize I don't need to be scared when he's around. He'll always be there to help me through those tough times. We face things together.

We complete each other in a way I never knew was possible. We've always been compatible, but our relationship now—aside from a few minor 'skirmishes', as he put it last night—is more stable and fulfilling than I could have ever dreamed it to be before.

"You're probably right," I relent to my friend.

"I know I am," Ryan tells me with a smirk on his face. "Now, back to our earlier conundrum. Is there anything I can do for you right now?"

I'm getting somewhat tired of people asking me that, but I know there really isn't much that I can do myself, from this hospital bed. I know I'll appreciate the support system that's shown up for me in the long run.

My mind whirs as I visualize the checklist that I've been forming, trying to narrow down anything that needs to be addressed. There's not much that Ryan can help me with on the home front. But I know he can help take some of the load off at work.

"Do you think you could call a few of my clients and let them know I'll be out for a while? Especially the Jackson Association; I was supposed to be drawing up plans by next week, and they're only half-finished."

"Consider it done."

"You sure you can handle that, Mr. Engineer? I know architecture is *way* below your pay grade," I rib him, bringing up our age-old argument.

Ryan rolls his eyes at me. "I will be an architect for you for however long you need me to, but I won't like a minute of it."

"You never know. I may convert you yet."

He laughs darkly. "Doubtful."

I laugh with him, and some of the tension eases from my shoulders. "Thank you."

"Of course. I'm happy to help. And hey, speaking of drawing up plans, maybe you should take a page out of my book and just rebuild your house, huh? That seems to be what we do around here," Ryan jokes with me, but pauses when he sees my eyebrows pulling together. I sit straight up in my hospital bed as my mind starts to work.

I know he was kidding, but... what if?

Memories of a previous conversation I had with Conner echo in my head. *A big open kitchen with a window above the sink.* I can see the blueprints forming in my mind and walls going up—in a good way. Ryan doesn't utter a word as I work out the details silently in my mind, the pieces coming together far too easily.

When I finally look back at him, my friend has a concerned look etched across his face. Meanwhile, I give him a Cheshire Cat grin and say, "Ryan Miller, you might be a genius, after all. Maybe there is something else you could do for me."

Chapter 33

Conner

"You swear your eyes are closed?"

I chuckle under my breath but bob my head up and down in a yes. "Jo, you put a black bandana over my face, so I can't see anything. But yes, my eyes are closed."

Josephine giggles from the driver's seat, and I smile underneath my bandana. She's been an unstoppable force since the house project has gone underway. It was rough for a while. When she initially got out of the hospital, the first thing she wanted to do was go look at the house. Against my better judgment, I let her.

I'll never forget the image of Josie standing all by herself at the curbside, looking at the charred remains of the home she built. Her arms were wrapped around her middle as if to hold herself together, her face impassive. However, I could see the hurt lingering behind those hazel eyes that give me purpose.

She stood there for a while. I was across the street, leaning against the side of my car, watching her, knowing that there was nothing I could do about this loss.

Then, as if a switch were flipped, Josie spun on her heel

and skipped toward me. She had that gleam in her eye that told me she had a plan, but she wasn't ready to divulge it yet.

Little did I know that she and Ryan would schedule a little dinner to talk about the plans that she had drawn up for our new house a few weeks later. When she told me we would be rebuilding the house exactly how she wanted it, I swear I could have cried. The expression on Josie's face was everything. This was what she did best. She was excited, she had something to work toward, she was ready.

Everything on the logistical side was taken care of. We called the insurance company and made a claim right away about the house. The police concluded that the fire was due to arson, but since neither Josie nor I actually lit the house on fire, we were able to get coverage for the loss. Alex, surprisingly, cooperated with the police and divulged exactly what happened. They determined that Alex wasn't at fault, but they haven't been able to locate who was responsible for lighting the fire. Alex bounced as soon as he was discharged from the hospital, and we haven't heard from him since, which, if you ask me, is perfectly fine. I'm sure he'll come moping about when he's ready, but you won't see me counting down the days.

So, now, here we are, a few months later. Josie, Ryan, and the construction crew have been hard at work, and Josie's bringing me by to see the progress. I've had a strict "no peeking" rule, as Josie wanted this to be a surprise. I'm excited to see how far the project has come.

The first two steps took the longest. Those involved cleaning up the rubble from the fire, sifting through everything to see if any of our belongings could be salvaged. At the same time, Josie was finalizing plans and running them by her partner, then submitting them for permits. After those came through, it was game time.

The car rolls to a stop, and I lean forward in my seat. I actually let her drive the Chevelle, which was a surprise in itself. I can't deny the anticipation that's sitting in my stomach, though.

"Okay, so it might not look like much," Josie prefaces, her voice wary. "There's still a ton of work that needs to be done, but I thought we were at a good point for you to see the progress."

"Can I take this off now?"

"Not yet," she says. I hear her reach to the back seat and grab something before she gets out and comes around to my door, opening it for me. I stand up and reach out with my hand to make sure I don't run into anything. Instead, I find Josie's outstretched hand as she takes mine to lead me. I step carefully as she drags me up through the grass.

Finally, we come to a stop, and Josie situates herself next to me. After a beat, she whispers, "You can take it off."

I do as she says, holding my breath until the bandana is off of my face. I'm hit with an incredible view. There's our house... except, not.

In front of me is the shape of a house, though it's only the frame. I can see straight through the lumber to the backyard. But despite there being no walls or siding, I can see it. I can see the dream that Josie designed in her head and brought to life.

"Wow."

She laughs next to me. "I know. I warned you it wasn't much, but it's something, right?"

"Josie, this is... wow," I say, at a loss for words.

Josie grips the straps of the backpack she's wearing so tightly I can see the whites of her knuckles. She's nervous. "Thanks. When Ryan was rebuilding their cabin, he brought me out to check over everything as soon as the frame was up. I thought it was cool to walk through it and imagine what it would turn into. I thought you might like it, too."

I turn to her and grin. "I do. Can we go inside?"

"I thought you'd never ask. Let's go!"

Josie leads the way toward the framed-out house. As we're walking, Josie's describing what her plans are for the exterior. I examine the place and start to fill in the blanks with what she's telling me.

Dark blue siding, with white trimming and shutters. A warm wooden door to contrast. We'll have a front porch, with white square pillars supporting the dormer above the door. The pillars will have bases made of a dark gray stone that will surround the whole bottom of the house—though she's not sure what kind yet.

We walk through the frame of the front door, and suddenly, we're inside our future home. I look around, seeing where the walls will go and what it will look like.

"I wanted the front living space to be open, so we won't have a hallway here anymore," Josie explains as she walks in. "A lot of the layout is the same as the old house, just more open. As soon as you come in through the front door, you'll see the living room, which will flow nicely into the kitchen.

"Then we'll have double French doors again, leading out to our backyard and patio. Here, I'll show you our room!" She skips off, and I suppress a laugh as I follow her. "I wanted to keep our bedroom on the main floor, with an en suite. I decided against keeping the ranch style and went with a second floor. We'll have a guest room, bathroom, and two office spaces up there for each of us!"

"What's this room going to be?" I ask her, pointing toward another door frame. This room is smaller. I think it's about where her office was before.

Josie comes up to my side and wraps her arm around my waist. "Well, this could be a few things," she says quietly. "We could make it into a library room or storage. Or I was thinking, maybe, a nursery."

I turn my head and look down at her, my expression softening.

"At some point," Josie adds quickly. She fidgets with the ends of her hair. "No rush."

I turn toward her and move my hands to cup her cheeks, tilting her face up to meet my eyes. "I love that idea, Josie. But don't feel like you have to make that happen for me to be happy. I'd be just as happy with it being a library."

We haven't really talked about the baby issue much since everything went down. It's been lingering in the back of my mind, and probably in the back of Josie's, too. The last time we had a conversation about adoption, it ended in a fight and our house getting lit on fire. I hold no grievances with her putting the subject on the back burner for now. There has just been so much going on. And besides, as of right now, we have nowhere to bring the baby home.

"I think it should be a nursery," Josie says with a hint of finality, her hazel eyes challenging me. "Someday."

"Someday," I agree with just as much conviction.

Josie steps up on her tiptoes to push herself further into me. I lean down and press my lips to hers. The kiss doesn't last long enough, but I'm the one to break it off. There will be time for that later.

We hang out in the framework of the house a bit longer. I ask her a few questions about the floor plan, and she answers enthusiastically.

"This is great, Josie. I can't wait to see it when it's finished," I tell her, letting hints of pride into my tone.

"Thank you," she responds, shuffling her feet. Then she perks up. "I actually have another little surprise planned."

"What is it?"

"Well, it wouldn't be a surprise if I told you. Follow me," she chirps, grabbing my hand and leading me out through what will be double French doors someday, opening into the back-yard. The grass near the house is torn up from the construction, but Josie leads me all the way back to the edge of the property line. She finds a good patch of grass and then drops my hand.

Josie shrugs the backpack off of her shoulders, pulling out a blanket and rolling it out on the grass. As soon as it's smoothed out, she sits down and starts digging in the bag again. I sit next to her, crossing my legs underneath me, as I watch for what she's going to pull out next.

Out of the bag, Josie produces a bottle of champagne and two stemless glasses, along with a tray of cheese and sausage slices and crackers. Then she pulls out some fruit to go along with it and a two-slice package of cheesecake. When I raise an amused eyebrow at her, she smirks.

"I just thought it would be a good time to have a little cele-bration," she explains as she pops open the champagne bottle and pours each of us a glass. After she hands me mine, she holds her glass in a toast. "To new beginnings, and to all the exciting new memories we'll get to make together."

"Here, here," I toast back, clinking my glass against hers. We both take a sip, smiling at each other over the rims of the glasses.

We dig into the snacks and drink our champagne as the sun sets below the horizon. Josie tells me about all of her plans in more detail: what kind of furniture she's going to get and what paint colors she's deciding between. She asks me my opinion, but I'm happy to defer to whatever she wants. This is her dream.

And she's my dream.

I'm happy to let her go wild with this project. It gives her something to put all of her energy toward.

We're lying on the blanket on our backs, looking up at the stars. It's crazy for me to think back just a few months, when we were doing this exact same thing together. But now, Josie's in much better spirits, and I believe we're staring down a new path with our relationship. The two of us have come so far from when we first started down this road together. We're both more open and trusting toward each other, free from the demons of the past. I'm not sure what our immediate future holds, but I know whatever it is will be a new adventure for each of us.

Whether that's going to be focusing on careers or working on starting a family is unknown. But either way, we'll do it together.

"What are you thinking about?" Josie asks me after a while.

I tilt my head toward her and grin. "You," I pause. "And me, I guess. Us."

"Good things, I hope."

"Of course," I say, letting out a happy sigh. "Mostly just what comes next."

"What do you want to come next?" she asks me hesitantly.

I'm quiet for a moment as I mull over her question. Finally, I roll to my side to face her, and she does the same, following my lead. Once we're face-to-face, I reach my hand out, tucking some of her wavy hair behind her ear.

"I want everything that you want," I say finally, unable to come up with a better answer. I suspect we're on the same page, though neither of us has outright said it.

What comes next? Our home, a ring, a wedding, a baby...

"You're so cliché," Josie teases me with a laugh. I grin back at her and take her hand, holding it between us.

"I don't want to jinx it."

"You won't jinx it. I think it's time that the universe cuts us some slack. We've been through it all at this point. Nothing else could phase me. So, Ace. I'll ask again. What comes next?"

I move, pushing her shoulder, so she's on her back again,

and I hover over her. I let my weight press into her slightly. Josie's face is glowing, looking up at me, and my heart explodes.

"What comes next is that I take you back to our hotel, and I kiss you silly," I whisper, leaning down and brushing my nose against her.

Josie wiggles beneath me. "Just kissing?"

I smirk devilishly. "Among other things."

"I like the sound of that."

"I'll kiss you and love you all night, then tomorrow, we'll start all over."

"Then what?" she asks breathlessly.

I take the plunge. "Then you go back to work, building our perfect house. Then we'll move in and make it a home." I bend my head, capturing her lips. I kiss her deeply before pulling back and pressing our foreheads together. "Then I'll ask you to marry me, for real."

"And I won't ruin it this time," she teases me.

"And you'll say yes. And we'll have a wedding, with the people we love most surrounding us and supporting us." I laugh under my breath.

"And then?"

"And then, we'll focus on building our family," I tell her quietly, holding her gaze steadily in mine. "If that's what you want."

Josie nods her head. "It's what I want."

"Me, too. I want it all with you, Jo. And now, I think we can finally have it."

From beneath me, Josie beams again, a smile spreading across her whole face. "Well, it's about damn time."

Chapter 34

Josie

"Okay, you can tackle the kitchen and unpack all those pots and pans. I'll work on getting the living room sorted out," I instruct Conner. He salutes me like a good soldier and sets to work.

This weekend has been a process of getting situated in the new house. We "officially" moved in on Friday. Still, since then, we've had an assortment of furniture deliveries. It's like playing a never-ending game of Tetris, as we try to maneuver around all the boxes of our new things.

Conner and I were grateful to have Ryan's mom and step-dad put us up in their home for the first few weeks after the fire. Since then, we have been living in an extended stay hotel. All the while, collecting artwork and decorations, along with any new clothes we wanted and furniture for the new house. Because we couldn't fit it all in the hotel, we got a storage unit and just stashed stuff in there until we were ready for it.

And now, we're paying for it.

I plop myself on the new living room hardwood floor and stare at the boxes and boxes of books that I now have to organize into the built-ins on either side of our fireplace. Conner and I went a little crazy at a used book sale a while back.

Right as I'm about to get started, I hear the doorbell ring. I look back at Conner, who has his hands full of pans, and I chuckle. "Don't worry, I'll get it. It's probably another Amazon delivery."

I clamber to my feet and get to the door, plastering on a big smile as I throw it open. The smile quickly diminishes when I register who is *actually* standing on my porch.

"What are you doing here, Alex?" I growl at the sight of my brother at the front door. "As you can see, we're a little busy."

My brother looks off to the side sheepishly and sticks his hands in his pockets. "Uh, sorry. I was wondering if we could talk."

"Who is it?" I hear a deep voice call from back inside the house. Then a loud clatter of dishes crashes to the ground. "I'm okay!"

I roll my eyes and then holler back, "It's Alex!"

I get silence in response, and then footsteps, as Conner comes to stand behind me. A happy warmth settles in my belly at the realization that he'd drop everything to make sure I'm okay. "What are you doing here?" Conner asks in a low, menacing tone.

"We need to talk."

"Only took you months to show up," I say to him. I lean my head out the door and make an exaggerated motion of looking up and down the street. "Is my new house going to get burned down again?"

Alex has the decency to look chagrined, and it helps relieve some of the tension balling up in my chest. He puffs out his cheeks and exhales loudly. "No, sorry about that."

I cross my arms over my chest and frown at my brother.

"You make it sound like a minor inconvenience. This isn't like those fights we had as kids. You destroyed my home."

"I know," he mutters as he looks at the new concrete of my porch. "To be fair, it wasn't actually me. Though, you can blame me, and that's fine."

"Right, that's what the cops said you said, but you couldn't give any names. So, are you here to tell the truth?" Conner prods him.

"Uh, I guess. Could we not do it out here, though?" Alex asks sheepishly.

I look at Conner at the same time that he looks down at me, and I raise an eyebrow, silently asking him what he thinks. He shrugs a shoulder and then turns and heads back toward the kitchen, where he's unpacking his assignment of boxes.

"You can come in," I grouse, pushing the front door open slightly so Alex can follow me inside. I hear his hesitant foot-steps behind me as he follows me into the living room.

A low whistle sounds from where Alex is standing behind me. I turn around to see him looking all around the new house. "Wow, this is amazing, Jo."

I fight to keep the scowl off my face. "No thanks to you."

"I suppose I deserved that."

"You, for sure, did. Now talk," I instruct, walking over and flopping onto my new fluffy couch. Conner sets a box down on the kitchen counter for later and saunters over to where we are, taking a seat next to me in solidarity. He drapes his arm across the back of the couch behind my shoulders and looks expec-tantly toward my brother.

Alex stands by the mantle of my fireplace, running his fingers over the distressed wood. Then he looks pointedly at Conner. "You remember I told you that things weren't handled last time I saw you?"

I look at Conner in question and see the exact moment his expression hardens. "And?"

"This was the fallout from that situation."

"You're saying our home got burned down because you couldn't pay back your debt to—what was his name—Jackson?"

"Jordy," Alex says with a grimace. "And yeah, more or less."

I raise my hands, and the two men look at me. "Hold on, I'm lost. Somebody fill me in on what's happening here."

Conner lets his head fall back against the couch and lets out a loud sigh. "You told me we weren't in danger."

What the fuck, I wonder as I narrow my eyes at my boyfriend. He clearly knew more about this than he was letting on. He and I might have to have our own little showdown after this one is done. I mentally gear up for battle.

"First of all," Alex says, holding a finger up, "no, I didn't. Second of all, I said that I *didn't want* anything bad to happen, which is why I left."

"So, you didn't go to a rehab facility across the country?" I accuse, finally somewhat catching up.

Alex looks at me with guilty eyes. "No. I left because Jordy's guys were onto my being here, and I knew that they would stop at nothing to ensure that their debt was paid."

My ears start to ring, and my head spins. "So, if you left, then why did they still burn my house down?"

"That's where it gets a little hairy," Alex mutters.

"A little?" I scoff.

"He knew I was staying with you. I got a threatening message from some of his guys, implying that they were going to start coming after people I care about if they didn't get anything from me soon."

"You ran away?" I ask him incredulously. "Why didn't you go to the police?"

"He's not the type of guy you go to the police to tattle on,"

Alex replies, seeming to be purposefully evasive. "Anyway, I thought they would have followed me away, and they did. I had been keeping track of the two guys on my tail for pretty much the entire time that I was on the run. Until about a week before everything went down, I noticed that they weren't around as much.

"I started trying to tail *them*. I knew that Jordy wouldn't just let me get away without paying him back in one way or another, so I started getting suspicious. That day I sent you the text was the day that I figured out they were coming for you to smoke me out," he says to Conner.

I look at Conner again, in shock. He's got a thunderous expression on his face, but Alex continues, "I hopped on a plane as soon as I could to get here, and I ran into Jordy's guys right outside. It was late, everything in the house was dark, and I didn't see Conner's car in the driveway. Unfortunately, right as I rolled up, Jordy's guys did, too. We argued out in the front yard. One guy threw a punch, I threw one back, then they went for the house.

"I tried to stop them. I swear I did, Josie. But they broke the door in and started spilling gasoline everywhere, telling me that this was how Jordy expected to be paid back. I tried to tackle one guy, but he threw me off and started punching me over and over. Then, next thing I knew, you were trying to wake me up, and the place was on fire.

"I swear that's the truth. All of it," Alex says, letting out a big breath and his shoulders slumping.

I watch him closely as he tells his story, looking for any hint of a lie or something to not add up with my own experience. But as far as I can tell, it was all right on track with my memories of that night.

"I believe you," I say finally, after a bout of silence. If possible, Alex hunches in on himself even more.

"I'm so sorry, Josie. Really. I never intended for any of this to happen to you. You weren't supposed to be involved."

"Alex, I was involved from the first moment you came and asked for money. I sealed my fate when I gave it to you." I laugh humorlessly.

Conner's arm tightens around my shoulders, and I shrug him off. He and I will sort everything else out later. But for now, I need to take care of my brother, who's breaking in half right in front of me.

"But I forgive you. It sounds like you at least made an attempt to keep this from happening. Though, I don't think really anyone could've done anything." Alex shakes his head *no* in agreement. "What's done is done. We got the money we needed from the insurance claim, and we've rebuilt. It's time to move on."

"I can't tell you how glad I am to hear that. It means a lot to me, Jo, really," Alex tells me sincerely.

I hold my stern expression on my face. "I forgive you, Alex. But that doesn't mean that I will forget. You don't get a free pass on this one. It might take time for things to really go back to what they were, but I promise I'll try if you do."

My brother nods his head. "That sounds like a deal."

"Good. Same with me. Conner?" I ask, looking over to Conner, who's watching the whole scene unfold warily.

"As long as you're happy, I'm happy," he says deadpan.

"Great," I turn back to my brother. "Do we need to hug it out now?"

Alex lets out an uncomfortable laugh, recalling how our mother used to do this when we would fight as little kids. "If you insist."

I get up off the couch and go over to my brother, wrapping my arms around him in a hug. We stay there, holding each other, before breaking apart and smiling awkwardly at each other. Alex looks around at all of our boxes and sighs.

"Well, I guess I'll get out of your hair. It looks like you two have a lot to do yet."

We say our goodbyes, both accepting the fact that we don't know when we'll see each other again, then Conner and I set back to work trying to get our house in functional order. There's so much to do and so little time. I turn on some music on a Bluetooth speaker, and we spend the rest of the day arm-deep in boxes, unpacking and organizing.

The whole time, my mind is reeling with everything I learned today. I've decided that, no, I don't think I blame my brother for this. I mean, of course, the fact that everything could have been avoided stings like a slap to the face, but here we are. Alex made his own decisions, and I suffered the conse-quences, but it's over now. There's nothing else to be said on the matter, as far as I'm concerned.

Ryan and Izabel stop by in the evening and bring us a few boxes of pizza, so we take a break and chat with them. Izabel's new baby is due any day now, so our get-together tonight is equal parts celebration for a new Miller as it is a celebration for our new house.

By the time we say goodbye and clean up, I'm beat. Today has been stacked to the brim, one thing after the other. And much to my chagrin, it seems like there's still one more conver-sation that needs to be had.

"You forgave him too easily," Conner mutters as we're getting ready for bed. He takes his shirt off and tosses it into the hamper.

"That's not for you to decide. And what else was I supposed to do?" I counter. "The police believed his story, so why wouldn't I?"

"Because he's the reason our house got burned down. Him and all his bullshit."

I glare at Conner. "You could argue that he's also the reason we have this new, beautiful home."

"Doesn't change anything for me."

"Well, then you're going to have to figure that out on your own. I'm not going to waste any more time or energy on him." I pause, pulling my own clothes off and stepping into my night-gown. "But also, I think you have your own groveling to do. What was that shit with you knowing about the trouble that Alex was in and not telling me?"

Conner stares at me incredulously. He looks ridiculous, standing there in only his dark forest green boxers and a stupid expression on his face. "What else was I supposed to do? He told me not to tell you."

"So, you kept the truth from me, and look what happened! I thought we were a team!" I shoot back, and then sigh as I rub my hand over my face. "Look, nothing about this situation is ideal. Everyone made mistakes. I gave Alex money when I shouldn't have, you kept secrets, and Alex got us into this mess in the first place.

"But it's over. We have our house and our future to look forward to, and we can't do that if we hold grudges or keep looking back. Do you understand?"

Conner grumbles as he crawls into bed beside me and snuggles under the covers. "Yes. I'm sorry."

"Good, then case closed," I say with finality.

Conner sighs heavily. A moment later, his arms snake around my hips as he pulls me to him. "How did you get to be so forgiving and good? You're an amazing woman, Josie."

"It's a gift," I tease him, mumbling into his chest. "I've learned from the people around me: you, Ryan, Izabel. That's part of life, isn't it? Always growing, always working on bettering ourselves."

"You're right," Conner relents.

"I know I am," I say back with a cheeky grin, even though he can't see it. Conner's arms hug me tighter to him, and I snuggle in against his chest.

Today was stressful, but my shoulders are lighter than they have in months, knowing that we finally put this issue to rest. Alex's and my relationship will likely never recover to what it was, but that's okay. All that is important is that I know he tried to do what was best and that I forgive him for his mistakes. All the rest is history. Nowhere to go but forward now.

Things in my life are finally coming together in the exact way that I always dreamed they would. I have the house, the guy, the friends. Only a few things are missing, but I know they'll come with time. There's no rush to happiness, but in every aspect, I'm already there.

Chapter 35

Conner

O_{NE YEAR LATER}

"Why can I *never* find my other boot?!" I hear Josie scream from the bedroom. I can't help but chuckle. I'm sitting on the two-seat swing that hangs from the roof of our porch, playing on my phone while I wait for her. The window to our bedroom is open, letting the house air out, while the day is slightly warmer. Josie continues to grumble as she gets ready for our date today.

Winter is just ending here in Tennessee, so for Josie, it's still 'boot season.' Though we've had a few warmer days–today being one of them–winter hasn't fully turned into spring. Time this year has flown by at rapid speed with everything going on. I never knew that building a house would take so long *or* be so involved, but Josie handled it like a champ. She made everything look easy, from getting the approved permits to managing all the construction and contractors.

And now, after we've moved in and had a chance to live in it, it's everything we could've dreamed.

We weren't able to salvage much from the fire, maybe a few items here or there, but nothing of significance—that *Josie's* aware of, at least.

The little black box presses against the pocket of my jeans, and I smile to myself. She has no idea that I discovered the ring while sifting through rubble and managed to rescue it.

She also has no idea that today is going to be more than a date. I've been planning this for weeks now. We're finally in the right place together to take the next step. We've been taking it slowly ever since the fire, which has worked out for both of us. We've had the chance to get more comfortable with ourselves and build a strong foundation for our family, whenever that happens.

It's crazy to think that all it took was one night for everything to start again, almost two years ago. And now, I'm getting ready to propose to her. This second wind of our relationship might not have been as long as some prefer, but I've always known that Josie and I were meant to be. There's no point in wasting time. I thought I lost her once, and now that I know she's still here, I'm never letting go.

I've decided to propose to her in a more private setting tonight. Though I know Josie usually loves to have all her friends around, tonight is for us. I want this moment to be intimate and memorable. I plan to take her to one of the fancier restaurants in town for a delicious dinner and then go on a walk together at one of the parks here in Cedar Ridge. That's where I'll ask her.

Josie finally emerges from the house and saunters across the porch to where I'm waiting for her. I stand as she gets closer and give her a good once over, appreciating the way her jeans flatter her gorgeous curves.

"You look beautiful," I tell her, loving the way her cheeks flush.

"Thank you," she says, playing with the hem of her shirt. It's a pretty lavender and made of soft material. "Are you ready to go?"

"More than you know," I tell her, sticking my hands in my pockets.

We walk down the front steps together and get into the car. She asks a few questions about where we're headed, but I don't give anything away. I want it all to be a surprise.

The restaurant is fancy enough that it has valet parking. Once I pull up in front of the entrance, I hurry around to open the door for Josie. She beams at me, taking my outstretched hand to help her out.

As I start to close the car door behind her, I hear a sudden ripping noise, and Josie lets out a gasp, turning to look at the side of her sweater that got caught on the edge of the car door. It now has a decent rip in the seam.

"Oh shit, I'm so sorry," I say quickly, moving my hand to cover up the hole. Thankfully Josie's wearing another layer, something white, underneath it, so she's not exposed.

In typical Josie fashion, she gives a shrug and grins at me, completely unbothered, and swats my hand away. "Oh, it's fine. This is an old sweater, anyway."

I frown slightly and ask, "Do you want to stop somewhere and get a new shirt?" I want tonight to be perfect for her.

"Nope," she replies, popping the *p*. "I'm ready to eat!"

I force a chuckle under my breath, trying to calm my nerves, and motion with my hand toward the front door of the restaurant, "After you, my dear."

"Wow, this place is swanky," she says softly once we enter the building. "I don't think I've ever eaten here."

"There's a first time for everything," I say, puffing my chest out slightly, proud of myself for doing something special for her tonight. I stroll up to the hostess and say, "A table for two, please."

I'm met back with a distressed expression. "Oh, I'm sorry, we're completely booked for tonight."

I deflate as if I was a balloon poked with a sharp pin.

"Are you sure there's not a table open somewhere?" I plead. I look over my shoulder at Josie, who's a few paces behind me, her hands clasped together. I turn back to the hostess and whisper urgently, though not loud enough that Josie will hear, "Tonight's *kind of* important."

"I'm sorry, sir, there's nothing open right now, and we're booked for the rest of the evening. I can make you a reservation for tomorrow night," the girl says to me. I can tell she feels terrible, but there's nothing more she can do to help. This is what I get for not making a reservation. I went back and forth on the matter and decided that we could swing it. I should've known better.

I sigh and decline, heading back to where Josie's waiting patiently. She looks at me with an eyebrow raised and a smirk. "No luck?" I shake my head, and she shrugs at me. "That's okay. I'm more in the mood for a good greasy burger than a fancy piece of lobster. How about Burger Shack?"

So, that's how we end up with a sack of greasy burgers to go, sitting in the Chevelle at the park. Josie wolfs hers down, groaning as she takes the first bite.

"Oh my gosh, this is so good."

I watch her in amusement as I eat my own food. I love that she enjoys the small delights in life. It makes the experience so much more fulfilling. When we're finished, we toss our trash away and head toward one of the trails.

"Let's play a game," I prompt once we've started walking. The sky has begun to darken slightly, and I frown to myself, praying that the weather will hold out for the remainder of our date.

Josie, oblivious to the quickly shifting weather and my equally shifting mood, turns her head and looks at me, a soft smile on her face. "What kind of game?"

I pretend to think about it, even though I've been planning this for a week. "Remember that game we played at the beer festival? Kiss or Dare?"

Josie throws her head back in a laugh and nods her head. "Yes, I do. Sure, Ace. Let's play Kiss or Dare."

"We should probably walk around a little bit. It might be easier to play that way than sitting," I say casually.

Our boots crunch against twigs as we shuffle along the path. Finally, Josie breaks the silence. "Okay, let's play this game, then. Truth or dare?"

I raise an eyebrow at her, amused. "It's *kiss* or dare. And kiss, definitely kiss."

Josie laughs at her mistake and smiles at me, stopping in her stride to press her lips to mine. She has to stand up on her tiptoes, but she manages. My hands rest against her waist as I kiss her deeply.

When we pull apart, her cheeks are flushed, and I know it's not from the breeze that's picked up. "Now you're making me not want to pick dare at all," she teases me, sounding slightly breathless.

I laugh and grab her hand again, entwining our fingers together as I lead us down the trail again. "Don't be a spoilsport."

"Fine," Josie grumbles good-naturedly. "Dare."

I dare Josie to attach herself to one of the trees by the path until someone notices her and asks what she's doing, then she has to respond, deadpan, with, "We are having a moment!"

Josie, never backing away from a challenge, does just that.

It ends with a very puzzled-looking older couple who just shrug our antics off as, "Oh, kids these days."

The game goes back and forth for a little while until we're laughing so hard our stomachs hurt. Between each kiss or dare, I double-check the dark clouds, growing ever closer. If I'm going to do this, I need to do it soon.

Josie's last dare was for me to ask another person walking on the trail for directions. After the person directed me which way to go, I politely thanked them and then turned and walked in the opposite direction. Then, when they called me out on it, I had to make a big show of acting embarrassed and redirect myself in the way they instructed.

I managed to complete it, and it took us a solid few minutes to come down from laughing so hard. The poor guy I chose as my victim was so shocked and confused that I nearly broke character during the dare. It was top-notch. Josie's always so creative.

Now she's looking at me expectantly for her next task. "Okay, Ace, your turn. Ask me."

I clench my jaw and wrap my hand around the ring box in my pocket. There's no way that any dare I could come up with would top that tree one, so it's gotta be now or never. "Kiss or dare, Jo?"

Josie pretends to think about it, tapping a finger against her chin. "Hmm, dare!"

My hand tightens against the box, and I start to pull it out. "Josie... I dare you to say—"

My words are cut off by a bright flash of light and an enormous crack of thunder simultaneously. Then, the sky opens up in a downpour.

Josie squeals and covers her head with her hands as she takes off down the trail, calling for me, "Come on! We gotta get back to the car!"

I let my head drop toward the sky, letting out an annoyed groan. *Of course.* The rain hits my face, and I take a few deep breaths before heading down the path after Josie. We run the rest of the way to the car, and I'm grateful that I at least made one good decision today in picking the shorter trail.

We both hop in the car. I pause for a moment before starting the car, considering asking her now, before I lose my nerve. I decide against it, quickly coming up with a more romantic approach for when we get home. I fire up the engine and take off toward home, leaving the park and my unsaid words behind us.

"I gotta admit, that was the most fun I've had in a while," Josie says half an hour later as she opens the bathroom door. I hear her footsteps on the carpet as she steps out, but she halts suddenly when she takes in my position. I'm sitting on the edge of the bed, head buried in my hands. "Ace, what's wrong?"

I scrub my face with the palm of my hands and then look up at her. Josie's watching me with wide, worried eyes, a towel scrunched around her wet hair. "Nothing went how I planned it today."

She's quiet for a moment, and then the bed dips next to me. "What do you mean?"

I laugh humorlessly and look at her. "I wanted to take you to a nice dinner, and they were all full. Then, with the rain." I shake my head. "Tonight was supposed to be perfect. You deserve that."

"Conner, what are you talking about? Tonight was perfect." With a sigh, I reach into my pocket and pull out the ring box. Josie's eyebrows shoot up on her forehead as she stares at it. "Is that...?

"Yes," I respond. Josie finally tears her eyes away from the box and looks at me. My heart skips a beat when I see they're glistening with unshed tears. Usually, that would worry me, but she also has a smile on her face.

"Is this what your dare was going to be?" she asks me, and I nod my head sheepishly. "Oh."

I hear her drop the towel onto the ground, and in a few quick steps, Josie's standing in front of me, her hands on her hips. Her hair is soaking wet and slightly tangled from the rain, but her cheeks are flushed and eyes are bright. I've never seen her looking so beautiful.

"Ask me," she says firmly.

I stare at her a moment before slowly standing from my position on the edge of the bed until we're face-to-face. I look down at her and ask her softly, "Kiss or dare?"

"Dare," Josie whispers back, a hint of anticipation in her tone.

Holding her eyes with mine, I lunge backward onto one knee. I grip the ring box and crack it open to reveal the ring inside—the very ring that I picked out just for her. I had managed to find it in all the rubble and chaos of cleaning up the burnt-down house, and I've been holding onto it ever since, waiting for the perfect moment to drop the question that's lingered on the tip of my tongue for months.

"Josie DiMarco," I begin, and then clear my throat when it cracks. "We've waited for this moment for what seems like our whole lives. You're my dream come true, and there's nothing more that I want than to call you my wife." My throat thickens as I hold her gaze. "I dare you to say yes."

Josie's lips turn up into a smile, and she falls to her knees in front of me. Both of her hands rise to cup my face, and she presses her lips to mine just once. "Yes," she answers, lingering above my lips. When she pulls away, I see a single tear slipping down her cheek. By the way her eyes are twinkling at me, I know it's a joyful tear.

"God, I thought you'd never ask," she says a little louder. "It would mean the world to me to call myself your wife, Conner Reynolds."

I grin back at her, my cheeks straining with the intensity with which I'm beaming at her. I move my head around and look down at the ring sitting in its box. I pluck it out of the velvet and grab Josie's left hand, slipping the sparkling diamond onto her ring finger.

Josie raises her hand up to inspect it. "This is perfect, Conner."

I brush a few strands of her hair behind her ear. "I'm glad you like it. This ring started out as a dream doodled over algebra equations, was strong enough to withstand a fire, and I think it finally found its home on your hand.

Her hazel eyes grow wide at my words. "You mean this is the *same* ring? How in the world did you find it?"

"Persistence," I say with a smirk. "It took a few hours, but you're worth it. I got this ring specifically for you, and I wanted you to have it."

"Ace, you're too much, really. Thank you," she says, tossing her arms around my neck and pulling me in for a big hug.

My own arms snake around her waist, and as I stand up, I hoist her along with me, spinning her around in a circle, my heart singing at the sounds of her laughter. When I set her on her feet, I lean down to kiss her again.

When I pull away, I have to laugh to myself, shaking my head as I gaze down at the woman I'm so horribly in love with. "Is this even real? When we were in middle school, I would practice asking you out in my bedroom mirror. And now, you've agreed to be my wife, in our bedroom, in our home that we get to create a life together in."

She gives me a wide grin, slowly nodding her head up and down. "And you're going to be my husband."

"I must be living in a dream."

"Maybe it is a dream," Josie asks, her voice taking on a content tone. "I think it's about time we had something good happen to us, don't you?"

"Definitely. And we have a whole lifetime of dreaming ahead of us."

"We'll do it together," she agrees, her eyes brightening. "Finally."

Epilogue

Josie

Two Years Later

"Josie!" The sound of my husband's deep voice echoes throughout the house as he barges in from the backyard.

"I'm in the kitchen!" I holler back, my hands sliding over the dishes as I try to wash out the remaining marinara sauce from the white ceramic. Spaghetti night is always my least favorite clean-up. I hear his footsteps, heavy on the wooden floors.

I look up just in time to see Conner bent over the kitchen counter. His face is flushed, and his breathing erratic. I turn to face him, my eyebrows furrowing in concern. The fact that my hands are soapy doesn't cross my mind as I walk toward him.

"What's wrong?" I ask, bracing myself for the bad news.

Instead, I'm met with his eyes lighting up and a crooked smile taking over his features. "It's time."

My heart suddenly drops into my stomach, and my jaw falls open. "It's time. Like *time*, time?"

Conner nods his head up and down, his smile growing with every passing second. It takes me a moment to get into action, but then I'm moving. My brain is running a hundred miles per hour, trying to think of everything I need to grab and who I need to call. I'm babbling sentences that don't even make sense. And finally, Conner rests his hands on my shoulders, turning me to face him.

"Jo, breathe. Everything's going to be okay. We're ready for this."

"You really think so? Things are about to change and really change. Like never-go-back change," I chatter.

"Look at me," he instructs, and I do. My gaze searches his face, and I find a sense of clarity when I look into his warm chocolate eyes. "Breathe."

I take a few deep breaths, in through my nose and out through my mouth, as he tells me to.

"Good. We've been planning for this for months. Everything's ready. All we have to do is go."

"You're right," I say on the exhale, my shoulders dropping slightly as the tension leaves them. Now that I have more oxygen in my brain, I can wrap my head around what's happening.

My face splits into a smile, and my heart takes off in a sprint. "We're gonna get our baby?"

Conner nods his head, his face mimicking my smile. "We are. Are you ready?"

I can't find the words, but I nod my head enthusiastically. Every nerve ending in my body buzzes in rapid-fire. I'm tingly and bubbly, like I could float away at any moment. I'm grateful for Conner's strong hand in mine as he leads me out to the car, grabbing my purse for me on the way out.

I'm jittery the whole ride to the hospital. We've both been

waiting for tonight for months, and now that it's happening, I can hardly believe it.

A year and a half ago, Conner and I finally decided we were in a stable enough place in our marriage to begin the adoption process. It took a long time, but eventually, we were selected by a birth mother after what felt like denial after denial.

Our baby's birth mother is so sweet. We met her when she was four months pregnant. Lauren just found herself in a situation where she couldn't take care of a baby at this time in her life, but wanted to give it the best chance she could. She explained that when she saw Conner and my application, she just knew we were supposed to be the baby's parents.

And now, five—or so—months later, we're finally going to meet our baby!

As we drive, I send a quick text to Ryan and Izabel about what's happening. I'm grateful that it's a weekend and that I've been lightening my workload at the firm, preparing for the maternity leave I get to take.

Though I'm not actually *birthing* my baby, like most mothers, I'm still determined to do whatever I can to bond with my baby in the first few weeks of their life. Conner's been able to take off a few weeks, as well, so he'll take a week off right from the start and then stagger his remaining time for when I have to get back to work.

Our nursery is all organized and ready to go. Izabel threw me a baby shower a few weeks ago with the theme "The Best Things in Life Are Worth Waiting For!" It was the perfect day, where all my closest friends and family could come out and celebrate with us. My parents showed up, as did Conner's parents. Alex even made an appearance to drop off a small gift.

Though my relationship with my brother has still been tense, we're getting along. He keeps to himself a lot these days, popping in every once in a while to visit. From what he's told me, he's made a solid effort to clean up his act. He's gotten a job down in Atlanta, and a new apartment that is in a better area. That's really all I can hope for him—that he's getting along in the best way that he can.

When we make it to the hospital, we're directed up toward Lauren's room. When we step inside, her brown eyes find us and go wide with relief. "I'm so glad you guys are here!" she says. I can see a sheen of sweat coating her forehead.

"How are you?" I ask her, hurrying over to her side and taking her hand. "Is there anything I can get you?"

Lauren rests her head against the pillow and shakes her head. I look to the nurse standing on the other side of the bed for clues, and she fills me in. "Contractions are getting closer together and more intense. She might like some ice chips to cool her down in between."

Conner runs off to get the ice chips.

It takes another few hours, but soon enough, our baby is born. We're standing in the room behind the privacy curtain when I hear his beautiful cry, and tears prick at my eyes. Conner grips my hand tightly, his eyes finding mine. I can see them glistening, too.

The following minutes pass slowly. But finally, the curtain is pulled open. First, my eyes go to Lauren, who's leaning against the pillows, her face flushed, but wearing a content expression. She looks back at me and smiles.

One of the nurses steps toward me, holding the swaddled baby in her arms. "Congratulations, Mama. It's a boy!"

"How—How does he look?" Lauren asks me once the nurse passes off the baby to me. She opted not to hold him first, which I respect, though she wanted to be with us when we met him.

I wrap my hands around the tiny human resting in my arms and hold him close to me. His pink face is all scrunched up, agitated from the process of being born and the bright lights and loud noises all around him.

Conner's standing just off to my side, his arms wrapping gently around my waist. His warm eyes look at our new son lovingly. "He's perfect," I tell Lauren. "Thank you so, so much. You did so well."

Lauren watches us with her baby for a few quiet moments and then says softly, "I knew I made the right choice. I always imagined this baby's parents looking at him the way you're looking at him now."

At her words, the tears that I've been managing to keep at bay slip out of my eyes. "I've dreamed of you, Greyson Reynolds," I whisper to the baby, who's now settled down in my arms. He blinks his eyes a few times at the sound of my voice, but then shuts them again, letting out a few squeaks. "You are my dream come true."

I look up at Conner, who's right there beside me, as he's been throughout this whole process. "Do you want to hold your son?" I ask him, and he nods, unsure. Carefully, I pass Greyson over to his dad. He looks tiny in Conner's bulky arms, but he holds him so gently, as if he might break.

"Wow," Conner breathes. "He's so tiny. But so..." His words escape him as he gets lost staring into our baby's face.

"Perfect," I fill in the blank for him. "So perfect."

I know several steps need to be taken over the next few months before he's entirely and one-hundred percent ours, but he's part of the family now, as far as I'm concerned. My heart is fuller than it has in the longest time. So full that I wonder if it will burst.

Conner hands Greyson back to me after a while, and I just can't stop looking at him. The nurses offer to take him to the nursery, but I shake my head. Instead, they lead us into another room to give Lauren some time to rest and recover. Once I'm situated, a strong hand wraps around my shoulders, and I turn to smile at my husband.

"Thank you," I tell him.

He raises an eyebrow at me. "For what?"

"For doing everything you possibly could to get this life for us. For never giving up." I shake my head. "For never letting *me* give up."

"We're a team, Jo," he says back, leaning forward and pressing our foreheads together. Baby Greyson chirps down in my arm and wiggles again before settling.

"And to think this all started because of a stupid broken window," I recall, thinking back to when my brother broke my window the *first* time. "I'm so glad I decided to call you."

"Me, too, Jo. Trust me."

"We've come a long way, don't you think?" I mutter, looking back down at the baby in my arms.

I glance back at him to see a soft smile on his face as he watches his new son. I maneuver slightly so that I can kiss Conner without moving the baby too much. As my lips press to his, Conner's hand comes to cup my face, his fingers dancing over the skin on my cheek. As soon as there's any type of distance between us, I flutter my eyes open and meet the warm chocolate eyes that are my home.

"I always knew that, someday, we'd be here," Conner's deep voice rumbles, beating me to the punch. "Is this life everything you dreamed?"

I give him a blinding smile, and say the words that have never felt truer in my life. "It's more. It's so much more."

Acknowledgments

Thank you so much for reading "Just Josie!" It really means a lot to me you'd take time out of your busy schedules and hectic lives to read my story.

Josie is a very important character to me and I'm thrilled to have been able to share her story with you.

If you loved this book, please don't forget to leave a review, and spread the word by recommending this book with your friends and family. Reviews and recommendations make a world of difference for independent authors like myself. Don't forget to buy your discreet cover paperback of "Just Josie" and "The Loathing Ryan Duet." Nicole with IndieSage really knocked the covers for this series out of the park. I'm so excited to see them all together!

There are a few people I want to thank for playing a large role in the making of "Just Josie"

My best author buddies, Alice Daniels and Kris Wood. These two are some of my closest confidants and biggest cheerleaders. Thank you both so, so much for always being there cheering me on. To those reading this, go check out their books too, you won't be disappointed!

Thank you to Kylie, who is also one of my best friends and trusted developmental editors. Your comments have taken this book to the next level!

To my editors who have worked on this story, Bailee and Sarah, thank you both so much for your time and care in giving feedback and polishing up this book to be the best version it could be!

And at last but never least, I'm always so grateful to my husband for encouraging me to tell these stories. I can't imagine life without you!

About the Author

Aria Harding is an up-and-coming romance novelist from the Midwest, USA. Aria has been a long-time lover of romance novels and is excited to join the ranks as a romance author. Her first book, "Chasing Infinity" was published in May of 2023 and there are many more exciting projects to come. Her goal is to write stories that make readers feel as though they are immersed in the world and experiencing the same highs and lows as the characters on the pages. Her favorite tropes to write include slow burn, enemies-to-lovers and second-chance romances. Aria always looks forward to hearing from readers, so feel free to reach out on social media and have a chat!

Instagram: @ariaharding_author